D1071584

AN HONEST WOMAN

Other books by Anne Christie

FIRST ACT
MY SECRET GORILLA

AN HONEST WOMAN

Anne Christie

St. Martin's Press
New York

Library of Congress Cataloging in Publication Data

Christie, Anne.
An honest woman.

I. Title.
PN6053.H68H6 1986 823'.914 85-30433
ISBN 0-312-38931-0

First published in Great Britain by Judy Piatkus (Publishers) Limited of London.

First U.S. Edition

10 9 8 7 6 5 4 3 2 1

For Mo, with love

AN HONEST WOMAN

Chapter One

Alison was sleepy and looked forward to her first cup of coffee from the thermos. She was never very alert at such an unearthly hour, and this morning it felt extra unearthly because it was so dark and cold; sparrow-fart, Philip called it. He, lucky man, was probably sipping fresh orange juice on a sunlit balcony in Trinidad.

The big Town Hall was already bustling with dealers unloading, and there were bangs and thumps as the last few of perhaps fifty trestle tables were set up along the walls. Alison's pitch was in a corner and well lit; she had been doing this particular fair once a month for over a year, so was an old hand amongst the changing faces of the other stall-holders.

'Hi, Charlie.' She smiled at the whiskery actor who sold records and books, and bumped into Hilary, dressed today in an even brighter magenta tweed than usual. Hilary, as ever, was the first there, and the first to have set up her stall, which was all silver and knick-knacks. A tiny pale woman of about sixty, very thin, with hair dyed as black as her face was white, butterfly specs and a slash of carmine lipstick, she intrigued Alison, not least because of her selling technique; often she even managed to sell Alison things she didn't really want or need.

Humming resignedly, Alison spread out the huge Union Jack which gave an attractive brightness and jollity to the stall. Deftly she set up her shelf-units for displaying the smaller pieces – ceramic figures, pieces of silver and a couple of old photos, one of a stern-eyed Victorian grandma. She always felt a little tense whilst she was unloading, and disliked leaving boxes of stuff unattended; people did steal at fairs. At last she was set up: she did a final check on a couple of price-labels, and changed one on a small soapstone cat from seven to ten pounds. She would keep it for a bit if it didn't sell, she liked its face.

'Mind my stuff for me will you, darling?' Hilary's bandsaw voice interrupted Alison's musings.

'Of course.' She focussed on the bespectacled face, framed by flowing scarves in clashing magenta and purple. If you put Hilary in a West End farce people would say she was over the top and unrealistic. She ought to be preserved in a museum, she was an art form all of her own, a happening.

Yawning, Alison sat on a chair between the two stalls and blearily unscrewed her thermos flask. She felt better after gulping down a cup quickly, and rose to have a good peer at Hilary's stall. As ever, she wondered where on earth she found her stock, and how she managed to keep her prices so low. Maybe her husband was a cat-burglar – that would explain it.

Enviously Alison shook her head over the vast collection of silver picture-frames her neighbour had on display; she picked up a couple, they always sold easily, and there wasn't a lot of silver back at the shop. Hilary returned, eyes glittering triumphantly. 'Look what I got, ever so cheap, I told her she was a silly girl!' She flourished a string of amber beads at Alison, who felt a frisson of annoyance that she hadn't seen them first.

'Very nice.' She examined the necklace – the beads were a particularly good colour. 'How much do you want for them?'

Hilary named her price, which though not cheap was less than Alison would ask. She bought the necklace and a couple of frames, and immediately regretted it, the profit margin would be too small for comfort.

Hilary, peering myopically at Alison's stall with the viewing-glass she used to read hall-marks, picked up a little brass and glass coffer and scrutinised it closely, holding it up to the light. 'What's your best on this, dear?'

Alison looked at the box, it was cheap enough, but weakly she dropped the price by a couple of pounds. Hilary's dark little eyes gleamed as she scrabbled in her bag, counted out the too-small sum, and walked victoriously back to her twinkling stall, clutching the little coffer.

Alison stood back to survey her own stall. It looked quite bright and interesting – she had one or two really good pieces of china in perfect condition – and she particularly liked the two-hundred year old Mocha-ware tankard, with its simple blue-grey stripes. She handled it fondly for a moment, then put it back, glancing at the big wall-clock on the far side of the hall.

'Will you watch the stall for me?' Alison asked Hilary who was avidly polishing her new acquisition.

'Off you go, dear,' she shrieked. 'Have a good time!'

Alison examined a pretty beaded bag on a stall under the clock, but discarded it reluctantly because the hasp was broken. Instead she bought a strange African carving, with a face like a flat spoon; it was black and about a foot high. She liked it and it was only a tenner;

she had seen one like it in one of her books she was sure. She would have to look it up.

Jo was supposed to be at school at nine forty-five; the team was playing an away match today. She had been quite nervous last night.

'Last time our team played them we got beat five one, and Micky said that half of them were giants.'

'Nonsense!' Mark had jeered.

'They were!' insisted Jo, shouting loudly at her brother. 'Real giants, with broken voices.'

Jo's blue eyes were extraordinarily dramatic as she described her matches: Alison shook her head and smiled bewilderedly to herself as she imagined her dimpled hoyden of a daughter pounding down the football pitch pursued by broken-voiced giants. Surely one day soon her tomboy would metamorphose into a different sort of adversary for the boys. She went to phone home.

'Hallo?' Mark's voice was very deep and gravelly this morning, like a grown man's. The fact of his growing-up never ceased to amaze her; it was so surreal that she, Little Alice – as Philip still sometimes called her in his fond but patronising manner – should be mother to this towering and beautiful young man over whom her friends were beginning to visibly widen their eyes.

'Hello, darling. Just a guilty mother check-call. Are you up? Did Jo get off OK?'

'Of course. She went ages ago. She was manically polishing her boots at seven o'clock. How's the fair?'

'OK. Quiet so far. Jo will be exhausted.'

'Stop fussing; she'll be OK. She's a wally.'

'Why?'

'Playing in a boy's team, it's not natural.'

'I wouldn't worry, love. She's all right, she's just a militant mini-feminist fighting for equal rights.'

'It's really embarrassing at school, people keep asking me if she's my kid brother or a flaming lesbian.'

The pips went. Alison fumbled for more money, but the line went dead. She put the receiver back on the hook and wryly imagined the breakfast scene with cornflake and toast crumbs everywhere. She hoped that Mark had fed the dog (Philip's dog, as she always thought of him). Pirate was a stupid dalmatian, thus named, not too originally, because of his black eyepatch.

The big main doors to the Town Hall suddenly burst open and twenty or thirty overcoated and muffled dealers of all ages and sexes surged past; Alison turned and moved quickly back to her stall where she met a triumphant Hilary, leering smugly, arms akimbo.

'I've sold your little box, dear. I knew it would go quick; it was a real old one. You've got me off to a good start and made me a tenner, so that's my stall rental paid.'

Trying not to feel miffed, Alison forced a smile. 'Well done.'

Then suddenly they were surrounded by dealers, examining, questioning, haggling. No time for talk. It was crazy time. Alison did well, but was frankly envious of the speed with which Hilary's stall so visibly depleted; Hilary, smugly polishing a sugar-spoon, shrugged: 'It's just experience and a good eye, you need to have a good eye in this business.' She paused to peer at Alison's African figure. 'What have you got there then?'

Alison handed it over to be perused with the viewing-glass, and Hilary shuddered. 'It's an ugly one, isn't it? They give me the creeps all these funny things you and Frankie seem to find.' She handed the carving back, then smiled to comfort Alison for her lack of taste and inferior talent. 'It takes all kinds, I always say.' She suddenly thrust a small, and to Alison, hideous, china parrot into her hand.

'Now that is really unusual. Nice, isn't it? You know that pair who always come – the ones with the green umbrellas? Well, she's a parrot collector. She's got over four hundred, I sold her two last month.'

Alison set her figure on a shelf beside an Imari bowl with a hair crack. 'Four hundred? You're joking.'

'Naeouw!' Hilary sounded positively Eliza Doolittle. 'I am not. You ask her, I've seen! At least four hundred. They're all over the house. She's even got them guarding the front door. She's got parrot curtains, a parrot bedspread, parrot teapots . . . it's amazing!' Again her vowels did a huge parabolic curve and Alison listened mesmerised.

Hilary paused in full flow to sell two brass candlesticks to an unshaven youth with quite cockatoo-like green hair, before she turned back to the waiting Alison.

'Where was I? Yes . . . to top it all she's even got two live parrots, and my goodness you should hear those birds squawk!'

It gave Alison the giggles: 'I don't believe you,' she gasped.

Hilary drew herself up to a dignified five foot three (she was about the same height as Alison), 'I'm telling you dear, it's the God honest truth. I've seen them.' She polished fiercely, then looked up.

'Psst!' she hissed, 'You've got a customer.' She rolled her head in a baroque wriggle. 'Very nice too.'

Still giggling at the almost apocryphal vision of four hundred parrots, Alison turned back to her stall and found a dark furry sort of man examining the African figure. He had piercing dark eyes, hairy wrists – she noticed them almost subliminally – and a very deep voice.

'How much is the Ashanti doll?' he asked, touching the spoon-faced carving.

She frowned, 'My what?' then understood. 'Ah . . . yes. The Ashanti – of course it is – I should have remembered. I was going to look it up.'

He held it fondly and smiled at her. 'What's your trade price?' She tried to remember; she had only paid a tenner, but it might well be a good one; this chap looked as though he might know about such things.

'It's twenty-five,' she blurted. 'I've only just bought it. I hadn't really priced it yet.'

'Ah, I'll forget about it then; that's a pity.' He was crestfallen, the beard positively wilted. He sounded a little foreign. She watched as his dark eyes lingered for a moment on the doll's strange flat disc of a face. 'Never mind,' he said. 'It's not exactly an essential ingredient for living, is it?'

He was Welsh, that was it. She was distracted by him; he ought to be called Esau, she decided, then tried not to giggle again – for Esau was an hairy man. She smiled instead: 'What isn't essential?'

He grinned. 'An Ashanti doll isn't.'

She found herself laughing quite loudly. 'No! I suppose it isn't.'

'Well . . .'. said Esau shyly, 'Never mind, thank you.'

He smiled at her again, and she longed to say something more to him, something witty or intelligent, something to make him stay; but he put his worn ex-army bag on his shoulder and walked away.

Suddenly bereft, Alison started to polish the silver on her stall. As she busied herself she thought wryly how very little, for a vicar's daughter, she remembered of the Bible, only the silly inconsequential bits like Esau, and the basics that everybody knew, like Thou shalt not covet they neighbour's wife – or husband? Sexist, the Bible was.

He looked like a family man, you could tell. She put down the box she had already polished twice, and sold a small bespectacled boy a Roman coin.

Later, as Alison sipped her third cup of coffee, Hilary asked her how it was going.

'So so.' Alison pendulumed her head unenthusiastically. 'I think the cold weather keeps them at home.'

Hilary clutched her bulging purple bag. 'Well I've had one of the best days ever.'

She said this so often that Alison and her partner, Frankie, used to chant it to cheer each other up when business was slow; Frankie could mimic Hilary's voice to perfection, almost as well as she could do Margaret Thatcher.

Alison hadn't done much more than cover the price of the stall and the things she had bought so far. The hall was quiet now – the mid-morning rush had died down to a trickle. She needed a sandwich.

In a small Italian sandwich bar across the road from the Town Hall. Alison totted up her sales. She had done better than she thought, and there were still a few hours to go; she bought a *Standard* and read her stars which advised her not to combine business with pleasure, or there would be disastrous consequences. Reluctantly she concluded that such advice was impossible to follow, and rose to go back to the fair. As she emerged from the shop there was a great kerfuffle of barking and leaping dog. Thrown backwards, she moaned in tired recognition and glared down at the excited dalmatian which stood barking manically up at her. The dog was attached to her tall panting son, who had obviously been drawn like a sledge behind the breathless animal.

'Ma,' said Mark urgently, as Alison ducked to avoid the dog's unwanted licks and leaps, 'It's Jo, she's hurt.'

Alison froze. Visions of cars and Jo's crumpled figure swirled through her head.

'She's at the school. She got kicked during the match; they rang and said she needed to be collected after the doctor's seen her. She's not badly hurt, nothing broken.'

Alison's fuses melted. Jo, the stall, the stuff. . . . She didn't know what to do.

'You go,' said Mark. 'Bring her home; I'll watch the stall. It's all priced, isn't it?'

She was touched by his grown-upness. She looked at him, his sweet anxious face, with her own big dark eyes – only he was tall and blond like Philip, not small and dark like his mother – and hugged him as the dog barked hysterically, as he inevitably did at any family demonstration of affection.

'Thanks, Mark. Keep a close account, numbers and everything, and watch the jewellery *all* the time. I'll try to be back in time to clear up.' Dithering, she turned to go. 'And Mark. . .' Handing her the dog, he nodded. '. . . If a bearded Welsh guy comes back – he's in an Icelandic jersey – tell him . . .'

'What?'

'It was about an African figure. . . . Tell him . . . oh hell, tell him that I'll come down on my price . . .' She was confused again.

He nodded. 'OK. Go. I'll manage.'

The dog dragged her to the car-park and leapt into the driver's seat. Alison swore and ordered him into the back; he obeyed reluctantly and gazed at her in pained disbelief as he sat there in injured isolation.

* * *

Jo, pale but mud-spattered, winced when she moved her impressively strapped ankle. It was a bad sprain, and she must rest it, the doctor had said.

'I told you they were giants,' she growled when Alison and the sports-master helped her to the car.

The sports-master was tweedy and cheery: 'Now Jo, remember that you said you wanted to be treated equally.'

'You just wait,' said Jo mutinously, 'I'll kill him; it was that great yob with the big nose.'

'Ah, Concorde.' The sports-master nodded, 'He is a bit big and rough; he's grown so many inches in the last year that he doesn't judge distances very well. He's actually a very nice lad – he was terribly upset that he had hurt you – and not a little confused to find that he was competing with a girl.'

'Huh.' Jo sniffed, then looked up at her mother and smiled her dimpled golden little girl smile: 'Guess what? I scored a goal.'

Back home the sitting-room was soon warmed up, and a film playing on the video. Alison felt torn.

'I've got to go back and pack up..' She saw that Jo's lower lip trembled a little as she pretended to concentrate on the film. 'Shall I get Jane from next door?'

'It's OK. I've got Pirate.' The girl frowned.

The dalmatian (Philip's damnation dog) looked up from where he lay by her on the sofa and wagged his tail so hard it hit Jo's tearstained face. She groaned, then wailed bleakly, 'When is Dad coming home?'

'Wednesday,' said Alison wearily. She kissed her tomboy and went to the door. As she closed it behind her she thought bitterly of her absentee husband; it seemed that he was never here for such family emergencies.

Mark, flushed with success, had just sold the Mocha beaker to an old Polish lady: 'She said it was for her muzzer,' he told Alison, amazed. 'If she really has a mother she must be at least a hundred.'

Alison nodded. 'She comes every week. She's a soapstone fetishist, but she nearly always buys something – last time it was an ivory monkey.'

'I've taken nearly a hundred and fifty quid,' he told her proudly. She grinned at him; it was a good day's business after all. Pleased, she fished in her pocket and gave him a fiver.

'Thanks, Ma.' He beamed, and she noted with a pang that the badge on his denim jacket said 'Give Life a Chance'.

He wrapped his scarf round his neck. I'm off to see *Sophie's Choice*.'

'It's terribly harrowing. Anyway, you aren't old enough.'

'Ma, stop worrying. I could get married any time if I wanted.'

She was looking, she realised, actually up at him – he was far taller than her. She felt all of a sudden small and frail. 'Married?' She felt shocked.

'Yeah, I'm sixteen.'

'Ah,' she paused, 'But only with parental permission till you're eighteen.'

He grinned, nodding. 'True, mother.'

Alison watched him go wistfully: the badge, with its implicit fear that for her children there might not actually be a future, had moved her deeply, and she felt vulnerable and wished yet again that she were not so often left alone to cope with her family. She was brought back to reality by Hilary's starting to pack up;

it was time, almost five o'clock. Wearily she began to wrap up her remaining stock. She was scrabbling under the table for a last cardboard box when Hilary jabbed her in the back and hissed under the Union Jack: 'That boy's back. You know, the nice one.'

Puzzled, Alison emerged, dusty from her grovelling, and there was the furry Welshman. It was Esau. Help.

He smiled tentatively, and his hand went out to the Ashanti doll, alone on the empty stall. 'Er, hello again . . .'

Alison swept back her hair, then wished she hadn't; she felt a mess.

'I came earlier, and the young man . . .'

'My son.'

'I thought so, he's got your eyes, like great black flowers, lovely . . .'

Alison hadn't blushed like this since she was Mark's age.

'What can I do for you?'

He was hesitant. 'I just came to see this again. Your son said you might let it go for less.' He held the figure up to show her; it suited him somehow.

She had paid ten, and quoted twenty-five off the top of her head.

'Make me an offer,' she challenged.

'I've got exactly fifteen quid.' He fanned three fivers at her, pretending not to look very handsome.

'I'm trying to become a rich antique dealer,' she said trying not to laugh.

'Oh.' He nodded a little sadly, and made to put his money away.

She took the Ashanti doll from him and looked at it. 'Are you buying it to sell?'

'No. I do deal, but mostly ethnographic or travel books. I actually want to keep this. I just like it.'

Suddenly she decided. 'OK. It's yours for fifteen quid. I've made a decent profit, and it deserves a good home.'

He smiled gloriously at her: 'Oh . . .' He made the single syllable sound deeply Welsh. 'Thanks, thanks very much indeed. It's lovely.'

He grinned into the dark disked face of the carving, then, eyeing her boxes and parcels, said, 'I'll give you a hand with these'. He was incredibly vibrant and warm. And before she could say him nay, he'd lifted up the biggest and heaviest carton, and she followed him as though hypnotised out to the cold and the car.

Chapter Two

Philip was due back from Trinidad tonight, and the fact that Jo was still off school, hobbling, and wanting a fair bit of attention didn't make Alison's life any easier. She had to view the local auction sometime before tomorrow's sale, Frankie needed a hand in the shop, and there was no food in the house.

'Mum,' Jo was calling from the sitting-room.

'Yes?'

'I'm bored.'

Alison walked through from the large kitchen-diner, burnt pot and Brillo pad in hand. Babs, the cleaning-lady's, absence through illness, had added hugely to her problems. Jo lay on the black leather sofa heaped high with books and felt-tipped pens. She was drawing as usual. The dalmatian beside her gazed sentimentally up from mother to daughter.

'Can I go swimming?'

'Better wait till the ankle is stronger.' Alison looked across the big all-white room to the window where there was a low glass and steel table laden with plants in white ceramic pots. Like herself they were drooping.

'How about watering the plants for me? You can sit in a chair; I'll bring you a jug.'

The goal-scorer's brows lowered as she grunted a mutinous acquiescence.

Alison filled a jug with water and walked back into the stark white room. It was Philip's room; he had insisted on being in charge of the decoration and enlarging of the house.

'Dammit, darling, we entertain so much for business, I must have a background that shows off my capabilities, it must have the Salveson stamp. It will be all-white, with perhaps a few accents of black or steel.'

And Alison had feebly allowed it to happen. 'A white carpet?' she had whispered uneasily.

'Yes!' Philip's blue eyes had had an almost manic fervour as he envisaged his priestly sitting-room. He never seemed to imagine Alison or the children there; but in a way it had paid off because the house had been featured in various magazines as the brilliantly converted, early Victorian semi-detached home of architect Philip Salveson, who had somehow eclectically combined Japanese and Scandinavian sparseness with a particularly English vernacular – or so the plump fellow who had written one of the articles had said. Alison had wanted her children in the picture, dressed in white if necessary, but Philip hadn't seen it that way. Instead he had gone out impulsively and brought back Pirate.

Alison remembered how he had gazed euphorically as the small black-and-white animal staggered across the white expanse of carpet: 'That's exactly what the room needed, just that texture of black and white. It's perfect . . .'

'But I don't want a dog,' Alison had wailed. Philip had put his arm round her – she almost slotted in beneath his armpit, he was so tall. 'Don't worry, darling. It's good for children to have a dog. I'll take him for walks. He'll be my responsibility.'

But there were always business meetings and architectural committees and prestigious happenings which took Philip away both mentally and physically, and the children were not keen to take the job of walking Pirate regularly, so, like a hundred thousand other things, Alison found herself doing it. She had just allowed it to happen by osmosis, by not being assertive enough to say no, by being feeble and feeling duty bound to do certain things. By trying to be a good wife and mother.

'M-u-u-m.'

'Yes, what is it?'

'Can I have some ice-cream?'

'Ice-cream?' It was mid-winter and mid-morning. 'There's some in the fridge.'

Ice-cream was almost the only thing left except for rotting coleslaw and a half-eaten tin of dog food.

Conceding for the sake of peace, she watched as Jo devoured two bowlfuls. Fortunately the ice-cream was vanilla and matched the carpet.

One day, thought Alison mutinously. She imagined the room painted brown, with kelims and pictures everywhere. She had given in to Philip's passion for plainness out of deference to his greater wisdom and talent; she had even enthusiastically hunted with him for the most minimal prints that they could find, which were mostly large expanses of paper, with small areas of almost invisible line or texture so that the icy wastes of wall were not disturbed by colour or tone of a distressing kind. But she had grown to loathe the room and its inhumanity. She loved when Jo brought in her football gear and the iconoclastically clashing colours of her felt-tips and toys brought some vivacity to the puritan white of Philip's sterile creation.

When Frankie, shortly after starting work in the

antique shop, had first set eyes on the house, she had gasped. 'My God, this is like a bloody museum. How can you dare to live in it or do naughty things like pee or eat? Or even breathe? It's so daunting!'

Alison had never voiced such thoughts even to herself, but daunted did describe exactly how she felt. Philip was so black and white, so adamant, herself so pathetic, so unassertive. If only she could be stronger.

'Mu-u-u-u-m.' Jo was still bored. 'Can't I come to the shop?'

'No, love, it's not a good idea. I'll try not to be long. I'll bring you something nice for lunch.' Alison hated herself for using food as a softener, but it seemed the only way.

'It's illegal to leave me before I'm fourteen,' Jo muttered.

Alison had to laugh. 'I'll quote you on that next time you're begging me to go out and leave you in peace.'

A rich smell of fresh coffee and beeswax met her at the shop. Frankie was already busy, towering, all five foot eleven of her, over a small pine chest of drawers which she was carefully burnishing with a yellow duster. She looked up, her head haloed by a leonine mane of copper curls, 'Hi Ally, how's things?'

'OK. Just preparing for Philip's return. I said I'd meet him at six.'

'He will be knackered after the journey. It's a long way, isn't it?'

'Yes.' Alison's voice was quiet as she disrobed. 'He always seems to be either knackered or not here.'

'Somebody needs a coffee, I'll get you one.' Frankie went into the inner recesses of the shop, a swirling tornado of lace and ethnic garments, and returned moments later with a large mug of coffee.

She watched Alison as she sipped. 'What's wrong?'
'Nothing.'
'Are you pre-menstrual?' Her Glasgow accent made her sound like a schoolteacher.
Alison smiled palely. 'My period just finished.'
'That's good. You can greet your beloved with a bloodless coup!'
'Bill and coo, you mean?'
'Very good,' said Frankie soothingly. 'We'll have us on the telly yet. The Magnificent Two. Ally 'n Frankie, the troglodyte and the giant, or the Muckle and the Wee – only that would have to be Frankie 'n Ally.'
Frankie had almost broken her heart when she had become too tall to be a dancer. As a small girl in Glasgow, she had obviously shown much talent, but alas, at fourteen she had suddenly started to grow. 'Like a bloody triffid,' she had told Alison. 'I could hardly see ma toes, and I used to starve myself to try to stop growing, but on and on it went.' So many of Frankie's stories were told with a sort of breathless Scottish hilarity, but Alison remembered how Frankie's face had looked when she told this one, and the memory of it still made her want to cry.
Today, as she polished, Frankie said again how much she missed her dancing. Alison tried to cheer her up: 'Maybe you'll become the greatest antique dealer in the world instead, the shop would collapse without you now.'
'Big deal,' grunted Frankie grumpily, then, leaping up, she grabbed Alison's scarf and whirled it round her head and crooned in her strong, pure and fascinatingly husky voice 'Or should I say . . . Big Dealer, big dealer . . .' to the tune of 'Big Spender'. She was terrific.
Alison clapped her finale, put on a butcher's apron

and set about unpacking a job-lot of china and glass. 'You're a hopeless case.'

'So you keep telling me.' Energetically, Frankie set to work again on her chest of drawers. They worked in companionable silence for a bit, and Alison dealt with an old lady who came in with a pitiful bagful of trinkets she wanted to sell. Occasionally wondrous goodies were brought in by sweet old ladies, but today's lot was painful and embarrassing; it was hard not to offer to buy the oddments simply out of charity. For an awful moment Alison thought the old lady was going to burst into tears at her rejection of her possessions, but she picked up her gloves and cheap glass jewels, thanked both women politely – as they exchanged agonised glances in an ornate gilt mirror – and exited with dignity on her complicated little criss-crossed black shoes.

'Oh God,' muttered Frankie hoarsely, 'that's what we'll be like.'

'Sooner than we think,' said Alison sonorously.

'Aw, come on, it can't be that bad.' Frankie lurched across like a grizzly bear to hug her. 'As long as we're in the same geriatric ward. And you can't really complain, at least you'll have a man in your bed tonight. Is that not good?'

Alison sighed. 'I suppose so.'

'I don't understand you,' said Frankie. 'You have positively the most handsome and talented husband that I have ever seen. He is fantastic, successful, pushy, bloody brilliant. And you've got Mark and Jo. What more do you want, woman? How dare you be unhappy?'

Alison shrugged. 'I don't know.' Her voice was quiet. 'I feel negated I suppose, like a sort of dung-heap for my children and husband to strut and crow upon. In a funny way the only thing I really enjoy at the moment is the shop, the stalls, the buying and selling.'

'Maybe you need a holiday?'

Alison sighed. 'Maybe.' They worked in silence for several minutes. Frankie stared out of the window at the passing cars, and across the road to the Cypriot fruit-shop where glowing tomatoes and peppers embellished the drear London grey.

'I'm nearly twenty-nine,' she said sadly.

'You're a babe,' Alison assured her. Frankie sighed.

'All my friends are either married or shacked up. I've only had one fuck in five months, and that one was pretty half-cocked.' She picked up a small glass paperweight and graphically drooped her wrist. 'He had a hang-up that would be better described as a hang-down.'

Five months? Alison could hardly imagine it; she found it bad enough when Philip was away for a week. Poor Frankie.

Frankie nodded, jutting out her lower lip in a clown-pout. 'Sometimes I hope I haven't sealed up, like your ears do if they're pierced and you forget to wear earrings for a time. Mebbe it's because I'm so bloody big; I sometimes think I frighten the wee buggers!'

'Listen,' Alison was serious. 'I think you should try *Time Out*.'

Taken aback, Frankie laughed awkwardly. 'You mean the lonely hearts?'

'Yes.'

'I couldn't. It shows desperation to do that.' Putting down the duster and tin of wax she stretched. 'I'm stiff, need to exercise the mighty body.'

She cleared a space on the shop floor by moving a couple of Edwardian handchairs and an aspidistra, and lay full-length on Alison's favourite kelim which was priced so high that it would always to part of the fittings. Alison never ceased to be impressed by Frankie's work-outs; she was amazingly supple and would quite happily do the shop accounts in the lotus position.

Frankie grunted, jack-knifed her body dramatically, then spread her legs wide and touched the floor between her knees with her great mop of curly hair.

'Are you serious about *Time Out*?' Her voice was muffled and breathless.

'I certainly am. I think it's a sensible and acceptable way to meet people in a big city; everything is so huge in London. You haven't been here all that long, and we're not much help to you because most of our friends seem to be married or gay. And we're older than you. Dammit, Philip's forty-four.'

Frankie sat up, red-faced. 'That's better!' she gasped. She stood up, panting. 'Is he really?'

'Forty-four last summer. I was twenty when we married, he was twenty-seven.'

'He's still a very handsome man.'

'So you keep telling me.'

'Ally, you're in a bad way. You seem to be on an anti-Philip campaign.'

'I'm not really.' Alison picked up a blue and white chinese bowl and felt its cool smoothness. Dreamily she looked at the clever dark blue design of criss-crosses and wiggles, then set the bowl back on its shelf and sighed: 'Marriage is a funny business. Somehow for most people it seems to become a sort of no-man's land of money, property, kids. Almost by default, people get bored with each other.'

Frankie was listening intently. 'No romance, you mean?'

Alison shrugged. 'I don't know. I shouldn't really complain.'

'You should count your blessings. My God, if I had what you had . . .'

Alison grinned and hummed and together they sang 'If I had what you had, and you had what I had . . .'

'Other people's lives . . .' said Alison wistfully. 'They always seem better; I suspect that the secret is to enjoy the now.'

'Aye, mebbe.' Frankie gazed earnestly across the room at her. 'May I ask you a very personal question?'

'You can always ask.'

'Well . . . have you always been faithful to Philip?'

Alison was surprised, and momentarily reticent. Frankie, sensing this, blushed as red as her hair. 'I'm sorry, it's none of my business.'

'It's OK, I don't mind.' Alison was almost surprised to hear herself say it. 'I always have been, yes.'

Frankie gazed at her admiringly. 'I think that's wonderful, fantastic after all those years.'

'I suppose it is,' Alison sat on one of the chairs and fondled a small Indian bronze of the god Krishna with a ball, an apple (or the world?) clasped in his hand. 'But sometimes I feel old and mouldering, and that perhaps I have missed out on the great outside.'

'But you weren't, you know . . .' Frankie's frankness had diminished slightly, '. . . a virgin?' She blurted it out.

'Oh no. I nearly married an Italian guy when I was nineteen. An engineer from Milano. I could have been a catholic Momma serving pasta to dozens of kids.'

'What happened?'

Alison still felt emotion when she remembered; hatred of her mother's manipulativeness, and contempt for her father's ineffectuality. And the loss, the pain of being parted from the dark warmth of Gino. She made a small sighing noise and stared into space above the table. 'Too much happened,' she said. 'Too much.'

She looked up again. 'But although I've remained faithful, I've been more than tempted a couple of times . . .' She brightened, 'I even arranged to go and have a drink once with a fantastic Irish actor I met at a party; he was lovely. So funny and intelligent and sexy. Oooh . . .' she moaned in memory.

'But you didn't?'

Alison giggled regretfully. 'No, it wasn't that. He didn't. He made a date to meet me in a pub in Hammersmith and didn't turn up.'

'How awful. Were you furious?'

Alison tried to remember; it was so long ago.

'I wasn't furious, I was sad and terribly frustrated – he was such a beautiful guy. So amusing, full of the blarney; I was dying for it, but in the end I was relieved. The kids were very small, and I was still mad about Philip – I think I wanted to punish him; it was just when he had started all that damned travelling and I felt utterly deserted and lumbered, and lost without him.'

Frankie looked at her curiously: 'And how about Philip?'

'What do you mean?'

Frankie shrugged. 'Is he faithful after all these years?'

Alison leaned forward, rocking, hands between her knees, eyes murky and looked meditatively at the little Indian bronze. 'He hasn't always been. Three years ago I discovered that he had been having an affair with a girl in Dublin – a honey-blonde.' She added the last bitterly. 'I felt shattered. Betrayed, full of hate. He had broken the bond.'

'What happened?'

'He swore it was over and hadn't meant anything to him. Just a screw he said, an aberration. He was lonely and working hard like he always does; he was very upset to have caused me such hurt, and swore it wouldn't ever happen again.'

'Do you think he has reformed?'

Alison shrugged. 'Who knows? All I know is that it has never felt the same for me since; my trust was broken.'

'But people do have affairs and it doesn't have to be the end of everything.'

'I know. I just feel that marriage should be sacrosanct, but maybe that is a hangover from my religious upbringing. Philip used to try to persuade me that sexual freedom might be no bad thing.'

Frankie looked deeply pensive. 'I don't know if I could handle monogamy, but I hate being without anybody.'

'You Frankie, you are young.'

'I'll be thirty soon, that's not young.'

'Of course it's young. And you are beautiful, talented, healthy and unattached.'

'Don't rub in the last bit,' growled Frankie. 'I'm all too aware of it.'

'OK. OK.' Alison stood up. 'I'm sorry. I am going to get that copy of *Time Out* and we'll draft you an ad.'

'I can't, Ally. I can't.'

'Yes, you can; we'll just do it as an exercise.' Firmly she disappeared into the back shop, and as she grovelled through the rubbish bag – she'd thrown away the magazine last night – she heard the doorbell tinkle and a man's voice speaking to Frankie. She held the magazine to her chest, but it did nothing to soothe her beating heart. It was him, she knew. Esau.

For a minute, she stood paralysed behind the thick blue velvet curtain which covered the entrance to the back-shop. He was talking to Frankie.

'Anything ethnographic, carvings, native stuff, and books I'm particularly interested in. Travel books, anthropology, pre-history all of that . . .'

'Have a look,' Frankie was talking. 'I'll ask my partner; she knows more about that side of the business than me. I'm stronger on Art Deco china and wee bits and pieces. Ally! Are you coming?'

Clutching the magazine tighter, Alison took a deep breath. She dashed to the little mirror set over the sink and blinked at her frightened reflection, big-eyed and elfin. Peely wally, Frankie was always saying she was, but right now she was quite pink. She marched out through the curtains and his eyes met hers full on and in.

'Oh . . .' he stammered. 'Good heavens, small world!' Then, embarrassed, he too blushed. 'I did wonder when I peered in the window, I thought I recognised a couple of objects from the Fair on Saturday.'

'Yes,' said Alison foolishly, nodding too many times. 'How's your Ashanti doll?'

He eased. 'Oh, boyo, she's lovely. My totem; she's supposed to be for good luck.'

'Really?' said Frankie.

'Well, they're actually made to encourage fertility, but I suppose it's the same thing, isn't it?'

They all three relaxed.

'This gentleman's looking for native things, and geography books,' explained Frankie.

'Ah,' Alison's business head had fortunately returned. 'I haven't much, only that mask, but it's not very old.' She pointed to the back wall.

He nodded. 'I saw that. It's not bad.'

Relieved to have something to do, Alison reached up

to a high shelf at the back of the shop. 'I've got these,' she handed him down a gourd with incised drawings of birds and little men round its side, and held the other one while he examined the marks.

'Nice.' He fondled the rounded gourd, and she was aware of the one she held, sensuous to the touch, warm and smooth, not cold like china or metal.

He peered at the price-label. 'I'm glad you don't have an obscure code. It maddens me when you have to ask the price of everything you look at.' He looked at the gourd Alison was holding, pressed against *Time Out.*

'Reading the lonely hearts are you? My favourite literature . . . . Can I have a look at that one?'

Utterly confused, Alison started to hand him the magazine, then stopped. 'Of course,' she smiled and handed the gourd to him. once again aware of the warm strong hands and the furriness. He was so dark he looked foreign, Jewish, or even Italian, like Gino.

He walked over to the window and peered at the gourds in a better light; they had been part of an emormous job lot bought at auction, and weren't priced very high, but even so, Alison willingly dropped a couple of pounds when he said he would like the pair.

Frankie wrapped them up and gave them to him in a Waitrose plastic bag. 'The wee birds on them are lovely, where do you deal?'

'Shepherds Bush, just from my house. I've not been doing it for long, I'm actually an unemployed lecturer. My Poly sacked half its staff under the government cutbacks, but it keeps me going between applying for jobs and going for interviews. I sell books by catalogue mostly – and . . .' he grinned proudly, '. . . I've just published a thesis on "Race, Riot and Urban Deprivation in Brixton".'

Frankie smiled at him. 'An intellectual, eh?'

He grinned. 'It was fascinating to do, it's what I like best, social research. I'm a social anthropoligist – lapsed for the moment.'

He went over to the far end of the shop to examine their books, and picked out a couple as the phone rang. Frankie disappeared into the back shop to answer it and came back for Alison. 'It's Jo. Wants her mummy.' Obediently, Alison headed for the phone.

The man suddenly looked at his watch 'Heavens, I must go home. My kids have a half day, I said I'd meet them.' He took the books and put them in his bag and made to go. Alison was back, 'I said I'd be home soon,' she told Frankie. 'She just told me the gas man had come and she wouldn't let him in.'

'Are you a one-parent family too?' asked the Welshman.

'Off and on,' Alison nodded.

'I'm getting paranoid. Sometimes I think there are only one-parent families.' He made to go, then felt in his pocket. 'That's my card. If you ever get any of the sort of stuff I'm looking for, I'd be glad if you'd contact me.'

Alison took it. He was called Gareth, Gareth Williams.

'Right.' She nodded again. 'I'm Alison Salveson, and this is Frankie Macgregor.'

They shook hands quite formally, and when once again their eyes met she felt both alarmed and excited.

'Goodbye then. I mush dash,' and he was gone.

'He was nice,' said Frankie.

'Certainly was . . .' said Alison a little weakly; Frankie stared curiously at her.

'I thought you fancied him. You could see he really liked you; you see you're not a dung-heap at all. I almost felt I ought to leave you alone.' She teased Alison with her huge green eyes.

'Shut up, you great Scots bint.'
'He's wee though . . .'
'What do you mean? He's about five nine.'
'He seemed small . . .'
'Frankie, you are obsessed about your height – it's because you're wearing high heels.'
'It takes a lot of courage for me to wear high heels.'
'You wear them. You look good. You're neurotic about being tall. It suits you, honestly.' Decisively, Alison reached for the copy of *Time Out.* 'Now, quickly, before I leave, let us draft you an ad.'
'No,' protested Frankie. 'Forget it.'
'Sit down,' said mother firmly. 'Here's paper and pen. Let us begin.'
Frankie peered at the magazine. 'Here's a hilarious one. "Jazz Musician, twenty-six, very attractive, wants to make music with guy." It must be a gay one.'
'I don't see what's hilarious about it.'
Frankie slumped. 'No, it isn't actually. I don't see any soul-mates at all. They all say they're very good-looking or highly attractive, but most of them sound bloody miserable, I can just imagine what pathetic wee nyaffs they are. And they all claim to be music-loving or theatre-going, it seems to be the thing to say. There's not a single one I'd like to answer except for the forty-two-year-old rumpled roué. He sounds quite funny – says he thinks the person who wrote the ads should write the whole paper. But forty-two is a bit long in the tooth for me. . .'
Alison chewed her pencil. 'I think you should actually put an ad in yourself; it' safer. You might meet a nutter with a hatchet otherwise. What about this "Weekends in the country, Mozart, good wine and food. It's lonely all by myself. Female (25-32) longed for by miniature painter."

'Show me.' Frankie looked at it. 'Yeah, could do, except that I don't know much about Mozart, except that your cassettes are pleasant enough. OK. I'll answer just that one, to get practised as it were.' She laughed, a little too loudly. Concerned, Alison put on her reading glasses and peered over them at her friend.

'Sex,' said Frankie simply. 'A good fuck. Maybe I could just put "Man wanted. Apply within." Her smile was painful.

Alison eyed her sympathetically. 'How about "Too tall to dance, but I can sing. Intelligent friendly man sought . . ." and put how old you want him.'

'Mmm . . .' Frankie bit her lips. 'Twenty-five to thirty-five I suppose – I like the intelligent friendly bit . . . .'

'How about "Antique-dealing lapsed dancer seeks whatever, age so and so"?'

'I like the "whatever" and the "so and so". Classy.'

'Shut up. I've got to go now. Promise me you'll send one. Use "intelligent and friendly"; it's good. You just have to decide what to say about yourself.'

'How about using the same for me, but say "Would-be dancer-dealer"?'

'Now you're getting places' Alison took a new bit of paper. 'OK. Let's put that down.'

'I will insert an ad,' said Frankie. 'I need to do something.'

'Good.' Alison got up and put her coat on. 'I'm late, must go back to my baby.'

'Some baby,' scoffed Frankie.

In the doorway Alison paused, puzzled for a moment. 'Why do you think that Gareth man asked if I was a one-parent family?'

'Wishful thinking,' said Frankie and winked.

Chapter Three

The Transcontinental lounge at Heathrow was crammed as Alison scanned the pale-faced passengers who walked blinking down the gangway, but there was no tall blond architect. She tried to make herself relax and think about tomorrow's auction, calculating her possible profit on the linen; it was an unusually large amount of stuff, and to buy it even at auction would require a fair capital investment. It could easily go as high as three hundred, but there were at least ninety things, some of which she could sell for a lot. If she were to be really bold she felt fairly certain she could double the money quite quickly, and if she waited longer for higher prices she could make much more, but she hated viewing in a rush as she had done this evening.

'Hi, darling.' Startled, Alison looked up into Philip's smooth, sunburned face. He looked very Nordic in his white suit.

'I'm sorry, I was miles away. Not of this world.'

'Lovely to see you.' He leaned across the barrier to kiss her. 'How are the young?'

'OK. Jo's foot still hurts, but she's back to school tomorrow.'

He frowned, his eyes tired: 'We'll have to stop all this butch football nonsense.'

'It will come to a natural end soon enough; we had to buy her a bra last week.'

Philip was astonished. 'A bra? Whatever for?'

'Her tits, what else?'

His bewildered look was to Alison the most aggravating of all his expressions. He seemed to her like a bad actor feigning disbelief – though once when she had loved that look, it had seemed to her both vulnerable and fetching.

'Come on,' she said. 'Let's get home. There's a roast in the oven.'

Mark opened the door to them. Jo, hobbling behind him, using an upside-down sweeping brush as a crutch, glowed to see her father.

'Hi, Pa. Wow! You're brown.'

'And weary, but all the better for seeing you.' The dog leapt and barked and tried to join the love-in as limbs, parcels and baggage tangled in a family cat's-cradle of greeting.

Then Alison saw Mark looking anxiously at her: 'What's wrong?'

The warmth of the house enveloped them as the door shut; Mark moved aside to let Philip unload his luggage and stood by Alison. 'It's Grandma – Molly phoned.'

This was unusual to say the least; Molly, Alison's sister, older by a millenial decade, never phoned or communicated except for a ritual Christmas card, and for the last couple of years Alison hadn't even sent a card. Their sibling bond was weak to the point of invisibility and revived quickly to near-hatred if they ever met for any length of time.

Confused by the conflicting feelings of guilt and non-confrontation which shrilled through her, Alison herded her family into the large white kitchen with its big glass oval table ('Like a great egg . . . the basic oval,' Philip had breathed messianically when he showed her his design). She bent in front of the oven to examine the crackling roast, then stood up with sinking heart to hear Mark say: 'Grandma's had a stroke – it sounds really bad – she fell and everything. Aunt Molly's had to take a few days off school to see Grandpa, he's sort of caved-in and can't cope.'

Automatically Alison reached for the carving-knife and fork. Philip sat at the table exhausted, pale blue tie undone, pale blue eyes trying to screw the family back into focus. Jo, crutch discarded on floor, leant fondly against his elegant side. She adored her father.

Alison wished that she hadn't given up smoking; she wanted a cigarette right now. 'I'll have to go down to Devon.'

'Molly asked you to phone as soon as possible. I told her when you were due back.'

Alison sat down suddenly, buzzing with decisions. Should she travel tonight? What about the auction? She hated leaving bids in case she ended up paying much more than she would have had she been there in person. The cleaning-lady, Babs, was still off work, and there was still no food in the house except what she had hurriedly bought for tonight; it was all too much. Abruptly she went to phone.

Molly's call was not unexpected; in fact, Alison realised dully, as she dialled the Torquay number, she had been dreading it for years. She had almost successfully brain-washed herself into believing that her parents didn't really exist for her any more. She had even ceased to feel guilty about her lack of feeling for the old retired vicar and his perennially-hatted and domineering wife, who seemed so alien to her younger daughter that she could hardly bear to think of her as her mother – she was more like an aloof and disapproving grandmother. The number was engaged; she re-set the receiver and waited a minute or so. It wasn't really as positive as a lack of feeling, it was plain disinterest she felt; dislike was too positive a term for it. She simply failed to carry her parents in her consciousness: the thought of them brought too many uneasy memories of her own feeble acquiescence to actions and attitudes that she inwardly despised. But right now she was not at all sure about her freedom from the parental bond; for the uncomfortable jangling sensation she felt within her solar-plexus tonight made her feel very uncertain as to the state of her unconscious. Fruitlessly she tried the number again. Maybe her mother was dead? She chewed her thumb, and called to the family:

'Please will somebody set the table?'

There was a clatter, and she heard Mark mutter: 'I ought to be re-christened "somebody".'

Her mother was seventy-nine now. Alison had been a very late child of a late marriage – an afterthought – who had caused great embarrassment coming ten years after the dragon Molly who, until Alison's untimely arrival, had revelled in being the adored only child of the country vicarage.

Philip used to tease her: 'Perhaps they had forgotten how to do it for all those years, when by chance the memory-penny dropped and out you popped, Little Alice, come to be the bane of the parental dotage.' She had laughed when he said this after first meeting her parents. It was Philip who had rescued her from her prison of dutiful daughterdom. At the time she had rebounded onto him, older, assured, handsome, a man going places; he had eased the pain of her bereavement for the forbidden Italian Gino. She had even thought she was happy for a long time, but nowadays she felt different: so many of her half-forgotten feelings of resentment seemed to be surfacing once more, and she often felt with Philip almost as helpless and weakly acquiescent as she had done twenty years ago in the idyllic setting of the Worcestershire countryside of her childhood and adolescence. Alison shivered, dialled again, and listened restlessly to the engaged tone.

Her father would be utterly helpless. 'The kitchen is your mother's domain,' he always used to say with his feeble little smile. 'I dare not enter.'

Even as a teenager Alison had despised his ineffectuality, his inability to be emphatic in any way, his domestic uselessness.

'Desmond wouldn't say boo to a goose.' Alison shuddered again as she remembered her mother's shrill autocratic voice repeat the phrase over and over, as, rubber-gloved, hair in a net, she ceaselessly tidied the hygienically spotless kitchen, where everything was controlled, except for the laugh at the end of the phrase which sounded like the mirthless shriek of a lobomotised parakeet.

This time Molly did answer; her voice was clipped and unfriendly. She who Britannia-like bore the responsibility and burden of their parent's demise, made her disapproval of Alison's detachment clear with every elocuted and self-righteous syllable.

'I'll come tomorrow, the one o'clock train.'

'You can't come sooner? She's in a very poor way.'

'Not really. Philip only came back from Trinidad half an hour ago, I'll come straight to the hospital.'

Molly didn't actually say 'I should think so too' to

Alison, but she was probably saying it to her desiccated lawyer husband now that the phone was down.

The meat smelt more than ready: Alison walked back into the kitchen and put on her oven gloves aware of a sinking feeling in her stomach that she hadn't felt for ages.

Frankie sat in her basement room in Bayswater, a few minutes walk away from the Salveson household and chewed her biro as she tried to compose her ad for *Time Out*. She felt honour-bound to hint at her great height, but wondered how best to word it. 'Lofty?' – that sounded unreachable, which was the last thing she wanted to appear. 'Five foot eleven?' It sounded too awful: people would think it was a joke, and it *was* a joke. She was a bloody joke to be sitting here so desperate for sex and affection that she had to advertise her loneliness to the whole of London. She tore up yet another piece of paper in disgust and threw it into the wastepaper basket. Maybe she should phone Alison, she would help; then she remembered that Alison would at this very moment be killing the fatted calf in honour of her man's return. Lucky things; she imagined the four of them, joyful, talking, unwrapping presents. Philip always came home loaded with goodies from the duty-free. And they would probably go to bed early to celebrate his return, who wouldn't? She untangled herself from the big striped cushion she was squatting on and stepped across an assault-course of discarded leotards and multi-coloured garments which fought for floor space with unwashed dishes and unframed pictures, until she reached a bamboo table, topped by a huge black cat and a vase of dramatically decaying tulips.

'Come on, Hamish, I need a cuddle.' She walked back to the cushion, the languid creature held against her sequined chest and sat down, a little forlornly, to continue her search for romance by advertisement in the fearsome anonymity of the 'Great Metrollops' as she called it.

The floor and table were strewn with Philip's home-coming gifts; big shells, white curved and translucent, plucked by some black diver from the depths of the Caribbean, lay entangled with a large bottle of rum, cotton shirts and brilliantly coloured pieces of cloth. 'I thought you would enjoy running up something with this,' Philip had said. He didn't seem to notice that Alison's sewing these days was almost entirely confined to mending pieces of linen or embroidery for the shop. In a year or so she would probably put the lengths of cloth onto a stall. The children had said goodnight and gone to their rooms. Philip came into the room.

'Has the dog been out?' Pirate leapt to the question and stood gazing up hopefully, his entire rear end wagging flirtatiously, then he barked and went to fetch his lead in his mouth.

'I'll do it.' She walked past Philip who was ruddy and newly-barbered from the shower, wearing a white bathrobe (he had switched it from the navy-blue one she had given him to off-set his eyes). He watched her let the dog out, and lifted up his pigskin document case: 'You coming up?'

'Yes.' She put out the empty milk bottles, locked the double mortice, and slowly followed her husband up to their large first-floor bedroom. Philip, naked, lean and sunburnt, stood on the far side of the room. She watched numbly as he climbed into the bed and patted her empty pillow. 'Come on, darling. I've missed you.'

It was a ritual; once it had been an entrancing exciting ritual – the first nights of Philip's home-comings had for several years been epiphanies of loving recognition – but tonight she didn't, couldn't answer that she had missed him too, because, she realised with a reluctant thud, it was no longer true. She pulled open drawers and counted out pants and jerseys.

'I have to pack.'

'Do it in the morning.'

'I've got an auction at ten, and Jo can't go to or from school by herself with that ankle. You'll have to pick her up at four.'

Panic registered on Philip's handsome features. 'I've got a big office meeting at two, to tell them about the pre-qualifying process. And you know what I'm like with jet-lag.'

For a moment Alison's own voice reminded her of her older sister's. 'I'm sorry, but it's your problem. She must have a lift, we also need a big supermarket shopping.'

'We'll have a take-away or a hamburger,' he said vaguely.

This was always his way, money and convenience foods, never his own self, she thought bitterly.

'I may need to stay in Torquay over the weekend if my mother is as bad as they say.' She couldn't bring herself to say 'Mummy' as Molly at forty-eight still did.

'Surely Frankie will help out?'

'She can't. We're very busy at the shop.'

'What about the cleaning lady? I'll be jet-lagged till Monday.'

He never, in sixteen years, had called Babs or any other cleaning-lady by her real name, and he was always travel-worn it seemed, or overworked.

'She's sick, not coming back till at least next week. You'll somehow have to cope, and don't forget that Mark has his mock O-Levels this week and next, so please don't lean on him *at all*.'

Philip frowned. 'OK, OK. I'm sure it's simply a problem of logistics. We'll manage. Don't worry.'

'Don't worry, I'm not!' She didn't mean to snap, but banged the suitcase shut for further emphasis. She stood near the door and started to undress. 'I'll write you a supermarket list, we're even out of dog-food.'

Philip lay with his arms behind his head, a handsome sight. He frowned. 'I have such a lot to think about.'

He watched Alison undress and admired her compact little body; his wife still looked surprisingly good to him.

Alison carefully folded her clothes and laid them on a chair. She, too, was now naked. 'I know you have a lot on your mind, but so have we all.' She took herself in to the carpeted and mirrored cool of the splendiferously designed en-suite bathroom and turned on the bath-tap full gush.

Immersed in the seductive warmth of the water she wondered about indispensability: if she were to go and never come back, if she were killed in a train-smash tomorrow for instance, Philip would have to cope, wouldn't he? He would have no option but to curtail his ambition; but it would take a major happening like death or a severe accident to make him do that.

She was almost asleep when she became aware of Philip, robed again, kneeling beside her. 'Don't worry too much, darling, it comes to us all.'

Startled, she stared up at him. 'What does?'

Embarrassed, he stuttered, 'You know . . . Death and that sort of thing.' He must have been reading her thoughts; hurriedly, she pulled out the bath-plug. He stood up, looking awkwardly at her. 'Your mother is seventy-nine. It's bad luck, but it can't be helped.'

'Oh.' She nodded, but she hadn't even been thinking of that, not so that you would notice.

Impressively, Philip was not too exhausted to make love to his wife; he even aroused her and it was good. As she lay with him spent and panting on top of her she was aware of his pulsing body, and thought hopefully that maybe she simply needed to sleep, and life would look easier in the morning.

Philip rolled away from her onto his side. 'Goodnight, darling. It's good to be home.' His back was towards her, and she missed him, as she often did when he was with her. Was it, she wondered sleepily and uneasily, because she was fonder these days of the image rather than the real Philip? She snapped out the light and turned so that they lay back to back, apart. As her memories of the day unreeled, she remembered, for no good reason, Gareth. He seemed so warm, so concerned, and her last thought as she drifted into an uneasy sleep, was not for her dying mother or for her domestic arrangements, but of the Welshmans' dark eyes.

Had he, she wondered, watched his children being born? She felt sure that he must have done; he was like that, you could tell. Not like Philip, who had said he would probably pass out, who was abroad anyway for Mark's birth (to do him justice, Mark had arrived two days early), and Jo had been a caesarean, so he couldn't actually have been present for that birth, but he hadn't turned up till eight hours after Alison had come to – site problems, he had explained as if she ought to understand, when he did finally appear.

I'd like to know, she thought. He seems such a sane guy. I wonder what happened to his wife?

Though it was long after midnight, the lights were still on in Frankie's flat, and the big cat watched expressionlessly as his mistress prepared herself for sleep. For Frankie, who hated to be cold in bed, this was an exercise which entailed her putting on more clothes than she took off. She started with a long pink vest with the wartime utility mark stamped on it; this was topped by navy-blue guernsey, so huge that the sleeves had to be rolled up to reveal her hands; her lower legs had Afghan legwarmers of rich pattern and colour, and above these she wore a worn pale blue cashmere polo-neck, upside-down like a pair of trousers, the neck hanging loose and suggestively comical.

'It's lucky you don't have to put a photo in with the ad,' Frankie said to the cat. 'It might cause a riot, eh?'

She climbed onto her mattress on the floor – the classic single person's double bed – one side obviously used for sleeping, and the other half heaped high with books (bottle-collecting, Japanese prints, and Art Nouveau jewellery). She reached for a pen and wrote out a cheque to *Time Out* for seventeen pounds fifty pence, which she carefully inserted into an envelope along with her ad which read 'Lapsed dancer, likes junk-collecting and theatre, seeks friendly intelligent humorous man, 25-35.' The age limits had been hard to decide, but she didn't want a boy, and there were some very nice thirty-five-year-olds about, indeed, even older people like Alison's lovely Philip. She wondered for a minute about expanding the age-limit, but decided not to. Decisively, she licked the envelope shut and stuck on a first-class stamp.

'Here's tae us. Good luck then.' She gave the envelope a smacking kiss, and rolled under her bright green duvet cover, reaching to put out the light as the cat padded over to preside on top of her huddled back.

Chapter Four

The train door slammed shut behind Alison just as the guard blew the whistle; it was a near thing, she had been sure she was going to miss it. Her heart pounding, she sat in an empty space and tried to regain her equilibrium. She closed her eyes momentarily and images of the last few hours fled past: Philip, helpless, searching for clean warm clothes, his mind befuddled by travel; Jo, hobbling, needing help to find her maths book, satchel, scarf, then needing a lift through the chaos of the morning traffic; Alison herself, rushing, tidying, trying to park near the auctioneers, getting a ticket for being one-third parked on yellow line. She had felt totally murderous towards the self-righteous traffic-warden – 'Please, please,' she had grovelled to the navy blue uniform, 'my mother is ill, I have business to do and a train to catch . . .'

'Very sorry, madam. We aren't allowed to make any exceptions.' With which the traffic-warden, pointedly not meeting her eyes, had torn off a sheet of paper from her clipboard and pinned it officiously to Alison's windscreen. Cursing, she had rushed panting and crazed to the auction room just as the large hamper of linen was coming up. She was furious, because she had left in plenty of time to be able to examine and count out the contents properly before bidding, but the auctioneer had started the lot off at thirty pounds, and it was leaping briskly upwards in five-pound hops. Alison had tried to stop panting and raised her hand. 'Sixty-five,' she had called firmly.

The bidding was fast. There seemed to be three contenders; she could see the very fat lady who sold classy linen at high prices, and sometimes did the same Sunday fairs as herself a few rows in front of her.

If there were really as many pieces in this lot as Alison had hurriedly calculated yesterday evening, even if she averaged only a few pounds a piece, she would net almost four hundred and fifty pounds – and there had been two or three really beautiful things – a nightie, a camisole top, and what looked like a ravishingly complex underskirt. 'One hundred and fifty,' she nodded to the auctioneer. It was now between her and the fat lady, who was relentless in her bidding. She never paused, and in a minute it was up to two hundred and fifty; Alison frowned. The bid was hers: she nodded, feeling the welcome surge of adrenalin that bidding always brought to her. She had decided to stop bidding at two hundred and sixty and it was there now, her bid. Bang snapped the other woman, 'Two sixty-five.' She obviously wanted to get it over with, by using short and snappy, aggressive tactics.

'Two seventy,' called Alison. There was a pause, the bid was slowing at last – the fat lady must have made the same calculations as herself.

'Two eighty-five . . . two ninety – and five. I have a bid of two hundred and ninety-five . . .' The auctioneer raised his hammer, 'The bid with the lady in the corner . . .' Alison was relieved to see him looking at her. She felt almost excited enough to bid against herself. 'Any advance on two-ninety-five?' A silence, and the hammer fell, as did Alison's heart, jumping with panic like a trapped rabbit. She had never bid so high. Was she mad? It was far above what she had decided was her top price.

'Gone, to the lady on the right, Name, please? Salveson – of course.' A wan smile of recognition. Maybe he would at least remember her name from now on, it was about time he did. She was a good customer.

On the train she wondered about the great quantity of linen: what if she had judged badly, and it was all tatty and torn or, horror of horrors, machine-made? She hoped that Frankie would remember to pick up the hamper as promised. Of course she would. Dear Frankie, she had thrust a small parcel into Alison's hand just as they parted, and Alison, rushing, had grabbed it unseeing. She examined the parcel now – an untidy brown paper pack in a polythene carrier-bag – and undid it curiously. Inside she found a feast, all wrapped up in a tartan paper napkin (Frankie teetered on being a tartan fetishist, and had a huge collection of tartan objects, from embroidered tartan aprons, and tartan Mickey Mice, to frilly tartan pin-cushions which said 'Frae Bonnie Scotland' in white stitching).

Gratefully she gnawed the chicken-leg, and uncorked the half-bottle of wine Frankie had also thoughtfully provided, along with a tartan knife-cum-corkscrew.

She could hardly imagine life without Frankie now, she had become such a friend and fellow-conspirator in the comparatively short time they had known each other. Frankie had swooped into the shop one bright day a couple of years ago, and they had got talking: the

Scots girl had been even more hectic and open than usual that day, having just missed out on an audition for a musical in a fringe theatre. In turn, Alison had forgotten her usual reticence, and had opened up to the big performer who could make her laugh like nobody else. In a matter of weeks they had become close friends. Frankie had an amazing talent for finding objects and junk, and was already an experienced dealer when they met – she had a weekly stall of china and amusing oddments at Camden Lock. At first she used to help Alison out two or three days a week, as Alison's original partner in the shop had left London to live a rustic life, but quite quickly Frankie had proved so reliable, independent and intelligent, that Alison had offered to share the shop with her on a more formal basis, which meant that they split the rent and bills between them.

In the car Frankie had said: 'You're in an awful state, please don't commit suicide or anything, or I'll kill you.'

The half bottle of red wine had a mellowing effect on Alison, who rarely, if ever, drank at lunchtime, because it sent her to sleep. But today that might be no bad thing. She dreaded seeing her mother and the dragon Molly, and felt in no way prepared for the family confrontation their meeting was bound to bring. Molly was full of righteous bitterness at her younger sister's total lack of interest in her parents, and who could blame her?

She lay back replete, and dozed, wondering how Philip would cope. He had looked so worried at the prospect of being domestically in charge; his helplessness made her feel intensely irritated. She looked out at the passing fields, peppered with frost and melting snow. She was sure that he would feed the children on takeways and have Jo picked up by minicab. Something stubborn within her wanted to force him to descend from his ivory tower, to grind his aloof blond face in the filth of domestic reality, and to involve him properly in the day-to-day grind of maintaining a lifestyle with house and family at the idealistic level he had so romantically yet autocratically structured theirs to be. She knew that she was being bloody-minded, but was nevertheless obsessed with a desire to force her husband into whole-hearted participation in family life before it was too late.

Maybe she was having a domestic breakdown, she mused as the train sped on its way. Her head dizzying from wine and conflicting emotions she dozed, savouring the soothing rhythm of the train and the fact that she had almost four hours to herself.

Gareth Williams sealed his seventy-fifth envelope of job-application in six months, and wearily wrote the address which was that of a small comprehensive school in North Wales. He would hate to go back to Wales, it wasn't even a job he felt eager to get – liberal studies for pre-school leavers – but he felt bound to apply for anything that might be remotely suitable. Anthropology had seemed such an exciting and interesting thing to study when he had chosen his course at Bristol all those years ago, but now, after almost eight months of unemployment, he wasn't so sure. He spent a lot of time in the library these days: it saved his heating bills and he could rake through all the relevant periodicals and journals for possible lectureships. He had enjoyed academic life, and hoped that it wasn't closed to him for ever; this business of having no job was growing hard to take, and the fact that he knew he was merely one of the nation's three and a half million unemployed was no comfort. His book-list was beginning to do quite well, as were his odd bits of buying and selling, but the loneliness got him down. Sometimes he found himself talking almost hysterically to the children, telling them exaggerated tales of his dealings, or trying to help them with their homework when they didn't really need or want help. It was pathetic, he recognised, but perhaps inevitable. He led an abnormal life at the moment, and it didn't look likely to change, not for some time.

It was nearly three years since Jan had dumped them all and left to go to Amsterdam with her Dutch lover. 'You keep your bloody kids!' she had shrieked, wild-eyed and terrifying. 'I can't stand your dreaming any more. You do it! You cope!' And she had left him, stunned, and literally holding the babies, who were at that time only six and eight. A bitch, like his brother had warned him; Gareth hadn't spoken to his brother after that till last year, he'd been so angry. A bitch, but by God she was lovely, one of the most beautiful women he'd ever seen, with all that blonde hair and those turquoise eyes like Bronwen's. Ceri, the boy, was as black-eyed as himself.

He needed a woman, needed one physically, though he ruefully wondered if he would remember how to do it, it was so long since he had. It was also the texture of woman he missed, the soft voice, the sense, the gentleness. Dammit, what he most of all missed was simply being cuddled, that touch of loving flesh, the comforting pleasure of another person's body, the closeness and kindness. The children were loving enough, but for them he was always the fountainhead, and often he longed to lose himself a little, to forget about his responsibilities for a while. Wearily, he put on his Icelandic jersey and wrapped a scarf round his neck. He reached for his old army satchel, picked up his letter of application, checked that all the lights were out, and quietly let himself out into the modest street of small terraced houses. He would tour the junkier Portobello Road shops today, and maybe look in on that pair of birds near Westbourne Park: the big Scottish girl was a laugh, and there was something terribly attractive and vulnerable about the small dark one, Alison, was it? They had an interestingly varied lot of stock, even if the Ashanti doll had not yet brought him any real luck.

Twenty years ago, when he had married her sister, Edward Rushforth had considered Alison to be a selfish and troublesome child; she was forever upsetting her mother, then there was all that nonsense of her nearly going off to marry some wop. Ridiculous. He stood now in the station at Torquay, searching for his sister-in-law's pointed little face until he found her, white, small, smiling a mirthlessly polite greeting to him.

'Alison, my dear, let me take your bag.' They exchanged ritual pecks and he ushered her into his car – a much polished old Rover.

'How is my mother?' She asked him at last.

'Ah, well. Er, not too good, actually. Awful bad luck, you know.'

'And Daddy?'

Edward cleared his throat noisily and glared at the road in front of them; he and Molly lived in a largish house in one of the more suburban suburbs of Torquay, where Edward was a partner in a legal practice.

'Well, ah, to tell you the truth, actually. He's um . . . all right, I suppose . . . A bit quiet maybe, poor old boy, and Molly of course is so good to him, but she's been fearfully involved at the school so it's all rather problematic.'

Alison's picture of her parents wasn't really any clearer from this explanation, but it was always thus with Edward, he would hum and haw, grunt, shuffle and frown, and you would be little better off at the end of it all. He was impossible and always had been in Alison's opinion, except perhaps as a chauffeur or slight leavener of Molly's blacker moods.

At the hospital Edward ushered her into a square small ward with three old ladies in beds and one sitting in a chair. Molly stood up where she had been sitting by a white-haired old woman in foul pink crimplene and glared at Alison.

'So here you are!' she said accusingly. Primordial guilt welled up in Alison, as she offered her sister a bunch of conciliatory roses. 'I brought these . . .' she said feebly. 'Where is she?'

Molly stared at her, a slightly mad look in her rather protuberant brown eyes (she was a much larger woman than Alison) then indicated the pink-crimplened old person at her side, whose back was to Alison and Edward. 'She's here, of course. What on earth did you think? For goodness sake give the roses to her, not to me.'

Alison was six again, trying not to cry because she had been discovered rummaging in her mother's dressing table, lip-sticked and happy, but wicked as her sister's pop-eyed rebuke told her. Things had not really changed, it seemed. Edward was ushering her rather firmly – his hand on her elbow really hurt – towards this travesty of her mother, this shrunken, lop-sided thing, who stared at the leg of the nearby trolley and dribbled from one side of her mouth. But things had in fact changed almost beyond recognition, externally if not internally. It was almost impossible to reconcile her memories of this woman who had terrified and hectored her throughout her adolescence, with the pathetically frail and undignified figure she now saw in a borrowed crimplene frock.

She knew beyond doubt now that it was her mother, normally so assured and manipulative in soft lambswool and muted tweeds, because she recognised her in the lop-sided face that was looking up at her now and making those terrible gasping noises of mutual recognition. Tears coursed down the pale, lined cheeks, one of which sagged horribly from the stroke. Edward let go his grip, and Alison tried to catch her breath; she was afraid of shrieking like a madwoman and wanted to run screaming from this nightmare scene, but she knew she must not. She was a grown-up, with children she loved. She must remember that this woman was Mark and Jo's grandmother, in fact there was a look in the wet blue eyes that reminded her painfully of Jo at her most vulnerable. She took two steps forward, showed her mother the roses, and knelt tentatively before her on trembling knees. 'Hello, Mummy, I brought you these.'

Her mother's head jerked up sharply several times, and strangulated noises emitted from the lop-sided mouth, whilst her helpless right arm twitched violently. Alison felt quite sick, but caught the flailing hand as gently as she could. This sudden decay of a once-powerful human being was almost too much to confront, but she succeeded in clasping the clawed hand and held it gently. 'The children send you lots of love,' she told the spectral face. There were more awful belly-wrenched grunts and spasms as her mother wept again, and her jaw searched upwards in a frenzied gesture as though she might hook some articulacy from the empty air.

'She's a bit livelier today,' whispered Molly. 'It's the frustration that makes her cry. Not being able to say anything. But . . .' She made her voice louder so that her mother could hear her and perhaps be of good cheer, 'things will get better they say, and she will learn to speak. We all need to be patient.' She put her hand on her mother's bony shoulder with a tired tenderness which left Alison feeling absolutely bewildered, and she herself burst into a violent weeping as she knelt in front of her mother. She stroked the old woman's gnarled and twitching hand, and as she sobbed she realised that her emotion was so mis-timed as to be of absolutely no use to anybody.

Behind her Edward grimaced at his wife who nodded vehemently. Edward's officer-training from the days of the Cyprus troubles came to the fore; authoritatively he bent over his distressed heap of a sister-in-law, and once again firmly gripping her elbow, he led her blindly out into the corridor, raising his brows as they passed Molly, in a tired 'I told you so'.

Philip knew by lunchtime that he couldn't possibly be back from his office in time to collect Jo from school as promised. Not only was he almost on his knees from tiredness, but there was the big office meeting this afternoon. He had to report to the other partners on his trip to Trinidad, where they were in the short list of an important competition for a local court-house. There was still much work to be done and money to be spent by the office, and even so they might not be the firm chosen to build the final structure, but so far – and no small thanks to Philip, their golden boy – they had done very well indeed. He yawned, and thought longingly of bed: Henry Kissinger, so he was told, never flew from West to East as Philip's body complained he had just done – he always made the sometimes very expensive point of flying from East to West.

'Are you all right?' Mary, his bright secretary-cum-PA, looked at him in concern.

'Just very sleepy. My diurnal cycle is feeling somewhat battle-scarred.'

'Shall I fetch you a sandwich? Coffee?'

'Lovely, Mary, thanks. I might lie down for a minute.' He walked over to the big sofa they normally reserved for clients, and lay resting under the large window which splendidly overlooked the Thames – the office was in Battersea, built cunningly in the shell of a discarded warehouse.

He lay alone and cogitated. The school, he suspected, would not be helpful if he asked them to order a mini-cab for his twelve-year-old daughter, though Jo, he was sure, would be perfectly happy with the arrangement. Frankie: she would be his salvation he decided. He stretched for the phone and dialled the shop number.

Frankie said hello in a polite little Glasgow voice.

'Is that the glorious Frankie?' Philip's voice dropped enticingly down the scale.

'Oh, hi, Philip. How was your trip?'

'Exhausting. But there we are, that's life and foreign travel.' He came to the point. 'Frankie, I need help. I said I'd collect Jo, but now I find I can't . . .' he spoke quickly, in his most charming voice.

'What time is she supposed to be collected?'

'Four.'

'I'm really sorry, Philip, but I've got two people coming in this afternoon to collect some furniture. I daren't go out, I'm sorry. How about Mark?'

'He's got a music lesson, he'll be home late.' Philip frowned, 'OK. Thanks, Frankie. Cheers, see you soon.'

Frowning, he put down the receiver to see Mary bearing coffee and a large sandwich. She smiled, 'I couldn't help overhearing that. Maybe I could help?' Philip tried not to look too eager.

'I could pick her up. I know what she looks like from the photo on your desk. It's Notting Hill isn't it? I've done all the hefty stuff for today, and posted the mail.'

'Mary, you are a saviour. That would be wonderful.' Gratefully he took the sandwich and bit into it, wondering if he dare push her goodwill further.

'What's the problem?' Mary sat down and gazed at him almost over-eagerly. Distrait, he smoothed his brow. 'Nothing really; it's just my wife had to go to see her ill mother, and I swore I'd do a vast shopping, but I can't quite see when . . . and there's supper . . .'

'Surely you can buy a takeaway for supper?'

Philip knew in his bones that Alison wouldn't like that one either. His Little Alice was becoming a difficult lady these days, not at all like the docile little girl of yesteryear.

'Yes, you're right. A take-away it must be. The shopping will simply have to wait.' He frowned again.

'What sort of shopping?' asked Mary.

Philip waved his hand vaguely. 'Everything: food, loo-paper, the lot. The house is empty – like Mother Hubbard's cupboard – but it's not your problem, I'll cope.'

'I'll do it,' said Mary. 'Just give me the money and some idea and I'll go.'

'Really?' He looked at her hopefully. She nodded firmly.

'OK. That would be a great help.' Relieved, Philip felt in his wallet. 'Here's fifty quid. Buy a bit of everything. We'll either devour it or freeze it.'

He watched as Mary carefully pocketed the notes he had given her. 'We also need dog food,' he told her. 'Dalmatian fodder, tins and biscuits.'

After she had left, Philip closed his eyes and dozed, musing about how rich the world was in fuckable women. He slept, and dreamed of England, and England's green and pleasant girls.

Alison's first impression of her father as he shuffled out to meet her in old carpet slippers and dark suit with the dog-collar he still often wore, was that he had been bleached and had shrunk in the process. He was smaller than she had ever seen him, and walked unsteadily towards her in greeting. Alison, who had stopped crying after five minutes of familial silence and disapproval in the hospital car-park, went to kiss his quavery cheek, and was hurt when this seemed to startle him.

'Hello, Daddy.'

He nodded palely. 'Have you seen your mother?'

'Yes, we've just been.'

'How was she?' His once-bright eyes looked somehow fainter too.

Molly answered before young Alison dropped any clangers. 'Much better,' she boomed. 'I helped her to eat some mince and very nice custard. She liked it.'

The old man smiled, like a child pleased with a story.

They went into the house proper. Edward poured sherries whilst Molly banged about in the kitchen, Alison fled from the pain of her father's tearful stare and offered to help. 'You can set the table. The mats are in the middle drawer,' she was told.

'What is the prognosis for Mother?' she whispered later to Molly in the kitchen. Molly thumped down a dish of fish pie and served it out bitterly.

'Nobody knows. She might recover a little, and learn how to walk and talk again, but at her age it will be heartbreakingly slow, and Daddy can't possibly look after her. On the other hand if she has another stroke it will finish her off, unless she's desperately unlucky and suffers an even worse paralysis.'

Alison shivered. 'What will they do?'

'Shuddering doesn't help,' her older sister said unsympathetically as she spooned Brussels sprouts onto plates. 'I don't know what we will do. I suppose they will both have to be here permanently. What do you suggest?'

It was Alison's cue, she knew, but could not take it. Her own and Philip's house was no good, there was only one spare room – which had been the au-pair's when the children were younger – and that was up a flight of stairs. When her mother had been well and able to travel up to London, she and Alison had wanted to scream at each other after less than two days. She looked at the food unseeing, and shook her head. 'It's awful.'

'Yes,' said Molly. 'But it comes to us all. You, me, the children, we will all be old one day.' She shook her head, 'When I remember her going off to her WRI meetings, always in one of her hats, I can't believe it.' There were tears in the pop eyes. Extraordinarily, Molly had always adored their mother. To see Molly crying was a rarity, and it made Alison feel even more helpless.

'Shall I take these through?' She lifted a couple of heaped plates. Molly sniffed loudly, 'Yes, thank you,' and blew her nose trumpet-like on a piece of kitchen roll. 'I'm not going to put them in a home,' she sniffed. 'I couldn't bear the guilt.'

Young Richard, eighteen, the baby of Mollys' three children, tall and curly-haired, with more life and fun in him than you would have believed possible with such conventional parents, saved the evening. He even made his silent grandfather give a thin little chuckle when he described his teachers and fellow pupils. Alison had always had a soft spot for the boy, who, despite the family rift, had come up several times to stay with them in London. They ended the meal laughing faintly at some joke of Richard's but Alison caught sight of her old father who was very quiet. He saw her look and whispered apologetically, 'If you will excuse me, I think I shall go and lie down.' He eyed Molly, like a small boy asking to leave the table, and she bellowed in her bossy way 'Of course, Daddy, off you go. I'll come and see you after we've washed up.'

Later, Alison crept into her father's room bearing a cup of tea, and was shocked to find him staring at his gas fire, weeping feebly, shaking his head. 'My poor Meg,' he moaned, over and over. 'My poor girl.'

Wrung by the sight. Alison closed the door quietly, and knelt beside the old man. She had for years despised his feebleness and indecisiveness, but now, seeing his heartbreak, in which she could share so little, she felt an uneasy sensation of not being very grown-up or strong in a situation which would, she presumed, be much eased by maturity. Indeed, confronted as she now was with her ancient parents, one speechless and smitten, the other half-dotty with despair, she felt guilty, devoid of proper feeling, and wondered what crass sort of creature she had in fact become. Philip used to call her a changeling, but it was a silly joke, because these people were indeed her parents, and she recognised that somehow she must come to terms with the fact, or she would never be properly grown up.

It was dark in London when Mark arrived home from his oboe lesson, and he was surprised to find several bulging bags of supermarket food spread out on the kitchen floor. On the oval table he spotted packets of halva and chocolate biscuits, a gigantic jar of mayonnaise, cheese, meat, wine, an unseasonably golden melon and lots of grapes and avocadoes.

Puzzled, he went through to the sitting-room where Jo, ensconced once more on the sofa, was sipping a Fanta as she watched the television.

'Hi,' Mark eyed her, 'where's Pa?'

'Working, I suppose.' Jo didn't turn round.

Annoyed, Mark turned down the sound, and she yelled angrily at him.

'Tell me,' said Mark, 'are we having a party or what? All that stuff, where did it come from?'

'Mary brought it.'

'Who's Mary, for goodness sake?'

'Shh,' Jo put her finger to her lips, 'she's in the loo. Has been for ages.' She giggled.

They heard the lavatory flush and the bathroom door open, and Mark saw a dark curly-haired girl in her twenties standing in the doorway. She was wearing an apron which had a smiley yellow sun on it, and said 'Happy Days'.

'Hello there.' She entered the room beaming. 'I'm Mary, from your father's office; he was held up and asked me to help with the shopping. I'm just going to unpack it and go. Philip will be home soon after six.'

Ungraciously Mark made himself a coffee and watched the girl unpack the many glorious goodies.

Then, unable to restrain himself, he asked if he might take some halva.

'Of course.' She handed him a whole bar. He nodded, tried to withhold a smile, and took himself off to his room where he drank his coffee and uneasily ate the entire block of halva. He didn't like coming home to find a stranger in the house, particularly not a stranger who used his father's name so freely. It didn't feel right, especially because she was wearing his mother's apron, the one he had given her last Christmas. Surely such things were not transferable.

Chapter Five

Alison put down the receiver and walked along the hospital corridor wondering why it was that everything Philip did or said these days seemed to aggravate her. On the phone, he had asked – surreally, it seemed to her – was it really necessary to par-boil potatoes for roasting, and although she was obsessed these days that Philip should be actively domestic, when he was, it often somehow irritated her beyond belief. She was too young to be menopausal; she had two lovely intelligent children, a devoted husband who was a good provider, and couldn't help being away on business so often, plus she had her own absorbing business outside the marriage. She had everything that most people longed for, so why was she such a malcontent? Why did it feel so empty?

There was a clattering of dishes in the hospital kitchen; she hurried because she was due to help the nurses by feeding her mother. Her mother still displayed recognition when she saw Alison, but didn't flail about as she had done on the first evening; today she stared at her in her lop-sided way and made noises, unintelligible and formless, whilst she groped faintly with her one live hand. Alison tried to look cheerful, but the sight still confused her with panic and horror. She also felt pity, of a tearing disembowelling sort, which made her want to escape screaming along the corridors of the hospital to howl on the windy moors and hills behind the town, expressing her outrage at a world where such things were normal everyday happenings. Lord, Lord, how are the mighty fallen?

'I've brought some nice soup for you.' Alison knelt beside the stricken woman and tucked a bib under her questing chin.

'Aaarghh . . .' said her mother, and Alison tried to find a pattern in the sound. Maybe she was trying to say her name.

'Did you say Alison?' She gazed intently at the ill woman.

Her mother was earnestly trying to tell her something, straining, stumble-tongued, muscles utterly uncontrolled. Tragic.

'I'm sorry, I don't get it. Here, try some soup. Automatically she tasted it to test for heat as you did for a baby. The sick woman painfully concentrated as the spoonful went down. 'Good.' Alison wiped off the surplus from that once fearsome, now pitiful, face. Her mother was trying to speak again.

'Gargh . . .' she said, and something in her expression communicated itself to her daugher. 'It's good, is it? You like it?' Alison tried to translate the sounds.

Her mother was smiling – she felt sure it was a smile. 'Oh good, I am so glad that something can give you pleasure.'

Biting back her tears, Alison gently gave the ex-ogress more soup, and felt moved as though a baby had smiled at her for the first time. Then, moments later – she didn't quite see what happened – but an out-of-control hand jerked towards the soup. Her mother made more noises, and the bowl went flying out of her hand and shattered into pieces along with the moment of recognition, spraying both her mother and herself with orange tomato liquid, and the old woman was once more transferred into an unintelligible weeping travesty of what once she had been.

If you can't beat 'em, join'em, Philip decided. So she was feeling hard done by, that she had been left for too long holding the family together on a day-to-day basis. Maybe it had been a strain, what with the emergence of her own business, and now the worry about her parents, but dammit, he only did it all for her and the kids, to give them this comfortable lifestyle with beautiful aesthetics to grow up in. He wished he knew what she wanted. Anyway, whatever it was, he wanted her happy, that was for sure. He lay in bed savouring the Sunday papers with a large cup of coffee and wondered what he could do to help. Flowers: that would soften her up – he would send Mark out for some – and he would cook: it would be relaxing, and might help to take his mind off the pressing problems of the big competition which was next on his agenda. He frowned at the thought of returning so soon to Hong Kong: it was only four months since he had been there in the faceless hotel, with the noise and the thronging millions in the streets. It was too soon to go again, but it was one of the most prestigious-looking jobs the British Consultancy Bureau had put him on for a very long time.

It was also a bore that he couldn't do any shooting when he was there; Philip's sport was to hunt game wherever and whenever he could. He belonged to a syndicate with several friends on an estate in Dorset, but had been so busy that he hadn't managed to get down there for over a year. In the old days his hobby had slotted in very well with the family, because Alison enjoyed coming to the country with the children but with her increasing absorption with her business the occasion never seemed to present itself any more. It was sad, it had done them both good: they had been happier then, less preoccupied with their own ploys. They both needed a break.

In the train Alison shut her eyes and tried to blot out the image of her mother's toiling inarticulate face she saw in her own window-reflection, but the vision remained inexorably burning like some ghastly turnip-lantern even when she drifted into sleep. The problem seemed to insurmountable, so awful, whatever view you tried to take. If her mother got even a little better, there was still her father to worry about; he seemed unable to open a tin or even make himself a cup of tea. Anyway, she couldn't really imagine her mother getting much better – her nervous system was pretty wrecked. And Molly? What about her? She would crack if the present business went on and on, but it might: people lived well into their eighties and nineties these days. Both parents might drag on for years. She groaned and put her hands to cover her face, momentarily enjoying the coolness and comfort of her own flesh. She was flesh of their flesh, her father and mother, whether she liked it or not, and a strange ache in her centre seemed constantly to remind her of the fact. A home? That was what Philip always talked about, but that was Philip all over – his own parents had died years ago in an accident – and he never spoke about them. 'Get the right person to do the job and you're half way there,' he always said, but it didn't feel right when the job was that of your own kin, even if you had hated them for years, and still sometimes wanted to scream at your doddery old father for being wavery and pathetic. Poor old man, he had only been trying to set the table for tea, but somehow he had done everything wrong.

There was no easy answer: as Frankie so often said when things looked black: 'There's not a lot you can do about it, dearie, life's a terminal disease, and that's all there is to it.'

A magnificent smell of baking bread engulfed Alison when Philip greeted her at the front door; he was wearing the 'Happy Days' apron with the smiley yellow sun, and held his arms wide to enfold her, carefully avoiding contaminating her with his doughy spoon or floury hand. 'Welcome back, darling, lovely to see you.' He stood back and beamed down at his little woman returned to the fold.

At the station, where Frankie and Mark had met her, Mark had presented her with a flamboyant bunch of white roses from Philip. It was strange, but she had felt a frisson of disappointment, a wish that sometimes he would give her brightly coloured flowers, red or orange. It was a ritual, an obsession that had gone on for too long, all this white.

'Lovely smells,' she smiled at her husband.

'I fancied making some bread, I used that nutty brown flour.'

The flour must be all of three years old, but Alison said nothing. Maybe the container had been airtight; it certainly smelled very good. In the old days before domesticity had palled for her, before she had discovered about Philip's affair, she used often to bake bread. It certainly made the house feel very welcoming.

'Come and have tea, you must be exhausted.' Philip led the way to the kitchen and laid down his wooden spoon in a bowl of batter. Then, after carefully washing his hands, he made a pot of tea.

'Anything I can do to help?' asked Frankie.

Philip pointed across the table, 'If you could pass me that lot . . .'

Frankie reached her long arm and handed him a large flat dish covered with a spotless dishcloth. He stood proudly by to make sure that everyone was watching, then, with a conjuror's flourish, whipped off the cloth, revealing a plateful of perfect flapjacks, brown and crisp.

'How about that?' His face beamed flushed and proud above the silly yellow sun.

The youngsters clapped, and Alison smiled, feeling terribly sad. Frankie's eyes widened in admiration. 'He's a wonder!' she said, jabbing Alison in the side. 'Where did you find him?'

Alison's icebergs of unease slowly melted in the comfort of food and family warmth. It was good to be home. The visit to Torquay began to feel like a very bad dream. She looked across the table to where Frankie happily munched a fifth flapjack. 'Where's the stuff?' she asked; she knew that Frankie had brought the hamper of linen.

'In the sitting-room. I looked at some of it; you'll make a bomb on it, there's an amazing embroidered farmer's smock that I lust after.'

'A proper oldie?'

Frankie nodded, flapjack-crumbed.

'It's terrific. Worth a hundred at least; it was

parcelled up in the bottom, inside a tablecloth. You did a real good deal.'

Excited, Alison went to look.

'Don't worry, darling, we'll wash up,' said Philip.

'Thanks.' It was good to know someone else was doing it – the eternal Someone Else, that He, or She to whom work could be delegated. There was a lot to be said for delegating sometimes, but like everything else it was essential to find a balance, a give and take. That was the real problem, to find the balance. She looked up and saw Frankie enthusiastically dancing around with an exquisitely embroidered white smock, long-sleeved, tough white linen, old, beautifully worked and perfect. 'Isn't it fantastic?'

Alison fingered the tightly woven fabric and wondered at the detail of the embroidery. 'It is stunning. It could be a museum piece.'

She was excited now, her worries about over-spending on the lot fading fast. 'What else is there?'

'There's loads.'

Jo was watching: 'Why don't you just tip up the basket and empty it all out?'

Frankie looked at Alison, and simultaneously they reached the hamper and heaved it up and over, spilling a mountain of white and frilly garments all over the unblemished expanse of virgin carpet.

'What a lot!' Jo gasped. 'There's hundreds of things.'

Alison grinned. She went to the wall-phone and took the notepad they used for messages, and a biro: 'We might as well catalogue it now.'

Frankie was immediately business-like and practical. 'Let's sort it into heaps, tablecloths, underwear, hankies and so on.' She squatted down and started dividing up the things, crooning often at some particularly spectacular piece. Jo spotted a camisole, frilly-armed, broderie anglaise, with a low neckline.

'Can I try this on?'

Alison nodded surprised and pleased, but she supposed that with Jo this came under the category of dressing-up rather than a feminine interest in clothes suddenly burgeoning along with her young body.

Jo ripped off her stripey jersey and put on the camisole top, turning self-consciously aside to hide her new-growing bosom. Then, grabbing a pair of long frilly drawers she tugged off her jeans, pulled on the white cotton laciness, and danced round the room, holding her blond ponytail up high with one hand behind her head, securing the frilly drawers with the other. 'Sous les ponts de Paree . . .' she crooned, swaying, grinning, suddenly a sensuous young woman, all in white, with a most appealing cleavage and thick woolly striped socks jutting out entertainingly from beneath the frills. Philip came through to watch, still be-aproned, cooking pot in hand, as Frankie, inspired by Jo's song and dance, put on the white farmer's smock and a woolly hat, grasped two white roses from the vase Somebody had so kindly arranged them in, handed one to Jo, and kept the other, then joined with her in a crazed, extempore dance, until they collapsed giggling on the soda. Philip and Alison clapped and cheered.

'I begin to understand why you go to the shop so much,' said Philip. 'Puts paid to architecture any day.' He grinned ruefully, still balancing his pot, which was full of water, and went back to the kitchen to continue his woman's work with all the clinical passion and absorption he normally applied to architecture.

By the time that Philip summoned them through to eat at the beautifully set glass oval table, so in keeping with the rest of the rather sparse high-tech room, Alison was justifiably jubilant. There were one hundred and seven items, the first sixteen of which when she totalled up what she thought them likely to fetch, added up to a hundred pounds more than she had so tremblingly paid out at auction.

'It's the best buy I've seen you do.' Firmly Frankie re-packed the hamper. 'Most of them have never been used, and you don't have to wash them all, just some of them. But you'll need to iron them all.' The way Frankie said 'iron', with a strongly pronounced 'r' always amused Alison.

As they sat at the table and watched in admiration as Philip, flushed from his culinary exertions, carried through a huge piece of crackling roast beef, roast potatoes and full trimmings, Alison felt a childish desire to giggle hysterically. These role-reversals viewed in her mother, husband and daughter, all in the space of a couple of days were positively dizzying.

'Dad,' Mark frowned as his father carved the meat, 'Are you going to keep that apron on all night too? You've been wearing it since breakfast.'

'Oh,' Philip seemed disappointed. 'I had grown rather fond of it. Should I take if off?'

'Yeah,' said Mark. 'You look a bit of a wally in it.'

Philip removed the apron with dignity, and wallowed as his work was consumed and admired. To Alison it seemed that he displayed such a desperate desire to please that she wondered momentarily if he were behaving like this from guilt.

There was a great clattering of forks and knives, amid exclamations of appreciation. Alison tried to eat, but something in Jo's absorbed face brought back the nightmare turnip-lantern grimace of her mother's speechless strivings, and her mood soured suddenly from hysterical laughter to tearfulness. Frankie caught her look. 'You all right?' she whispered.

'Not really . . .' Alison put down her fork and knife. 'It's been quite a few days . . . . I'm tired.' She pushed aside her brimming plate. 'I'm sorry,' she said. 'I'm just not hungry.'

Abruptly she rose from the table and moved clumsily to the sitting-room where she stood blindly, her back to them all, sobbing helplessly. The family and Frankie looked anxiously through the door. Jo came and put her arms round her mother; they were almost the same height, Alison noticed subliminally.

'Don't cry, Mum. Maybe Grandma will get better.'

Alison sobbed louder and shook her head. 'She's so ill,' she bawled.

Mark now stood beside them. He touched Jo's shoulder. 'Grandma's really old, Jo,' he told her earnestly.

Jo looked very young and worried. 'Will she die?' she asked, looking up at Philip who now stood helplessly by. It was Mark who answered her.

'Jo. It's natural. People have to die when they are old.'

Turning to Alison he held her elbow tenderly. 'Ma. Please come back and be with us; we do understand.'

Silently they returned to the table and resumed the meal, with Alison taking token nibbles. The dog beneath the table, encircled by ten legs, was euphoric, served delicacies in secret by five clandestine hands, the owner of each one believing him or herself to be the sole canine benefactor at the meal.

Later, Alison went to see Frankie out. The Scots girl started to walk down the front path, then turned, lit by the lamp outside the front door.

'By the way, that bearded Welsh guy looked in again. Bought a whole lot of those old Australian postcards of naked aboriginals – the naughty ones.

Seemed very pleased with them. I did my best to chat him up – he's awfully nice – but he wasn't interested. You could tell he was disappointed.'

'Disappointed? Why?'

Frankie grinned wickedly in the yellow light. 'Because my partner wasn't there.' She waved her brightly mittened hand in bravura farewell as she walked away, 'Byee!' she called, teasing, and was gone into the night.

Smiling, Alison shut the door, and re-entered the house. She shook her head: Frankie was daft, daft as a brush. Saying that about Esau: he probably didn't even remember what she looked like. She could remember him though, and could even imagine him with red roses.

Chapter Six

At the riverside offices of Salveson, Robson and partners, Architects, Mary Henderson frowned and tried not to let herself be distracted by the infinite soothability of senior partner Philip Salveson's smooth blond brow, as he in turn frowned and concentrated in higher things. He was dictating to Mary, who crouched over her shorthand pad, keen to please her unattainable but alluring boss. Philip stopped dictating, opened his pale eyes and gazed out across the Thames; it was a fine view, even on this grey winter day, a generous, spacious panorama, with the great river, small boats, bridges busy with traffic, and the trees, stark and beautiful, across on the other side. He had chosen the site well.

'Get those typed up and ready to sign by lunch, will you, Mary? I shan't be here in the afternoon; there's the Hong Kong prime-up at the Hilton'

The girl nodded, and started to organise papers.

'And Mary?' She looked up, hoping the flush she felt when she confronted him full-face didn't show. 'Yes?'

'Are you doing anything tonight?' He was smiling straight at her. She gulped, and wanted to put her hand on her chest to try to quieten the pitter-pattering, but thought better of it. 'No, I don't think so . . .'

'I was asking because we're a bit stuck again . . .' said Philip, and her pitter-pattering sputtered to a stop. 'My wife has to go out to a meeting.' When Alison had said what the meeting was, Philip had actually roared at the nonsense of it. 'A nuclear disarmament meeting? Are you mad? It's bad enough Mark wearing these silly badges, but one expects such behaviour from adolescent children. Surely you are old enough and intelligent enough to know that we can't possibly do without a proper defence system and decent deterrents. It is child-like!'

Alison had stared stonily up at him, her dark eyes larger and unfriendlier than he had ever seen them. 'I told you days ago that I had a meeting tonight; it is something I want to find out more about. I need to know.'

'But I have an Architectural Committee tonight.'

'You didn't say so before.'

'It's always on the third Thursday of the month.'

'You missed the last two.'

'Anyway,' Philip had glared 'Mark will be in, won't he? Then there's no need for a sitter?'

'He's got a school theatre trip.'

'How about Frankie?' (Frankie often stayed with Jo if she were by herself.)

'Frankie's coming with me.'

'Dammit!' Philip had clutched his head. 'I must go, I'm late!'

'So am I.' Alison's voice was cold and computer-like. 'You will have to arrange for somebody; I did warn you that I'd be out.'

'You mean you need a baby-sitter?' Mary's smile dimmed sharply as she met Philip's apologetically persuasive gaze.

'Yes . . . . Jo will be alone otherwise. She's perfectly capable, but just too young to be legally left utterly alone for an evening. Any chance? We will reward you of course, my dear.' He flirted now, automatically. She was very pretty.

Mary's pitter-patters started up like an engine which suddenly goes strong and smooth with the choke pulled out.

'Of course I'll help. What time would you like me?' She wanted to be involved with Philip on any terms. This was better than nothing, and might lead on to greater intimacies.

'Good girl! I knew I could rely on you!' He was out of the room in a moment, leaving her reeling from the memory of his tweedy hug. Blinking, she settled down to transcribe his words onto the architectural notepaper with the sparely designed office logo. She wanted Philip like she had never wanted anyone, and she intended to get him somehow, if necessary by proving her indispensability to him.

Alison arrived late at the shop, greeted Frankie with a glower, and hung up her coat so angrily that it fell to the floor almost immediately.

'What's up?' Frankie went automatically to fill the kettle as her partner flopped herself down on an elegant brown velvet love-seat and shut her eyes.

'Is it your mother?' Alison's head shook.

'The kids?'

'No . . . it's just . . . just that I've had enough!' Angrily, Alison beat the brown velvet arms of the love-seat and sobbed. Frankie, worried, sat in the empty side of the love-seat – which, from above, was S-shaped, so that if two people sat in it, they were shoulder-to-shoulder, cheek-to-cheek intimate. She touched Alison's arm gently. 'What's going on?'

Alison's eyes were still tight shut as she grasped to define her rage. 'I am sick of being a second-class citizen. Sick of being treated as a rather sweet but silly girl – not even a woman. I am sick. . .' Frankie watched in alarm, as her friend stood up, her face tense and pained, and shouted 'Sick to death of being smothered! I want to be me, to be free, to be my own keeper!' She sobbed breathily.

'Help, murder, Polis!' muttered Frankie to herself. 'This is bad.' She patted Alison. 'Sit down,' she said. 'Have some coffee.'

Alison felt all of a sudden very weak, and Frankie saw how white she was as she sighed tiredly, emptily. 'I'm sorry. I'm just in a state.'

'I can see that, dearie.' Wordlessly Frankie handed Alison a steaming cup of comfort. She took it gratefully, and noticed as she did so that Frankie was wearing a black and white CND badge. She sipped her drink, eyeing the badge, red-eyed.

'Do you think it's wise to wear that in the shop?' she asked.

'Why not? I could put it upside-down so it means 'Ban Y-fronts' if you'd prefer?'

Alison almost smiled. 'It's just that people are funny about coming into shops; I would prefer that you didn't actually wear it here, it's unbusiness-like.' She felt a little puzzled by her own feelings, and, remembering Philip's paternalistic and scathing comments about the irresponsible zealotry of the anti-nuclear brigade, and her own decision to go to a meeting tonight, started to laugh weakly at her own confusion of ethics. Tears were still not far away.

Frankie surveyed her. 'You are in a helluva bad way,

Mrs Salveson. OK, if it troubles you, I'll not wear the badge in the shop, but I just feel that I need to stand up and be counted. I was talking to your kids the other day when we were waiting for you at the station. It's terrifying; they don't think they will have a future, a world to live in. They're so sad and pessimistic about it. I'm telling you Jo is really scared.'

Alison nodded wearily; she knew all too well Jo's dark and fearful side. Once it was ghosts, but now it was for her own future she feared. And Mark? His badge stated his fear. And Alison? She who had just asked Frankie not to wear her badge, her statement of belief. Where did that leave her?

Her doubts were momentarily interrupted by the first customer of the day, a well-suited man, a dealer from the posher reaches of north London, who usually bought and spent generously. He was immediately taken by Frankie's Clarice Cliff teaset.

'Nice.' He handled the – to Alison, crudely decorated – pieces, and peered at the label. 'What's the best you can do on that?' Alison summoned Frankie and left her to it; Frankie hummed and hawed, and said she would drop a fiver. The dealer put the teacup down and examined something quite different – this time an Art-Nouveau silver frame belonging to Alison – which was also priced high, but was unusually pretty, a complicated design, well-made and perfect, worth its money.

The dealer smiled, jolly and friendly, and made an offer for the teaset and picture frame which was about twenty per cent below the asking price. Alison shook her head behind his fat, well-tailored back.

'No,' said Frankie, and Alison noticed with amusement that she subtly held her scarf over the black-and-white badge. 'But I'd do the pair for a tenner less.'

'I'll think about it,' said the man.

Fed up at losing what would have been quite a good pair of sales, Frankie gave a momentary pout of regret in Alison's direction as the man finished looking round the shop and left.

'Damn.' She frowned after she had closed the door behind him. 'I was absolutely certain he would buy those.'

'Me too,' Alison shrugged and sighed.

'Ah well, you can't win them all.' Frankie sat down spreading her limbs out wide, and stared out of the window. 'It would be nice to be a really successful dealer with one of those great wads of notes like he had.'

'Underneath your CND badge? Close to your heart?' queried Alison. 'I saw you hide it.'

Frankie blushed. 'I suddenly saw what you meant; he was the kind who would have stayed on to tell me how stupid and childish it all was.'

'Like my husband,' Alison's voice was quiet.

'Alison, you're being too hard on poor Philip.'

'It's just how I feel.'

The phone rang: Alison leant across to answer it. A polite male voice, well-educated, deep and friendly, asked to speak to Frankie. Alison handed the phone to Frankie, who looked surprised.

'Hello?' She listened, then, a little embarrassed, glanced at Alison and turned away. Sensing her friend's need for privacy, Alison went over to examine the rail of linen near the door, and checked through the prices. As she fiddled and Frankie burned – her cheeks were flaming – another customer, a youngish American dealer whom Alison recognised from Market days, came in and carefully looked through the rail of linen before picking out half-a-dozen of the better pieces; 'I also like the man's smock,' she said, 'but it's a lot of money.'

'I have never seen one as good, except in the V & A.' Alison pulled the heavily-embroidered garment out on its hanger, smoothing it seductively in front of her. The American looked long and carefully. 'Yeah, it's beautiful, but out of my league, unless you go down a whole lot.' She bent over the heap she had picked out, and together they added and haggled, gently, friendly, and in the end were both pleased.

When the woman had left, her hold-all bulging with carefully folded linen, Alison brandished her three-figure cheque in triumph at Frankie, who didn't seem to be concentrating. 'What was the phone-call?' Alison asked, remembering.

Frankie expressed embarrassment, excitement and terror all at once, with breathless squeaks and gestures. 'I've got a date.'

'Already? From your ad?'

'No. I answered that nice-sounding one. The miniature painter. He even lives not far away, just across the park in a basement flat with a studio in the backyard. He sounds really nice.' She was quite starry-eyed. She pronounced 'really' like she sounded, reeling.

'When are you going to see him?'

'Tomorrow night. We're meeting for a drink in Queensway.'

'Well done!'

'He's got a lovely name.' Frankie was far far away. 'Anthony Brownstone . . .' She savoured it, daydreaming.

Alison tried to bring her down to earth. 'What will you wear?'

'Could I borrow the white smock?'

'Certainly not. What if you spilt wine on it?'

'I would look all virginal and bridal if I wore it.'

'Enough to terrify anybody who had been so lonely-hearted as to put an ad in a magazine.'

'Oh dear,' Frankie was properly worried. 'What will I wear?'

'Oh come on, just what you feel really you in, and not too outrageous. Don't wear all your tartans at the same time.'

'OK.' Thoughtful, she turned to Alison. 'Listen, are you all right? You were in a bad way before that dealer arrived. What happened this morning?'

'It wasn't just this morning. It's all the time; Philip and I seem to antagonise each other simply by being ourselves.'

'Oh come on. That's not funny; you two have everything going for you. You're in a strange mood at the moment: it's probably to do with your mother being so ill, and the children growing up. They don't need you so much these days, and it gives you too much time to think.'

'It certainly does;' Alison, seated once more on the love-seat, was very sad. 'Maybe I ought to take alcohol or drugs, and try to escape reality.'

'I think, therefore I drink, eh?'

Alison smiled bleakly and shrugged.

'Here,' said Frankie, reaching into the depths of her bulky embroidered jacket. 'This is what you need.' Tenderly, she handed her friend a packet of polo mints. Alison took one and sucked it, then took two of the small white circles of sweet and inserted one in each eye. She looked as though she was wearing a tiny pair of thick white spectacles.

Frankie laughed: 'That's better!'

Alison at last stood up; she sighed, removed the polo mints and put on her coat. 'I must go and do the rounds. See you later.'

‘OK. Good hunting.’ Frankie looked up: ‘You are going to the meeting tonight?’

Alison’s dark eyes flashed. ‘Of course! I will no longer be dictated to for anything! Sheep’s lib! M-e-e-eh!’

She came to the Hammersmith roundabout and drove south until she reached a grotty side-street with two shops where she often junk-hunted. She always felt a frisson of excitement when she came here; over the last two or three years she had found one or two astonishing bargains, though not in the last few months. She wondered what goodies she might find today, especially as she was flush for a change. Just lately, she had had the feeling that she and Frankie might be about to move up a notch or two on the success-scale; it was an exhilarating thought. As she peered in the window, piled high with an incredible assortment of objects – a solar topee nestled with a stuffed, headless swan, and heaps of cracked china plates supported old hockey-sticks, an interesting-looking crystal inkwell and plastic shoes. Excited, she pushed her way into the shop where a weary-looking man in a blue pin-striped suit and tattered floral shirt, eyed her sleepily, and nodded recognition. Alison spent an entertaining twenty minutes or so grovelling, pulling things out from their retaining tangles of alien objects, and came up with several reasonable finds. The inkwell, which had silver fittings on well-designed crystal, might well have been worth quite a lot of money, but it was chipped. She spotted, high up on a far shelf, a large bundle of African jewellery, beaded necklaces and cache-sexes, and several brass and copper bracelets, all very dusty and messy, but interesting. She liked their sculptural shapes, and pulled the bundle down to have a closer look, but her gesture suddenly animated the man who looked up and shook his finger at her.

'No darling, not vose, vey're laid aside for a fella, a local fella, buys all vat native stuff.'

'Oh.' Disappointed, she saw that the beaded necklaces were particularly complex and the beads were the old hand-made kind, all slightly different.

'Sorry about vat, dear, but 'e comes in most days. Only lives round the corner.'

The penny dropped. It must be that guy, that nice one. 'Has he got a beard, this fellow?'

'S'right. Very dark, sounds Scottish or something.' The man sniffed, and re-read his *Standard* for the third time.

Alison reluctantly put back all the African things, and pulled out a Staffordshire figure of a highwayman. It wasn't a particularly nice one, and was also damaged, but she bought it. She also bought a couple of glass necklaces, a battered mother-of-pearl knife (silver), and the solar topee, Frankie would like it. She would probably threaten to wear it for her lonely-heart meeting.

She paid the man after a ritual haggle, and put the various things into her battered leather bag. It was heavy and strong, but tatty; she didn't like looking too opulent when she went out to buy.

She moved on to the next shop several doors down, where she found nothing of any interest, only dusty clothes and pee-smelling carpets. She drove two or three streets further on, and here she found quite good pickings, including a good pine chest of drawers, which needed to be stripped, but was very sellable. On the whole it was a good day's hunting, she was pleased, and forgot about the growing sense of isolation she felt within her marriage for all of an hour or two.

At supper Alison ate with Mark and Jo, and Jo expressed her displeasure that she would be subjected to young Mary's company for the evening.

'She talks all the time, never stops. Keeps asking me about school and pretending to be terribly interested – she even collects dolls – yuck! You can tell she's an imbecile; fancy collecting dolls at that age. She's about twenty-four; must be mad!'

'I sell lots of dolls to grown-ups – men, women, all sorts,' said Alison trying to pacify her. 'I sold a teddy to quite a famous actor only last week.'

'Proper old ones are different. She has Snoopy dolls even – she told me – seemed to think I'd be fascinated.'

'I'm sorry, love,' Alison said as she finished wiping crumbs from the table, 'but it's for our own peace of mind. Soon you will be safe on your own, but not quite yet. I'll try not to be too late.'

'You're always out these days.' Pouting, Jo bounced a white football round and round the table, missed, and it went flying onto a heap of crockery on the sink, making great noise and smashing a mug.

Alison shrieked with rage. 'For heaven's sake! How many times have I told you not to play with that bloody thing inside the house. Go outside if you must let off steam!' Furious, she slammed the crockery into the rubbish bin. Sometimes, when her daughter was in this sort of mood, she wished she *would* play with dolls for a change.

'Anyway,' Jo glared, tears not far off, 'you *are* always going out. All you ever think about is antiques!'

'What?' Alison reared up, the bait taken good and

proper. 'What do you mean? I have a job to do, a shop to run. I haven't been out except to work or to go down to see poor Grandma for ages. How dare you say that!'

'And Dad's always out or away.' The blonde fringe was askew, the tomboy crying. Red-faced, Jo slammed out and there was a bang of the bathroom door and emphatic click of the lock. Alison rushed after her and beat on the door. 'Jo, come out, please, I want to talk to you!'

'Go away!'

Alison gestured helplessly towards the ceiling, God or the sky. Mark, who had been silent throughout their exchange, reached for his coat which was slung over a chair-back. 'Just leave her. She's been in a funny mood ever since she came home. The girls have been getting at her for all her football stuff.' He looked at his mother who was also tearful now. 'Honestly Mum, you take things far too seriously. Just go. Jo will be fine once you've gone. She doesn't have to talk to that twit.'

'Is she a twit? Dad said she was very bright.'

Mark didn't answer, but grinned a silly smile.

'What's wrong with her? She seemed OK when I met her at the office party.'

The boy shrugged. 'I dunno, she just seems a bit well, you know . . . keen.' Hurriedly, when he saw that his mother wished to be enlightened further, he pulled on his over-large army greatcoat. 'I've got to go. I'll be late.'

Alison finished clearing up, confused, as she so often was. Was it fair to be out when Jo obviously needed attention, and so disliked the girl who was coming? Was it really necessary to go to a nuclear disarmament meeting because Frankie had got her enthused? She slammed the cutlery drawer shut: of course she must go. It was important to her, and, obliquely, to the children. Very. She decided to spend time with Jo at the weekend; maybe they could all go out on Sunday – the whole family for a change, like they used to – and take the dog to Richmond. Then she remembered that Philip was setting off again on Sunday, this time for Hong Kong. Sighing, she went to open the door to the ever-bright and sweet-smelling Mary.

'Good evening, Mrs Salveson; your husband asked me to come about seven, I hope that was right?'

Alison felt rather drab in her brown skirt and jumper beside Mary's bright red very mini-dress and high shiny boots. Even her own favourite boots, in burgundy leather, suddenly seemed middle-aged and boring as she helped the girl with her coat.

'I'm just about to go off, but I'm afraid that Jo and I had a contretemps . . .' She lowered her voice. 'She's locked herself in the loo.'

'Oh dear!' Mary's father was colonel of the regiment, and occasionally it showed in his daughter's intonation, when a sort of military jolliness obtruded.

'Just like the three old ladies!' she shrilled. 'Don't worry,' she assured Alison, 'I know my way around; I'll cope, and get her chatting.'

Alison paused as she wrapped her own outer garments round herself. 'I didn't realise you had been here before.' Her tone was interrogative, her antennae trembling.

'Oh?' Mary hooted again, a nervous jolly hoot. 'Didn't they tell you? When you were away? I helped out with shopping and things because Phi . . . er, Mr Salveson, was jet-lagged and had a meeting. And I picked up Jo from school.'

'Ah,' Alison nodded, and yashmacked herself with the big red scarf: 'I hadn't realised; I had been rather impressed with the unusual display of domesticity.'

Mary grinned nervously, just as Jo emerged from the bathroom with her hair wrapped in a towelling turban. She grunted as she walked past the two women; Alison reached out to touch her shoulder affectionately, 'I'll see you later, darling.' Jo avoided her touch, and wordlessly went to sit on the sofa beside the dog. Alison's last picture of her turbanned mini-virago was of her gnawing her thumb, concentrating on the television screen as she used the remove control panel to swing from channel to channel.

As Alison opened the door, a thought struck her. 'Mary?' she looked at the girl's huge frank eyes. 'You didn't bake the bread, did you?'

'Bread?' the girl was obviously nonplussed.

'Forget it.' Alison had the grace to grin, and left.

Chapter Seven

The small church hall was crowded when Frankie and Alison arrived at the nuclear disarmament meeting; they squeezed their way in to a couple of empty seats and eyed their neighbours. Neither of them knew anybody well, though Alison vaguely recognised a couple of people from the shop and one or two parents from the school. She was impressed by the age range. There were a few very old people; one knobbled, arthritic woman in a Chinese jacket, embroidered white on blue, with a pale blue hat, looked bright eyed and eager, and wore her black and white CND badge with pride and elegance. There were several young people in their twenties, earnest and concerned, and a beautiful pregnant girl, whose dignified profile over her swelling belly moved Alison with its purity.

Leaflets were being passed round, and an anxious man in flared trousers and glasses held up a blue and white poster with sort of childish cut-out shapes of people holding hands. 'Can any one of you display them? It's the Easter Friday demonstration. There's going to be a fourteen-mile-long link-up of people from Greenham Common to Aldermaston, right across the Downs. Please come, we need as many people as possible, there may well be a turn-out of a hundred thousand; we have groups coming from all over the country.'

'That sounds fantastic,' said Frankie, 'especially if it's a lovely day. Let's go!'

'It's Good Friday. The kids will be off school; I don't know . . .'

'Young Mark told me he'd fixed to go anyway with some friends. He's camping nearby.'

'I hadn't realised he was going on the march. I knew he was thinking of going for a cycle trip with tents . . .'

'He would have told you. You've been a bit taken up with your own problems,' Frankie whispered.

The leaflet man was looking down at them. He held out the posters. 'Would you like to display one?'

Frankie looked at Alison; it was quite a sweet poster, innocuous. Alison paused, 'All right. But just a little one.'

'Good girl.' Frankie patted her arm, and took one.

The lights were suddenly put out and a large television turned on. They were to watch a documentary film made in Edinburgh; the operator of the cassette apologised for the quality of the film, and Alison's heart sank as snowfields of grotty flak drifted across the screen, but then a woman doctor, an Australian, who informed them quite soon that she was forty-two, came into focus through the flak, and Alison was riveted, enthralled by the sense and straightness of the woman's talk, and horrified almost to tears by the content of what she said.

The doctor on the television was dressed simply and smartly, and looked tidy and exceedingly sane. She commenced by telling her audience that there was really no separation between so-called peaceful reactors and the creation of nuclear weapons because a nuclear power-station built for peaceful purposes was in fact producing the essential radioactive ingredients which are needed to manufacture bombs and missiles. And now, she said (and the film was already a couple of years old) there are thirty-five countries with the capability of producing atomic weapons because they have the set-up with their peaceful nuclear reactors.

She went on to describe the various kinds of radiation that exist, starting with X-rays. Alison tried to remember them all but couldn't quite, but she did take in the comment that all five sorts damage the structure of whatever genes they are exposed to, and that it can take up to fifty years before that radiation which has lain dormant in effect goes berserk and causes uncontrolled cell division and cancers – which fact, the speaker chillingly pointed out, leaves the physicists free to wreak more long-term havoc. Because of the huge time-lag they feel no guilt or come-back.

Frankie, listening intently, bit her lip, and caught Alison's eye a couple of times in agonised helplessness. The doctor went on to describe, in her matter-of-fact way what radiation sickness was like, how your hair falls out, you get ulcers, mouth ulcers, subcutaneous bleeding and vomiting, none of which is treatable medically. She spoke of the present epidemic of cancer, which in the States was one in three people. 'Plutonium,' she said, 'is thalidomide for ever.'

Then she said that the Joint Chiefs of Staff in the United States had said recently that they considered there to be a fifty-fifty chance of nuclear war by 1985. Alison Salveson felt sick and thought of her children, Mark with his 'Give Life a Chance,' and Jo, kicking and fighting her own aggressive way through life. Maybe her own mother was lucky to be near the end of her life.

'It doesn't matter,' said the woman doctor, still

sounding totally sane and intelligent. 'It doesn't matter if our kids brush their teeth or have good food or if you are having good marriage relationships. The only thing that matters is that we have less than forty per cent chance of reaching the year two thousand and what are we going to do about it?'

Philip let himself in to the house quietly; his meeting had finished early and he had decided to come straight home as he was hungry. He hung up his sheepskin jacket and went into the sitting-room where he found Jo and Mary sitting on the floor, absorbed, surrounded by dozens of remnants of cotton cut into neat hexagonal shapes.

'Hi, Dad.' Jo looked up for a moment, then dropped back to concentrate on cutting her piece of cloth; Mary, at a disadvantage on the floor, blushed and smiled, and tried to rearrange her legs in a more attractive position.

Philip walked over to see. 'You seem very busy; what are you doing?'

'A patchwork cushion. Look.' Jo held up a brightly patterned grouping of hexagons. 'I've done all that this evening.' She beamed as though she had scored a goal. Jo always seemed to need to compete, if only with herself.

'Lovely,' Philip nodded, pleased to see his hoyden thus domestically occupied; she looked very pretty with her blonde head bent over her needle and thread – peaceful and eternally feminine – it made a pleasant change. 'What did you have for supper?' he asked, 'I'm starving.'

Mary leapt up, spilling cotton patches and thread, and stood, her fine legs well-displayed by the mini. 'Can I help? Make you something? Coffee?'

'We had chicken,' Jo told him. 'We left you some.'

'Sounds good.' Philip went to pour himself a vodka. 'I'll manage, thanks. But can I offer you a drink or some food?'

Mary picked fluff and pieces of thread off her scarlet bosom and thighs.

'No, honestly thanks . . . . I ought to go . . . . I've got things to do.' She grinned pinkly, and could have bitten her tongue off for refusing, but it was too late. 'I'll be off.' Flushing, she bent to gather her things into a basket, whilst Philip, absent-mindedly sipping his drink, admired her youthful contours.

'I'll leave all these bits with you, Jo, so you can finish your cushion cover.' She laid a heap of scraps at Jo's side, and the girl nodded, frowning intently as she turned a tricky corner with her needle.

'Say goodbye to Mary,' her father muttered when Mary went to find her coat.

Jo stood up, leaned sleepily against Philip's side, and brushed back her yellow fringe. 'Bye,' she said shyly, 'and thanks. I think I'll make a bedcover out of patchwork, a red one, with big square patches.'

'I'm very impressed with her doing all that in one night. She's really fast,' Mary told Philip.

'You should see her on the football field,' said Philip amused.

Jo returned to her obsessive needlework whilst Philip saw Mary to the door, pulling out a fiver as she was about to depart.

'Please no.' She was very embarrassed now. 'I truly don't want any money. It was a pleasure; I'll help you any time. Really.' With the last two syllables she contrived to gaze into his eyes, hoping that he would understand how sincerely she meant it; then, wrapping her coat collar tight round her neck, she nodded to him, so tall, so aloof, so vulnerably unattainable, and turned abruptly to go, struggling clumsily with the door-handle which would not open.

Philip leaned across her. 'Let me,' he said, laying his cool hand on hers. 'And thank you again, Mary. You've been more help than I can say. Goodnight.' He opened the door, looked into her eyes and she fled, dithering with excitement and regret to her parentally-funded flat in Holland Park where she lived with a King Charles spaniel and a large collection of dolls and stuffed toys. Here she sat drinking cocoa, a Snoopy doll clutched to her swelling bosom, watching the late-night movie, trying not to dwell on her unrequited love for Philip Salveson, architect, and father of two, who was at that moment wondering if the office would agree to Mary's accompanying him to Hong Kong. The girl could be very useful. He gnawed his chicken-leg thoughtfully, enjoying the pale flesh. Then he put down the chewed bone and wiped his mouth. No, he decided, it was a bad idea. Too messy.

Alison had cried last night at the meeting; Frankie remembered her face when the lights were put on at the end of the second television tape. That had been horrendous; she and Alison had both been very moved and convinced by the arguments of the Aussie doctor who had given up her medical practice with forty dying patients in order to talk about the nuclear threat and to try to rally women to use their female instincts to change things in the arms race. 'We must take over the system,' she said, and she had borne her mixed audience along with her. 'The present system is necrophiliac, and knowing that, what else could I do but go and fight?' And, she had said, 'Women cry at meetings like this, and men say "They're wrong, we need so and so many missiles . . ." and they argue this and that with technical facts . . . but women must make their voices heard if we are to survive . . .'

As she remembered this, Frankie pulled off her bright green baggy trousers and tried on her purple and blue striped dress, then looked in the mirror and shook her head, it looked just as bad. She was beginning to panic, she had only twenty minutes till she was due to meet her blind date. It was a five-minute walk to the pub, but she still couldn't decide what to wear. Twenty minutes: it was unbelievable, but that was all the time it would take when somebody did press the nuclear button. No time for anything, and, as the speaker had said, the chance of being near a loved one or being able to contact them was pretty remote. She ripped off the dress and reached for an embroidered Indian skirt; Alison always admired it. She tried it with her red billowing blouse and some long silver earrings; not bad she thought, looking critically at herself in the mirror. A bit of eye make-up and the earrings and she might pass.

Twenty minutes to completion, and everything would be dead, even the cat.

Frankie now only had twelves minutes: Shuddering, she clambered over the multi-coloured mountain of discarded garments which had accrued on the floor, and, giving her large black cat which sprawled sybaritically on the unmade bed a passing fondle, she grimaced at her face in the mirror, and put on eye-liner with a lot of translucent greenish eyeshadow. She patted her newly-washed hair, trying to make the orange curls flare out sideways rather than upwards so as not to add to her great height, and searched for her favourite flattest boots. Should she, she wondered for a wild moment, even take her dusty cap out of the drawer? That is, if she could remember where it was after her six-month sexual drought.

'Come on Frankie, you're gonna be late,' she muttered. She pulled on her poncho, and, seeing through the dark window that it was wet outside, took her big tartan unbrella.

'Avanti!' she flourished it at the disinterested cat. 'Wish me luck, Hamish!' and, looking at her watch, exited from her flat and ran down the wet dark road trying to remember what her date had said about himself. Dark haired, that's what he'd said, wearing a leather jacket, and he would be carrying a copy of this week's *Time Out*.

When Alison had returned home late from the nuclear disarmament meeting Philip had been already in bed, deeply ensconced in matters architectural arising from his day's meetings; Alison, moved and alarmed by what she had seen and heard, was glad that tonight he was incommunicado, as she wanted to think about what had happened. She would not have borne to have an argument with her husband about military strategy and the obviousness of the country's needing a good defence system. She just kept remembering the figures the Australian woman had given: that America had over thirty thousand hydrogen bombs ready and waiting, that Russia had over twenty thousand, that American had forty times overkill – which meant enough to kill every Russian forty times over – and Russian had twenty times overkill, all of which added up to enough to kill everybody on earth twelve times – and this was two years ago. It was mad, obscene.

That speaker was an amazing woman; she looked so

good, so normal, so un-neurotic. Yet she had had the courage to drop everything in order to go and try at this late date to harness the human survival instinct which seemed to have got lost and sick. 'A terminally ill planet,' she had called it.

Frankie had winked during the coffee-break last night and pressed a very small and discreet badge, silver and black, with inverted 'Y' of the peace movement into Alison's hand. 'A wee present; I know you don't approve, but you look like you need one.' Today, as she prepared breakfast for her sleepy family, Alison reached for the 'Happy Days' apron and pinned the badge onto her chest: she wanted to wear it. It seemed the very smallest thing she could do; she had also booked to go with Frankie in a couple of weeks' time on the big march planned for Easter Friday.

'Breakfast's ready!' she called, and plopped tea-bags into the pot. 'We have become passive. We are sick, we must become passionate; we women could take the lead. We need to harness our women's passion.' Alison remembered the woman doctor's words, her passion, her hope.

'They are sick,' she had said, 'those who say it will never happen.' Like Philip, thought Alison, as she poured herself tea and buttered a piece of toast, but she didn't take more than a small bite. Her mind was filled with the awful pictures of her own ill mother, mixed up with the people of Hiroshima with terrible unhelpable injuries, the mothers and babies speechless with pain, and it was still going on, and would until they were released by death. Pregnant women in Hiroshima lived in terror of what might come from their irradiated wombs. Like the woman doctor had also said last night, the politicians, scientists and military people who had brought us to this pass had the arrested development of a thirteen-year-old boy – the war-like games, the obsession with power, death and ego. Male principles all. She thought of Philip and his love of guns and hunting, and shuddered.

'Mum! Toast's burning!'

Alison opened her eyes, and remembered the terrible description of the people who had seen the blast in Hiroshima, whose very eyes had melted, so that the fluid ran down their cheeks. Philip was peering at her. 'Are you all right?'

She blinked, back into her high-tech kitchen, and clattering family. One bad thing about the plate glass table-top was the noise – that and the white ceramic floor-tiles where everything that dropped smashed to pieces. She got up and passed the cornflakes to the sleepy Jo; Philip was still looking at her.

'I'm all right.' Her mouth twitched in mirthless smile.

'You aren't going to take to wearing badges and becoming a zealot, I hope? It's not your style, darling.' He smiled, an almost patronising smile.

Alison glared at him, 'I just might be from now on. Last night was a pretty shattering experience, and yes, I do intend to get involved.'

'You can't only look at one side,' said Philip blandly. 'You must read up all about all points of view, otherwise it is simply meaningless. The government and the military do actually know that the real problems are. Dammit, darling, do you want us to be like Afghanistan or Poland, and just allow people to walk in here and flatten us? You must be sensible and see this whole business in perspective.'

Alison funked it again, and muttered something like, 'I know, I intend to find out,' and went off upstairs to finish getting dressed; she felt too fragile to argue with Philip. As the Australian doctor had said, women, because of biology, and always having or rearing children, have accepted second place, but they must learn to become passionate. Somehow they must take over the system, or there will be no world. It was hard, and years of ingrained habit of accepting second place made it very difficult to start changing, but she intended to try.

She reached for her brightest green sweater and her favourite skirt, and smiled encouragingly at her pale little face in the mirror. Actually, the eyes were still pretty good, but like the woman had said, nothing mattered except the imminent holocaust, not your work, not your children, not your love life. She was sure she was right, but she wasn't so sure that she, little London Alison, quite knew what she could usefully do about it, because all those things that the woman doctor had said did not really matter, did actually seem important, though of course they wouldn't even exist if the ultimate preventative medicine of closing down the reactors was not somehow applied. It was frightening and bewildering.

Frankie was a couple of minutes late when she reached the very crowded pub; she looked round as she shook the rain off her umbrella. Then she saw him sitting on a stool by the bar; he caught her look and smiled shyly over his half pint of lager, and she saw that he was rather nice-looking, with bright dark eyes, a leather jacket and a copy of the weekly matchmaker tucked under his arm. As she walked towards him, he grinned and gestured towards an empty stool he had obviously been guarding beside him. Clumsy with shyness, Frankie almost tripped over her umbrella and then the stool, and he, also shy, caught her arm, and said 'I hope you really are Frankie? I have already accosted two strange women.'

She warmed to him, then, to her horror, he got off his stool, and whereas up till now he had been on a level with her height-wise, she found she was staring down at him. She hoped her dismay didn't show, but at the same time longed to simply disappear. He was a miniature painter in every sense of the word. Her internal kilted clown wailed with painful laughter.

He peered anxiously at her. 'What can I get you to drink?'

Frankie's mind went blank.

'Wine? beer?' She had never felt so tall and gawky, not since she was fifteen. Then she remembered what Alison had advised – drink only soft drinks until you had them sussed out – keep your head.

'Perrier, please,' she said distinctly.

Anthony Brownstone looked a little surprised. 'Sure?'

Frankie nodded, though she loathed Perrier, and dropped her umbrella as she slid onto the stool; Anthony bent down to retrieve it for her, looking even smaller, doubled up and grovelling. It was no good, Frankie knew she had to go; people would laugh if they saw them standing side by side. He was ordering her Perrier and another lager for himself. He was excited, and thought Frankie was absolutely stunning, even though she was so tall. He climbed onto the bar stool. Face to face like that it was much more comfortable.

They both talked at once – 'What?' 'How?' – then stopped, embarrassed. Frankie wondered if she could go to the Ladies and escape, but had a vision of Anthony running after her, and couldn't confront the possibility. She would have to go through with it at least until her Perrier was drunk.

'Do you . . . um . . . do this often?' Frankie asked at last.

'Putting in ads, you mean?'

Frankie nodded. Anthony looked serious; 'Once before. And I had a three-year relationship from it.'

'What happened?'

'Somebody bigger and better-looking than me turned up. I've applied for a body transplant, the rest's not bad. Cheers.' They clinked glasses. 'What about you?'

'This is my first blind date,' Frankie confessed. She couldn't invent lies, he was a nice wee man, but it could never work. She did not, could not, ever fancy him.

He eyed Frankie, all those orange curls were amazing; she would be glorious to draw. 'You're Scots?'

'How did ye guess?' She put on her broadest accent, gulping down the Perrier so fast that she choked. He reached over to pat her back, admiring as he did her well-made frame. 'You can see that you're a dancer. Do you do lots of work-outs?'

Frankie nodded. 'But I don't dance anymore. I sell antiques. I got to be too big to be a dancer.'

Anthony laughed. 'And I wasn't allowed to join the police force when I was young because I was too small! Farcical, isn't it?'

Frankie was amused. 'You surely didn't want to? I thought you were an artist?'

'I did at eighteen, and when I did grow tall enough to join I had started painting. My old man was a copper. Longed for me to follow in his footprints; he was a good man. I admired him a lot, but I always wanted to paint.' He was looking at Frankie with such undisguised admiration that she felt embarrassed; it was no good, it could never work. She felt like a giant, even his hands, though well-shaped, looked tiny. She got up suddenly from her bar-stool and looked at her Mickey Mouse watch. 'I've got to go,' she said abruptly.

He was shocked. 'Already? We have barely met . . .' He was obviously hurt and she now felt guilty.

She grabbed at her unwound poncho and leather handbag; 'I'm sorry, I simply have to. I'd forgotten that I'd promised to be somewhere . . .' She looked very embarrassed, her eyes almost tearfully bright. She knew that he knew she was lying. 'Goodbye,' she gasped politely. 'And good luck. I'm sure you'll get lots of answers . . .'

He slipped down from his stool and looked at her, very sad.

'I am sorry,' he said simply, 'very sorry. I think you are absolutely lovely, and I'd like to know you better. Maybe I should go home and drink Baby Bio and put some manure in my boots.' He smiled a half-inch one-sided smile, one that she suspected might be habitual; he did seem very sensitive, a real wee laser beam.

'Anyway,' he held up his hand, 'my mother always used to say that dynamite is sold in small sticks. And may I say to you that the bigger you are, the more there is to appreciate.' He looked so very straight at Frankie, that she couldn't look back. Instead she fumbled with her colourful fingerless gloves, blushed again, and fled, leaving the artist staring gloomily at his half-empty glass of lager.

Back at her flat Frankie cuddled the cat and tried not to cry. She had behaved appallingly, she didn't really know why. It had suddenly all seemed too macabre; she had been so excited and hopeful until she had seen how short he was. He was nice though, perfectly made, with a fine head, intelligent and good-looking. The cat didn't like it when Frankie clutched at him like this – it was both alarming and noisy. He shook himself and flicked his elegant black tail uneasily; he didn't like those warm drops of salty water on his back either. Suddenly the animal leapt away from his mistress, puncturing her flesh with his claws; he went out and she heard the single clang of the cat-flap toll her loneliness and accentuate the silence which was broken only by her wistful sniffings.

In the Salveson household the various members of the family were busy in their own rooms, each one absorbed with his or her preoccupations. Mark was sprawled on his floor surrounded by camping and cycling gear; it was early to be packing for his weekend trip, but he liked to be well-prepared. He had a pair of black trousers and an old black sweater laid out like a fallen body on the carpet, and was deeply absorbed with a tin of paint and a half-inch brush with which he was painstakingly applying white lines to the black fabric. Beside him were a canteen of cutlery, an opened-out tent, and a puncture outfit. He wasn't sure what to do about sleeping bags: originally he had simply planned to take the warmest cleanest one he could find in the linen cupboard, but his friend Pete had joked this morning about taking two; you could zip them together, he said, to make a double sleeping-bag, then he had laughed very loudly, 'By far the best way of keeping warm.'

Mark dipped his brush and wiped it carefully on the side of the tin: Susan Richards was going on this trip. The giggly lively Susan, who was also very clever at almost everything, and played the violin in the school orchestra. He smiled as he painted white concentric curves on the black fabric of the stretched-out sweater;

he wouldn't mind sharing a double sleeping-bag with Susan.

Jo, in her bedroom, presided Atlas-like over a strewn archipelago of multi-coloured patchwork hexagons, the piecing-together of which had become an obsession since Mary had taught her how. Tonight she was making a small piece for her grandmother who was so ill that Alison seemed to be constantly bad-tempered and upset or on the phone to Devon. It was to be a small intricate round patchwork to make a cushion for the old lady's white head when she rested in an armchair. Jo carefully chose a piece of cotton with tiny daisies that had once been a summer dress when she was tiny, and there was another scrap, very pale, with green rabbits that Mark – her mother swore – used to wear as a shirt when he was little. He had been very angry when Jo threatened to take it to school and show his friends. He had thumped her really hard when she had said she thought Susan Richards would like it; she rubbed her shoulder under her striped football jersey, it was still quite bruised. She giggled, poor Mark, he looked very funny when he went all red like that.

Philip raked through his drawers, preparing his luggage for the Hong Kong trip; there was much ironing to be done, about eight shirts. He would need them all; he did wish that Alison hadn't so dramatically stopped doing things like ironing just when the cleaning-lady was ill again. In the old ways Alison had never complained; it had been good to come home to that welcoming smell of clean steaming linen and comforting to see her, flushed from the ironing, smiling up at him from a growing heap of beautifully pressed and organised garments and tea-towels. He kicked a drawer shut with his stockinged foot, and melancholically set up the ironing board in the utility room attached to the kitchen. Gone, gone, he mused, were days of happy domesticity, and quite right too, he supposed, when he thought about it. Women had always been subordinate, from biological necessity, but now with the invention of the Pill and proper education, times must change, and people like himself had no option but to adapt to the times, however difficult they might find it. He switched on the iron, put water in the steam compartment, tested the heat with his finger, and set about flattening the first of the eight shirts in his cool methodical way.

Alison, tired, had retired early to bed, where she sat reading through a heap of anti-nuclear leaflets and magazines. She found it hard to concentrate, and kept dozing. She had spoken to her sister earlier in the evening, and Molly, strained and abrupt, had said little, except that their mother, who was no better, was now out of hospital and permanently based at Molly and Edward's house; her dying, it seemed, was to be a painful and protracted business. Alison remembered the Australian doctor once again: she had talked of death, and had seen many people die, she said, and 'The living will envy the dead.' Alison shivered, she had never seen anybody die, and certainly had no desire to. The people who find it hardest to die are the selfish ones, the doctor had said. Those who have loved die gracefully. And she had ended, trying to rally woman power, saying 'We are here to help other people, not ourselves.'

It was probably all true, but also confusing. For instance, Alison herself, where was she in the love-stakes? She had loved passionately and deeply, first Gino her forbidden Italian, and then Philip – her love for him had blossomed and she had adored him blindly for years – but nowadays it was different, she barely noticed his absences now, except sometimes in bed. Often his presence seemed an irritation, an interruption of her life. Since he had come home from Trinidad they had barely made love, apart from the home-coming fuck. They had been too fraught, too preoccupied with other things; they had felt apart, so where was love left now? Would Alison die gracefully? Did past dead love count?

In the old days, the bliss of early love and marriage, she used to hate it when Philip was away on business, and they would make love with much passion before he departed; there was too always an added poignancy because of the unspoken fear that his plane or train might crash. She used to ache for him when he was away. She felt sad tonight when she remembered, and wanted him suddenly. Philip coming back into the bedroom with his smooth newly-ironed shirts, was surprised when his wife rose from the bed and came to embrace him long and hard. 'What is it?' He put down his white, crisp burden on the chest-of-drawers, and enfolded her. Her voice came, muffled from his chest, 'I just needed a hug.' Philip was both touched and pleased; she hadn't been so demonstrative for a long time. Hopefully, he began to unbutton and take off his clothes.

Chapter Eight

Anthony Brownstone frowned with concentration as he dipped his number six fine Kolinsky sable brush in a pan of cobalt blue and painted in a rich night sky behind the head of the mythical princess; her curly head reminded him of Frankie, and he wondered yet again how he could possibly attain the Scots girl. He had a strong suspicion that she would never agree to come out with him even if he did contact her again. But he did have her umbrella which she had forgotten when she fled from the pub. It sat, a large tartan reminder, in the corner of the room.

He gazed out of his window, through the avocado plants and jungle greenery with which his converted basement greenhouse-studio was rampant, and pictured Frankie here. She would look magnificent in his white-walled setting, filled with interesting objects and his own decorative and highly-detailed paintings, but then the big Scot would look beautiful anywhere. If only he could meet her properly, and like Rapunzel she would let down her red hair, he could climb up it and nestle in her bosom, would it not be bliss? He sighed, washed out his brush carefully (it had cost twelve pounds), dipped a slightly smaller one into his jar of water, and began carefully to mix together raw sienna, cadmium red and his favourite deep yellow to try to capture the colour of the princess's hair. Maybe he would succeed in summoning up courage to contact her again. It was worth a try.

Easter Friday had dawned, dull and grey, when Frankie and Alison met up at the appointed place in a quiet street near Shepherd's Bush for a bus to take them on the protest march. Frankie, who looked very striking in a billowing tartan cloak and red boots, had equipped herself with a Balmoral and a tall stick.

'What's that for?' asked Alison.

'It's a cromach,' Frankie told her, and sang 'As step I with my cromach to the road . . .'

Alison was glad to see her in cheerier mood than of late. She had been quite depressed recently.

'Hey, you never told me about your date with the miniature painter; what was he like?'

Frankie grinned ruefully and adjusted her black Balmoral, which had a CND badge placed firmly in the centre of its chequered headband.

'Honest,' she said earnestly, 'he was so wee that he wouldn't have to turn upside-down for cunnilingus.'

Alison snorted, and they hugged each other. When they had got their breaths back, Frankie looked at Alison.

'Did you not bring a hat?'

'I couldn't find anything that Jo didn't jeer at.'

'You mustn't let your children terrorise you. Here, try this.' Frankie felt under her cloak and pulled out a magnificent mohair beret with a massive pom-pom, blue, green and red, and very pretty – Alison's taste exactly. She pulled it on and adjusted it in a hand mirror; she felt really good. 'Where did you find it?'

'If I told you you wouldn't wear it.'

'You been rummaging in the rubbish-bags again?'

Frankie nodded blandly.

'You're a genius.'

'I know, but I'm wasted on you, hen.'

There were now about two hundred demonstrators gathered; the buses at last arrived, and people started climbing on; Ron, the organiser, a worried-looking man with a clipboard, was anxious because there were more people than seats, the clipboard list was a muddle of names and numbers. Alison was bending down to pick up her picnic bag, when she heard Frankie in her most enthusiastic voice saying, 'Hello there!'

Alison lifted the bag up, and looked round, enjoying the feeling of her new hat, and there grinning at herself and Frankie, was Esau, the hairy Welshman.

'Surprising who you come across on such occasions,' he said easily.

'Isn't it?' she smiled and didn't know what else to say. He seemed to be alone. 'No family with you?'

'No, I'm a bit bereft, but my sister said she would take my youngsters for the weekend. I had to stay in town as I'm doing a market tomorrow. How about you? Your family here?'

'No. Half of them don't approve, but my son is already there, camping near Aldermaston.' She was proud of young Mark.

He nodded a little shyly. She could see a thermos poking out of his old canvas bag.

Frankie was looking round, 'Come on, you guys, we'd better get going or we'll be left behind.' She looked at Gareth. 'Will you join us? We can talk junk whilst we protest.'

'OK. Thanks. I'd like that very much.'

Alison dropped her scarf in the scramble to get on

the bus, and when she had picked it up, she saw Frankie gesticulating that she had found seats; Gareth was sitting across the aisle from Alison when she plonked herself down beside Frankie.

The bus set off; Alison yawned, sleepily. Philip had got home yesterday afternoon from Hong Kong, and she had left him snoring. She had hardly spoken to him, they had rolled into bed together and embraced as usual, but it had felt anonymous and empty, dutiful sex.

'Would you like some coffee?' She was startled by Gareth's deep voice, rich and Welsh, at her shoulder, he was holding a plastic mug of aromatic dark coffee towards her. She wished she didn't blush whenever he spoke to her, it was ridiculous at her age. 'I'd love some, but we've got . . .'

'Maybe I can have some of yours later; I have got lots.' Gratefully she took it, and was very aware of his dark-haired wrist and the way his strong hand cupped the steaming mugs. He was a very beautiful man. She sipped and smiled at him, 'Much needed,' and handed the mug for Frankie to share.

Frankie leaned across Alison: 'How's your job-hunting, Gareth?' She handed out apples, which the three of them munched.

Gareth held up his hands dramatically: 'Terrible! I've been short-listed six times now, trekking all over the place, up to York, back to Wales, Southampton even, I'm beginning to think I may have to go abroad. It's driving me potty. I actually had five interviews for one job I didn't get.'

'What about the kids?' asked Frankie. 'Do you live alone with them?'

He nodded, crunching Granny Smith. 'It's a big problem. I may have to try Canada or somewhere like that, or the States, but I like it here.'

Alison was longing to ask about Gareth's wife, but didn't quite know how to put it. He told them gradually; he seemed very at ease with the two of them. She was aware of Frankie leaning across and laughing, trying to hear what he said; maybe he would do for Frankie, she obviously liked him a lot, and no wonder, he was such a warm guy, but in her bones she knew that he didn't want Frankie, nor did Alison want him to if she were really honest.

'I could take the kids abroad because I have no ties here since my divorce. My wife . . .' (he said the word with a spat-out bitterness) '. . . pushed off with somebody and now lives in Holland, but she has relinquished all interest in the children.' He shook his head. 'Not funny, it wasn't.'

It was a double negative, but they understood, Alison wished that she and Frankie could change places, so that Frankie could act as a buffer; she found the physical presence of this man totally disturbing. She had never, since her early years of courtship, first with the Italian, then later with Philip, felt this sort of pull; she simply wanted to hug and comfort him and in turn gain comfort in his arms, but she was a married woman, mother of two, and a faithful, if not blissfully happy, wife. Frankie was nudging her. 'Shall we eat our sandwiches now?'

'Better wait. It's a long walk ahead of us.' She leaned back and looked from Frankie to Gareth, 'I'm going to have a sleep.' She shut her eyes, hoping it would cut her off from the disturbance she felt within her, but it didn't work; instead of the physical actuality of the man next to her causing her to thrum, she saw in her head montage images of his big dark eyes and furry skin, juxtaposed against pictures of Philip, pale, blond and smooth, his aloofness as different to the Welshman's warmth and humour as was his skin texture and colouring. The bus roared on its way; they would soon be there.

The wooded lane Frankie, Alison and Gareth were now walking along with several thousand other demonstrators, carrying banners, babies, knapsacks, all hatted and booted, was dark and gloomy. They were in a group, following the worried-looking clipboard man, Ron, dressed in yellow PVC. The hundreds of buses which had disgorged the marchers had driven further up the narrow road in order to turn, with the result that the crowds of walkers were now forced back against the hedgerows, often precariously, as the buses lumbered by spewing out awful fumes, which lay heavy on the murky leaves and oppressive air. At this rate they might well succumb to lead-poisoning from the thrumming exhausts; Alison felt quite claustrophobic, but there was no way of escape through the surrounding greenery, which was firmly fenced off. She found herself walking side by side with Gareth, who mimed choking and made noises of disgust.

'This is a thoroughly apocalyptic start to the day. It's almost as if the end of the world has already come.'

She nodded, 'Quite frightening. I hope my son is OK in this crowd.'

'He'll be all right, he's a good lad. I was impressed with him at the market; he knows what he's doing as well as anybody. Don't you worry.'

They walked for a mile or so, and gradually the traffic congestion began to clear, but it was slow going.

'The cyclists are the wise ones,' said Gareth, gazing enviously at the many young people who swooped speedily and easily past the massive crawling crowds. 'I wish I had brought my bike.'

Frankie walked with them for a while, and they all admired the rich folk art of the peace symbol which was to be seen everywhere: people had knitted complex and original sweaters, hats and gloves with nuclear disarmament symbols. There were images of suns, trees and wicked mushroom clouds in all sorts of unexpected places, embroidered, painted and modelled on garments, banners and faces. Many of the youngsters had an almost tribal look, like the wondrous court-jester-like punks with green or orange hair that they had seen earlier on the bus, who were still near them, happy, singing, cohesive. It still surprised Alison to see punks on such an organised thing as this march – somehow it didn't fit with her preconceived image of such youngsters that they could organise themselves and care enough about anything to make the communal effort to be here. She was moved and found them beautiful. Painted faces were to be seen everywhere: people had CND symbols in green or blue on cheeks and foreheads, and some had painted fearsome death-masks on their faces. There must be thousands of pretend skeletons walking in the crowd – people in black tights and sweaters, with bones painted dramatically in white, topped by skull-heads or masks. It was impressive that such creative effort had been expended.

'Somebody should do a book on it,' said Frankie. 'The Art of Protest. It could be terrific; just the bicycles alone . . .'

The bikes were splendid: people had erected great bamboo poles and flags on their bikes, and streamers fluttered on the wheels, and flew past the struggling crowds like extraordinary visions out of a painting by Bosch or Breughel. None of their group had ever experienced anything like it; they walked silently for a while, then Frankie voiced Alison's thoughts almost tearfully.

'It is so sad when you think why in fact we're here. That all this inventiveness and creativity, and . . .' she struggled for a word. 'Love! That all this might be lost because of our own stupidity. It is crazy! And these trees and flowers . . .' She gesticulated with her cromach. They walked on for a mile or so, then, miraculously, the sun came out and was greeted with a cheer that echoed up the road for miles. Alison felt happier as she walked, at least the atmosphere was no longer gloomy. The trees lining the roadside were smaller and less overpowering at this point, and there were primroses everywhere, sparkling under the fresh blue sky which had at last appeared. She enjoyed the sun and the spring flowers, and felt a pang as she remembered her parents and her mothers' illness.

A small aeroplane puttered overhead trailing a white streamer. How clever of somebody thought Alison as she strained to read the message, but there was a groan, such as follows a bad joke when the people nearest her made out the black print. 'CND KREMLIN'S FOOLS,' it read.

'It takes all kinds of silly buggers to make a world,' muttered Gareth.

Frankie was pounding along beside him. 'Gareth,' she asked suddenly, 'I've been thinking about all these symbols people have covered themselves with today. It's sort of safe here, because we all think more or less the same, but do you, for instance, wear your badge all the time?'

'At home and work you mean? At least when I had a job . . .'

Frankie nodded. Intrigued, Alison listened.

'I do actually,' he smiled. 'But I'm known for being a

cussed so and so, I even wear it when I go for interviews. Maybe that's why I'm only ever short-listed, and never get a job. I'm very well-qualified.'

'That's brave,' said Alison. 'I'm not so brave.'

'Or foolhardy. Probably the latter; but I have thought quite hard about it. I believe it was Dante who said "The hottest place in Hell is reserved for those who stay quiet on a moral issue." I felt I could not be one of them, I want to stand up and be counted, not that I do much else, apart from delivering a few leaflets, and I've done training in civil disobedience, you know, passive resistance.'

There was a young father, blond-bearded, in front of Alison; she watched his baby, sprawled across his shoulder, sleeping, lids almost blue, mouth sweet and half open, tender and ravishing. It almost made her feel broody. Frankie had wafted off again; Alison glimpsed flashes of tartan cloak, Gareth was still beside her.

'How long have you been in antiques?' he asked.

'I've had the shop for almost three years, and before that I did stalls a couple of times a month. I just loved it; I liked having something of my own to do and getting away from domesticity.'

He nodded. 'It's good fun, the unpredictability of it. It's like an eternal treasure hunt; I find it soothes the child in me. It's hard work though, and it can be so boring on a bad day.'

'Very,' she agreed vehemently, 'and so uncertain, and I hate the filth. I used to work in an auction house in Worcester, when I had just left school, so I knew a bit about it, and always liked beautiful things and odd pieces of china and furniture. That's how it all started.'

'Your husband, is he in the business?'

Alison giggled. The thought of the fastidious Philip with all the dirt and mess involved in buying and selling was incongruous. 'No way. He's an architect.'

'Ah,' Gareth nodded.

'And absentee father . . .' she added bitterly, half under her breath, then, uncomfortable at her disloyalty, 'I didn't mean that, it's just that he has to be away a lot, abroad mostly. It can't be helped, but it gets me down sometimes.'

They passed by some enterprising vegetarians at the side of the road selling wholemeal pittas filled with savoury amalgams of nuts and vegetables.

'That smells good,' said Gareth. 'Would you like one?'

'I've got sausages . . .' she said dubiously. But they smelt wonderful, so Gareth smiled and bought a couple. They walked along munching, bean-sprouting mouths grinning.

'Excellent.' Alison wiped her mouth. 'Thank you. I'll give you some sausages later.'

'Promises, promises,' said the Welshman, and, once again she was aware of her uncontrollably suffusing capillaries.

They passed a fir wood where people had made small encampments under the trees, and were brewing tea and feeding babies. There was a lean dark man standing on the grass verge playing an accordion; he was quite young, his eyes were shut, and he played with great concentration and sweetness as the thousands of marchers filed past, peaceful, happy, conjoined, all moving hopefully towards the great goal of peace. There were many religious groups bearing crosses, Quakers, doctors, gays. All the world seemed to be there. The music was so haunting and eloquent that Alison paused to listen. Gareth stood near her, looking with great seriousness first at the oblivious musician whose contribution to the day was his very self, then at Alison who had an expression of such intensity and sadness that it was all he could do not to enfold her in his arms. She turned to him, her eyes bigger and darker than ever.

'Do you think there's any hope? I cannot encompass the thought that all this really might be destroyed, but I don't see that we have much chance of continuing.'

Gareth firmly pocketed his hands. 'I don't know,' his voice was husky and deep. 'I watched both of my children come into the world, it makes you think, actually seeing a child born, all that pain and danger, then all the loving, the nurturing and effort they need until they are independent. Sometimes I think my view is extra black and pessimistic because I'm divorced and jobless. But at other times I think there really isn't much hope. I don't see how we can possibly avoid an accident simply in the normal run of things. Whether the accident is caused by human or mechanical failure is irrelevant; the damage will be done. I think it may already be too late to stop it, and I too have very little hope.' He looked across to her with a lopsided smile. 'Gloomy Welsh Jeremiah, amn't I?'

'A realist, I'd say.'

He shrugged. 'Maybe. But it is an unbearable, unimaginable reality; the worst thought of all for me, for any human being with children perhaps, is the realisation that there may well be no grandchildren. That is almost too painful to confront.'

The crowd had thinned out, and people were beginning to stop by the roadside in preparation for the link-up; Ron, their mother duck, who looked too hot, and more worried than ever in his yellow PVC, stopped at an unoccupied few feet of grassy verge. He nodded to Gareth, and Frankie and several others of the original group appeared. 'How about stopping here? It seems as good as any; it will soon be time.'

They stood along the road, and some of them sat to eat their picnics; there was a strong feeling of growing excitement, and guesses were hazarded as to the numbers. Eighty thousand? A hundred thousand? Obviously this was a massive turn-out, beyond any expectations, and if there were people lining both sides of the road it would be a double chain. It was a vibrant concept; Frankie took off her tartan and relaxed in the spring sun. Ushers cycled past quite frequently, and others discreetly picked up any litter and put it into black refuse sacks.

'It's so civilised,' said Frankie. 'It's tremendous to be part of something as big as this.' They lay back and watched the occasional official car, usually old, battered and plastered in peace slogans, pass by, and admired a group of three cyclists, obviously quite young, who swooped past all dressed in black and white skeleton outfits, with strange banners and scythe-like shapes streaming high and dramatically from the backs of their machines.

'Marvellous they are,' said Gareth, and the waysiders smiled in admiration at the artistry and inventiveness; it was like a circus. Alison, loving it all, was astonished when one of the skull-masked, black-clad skeleton-cyclists made a sudden U-turn and skidded to a halt literally at her feet. She was sprayed by gravel and drew back her legs in alarm. The cyclist who was male, stood looking down at her through his terrifying papier-mâché skull which covered his whole head. For a moment Alison felt a frisson of fear, then the skeleton swept off his mask and said 'Hi, Mum.' Mark, hot-faced, stood grinning down at her. 'Fancy meeting you here!'

Alison shrieked, clutching a hand to her chest. 'I don't believe it!' As though to test her sanity, she stretched out to touch his solid black leg graffitied with great white bones. 'I had no idea you were going to be here all dressed up.'

Mark knelt down, nodding a shy recognition to Gareth; Frankie handed him a chicken leg which he gnawed hungrily, handsomely blond like a young medieval knight in black and white livery. Abruptly, he stood up. 'Must go, we're checking the whole route. I'm miles behind Susan and Pete.' He looked along the road where his fellow skeletons, one of each sex, were waiting for him. 'Bye,' he said, 'thanks for the food,' and, pulling on his mask like some diver about to descend to a watery hell, he nodded, unrecognisable once more, mounted his amazing bike and was soon invisible to his proud and astonished mother.

Word came down the line that it was nearly link-up time; they stood, and Frankie put on her cloak once more. There were a couple of false starts, and many of the demonstrators stood holding hands with their neighbours, whoever they happened to be. Alison, her hands in pockets, stood wedged between Gareth and Frankie. She was bubbling from seeing Mark, it had been so unexpected and exciting. Gareth smiled at her obvious emotion.

'Happy?' he asked. 'You should be with a boy like that. You need never worry about him. That was a nice class of female skeleton he was with, too.'

Alison beamed a wordless agreement, and Frankie leaned across to her: 'I think we should present Mark with your solar topee as a reward for ingenuity. That was fantastic.'

Ushers came by in a van and leaned out of the window: 'It's almost complete, the chain, but there's a gap a hundred yards down on your right . . . can you all move down a bit?'

They shuffled good-naturedly, hundreds of people. There was a pale French girl playing a penny-whistle, and some youngsters were dancing up and down the roadway. An elderly man, absolutely bald, wearing long baggy khaki shorts danced with a small blonde Swede, holding his shorts up like a skirt, and the people near them clapped in time to the tin-whistle. More rumours came up the line: 'It's time! Link-up!' The shout echoed up and down the fourteen miles of people – twenty-eight miles of peaceable individuals – of all colours, ages, beliefs and backgrounds, as they lined both sides of the country lanes linking the atomic weapons research establishment at Aldermaston with the US air force base at Greenham Common and the bomb factory of Burghfield.

Frankie heaved Alison's left hand out of her pocket. 'Come on, hen, link-up.' Alison took her right hand out of her other pocket and stood shyly for a moment beside Gareth. It seemed to each of them that they must be the very last two individuals of the hundred thousand standing there in the green-sprouting English countryside to touch hands. Gareth looked at Alison, and she at him, both shy, almost afraid of the inevitable, and as their hands grasped each other, warm and firm, and two hundred thousand other hands were linked in peace and love, the look they exchanged was one neither of them would ever forget. It was for each of them as though they saw into the other's soul. There were no barriers between them, and a physical charge like electricity passed from one to the other. Alison felt as though she could see how Gareth thought and felt, almost as though she were him, and each one knew what the other knew and wondered fearfully what was to come.

'There's the balloons!' people shouted, and at

various points along the line great flocks of silver balloons sailed upwards, marking that the event they had all come for had taken place.

'Isn't it great!' called Frankie, arms outstretched, cromach at her feet. She was surprised when Alison didn't answer, and peered round to see if she had heard her and realised that her friend was not of this world, any more than the Welshman was. Frankie's good Scottish alarm bell went, shrill and loud; she looked at Alison anxiously. 'Listen,' she said, shaking her by the shoulder, 'I think Ron's going to move us on. It's going to be hell finding the bus.'

Alison and Gareth let go of each other's hands simultaneously, both still in a state of shock. They studiously avoided more eye or body contact, and tried to chat with other people as they walked further along the route which had now become very crowded as people swarmed all over the road, into the woodland along the wayside. It was so congested at one point that Frankie led the way across a ditch and for a while a group of them walked in the small fir forest, soft underfoot with pine needles and fir cones. All along the way there were small encampments with fires and groups of peaceful friends, where children played and babies slept or burbled. Alison felt a great yearning to lean against the pink bark of the trees, to embrace the pines and lose herself as she stared up through the sombre branches which cathedraled the many nuclei of quiet people below. There was everywhere a feeling of being united, of being linked with everybody here and with nature and the beauty of the unfolding spring which surrounded them. It was as near to a mystical experience that the agnostic Alison, the vicar's daughter, had ever been. She found Gareth once again walking beside her; they had gravitated wordlessly to each other.

'I wonder if we'll ever get home?' Alison said.

'We still have three or four miles to go. We have to go round the perimeter fence of Aldermaston; I guess we are nearly there. God knows how we will find our bus.'

The crowds soon became so dense that even Ron's yellow PVC was lost to sight; Frankie, Gareth and Alison searched for about half an hour, then gave up. They walked along the wire-netted perimeter of the air base, which stood bleak and sinister in the midst of innocently pretty countryside. All along the fencing people sat in groups, singing, resting, talking. It had grown suddenly much colder, and some had lit fires. It even rained a little. Every few yards they would admire some flowers or bunting woven into pictures and slogans in the netting; there were spiders' webs of dark string, coloured ribbons, CND signs, messages, jokes and flowers, hundreds of thousands of them, decoratively daisy-chained with wit and beauty into the stark military mesh.

As Alison slept on the coach home, her head drooping onto Frankie's shoulder, Frankie looked at her unconscious friend and felt concern; Alison looked so fragile sometimes, especially of late. She saw Gareth also looking at her with a dark brooding look, in-turned and private. He caught Frankie's glance and smiled, a gentle sleepy smile, enough to break anybody's heart. Momentarily she wondered what he would do when he got back to town, with his kids away, and wistfully toyed with the thought of asking him to her place to share a take-away, but something warned her that this was not a good idea. She knew that he wasn't really interested in her and she fancied him all too much. Better to keep away.

Philip had slept off his jet-lag, and was quite bright when the tired, wet Alison got home. He had watched the march on telly, and was grudgingly admiring of the numbers, but basically somewhat avuncular in his attitude to her outing. He listened with some interest to her description of Mark's extraordinary unveiling, and smiled coolly. 'It's a phase, but I'm glad he feels passionate about something, and you, darling, it's good for you to have an interest as well as the shop, but I'm going to get you some books so that you really understand both sides of the argument. You must do a bit of homework you know; emotion is all very well, but facts are facts, and the country must have a proper defence system.'

Alison wanted to scream; she wished she could play the video-cassette of the Aussie doctor to Philip, over and over, so that he could understand, would rediscover his passion and feelings, and would stop being so bloody cool and logical all the time. To prevent herself from yelling at him, from attacking his detachment and male arrogance, and perhaps to prevent herself from then being demolished by his icy logic, she fled to the blissful solitude of the bath, where she lay immersed, the day's film unreeling through her head. She wished that she could stop wondering what Gareth was doing. He was just a man, with his own life, and it was nothing to do with her; her life was here with Philip and the children, and she must not forget that. But what about that extraordinary moment they had shared? She tried to dismiss it as part of the whole group emotion of the link-up, but she knew it had been different, specific only to herself and Gareth.

In the kitchen Philip was busy, chopping, mixing, humming; he wanted to try to regain some lost ground with his wife – they seemed to be flailing about on a sort of emotional No Man's Land at the moment, and, to be honest with himself, he felt a little guilty that the Hong

Kong trip had been so long. He wielded his razor-sharp five-inch Sabatier knife with precision and care, piling the chopped vegetables into an aesthetic arrangement on the white Finnish plates. It had taken months to make up after Alison had discovered that he had been affairing with the honey-blonde architect in the Dublin office three years ago. Things had never been quite the same, and to be honest he still felt a bit of a shit, though these things happened all the time.

Upstairs, to the music of Haydn, Alison pulled the plug out of the bath, and dried herself as the water gurgled away. Bed would be welcome: she walked naked and sleepy through to the bedroom and was amazed and touched to find her husband standing in the doorway bearing a tray with glasses, a bottle, heaped plates of salad, smoked salmon, avocadoes and prawns. Food for love.

Philip, aproned, wearing an open-necked white shirt, smiled at his wife and walked towards her beaming: 'Champagne for Madame.'

They ate and drank and spoke of this and that, mostly their children. The food was delicious, and Alison, tired from the day's events, felt almost instantly drunk.

'I thought we should celebrate being alone for once,' said Philip, sipping the cool champagne fervently. 'We seem to really talk so seldom now.' He turned her face towards him with his free hand and looked bleakly into her serious eyes. 'I missed you like hell today.' He kissed the tip of her nose. 'I love you, Alison.'

Alison gulped down a second glass fast, moved by his obvious emotion. He looked so like Mark tonight, vulnerable, and somehow younger than usual. She buried her face in his pale smooth chest, where she had lain with love and tenderness for all the early years of their marriage, and mumbled, 'I don't think I'm very loveable these days,' in a sad small voice.

He kissed her more, and fondled her, and she caressed his strong satin-smooth body which so patently yearned for her loving, and they made love with the habit and expertise of years together. As always, he made her come, though tonight it seemed to take forever. As Philip came, he gasped his love for her with a poignancy and desperation which made her feel afraid. When it was over, she felt utterly empty, as though she had forever lost something which had been precious. They were both half-asleep when the phone rang: it was on Philip's side of the bed. Blearily he groped for it, and Alison looked at her watch: half-past eleven. She hoped Mark was all right.

Philip said hello, then listened for a moment. He looked serious and held his hand over the receiver.

'Darling, it's Molly. She wants to talk to you. It's bad news.'

Alison was immediately wide awake, chilled. She took the phone almost reluctantly. 'Molly? Hello, what is it?'

Molly sounded weak and abrupt. 'I'm sorry to have to tell you, but Mummy died half an hour ago. I felt I had to let you know as soon as I could.'

Alison felt as though her heart had stopped. 'When?' she said weakly.

'Eleven o'clock. Here, at home. Daddy is very shocked. I can't talk for long. The doctor's here.'

'Was it quick?'

'What's quick?' snapped Molly wearily. 'You know she's been ill for months now.'

'I know . . . I meant . . . in the end?'

'Yes. Pretty quick and dreadful. I'm sorry, I must go. Let's speak tomorrow.'

'Yes,' whispered Alison.

'Alison?' Molly's voice was loud.

'I'm here.'

'I'm sorry, I didn't know how to tell you. . . . Goodnight . . .' She was howling, and rang off. Alison sat frozen, receiver in hand, until Philip gently took it from her.

'Your mother?' he queried. She nodded dumbly. 'Half an hour ago, when we were making love.'

'Darling, I'm sorry, but it had to be, and it's better for everyone that it's over. It sounded awful, what you told me of it.'

'Awful,' she agreed, still numb. She stared at the end of the bed, and reached for her glass to drain the last half-inch of champagne. 'I hated her for most of my life, for almost as far back as I can remember.'

'Darling, it's no good thinking like that.'

'Like what? It's the truth.'

Philip lifted his head and sniffed. 'Do you smell burning?'

'What?'

He sniffed again. 'There's definitely something burning.' Suddenly he leapt out of bed stark naked. 'Hell! It's my bread! I completely forgot about it!' Bending down, he picked up the 'Happy Days' apron from the floor, and rushed out of the room adjusting the garment over his manhood as he went.

When her husband was downstairs battling to salvage his scorched staves of life, his symbolic marriage-cementers, Alison let go her tears. She roared and groaned and Philip returned to the nuptial bed to find her crumpled and sobbing like a mindless child. Filled with love and pity, he put out the light and climbed in beside her, where he took her small exhausted body and tenderly embraced her once again, but this time he cherished her protectively, willing her to peace, cuddling her gently, as a mother does a weeping heartbroken infant.

'Mummy!' she cried, 'Mummy', and clutched at his flat hard chest.

'Oh my baby,' he said, and smoothed her with his sweet coolness. 'Little girl. Don't worry.'

Chapter Nine

On the night that his grandmother died Mark Salveson went alone to bed in a double sleeping-bag in a tent set in a corner of a Berkshire field not very far from the pretty English village of Aldermaston; he felt happy, his mind overflowed with images of the day, the thousands of people on the march, the exhilaration of being part of it and roaring along on this bike, with his posse of fellow-skeletons. It had been fantastic, but by far the best bit had been at night, when the seven youngsters who formed the small four-tent encampment, had sat beside their campfire still in their skeleton-suits, but minus the skull-masks. There, lit by the tongueing flames, they had eaten sausages and roared with laughter, giggling, singing, full of surplus energy. Mark had even managed to sit for quite a long time with Susan Richards' warm young body encircled by his arm. It had been pretty exciting too, when they had gone to find some more wood for the fire – she had let him go quite far. His enthusiastic young member tent-poled the sleeping-bag at the memory. He rolled over and fondly put it through its paces, until it subsided, exploded into blissful peace. It was a pity that Susan hadn't wanted to share his sleeping-bag, he mused sleepily; but there was still tomorrow, maybe she would change her mind. He dozed, smiling at his hopeful fantasy of Susan's tapping on his tent, and her still small voice in the wilderness of the chilly rural night, whispering 'Hey Mark, I'm freezing, can I come in?' Outside, the last embers of wood hissed to oblivion in the rain, and a few miles away the myriad flowers and ribbons which decorated the grim perimeter fence of the nuclear establishment, drooped and grew bedraggled in the black downpour.

Alison woke with a thud to the realisation that her mother was dead; she lay with her eyes closed, aware of a great feeling of grief and guilt, and a sensation of emotional depletion and bruising that was quite overpowering. Logically, considering the tenuousness and the dislike that had been apparent in the relationship with her mother for so many years now, it was surprising that she should feel so thunderstruck; she ought by rights to feel relieved, if not euphoric. Instead, her very genes seemed to scream for comfort, and she was still haunted by a perserving image of Gareth which seemed to sit in front of her, like an after-image of the sun, and was obviously determined not to disappear whether her eyes were shut or open.

On the Sunday afternoon Philip and Alison prepared a large family meal for the children's return. In Alison's childhood home Easter had always been terribly important: her father had looked hunted for weeks and locked himself up trying to write a particularly inspiring sermon to celebrate the resurrection of Christ and Nature. As she peeled potatoes, she remembered how aged thirteen, she had gone to listen to his Easter sermon, keyed-up and hopeful, full of her own excitement at comtemplating spring and the annual miracle of rebirth. But he had been so boring, inaudible and hopeless, that it had been the final severing of any respect she had for the old man. He simply couldn't do it, couldn't do anything by himself as far as his critical daughter could see. She had decided then that she must be a changeling, and had emotionally disowned her parents from that time, painfully sloughing off the smothering swaddling-clothes of religion and convention with which they struggled still to imprison her.

She was weeping by the bedroom window when she saw her children arrive home almost simultaneously. Philip, unusually sensitive to her despair, brought her a cup of tea.

'I've told them about Grandma,' he said. 'Can you come and see them? Jo is very upset.'

She wiped her face and descended to find Mark and Jo on the sofa, sunburnt, but silent and woebegone. Mark rose to hug her. 'I'm really sorry, Ma. Poor Grandma.'

Jo had been crying and was clutching the dog, who looked uneasy and leapt to lick her tears, then barked, sensing the odd atmosphere.

'I really loved Grandma,' she said, sniffing. 'I hated when you had fights. She was kind to me – she taught me to knit and crochet . . .' her face crumpled and she bawled until Alison hugged her to an intermittently sobbing peace.

'It's rotten,' said Mark. 'I hate old age.'

'Comes to us all.'

'That's why I hate it most.'

Later, when the children had washed and changed,

Jo, who had cheered up, expanded on her weekend in the country.

'I shot with an airgun, lots,' she announced proudly. 'We put pennies on trees for targets.'

Philip, always interested in firearms, asked if she had enjoyed it. He was a trifle surprised by the never-ending butchness of his little princess, but always entertained by her. Jo grinned, eyes shining. 'Yeah! I beat all the boys!'

'Bet you were popular.' Mark cuffed her straggling hair.

'Course I was.' She thumped his ribs.

Philip summoned the four of them: he poured glasses of sherry and carefully handed them round. Jo went quiet. 'It seems strange,' she said at last, 'to be drinking here when Grandma's dead.' Alison hugged her wordlessly.

'She didn't even get my patchwork. It can't have arrived in time.' She gulped down her sherry rather too quickly, then looked up guiltily. 'I did something horrible.'

Alison looked at her anxiously. 'What was it?'

The girl frowned. 'I killed something.'

'You shot something?' Mark was sprawled on the sofa, the dog laid across his knees, blissful. Jo nodded.

Mark laughed. 'A cow? A sheep? Your hostess? Tell us, for heaven's sake.'

She clouted him. 'Shut up.' She glanced from Alison to Philip. 'I shot a rabbit.'

'Well done, girl,' applauded Philip. 'You should have brought it home for the pot. That's what rabbits are for.'

Alison was aware of her daughter's unease. 'Did you mean to kill it?'

Jo shook her head and remembered – the bloody

eyes, and her longing to unlive the moment of horror. She had thought it was just like another target before she had aimed and pulled the trigger. Then the animal had plopped over on its side dead. Tom, her friend's older brother, had been impressed: 'You really are good,' he had said, and he had stunned her by suddenly kissing her firmly on the nose, adding 'I like your freckles too.' Grinning, he had handed her the still-warm corpse of the rabbit, head down-hanging, blood dripping from its mouth. She had felt very surprised, then wished he would do it again, but on the lips this time.

'Don't feel guilty,' said her mother gently. 'After all we are carnivores, somebody has to kill animals.'

Jo frowned. 'I've been thinking about that, and I'm thinking of turning vegetarian.'

Mark winked at Philip. 'When are you starting?'

'I only had eggs for lunch . . .'

Philip rose cheerfully to take the sizzling turkey cadaver from the oven.

'What would you like instead?'

Jo, eyeing the bacon rashers on the breast of the bird, sniffed the heady splendour of meaty smells. 'I think maybe I'll start tomorrow,' she said feebly.

Alison was in the shop on Tuesday morning waiting for Frankie; she was pleased because the American dealer had just come back and had actually paid out a hundred and forty pounds for the splendid embroidered man's smock. The minute she had sold it Alison had felt the usual pang of regret – she always wondered if she could have got more at such times. Selling and pricing had as much to do with confidence as anything else. Still, she could hardly complain, even if the dealer did immediately go and sell it to the Boston or New York Museum for three times as much. She had made an astoundingly good profit. Business had never been so good, but of course it wouldn't last: it always came in spells. Alison hadn't seen Frankie since the march, so when the big Scots girl swooped in like a multi-coloured tartan tornado, she found herself enveloped in a massive loving hug. 'You poor sod. I'm really sorry about your Ma,' said Frankie simply. 'How's the kids?'

Alison shrugged, wet-eyed, and sniffed. 'They're great really; they were upset, but they didn't see my mother often. It's just such a shock.'

They gulped coffee companionably, and a couple of customers came in to browse but bought nothing. Alison was poised to leave when the phone rang. She picked it up, 'Hello? Two Birds Antiques.' She listened, then handed the receiver to Frankie, the mouthpiece covered with her hand. 'It's Anthony Brownstone,' she hissed, and tried not to laugh at Frankie's lack of surprise and horror as Alison mimed painting a very small picture with an even smaller brush.

'Hello?' Frankie sounded guarded, and listened carefully to a lot of talk. 'I'm not sure,' she said hesitantly, not looking very happy. There was more talk, then Frankie gasped. 'My umbrella? Ah yes, I wondered where it was . . .' More talk then 'OK,' she said, 'Why not, if you promise that your intentions are purely plutonic.' Anthony spoke further and she nodded to the phone. 'OK,' she said again. 'Friday, six-thirty. The Curzon, *Heat and Dust*. I'd quite like to see that.' Sighing, she put down the phone. 'Why can't I learn to say no?' she asked. 'It's that wee guy I ran away from. He's got my brolly. Shit. Why is it that you hardly ever fancy the people that fancy you and vice versa? It's a bad bloody joke.'

'He sounds very nice,' said Alison. 'Maybe you'll enjoy it.'

'I doubt it,' said Frankie bitterly. 'I should have asked him to wear stilts or mebbe I could cut off my legs below the knee.'

'Frankie that's sick; can't he simply be a friend?'

'Can friendship exist between men and women?' Frankie sounded dubious.

'Of course it can.' Alison tried to cite some examples, but not many sprang to mind.

'Robert Louis Stevenson said marriage could be regarded as a sort of friendship recognised by the police,' said Frankie. 'I read that recently; it's a good definition, isn't it?'

Was Philip her friend, wondered Alison. For years he had been, but these days the relationship was no longer simple like it used to be when they could take each other for granted. She remembered his agonised behavior at the Easter meal. He had seemed so over-excited, so full of effort and forced cheerfulness, hectically trying to display family togetherness. It had been quite uncomfortable. Gareth now: he felt like a friend, she longed to talk to him, to share his thoughts, but peacefully, alone. Was that friendship? Frankie interrupted her rudely.

'I worry about you. You are away with the fairies. Are you in love or something, you silly bitch?' Her concern made her sound cruder than usual. Alison came to, her vacuous smile fading, and for months afterwards, she was to remember the unsmiling expression on the usually jokey face of her friend. Frankie was trying to tell her something important, but Alison was beyond being able to listen. Already she could see irresistible joys on the horizon, and though she feared them, she knew that she must experience them fully for herself. It was Eve and the fruit of Good and Evil all over again, and although to eat of the Tree of Life was forbidden, she knew that she must taste its fruit for herself. It was too seductive to refuse.

It was dark and late when Alison and Philip met at the station. Philip, having worked late at the office, looked shattered. He sighed as he wearily removed his jacket in the congested space of the sleeping-compartment.

'Did you bring my suit?'

'Of course.' Alison sat on the lower bunk to ease off her new black boots bought in a hurry at lunchtime.

She was dressed all in black; Molly could surely find no fault with this outfit, though she usually did have some sort of comment on Alison's clothes, like 'Very smart in London, I'm sure, but not quite the thing down here . . .' or 'Unusual . . . . Mmmm . . .' a sort of mildly disapproving hum. It was silly to think about it, it didn't really matter a damn what Molly thought, though Alison felt a definite weight of unspoken guilt when she thought about her mother. Their relationship had seemed so insolubly hopeless, but somewhere inside herself she had always vaguely hoped it would get better with the passing of time and the resultant mellowing of the two life-long protagonists. But now it was too late, and that particular recognition scene could never be played. She shivered: a parent's death brought you one step up the ladder, or down, as the case may be.

She rememberd a card Philip had once sent her from Sweden, a Dalarnatrappe, it was called. It was a Swedish folk-image of the journey through life, and showed a sort of decorative staircase, like four children's building blocks – a big one on the ground, painted with blue curlicues, and three smaller ones set on top of it – in different colours – like a stepped pyramid. She remembered that on the left side there was a little tent with a nursing mother with a baby, then each step was occupied by a little person, starting with the child, aged one to ten, hopping up in decades – a decade to each step – till at the summit the man and woman stood together, marked fifty years (in the briefer Swedish), then down they went on the right side, growing progressively bent, decade by decade, with walking-sticks in their hands, from sixty on, till at the bottom was a bald-headed old centenarian, about to walk off the side of the picture. It had seemed amusing when first she had seen it; she had pinned it up in the kitchen until it became obliterated by phone-messages and scrawled numbers. It was decorated with flowers and tendrils, and looked beguilingly cheerful, but when you really thought about it, it was frightening.

'Penny for them?' Philip, already in his white pyjamas, knelt beside her bed and touched her knee tentatively.

She came back to reality. 'I was thinking about life,' she took off her tights, 'and death, basic thoughts like that. Fearsome stuff if you think about it properly.'

She pulled her jersey over her head, and felt Philip's hand creep round to help her undo her bra; but she drew back, 'I haven't brushed my teeth.' She got up and fumbled with her toilet-bag, wishing that she was alone. She felt claustrophobic in this space, and wanted to be left with her thoughts; Philip seemed to get the message, and climbed onto the upper bunk, where he unfolded the evening paper and became immersed as she padded about, hanging up clothes, even hanging up her husband's discarded shirt. He saw her and said 'I could do that darling,' and she smiled, embarrassed that he felt he had to say it. 'Don't be silly, stay where you are.'

He gave her a small shy grin, and read on, then looked up again. She was in her nightie, her nicest softest one. 'When is the funeral?'

'Twelve, then lunch at Molly and Edward's.'

He folded the paper and put it away, then reached out again to Alison, and gently touched her cheek. 'You OK?'

She nodded, 'Tired, that's all. Need my bed.' She made to climb into the lower bunk, when he felt under his pillow. 'How about this to help you sleep?' He held up a bottle of best Glenfiddich whisky, and she was surprised, but thought how welcome a small Scotch would be, 'Lovely, Clever you.'

'Got a crate from a client today; pass the tooth-mugs.'

She did, and he patted his blanket. 'How about hopping up here? There's more headroom.'

She hopped, and he poured; the first glasses were drunk very fast. 'How's the tiredness?' asked Philip, reaching once more for the bottle. She beamed, the whisky was exceedingly cheering. 'I think it has almost gone. How's yours?'

'Gone I'd say, but I have a terrible thirst.' He poured two more large glasses, which they gulped. Alison asked how Philip had felt when his parents died. He had almost never spoken of it, he had only been eighteen, an only child, when they were killed in a car smash on holiday in Scotland. He told her, in detail for the first time, how he had had to go to Inverness to identify the bodies, and even now, she felt him stiffen with horror at the memory.

'It doesn't help to think about these things. Put them

aside; get on with life.' He grunted almost angrily, then took a large slug of alcohol, and turned to Alison, his eyes an intenser blue than ever. 'Life, that's what matters. The here and now. You, me, bodies, the family, and work. Work is the great comforter. And sex . . .' Putting his glass down he reached for his wife, nuzzling her breasts, holding her, stroking, as the speeding train roared and rocked through the night.

She looked down at his blond head, noticing the slight thinning on the crown. She caressed his hair slowly, then his face, which was full of pain. She tried to imagine her mother lying in her box: was the lid already screwed down? The last screw, she joked feebly to an invisible Frankie. Shuddering, she remembered her mother's helpless, half-faced grimaces. But her mother was dead, gone, silent, for ever; Philip's hands warmed and pleased her. Wordlessly they pulled off their night-clothes, and he looked into her eyes, pleading for love and comfort as they caressed and tongued and kissed, excited by the whisky and the rhythms of the train. Their bed was a flying limbo, far away from arguments and disagreements, there was only this speeding compartment in which they were transported into another country of touch and thrumming joy. He knelt above her, wordless with passion, and they sipped, sharing a single glass, and passed the whisky's sweetness back and forth with ambered kisses.

They laughed for joy, abandoned, their loving which was like it had been years before, giving, taking, floating. She opened herself to him. 'Fill me with whisky,' she commanded, smiling up at him, wanting to suck him into her.

'Down there?'

'Yes . . .' She pulled him to her, and carefully he

poured the golden malt liquid into her secret cave, and drank at her fountain, and she was paradised by his lips, speechless with her need of what he could give her at this moment. At last, sated, he leaned back above her.

'My cup runneth over,' he told her, happiness flowing from him. Then, anxiously, 'Didn't the whisky sting?'

She shook her head and stroked him gently. 'Not a bit.'

Chapter Ten

It was still virtually the middle of the night when Philip and Alison were jerked awake by the train guard knocking them up at Newton Abbot. There was barely time to dress and blearily inhale their tea or nibble the unwanted British Rail biscuits, when they found themselves blinking on the black deserted country platform. Molly had said she would arrange for a taxi to take them to the house as it was too uncivil an hour for her or Edward to collect them. 'I'll leave the key for you; come in quietly and go into Emma's bedroom. We'll see you at breakfast.'

Hours later, in her sisters' house Alison, unrelenting in black, and Philip greeted the rest of the family. Molly offered a glacial cheek for her younger sister to do obeisance to, and Edward rose from the breakfast table, wiping his mouth hurriedly. 'Morning Philip, morning Alison. Do sit. I'm off to the office. See you all later,' and, lucky man, he was gone.

Molly noted the black clothes and said little, other than to offer tea or to pass toast; she was still in her dressing gown, and looked pale and worn. Her daughters, Emma and Sarah, older than Richard, and more conventional, appeared, and at least it became slightly easier to chat.

Having finished eating, Alison asked when her father would appear.

'He wakes very early, I gave him breakfast ages ago in his room, but he might like some tea if you care to take it through to him.' Molly poured a fresh cup and handed it to Alison, who took it and went to her father's bedroom where, with some trepidation, she knocked on the door. His reedy voice called her to enter.

The retired vicar was sitting in an armchair, almost engulfed by its green moquette wings; he looked tiny, even littler and paler than he had the time before. She walked towards him, bearing the cup and saucer. 'Hello, Daddy, I brought you a hot drink.'

He didn't seem to register who she was, but looked vague. 'Put it down there . . .' He pointed to a small fireside table beside him; she stepped forward and knelt to put it by him, then reached for his shiny-skinned blue-veined hand, which felt cold. 'Daddy, it's Alison, I've just arrived. I've come to be with you.'

He looked dreamy, surprised a little, then pleased. 'Alison?' He glanced, a little vaguely, at her fingers, and sipped his drink with his free hand. She patted him, terribly moved by the sight of him, and was uneasily aware of the two beds in the background, one screechingly uninhabited, spotless, with a tight-stretched pink chenille bedcover, the other unmade, with her father's striped winceyette pyjamas sprawled on the white sheets. How terrible for him to have to confront this emptiness on waking and sleeping, after fifty years.

He looked at her at last, and stroked her cheek. 'You must look after yourself, you are tired.' She closed her eyes, pained by his, for her, new-found sweetness.

Then he took his hand away and fumbled for his spectacles, gold-rimmed, which he put on. 'That's better,' he mumbled, peering round the room, his eyes now seeming enormous. 'Is Philip here?'

'Yes, he'll come and see you in a minute.'

'And the children?'

'They aren't here.' She wished they were. It had been a bad idea to leave them, but she had weakly succumbed to Philip's insistence that the youngsters were best kept out of things like funerals. The old man got up slowly and shuffled in worn slippers to his unmade bed, where he found his ancient watch with Roman numerals, and painfully fixed it on his wrist; it took time. Then, in front of the mirror over the pink-painted mantelpiece, he brushed his thin white hair carefully, and turned to his youngest daughter. 'You knew of course that your mother wasn't well?'

Choked, Alison rose and went to him, and embraced the frail shoulders. 'Daddy, of course I knew; I came down to see her. And I'm sorry, so very sorry that she has gone.'

He blinked. 'I never thought she would be the first to go. She was younger than me, you know.' He shook his head. 'Strange.'

'Oh Daddy.'

'Never mind, my dear. Never mind.' It was ridiculous, he was comforting her. She sniffed, and he handed her a hankie, with which she trumpeted an end to her weeping. There was a tactful knock on the door, and Philip joined them. The two men gently discussed the train-journey and the wetness of the weather, until Alison had to get out. 'I'll go and help the others with lunch,' she said, touching each of them as she spoke.

Alison was shocked afresh by the bent smallness of her father when she saw him getting into her brother-in-law's car; she felt a momentary pang that she was not to travel with him to the funeral, feeling both that she had been demoted, and that perhaps she could have boosted his frailty, but Molly had organised that Molly, Edward and the old man should travel with the two girls, and Richard, who had tried to make his unruly mop of curls look acquiescently funereal, and was wearing an unaccustomed grey suit – obviously acquired for the occasion of his grandmother's demise – was to drive Philip and Alison in his old Mini.

Alison couldn't shake off the feeling that she and Richard had been put together like naughty children. 'Have your parents forgiven you yet?' she asked. She knew that he had got drunk at a party last weekend, and was in disgrace.

'I think so,' Richard nodded. 'I'm working to get my gold star, being ferryman for you two.' The rain thrummed on the roof. 'I can hardly see out,' he complained, then swore as the car juddered then bumped, and slowed to a halt.

'What is it?' Philip leaned forward.

'Shit!' Richard pulled on the handbrake. 'It's a puncture. Sorry folks; but I'll just have to mend it very quickly.'

'How long have we got?'

'Twenty minutes, which gives us about five to do the job,' he shook his curly head and laughed. 'Honestly, Ma is sure to think I did it on purpose.' He got out of the car, pulled up his anorak collar and went to drag out the spare wheel and tools; Philip, grabbing a large black umbrella climbed out to help him, and Alison, taking her umbrella (a highly unsuitable golfing one, a gift from Frankie), also got out, and stood in the village street watching the men at work. It was still gusty, and suddenly her umbrella turned itself inside-out. Philip looked up at her, his hands black and dirty from struggling with the wet wheel, which seemed to be jammed. 'You'll get soaked. Go and shelter in a doorway,' he called.

'Nothing I can do?'

Richard looked up. 'Could you buy me some cigarettes?'

'I didn't know you smoked.'

'Never in the bosom of the family, but I do, and I need one now.'

She went into the small general store and bought a twenty pack of the kind he wanted, and some matches. Deciding that she could do with one herself, she lit a couple in the doorway before joining the heaving, cursing men. 'How are we doing?' She handed Richard a cigarette, and Philip looked up at her in dismay.

'Alison, what are you doing?' She hadn't smoked for years, and then only briefly, when she first started having antique stalls. She inhaled headily: 'I need it, just for today. It's not a common occurrence, one's mother's funeral.'

The two men pulled together, trying to move the nuts on the punctured tyre, but they wouldn't budge. Alison, frustrated at not being able to help, looked at her watch: they were going to be late. She eyed the nearby shops, and her attention was caught by one coyly called 'The Captain's Cabin'. Her heart leapt when she realised it was an antique shop, new to her.

'I'm just popping in here,' she called, as a cheer came from Richard as at last a nut shifted.

It was a delightful shop, and in moments she was in overdrive, adrenalin making her decisive. Four minutes later Philip stared in astonishment as his wife emerged from the shop clutching an enormous blue and white vase, all of thirty inches high, and very handsome. 'Are you crazy?' he asked, exasperated, his bland brow slashed with black oil. 'You can't arrive at the church with that huge great thing.'

'It is a bit big,' said Richard, amused. 'I can just imagine my mother's face. Here, you'd better hide it in the boot. Wrap it in the old blanket.'

Carefully Alison laid down the vase, and took a final drag of her cigarette. 'I'll just be two seconds; you two get in and start up.' She dashed back to the shop where the appalled Philip saw her receive an even larger object from the dealer in the doorway. This time it was a sort of Victorian tricycle, shaped like a horse, with wheels beside the galloping legs, carefully painted dapple-grey.

Richard admired it, and opened the car door to help her put it into the back seat, then, when everybody was in place and the doors all slammed shut, he said, 'Right. Hold tight. We're off!'

Philip didn't actually complain – in fact she hadn't held them up at all – but his disapproval was evident in his chilly silence. He mopped his dirty hands and face with a cloth, whilst Richard skeetered round corners on squealing brakes. They were six minutes late when he at last lurched to a stop in front of the little village church; Alison prayed that her blue and white vase was safe: it had cost seventy pounds, but she had an excited idea that it might be worth very much more, and the 'horsicle' as the ex-naval dealer had cheerfully called it was in very good condition. The three of them ran up the church steps, and she was aware of organ music playing; they were ushered into the front pew, where Alison flinched again from the sight of her huddled father. Molly glared along at them, and Alison whispered 'We had a puncture – sorry!'

'What did you say?' asked her father in a very loud voice.

'We had a *puncture*,' hissed Alison.

'Ah,' he nodded and kept on nodding dreamily until Alison felt quite anxious. She held his arm, and he patted her hand.

'I'm glad you weren't hurt,' he said. 'We were worried about you. Is Philip here?'

Alison nodded. She was still breathless from the rush. She caught Philip's eye and he winked, which surprised her. He looked very beautiful, pale and dignified in black and white, almost episcopal. Memories of their abandoned love-making on the train filled her mind, and she tried to rid herself of them as the young balding vicar who stood in front of the small congregation began his funeral address.

My mother is dead, Alison told herself over and over.

'We are here to mourn the passing of our dear departed sister Margaret, who gave so fully to the work of the church and the community, who was a respected and well-loved wife, and the mother of Molly and Alison.' He chanted her name so that it sounded like 'Alisong', and she wished that what he said were true, and that she had really loved her mother. It made all this living business so empty when there was no love.

She felt her father rise, and followed suit, fumbling for a prayer-book. As she stood up she met Richard's eye: he was standing at the end of the row. He grinned conspiratorially at his aunt, and wiped his brow with an invisible handkerchief.

She smiled back, he was a lovely boy.

The congregation sang Hymn 399. 'When our heads are bow'd with woe'; and a thousand childhood memories flowed over Alison, of all the services she had ever been forced to attend and the hymns she had sung. She had discarded her Christian upbringing, and viewed it as so much mumbo-jumbo, but the one bonus from her childhood – her only legacy from that seemingly interminable churchgoing – was her love of music. Gradually over the years she had become familiar with all the hymns and psalms, musically if not verbally. She seemed to have a mental clampdown on the words, and rarely remembered any of them, but mention a melody and she could hum it, and waft off on its stream. Her mother had been a good singer, and had led the choir for many years. Music was pretty well the only thing they had had in common, other than the inescapable fact of the shared genes.

The young vicar was rambling on again. Alison looked across to the small choir who had come to sing for her father's sake – both he and her mother had been much involved in church activities here, even after his retirement. She noticed a stocky man with a black moustache standing in the choir, and was startled for a moment by his resemblance to Gareth: he had the same piercing dark eyes and level brow. She looked away, disturbed by her memory of the Welshman; she had been free of his haunting for all of twelve hours, since getting on that train with Philip. They were praying now: it was painful to watch her father struggle to kneel on to his hassock, the sight made her want to weep. The whole family except for herself was on its knees, even Richard and Philip: Philip never went to church either, but she supposed he felt more comfortable behaving like everybody else. Still choked, Alison felt self-conscious, sitting upright in her pew, but she couldn't bring herself to kneel, it would feel false. Dutifully she shut her eyes and remembered again the boredom of her father's preaching, and how she used to peep out between her fingers until her mother or Molly's disapproving stares had forced her to stop looking. Things hadn't changed much. She still felt like Molly's naughty little sister.

Once more the congregation rose, and Alison was pleased and surprised to note that the next item on the agenda was 'I know that my Redeemer liveth', from Handel's *Messiah*. It was an unusual thing to be sung at a funeral in a small country church, an oddly unconventional choice. She remembered that Molly had said something about taking her mother in her wheelchair only last week to hear the *Messiah* in Torquay, and that it had been superb; her mother had shown great pleasure, maybe that was why. She wondered which of the rather dreary women in the choir were going to sing the solo, when there were shuffllings, and the dark man with the moustache suddenly stepped forward. He stood alone, looking intensely serious and even more like Gareth, gazing into the air in front of him; then the organ struck up the sweet and haunting melody. Handel always got to Alison: no wonder Beethoven had said he would kneel in homage at his feet, he was indeed a genius. The dark man looked up and began to sing, and an extraordinarily beautiful high voice emitted from his undeniably male body. It was uncanny, he sang like an angel, but a female angel. She had never heard the piece better sung, and at last wept freely from the sweet pain of the music, and from the unfinished business of her relationship with her mother. She felt for her father's hand, and willingly he held hers in his papery fingers, whilst the music swelled and lifted all the people far above the little grey cloisters of the church and small green churchyard where the coffin lay awaiting its chill covering of clay.

In his small terraced house in Shepherd's Bush, Gareth wearily hung the last wet garment on the pulley above the bath. He was sick of the endless washing and ironing, though the children, to do them justice, were learning, even at nine and eleven, to help him with many of the domestic tasks. Holiday times were always a problem: he couldn't really go out job-hunting as he usually did, nor could he spend all day in the library, because the youngsters got bored, and the boredom showed. They had come back yesterday from the weekend with his sister in Lewes. He had been pleased to see them back, because the house had felt screamingly lonely since all that togetherness on the march last Friday.

He had spent a strange weekend, half-mad with isolation, ringing up various friends to find something to do on the Sunday. Saturday hadn't been too bad; he had done a stall in the Red Lion pub in Hounslow, and had pulled in a surprising amount of money considering the simple odds and ends he was selling. His sister had asked him down to Lewes but he didn't want to impose his black mood upon her. In the end he had spent Sunday mostly in bed reading, and his neighbours had given him supper – they were marvellous neighbours, never nosey, always ready to help. Often the woman would make sure his children had lunch and someone to talk to if he had to be out selling, or travelling overnight to one of his endless interviews.

It was raining heavily outside, Bronwen and Ceri would be soaked: he had sent them off to the Science Museum this morning, hoping to get through the piled-up chores. He went to the fridge and made himself a cheese and pickle sandwich, and decided to have a beer. It would probably send him off to sleep, but that might be no bad thing, he just felt so bloody black. He pulled the ring off the can and drunk ruminatively, wondering how on earth to keep the youngsters entertained, not too expensively, in this depressing weather.

He glanced moodily at the Ashanti fertility symbol on the mantelpiece; that had been his first glimpse of Alison, when he so hot-headedly bought the figure for himself. It was beautiful though, as she was. He wondered how Alison was getting on. She was obviously in a vulnerable state at the moment – sometimes she looked almost as lonely as he felt. He sighed, suddenly overcome by a great longing to see her; he felt that they had such a huge load of things to discuss and exchange, and by God, just to talk to a sympathetic, intelligent and attractive woman, what bliss that would be. He drained the can, and when his children came in an hour later, they found him snoring slightly, sprawled in the big chair beside the gasfire.

The funeral lunch consisted of cold cuts in every sense of the phrase, slices of ham and chicken, and chill looks and words from Molly, who was obviously used-up, like a boiled bone; all the goodness had gone from her, at least for now. Alison felt uncomfortable in her sister's house, and looked forward to escaping onto the late afternoon train. She stood furtively smoking a cigarette with her nephew in the garden, where seagulls wheeled and the pale spring sun embroidered the dripping buds and branches of the awakening greenery. Richard asked her what she had thought of the service and she shrugged.

'The usual. Whenever I hear a church service, I'm glad all over again that I don't belong, it feels alien to me, but the music never fails to move me.'

The body nodded, exhaling smoke. 'Me too.'

'As for that singer, I was astonished. He was fabulous.'

Richard grinned, 'I nearly got the giggles. Old Mrs

Martin, the one in the pale blue flowery hat, said she saw that I was quite overcome, because my shoulders were shaking. Little did she know. But that chap's OK, you know.'

Alison didn't understand.

'He's normal, married, got four kids.'

'Ah.'

They watched the shrieking gulls fight, squawking over some bread on the wet grass. 'We'd better go back in,' said Alison.

Richard nodded. They went back into the house and Molly met them in the kitchen. She stared, white faced and dead-eyed at her sister. 'Oh. There you are. We have been looking for you everywhere. Daddy is tired, he wanted to see you.'

'Sorry,' mumbled Alison, a naughty little girl again. 'We needed some fresh air.' Molly's gaze raked the two nicotine delinquents with bullets and left them dead and bleeding on the spotless yellow vinyl of the kitchen floor. Alison fled to the frail harbour of her father: he was already in his room, sitting alone. Quietly she shut the door behind her, and he looked up, a little startled, when she touched his arm. Patting her hand, he motioned her to an upright chair beside him. 'Good to see you my dear, I thought you had fled all the Good Workers.'

Alison was surprised; in a way this was exactly what she had done. All those robust well-hatted ladies, so full of praise for the good works of her mother, had become quite suffocating after two or three sherries. She flashed him a small grin, 'I hope you didn't mind?'

'Why should I? I've just fled them myself. Such ladies are both the bane and the bulwark of Church life, but I had had enough of them for today of all days.'

'How are you feeling?'

He looked at her, his eyes seeming to fill the round gold lenses, then looked away, sad. 'Empty, I suppose. There seems to be very little point to anything now.'

'Oh Daddy, you will feel better.' She stroked his hand, flaccid on his knee. He nodded, teetering on tears, then smiled a little.

'What did you think of the Handel?'

'I was amazed to hear a solo from the *Messiah* at a funeral. Surely that is unusual?'

He looked almost impish. 'It was. I specially asked for it. I had my reasons.' He looked straight at her, quite pleased with himself.

'Tell me.'

He pulled himself out of the chair and pattered about the room, then looked out of the window down towards the harbour and the sea. 'A lot of white horses today. It's very rough, I wouldn't like to be a fisherman.'

'Daddy, tell me about the singing.'

He still stood with his small dark-suited back towards her. 'The first time I ever saw your mother she was singing "I know that my Redeemer liveth," in Tewkesbury Abbey. I was doing a lay-preacher job there and went to an Easter peformance of the *Messiah*. Nineteen thirty-four it was.'

Alison had never heard this story. It was a mother she could hardly imagine. 'I didn't know she was good enough to be soloist. Why did she stop?'

'The war, worry, Molly's birth and then you, little thing, arrived. She worried, you know. Worried that everything should be just so. Insecurity. It seemed easier to sing in the choir.'

Do insecure people become manipulative? Alison wondered. It certainly was one way of viewing her dear departed parent. She remembered the singer, and his sweet rich voice.

The old man was silent for a while, then nodded, and looked at his daughter again. 'Do you know,' he said earnestly, 'the most odd and wonderful thing?'

Alison shook her head.

'When I shut my eyes and he was singing, it was strange . . .' He shook his white head, smiling a little puzzled at the memory. 'Very strange.'

Alison looked at him expectantly.

'Well,' the old man took a big breath, 'he sounded, that man, that singer with the black moustache, exactly like your mother did, all those years ago, that very first time I heard her singing, or even clapped eyes on her. Odd, isn't it?'

Alison found it too much, and saw tears trembling in his eyes; she moved across to him, and embraced his frail body, and rocked him as he sobbed. At last, he subsided, and blew his nose noisily. 'I do apologise. I didn't mean to give way.'

'You are supposed to at times like this.'

They sat together in silence for a while, then he looked at her again.

'I miss her, you know.'

'I know. You must have missed her all the time she was ill.'

'Yes.'

There was nothing more to say; Alison helped him to undress and saw him into his bed in his long woolly underwear and striped pyjamas. He took his glases off carefully, and laid them on the bedside table, which was full of medicine bottles and a water carafe. She leant over him. 'Are you all right?'

'Yes, thank you.'

'Philip and I are going soon. I have to say goodbye.'

'Goodbye, little Alison,' he smiled and shut his eyes and seemed to be asleep. She tiptoed out.

The guests had all left by now; Emma and Sarah in smocked floral dresses were clearing up the debris whilst Edward and Richard washed up. When Philip appeared with their luggage, Molly, half-asleep in an armchair, looked up hopefully.

'Is it time for you to go?'

'Almost.'

Edward welcomed the chance to remove his yellow rubber gloves. 'I'll go and get the car,' he said eagerly.

Alison, standing in the kitchen, caught Richard's eyes in a panic. The things? The huge vase and the cumbersome wheeled toy? Neither Molly nor Edward must see them. Richard nodded at her, and whipped off his apron. 'I'll take them,' he told his father. 'I'd like to.'

To his sister-in-law's relief, Edward conceded, and after awkward farewells – in which Molly stood regally impassive, enshrouded in her invisible but bulky mantle of matriarchy, grudgingly ready to receive a token kiss on the cheek – they found themselves once more on the train.

Philip was sitting self-consciously beside the big Japanese jar. It was a splendid object; she felt certain that it was Arita ware, and if that were so it could be worth thousands. She would have to have it authenticated by Sotheby's or Christie's – a similar one had sold recently for ten thousand pounds.

'If the train fills up, what will you do with these?' he asked.

'Sit and hold them, I suppose.'

Philip rolled his eyes upwards; he was not amused. Alison sighed and gazed out into the dusk, dark and mysterious, with occasional lights flashing by and silhouetted trees. She felt very separate from her husband as she watched him sleep; he looked positively translucent from exhaustion. He needed a respite.

Once more in the train-window Alison's own reflection blurred into a nightmare image of her mother's face in her last illness, the agonised grin of effort; then, as sleep began to overtake her, the face changed to that of Gareth, dark, kind, concerned. Her eyes tight shut, she frowned in an effort to dowse the image, and turned away as though to shake it off, but it remained inexorably there until she slept, like some benign sun, warm and welcoming, infinitely, irresistibly alluring, drawing her to its hot consuming centre.

Chapter Eleven

'Please at least go in late to the office, if you can't take a whole morning off for once,' Alison begged Philip in the morning. Still in bed, they both ached with tiredness; neither of them had slept well after coming home from the funeral. He shook his head, yawning.

'No way; I've got a meeting in Maidenhead.'

'Maidenhead? Why there?'

'There's a big construction firm there that's involved in the Hong Kong project. It could be our biggest scheme ever; I need to work full-belt until it's under way.'

'But you promised to take some days off during the kids' Easter break, before they both push off by themselves.'

Philip, embarrassed, was silent.

'Philip, you did! You swore to take some time off this week and over next weekend.'

'I know, I'm sorry.' He sat in bed frowning at the duvet.

'Sorry? We live a totally crazy life! You are hardly ever here, and when you are, you are exhausted and stressed, or manically trying to pretend that everything is fine by hi-jacking the kitchen and baking bread to prove that family life is alive and well, flourishing as the yeast rises. It is insane. I am sick of it, sick of having you as a sort of remote figurehead who sets us up for ideal family life in the perfect aesthetic setting, like programming some bloody computer, so you can go off and gallivant in Hong Kong or Trinidad.' She was getting angrier and angrier.

'Gallivant! Did you say gallivant?' roared Philip, glaring back at her. 'Jesus Christ, woman! You should try one of my business trips sometime!'

'I wish I bloody could, I'd like a break from routine, from all the decision-making and nurturing I am left to do by myself, month after month, year after year!'

Philip stared at this spitting stranger in his bed: 'If you knew . . .' he said quietly, 'how boring my trips are; how empty of people I can in any way relate to, how foul and anonymous I find even the most exotic hotels, and how dull and tasteless the finest foreign food can be when you have too much variety and choice. If you had the remotest idea of the emptiness of my life on these goddamned trips, you would not use the word gallivant.'

A brief image of a long-legged American danced before his eyes, but he dismissed her as a rarity, a soon-to-be-forgotten bonus, not worth mentioning.

Alison stared at him: 'Stay then! Let's try some proper family life for a change. Send somebody else, somebody younger, or somebody who realises that what he really wants to do is to escape reality, and doesn't – like *some* . . .' she hissed the last word bitterly, '. . . harbour some pure white fantasy of the glorious family, the holy quartet complete with divine dog – *your bloody dog!* – that I have to walk and feed and rescue from crapping in the neighbours' gardens and breaking their blessed plants!'

Philip shook his head, pained. 'This is madness.' He put a hand across his brow, then looked at his wife, who was steaming hate.

'I love you, woman.' he put his hand out to touch her fingers, but she snatched her hand away, breathing heavily, eyes hot. He tried again: 'On the train . . . not many people have it like that.' He appealed to her shared fuck-memory; she looked away, her Achilles heel smarting.

'That was . . .'

'That was what?'

She shrugged. 'I don't know . . .' She thought hard: what had it signified? 'We needed each other; we succoured each other . . .'

He tried to make her laugh, and nodded, daring a smile, 'We certainly did . . .' in every sense of the word . . .'

She didn't react, but stared ahead of her, not amused.

'Things have got to change,' she said. 'You can't keep being away so much; it will bust us. You have got to do some of your famous delegating.'

'Darling.' This time he took both her hands in his, but they lay unresponding, like empty gloves. 'At the moment the partnership is involved in difficult negotiations in Trinidad and Hong Kong. I cannot delegate or renege now; it's too tricky. Also, I handle these situations better than anyone in the office.'

'*Will* not delegate, you mean. It's a matter of priorities. Philip, and yours and mine no longer seem to be the same. For you it's work first, and ambition – far and above all the other things like spending time with the children, helping with major decisions, organising holidays, car, dog or house-maintenance, the lot. It all rests with me. Without me nothing would happen in this bloody place, except when you happen to fly in like some flaming angel in white to bake bread or cook a bi-annual feast. It's all for dramatic effect, and has little to do with real life. It's a set-piece, an image, not a reality.'

Philip was silent, now fuming; he dropped her hands which lay abandoned where they fell, as though they were not her own.

'I know all that,' he said distinctly. 'I know that you handle it all, but you are my wife, and you do it wonderfully, and . . .' He only just managed not to shout the next sentence; 'I love and admire you; you are efficient, intelligent, admirable. That's why I married you. We make a good team, the two of us.' He paused, gazed at her triumphantly, then added fiercely, 'Both in and out of bed!'

Alison wanted to scream: it was all true, but it was all untrue as well. She was not happy: she did not like the life she had acquiesced to. She wanted more independence, more support on the human things, and Philip's proper acknowledgement that her work was important too. But it was so hard to express; she remained imprisoned by her own inability to communicate her needs and wishes.

Philip got out of bed and started dressing. 'You seem to think I lead the life of Reilly. Do you really think I enjoy these endless trips? I sometimes get so lonely I feel half-mad; it's tough for me too you know. Empty relationships with strangers – life is hard for most people, and you have it pretty good here, you know. You don't have much to complain about.' He gestured grandly round the mirrored wardrobes and white-carpeted splendour of the bedroom, and went to the bathroom. He came back, brushing his teeth, and waved his frothy toothbrush at her: 'Dammit, woman! Can't you see I only do it for love of you all? I do everything for you and the children. I would give anything to be home more and lead a domestic existence.'

Anything except himself. Alison stared stonily at him. 'I think you like to go away: it keeps you in your ivory tower, and that, if you are honest with yourself, is the place you most like to inhabit, except for occasional forays into real-life, preferably into a master-planned set-up – preferably all-white.' She sounded precise and judgmental, like a schoolmarm.

Philip was lost. 'What's this about all-white? You seemed as eager as I was when we chose to do everything white.'

Alison shrugged, 'There seemed no other way to be, in the face of such manic fervour. After all, I'm not religious.'

Philip snorted like a puzzled bull. 'Come off it, woman. You have as much say as me in all these things.' He started at her perplexed.

'Theoretically, maybe, put in practice no,' said Alison. 'I suppose I thought it was more peaceful to let you have your way. But I regret it now.'

'Good God, you make me sound like a bloody tyrant.'

'No,' she shook her head. 'I think it was more to do with my own apathy, but I am changing, have changed.'

He clasped his head, groaned, and began to dress. He immersed himself momentarily in the oblivion of a jersey, until his bewildered head popped out. Ruffled, he glared at her. 'So what happens now? Are we to have a blood-red sitting-room as a sign of your advancing psyche?'

'It might be interesting.' Alison watched coolly as he adjusted his shirt collar and brushed his pale blond hair. 'Anyway, we can talk about it more peacefully when you aren't rushing off to work. How about trying to go down to Dorset at the weekend, or early next week? The kid's school trips aren't for nearly another week.'

Philip stood frozen, hand with hairbrush in mid air, 'I ah . . . meant to tell you . . .'

'What?' she snapped, hackles rising. He had promised a respite, days together.

'I didn't tell you because of the funeral and everything . . .'

She looked at him in an expectant, but not friendly, way.

'I have to be off again on Sunday, Hong Kong: for a long stint. Almost a month, certainly three weeks.'

'You bastard!' She stared at him in utter disbelief, betrayed. 'You promised to be home for a decent spell, to take time off.'

'I'm sorry, I'm really sorry, but there are huge problems that need to be sorted out. I felt I couldn't tell you until now because of your mother.'

'Send young Williamson, or Hawkins, or somebody from the main team.'

'I can't; I made all the contacts, they are tricky people. I must see this project through, too much depends on it. I only heard on Tuesday, just before we set off for Devon, I didn't want to upset you.'

'Well, you bloody have!' She really wanted to hit him, to cause injury. Instead, she hurled off the covers and stormed in to the bathroom – much in the manner of her daughter a few nights ago – where she wept and beat the cool porcelain of the basin with angry impotent hands, while Philip knocked on the door and said, 'Alison, please let me in.'

'Go away,' she called, and wept afresh when she heard that he had gone. He must have known this when they made love on the train. The traitor. She groaned and heard first the bedroom door, then the outside door bang, then the car started up, and she knew she was alone, until she heard Jo's voice, sleepy, questioning; 'Mum, Mum! What was all the shouting about? Where's Dad? He's not had breakfast . . .'

'It was nothing. We slept in. Pa was late for the office; we were tired and bad-tempered, that's all . . .'

She wished it were true, that that was all it was; but she was aware of a growing and bitter resentment of Philip's ambition, of his putting work first, whatever. The trouble was that the summit of the particular mountain of ambition/success that he was climbing, never appeared, in fact it seemed to be unattainable, and every time Philip thought he had reached that summit, he would discover that it was further on, higher up, so he had to keep on winning, travelling, climbing, whilst his family on the foothills and the plains, carried on regardless, unheeded except for his occasional descents into what Alison considered to be real life.

Her feeling of dissatisfaction was deep and powerful; though she knew that from the outside she probably appeared spoilt, mad and selfish, for her the present system no longer worked, she was empty emotionally towards Philip; their love had become a duty, a habit. She no longer felt as though they were travelling on the same road, and Philip's particular journey was one she secretly despised anyway. She did not even especially admire the buildings he designed. His ambition seemed to be so consuming that it ate up life, so what was it for if there were no life left over to enjoy as the fruit of the ambition? When she was younger his strength and determination had been so powerful that she had accepted them as forces which could also govern and structure her own life, which up till then had been pretty formless and ruled by others – starting with her mother, then Molly, and school. She had unwittingly allowed herself to be dominated, but today's Alison was a different person, her mother was dead, and so, she suspected, was the meek Little Alice of yesteryear, but, like her mother, only just.

Anthony Brownstone listened blissfully to the fluted music from Thomas Tomkin's *Book of Songs*, 1622, and hummed along with the radio. His coffee tasted particularly sweet this morning, and the spring sun even reached down into his basement where it bewitched his avocado plants and hanging ivies. Frankie was a super girl, such a bundle of contradictions, so filled with uncertainty about herself, yet so earthy and amusing. They had gone to see *Heat and Dust* at the Curzon, and had come out filled with images of India. After the film they had eaten a Chinese meal and talked a lot; she had told him of her longing to perform, but how little luck she had had. He, high on being out with the huge and wonderful Scot, congratulated himself that he had been at his wittiest. She had roared with laughter, and they had drunk two bottles of wine; when they said goodnight outside the restaurant – Frankie had insisted on going home alone by tube – she had even, giggling, agreed to come with him to his painter friend Jay's party next week, though she still made it very clear that she was not interested in him sexually. The madrigals were still playing: Anthony closed his eyes and swayed to the sound; he could wait. She was a special sort of person, worth waiting for, if he could only manage to keep his hands off her beautiful mighty body. She must ultimately be assailable, he smiled to himself. 'Patience, Brownstone, your time will come.' He would take her to the party and make sure that she could relax with him, and he wouldn't even make the tiniest pass until he felt sure she was ready. It was after all a miracle, that after her running away from their first meeting, she had agreed to come thus far.

It seemed to Alison to have been a particularly fraught few days: there had been that tremendous fight the day after the funeral, the aftermath of which had hung over them till Philip left on Sunday, then there had been frantic shoppings with the children, trying to find jeans and training shoes which both fitted and suited the fashion decreed by their peers. It drove Alison nearly mad, having to stand in shops with her offspring whilst they discarded and rejected what seemed to her excellent, practical and highly desirable garments as being too baggy, too tight, or the same as somebody else's. At last they were kitted out, passport found, bags packed, and she took them to their bus and train, and she was alone.

It was strange with both children and Philip away; she was glad to have an antique fair at the weekend, even though it gave Two Birds their worst business day ever. 'Seventeen pounds,' said Frankie in dismay. 'And we paid twelve for the stall, and I spent eleven buying those silver rings from Hilary.' She slumped in her chair gloomily. 'It's been a total waste.'

Alison sighed. 'Maybe we're losing our touch.' She had shown Frankie the big blue and white Japanese jar she had bought in Devon, and Frankie had been dismissive. 'Bet you it's modern,' she said. 'I've seen these before. They're very clever, but old they are not.'

Alison sagged frowning, 'I thought it was just like that one sold for thousands just a few months ago.'

Frankie nodded 'Gold star to you, hen, it *is*. That's why! They started making them after seeing that one fetch such a lot.'

Alison looked at the big vase despondently. 'Seventy quid I paid. I thought it might make my fortune.' Today the object lacked lustre, and the texture was wrong; uneasily she suspected that Frankie might be right.

It was still early when Alison got back to the empty house where she was greeted by a very worried dog, who, seeing everybody depart with bags and suitcases, and finding himself alone in the house, had decided that the end of his world had come. He lay shivering with misery in his basket, bereft and terrified until Alison's return rendered him utterly hysterical with joy; he leapt, barked and licked, so that she had to shout at him to desist.

For her lonely Monday breakfast she made herself tea and toast, and melancholically ate a grapefruit; she didn't remember ever being alone for so long. Usually the children were here when Philip was away: it felt very weird. She patted the dog, huddled at her knees, and wondered how she would cope with ten days of total silence. When the phone rang she was delighted to hear Frankie's voice, excited and gleeful.

'They've come!' she was shrieking. 'Lots of them!'

Alison didn't know what she was talking about.

'The letters! My answers! It's amazing, there's lots. It will take ages to sort out. Will you help me?'

'Of course, come round tonight when you get back.' Frankie was going down to an auction in Kent today, borrowing the car.

'OK,' Frankie was whooping. 'I can hardly wait! There's a few weirdos. Two of them thought I was a man, and one of them's really filthy.' She hooted joyfully. 'Anyway, I'm off. See you tonight.'

'I'll feed us.' Alison smiled as she put down the phone. It would surely be an entertaining evening.

She was half an hour earlier than usual when she set off for the shop, and was driving down a quiet back street when she noticed a flash of headlamps from a little yellow Citroen. She flashed back a greeting almost before she had consciously realised that it was Gareth in the other car. They passed each other, drove on a few yards, then, simultaneously applying their brakes, both went into reverse. The street was virtually empty, and she found herself stopped side by side with Gareth whom she hadn't seen since the march. They wound down their respective windows and she saw that he had two children in the back – a boy and a girl – both grinning shyly, each as beautiful as the father.

'Hi there,' he said. 'I was sure it was you. How's things?'

'I'm reeling, to be honest.' She told him about her mother and the family being away. 'So it's just me and the dog – a strange sensation.'

He made comforting noises and thought quickly. 'Listen, I'm taking this pair to the baths. Come and have a quick coffee, it's not far from your shop.'

Cars were now moving awkwardly round them, and a couple hooted. Alison, flustered, glanced at her watch. She was very early. 'OK.' She smiled. 'I'll park and see you there.'

He was standing at the pay-desk with the two children when she arrived after a breathless battle to squeeze the car into too small a space; the boy looked friendly and grinned at her, the girl, with blue almost turquoise eyes, was less forthcoming. Gareth, hands on their shoulders, introduced them: 'Alison this is Ceri and Bronwen, my wicked offspring.' The girl tried not to smile, and looked down, embarrassed, playing with her rolled towel. Gareth handed them tickets. 'OK. Off you go, you two. I'll be in the café and I'll come and watch you.'

'Are you not going to swim?' asked Alison. He shook his head. 'I can't be bothered today; usually I do, I'd rather talk to you.'

There was no coffee, so they sipped frothy chocolate, super-sweet from paper cups, and sat side by side above the pool watching the children giggle and learn to dive. Momentarily Alison felt as though she had a surrogate family, and was reminded of her own two, three or four years earlier. Gareth eyed her: 'Did you go down for the funeral? Devon, wasn't it?'

She nodded.

'Bad, was it?' His voice was deep, enfolding.

'It was very upsetting. It brings it all closer; we didn't really get on, and I still feel guilty about that. I don't know . . .' she trailed off, and sipped the comforting sweet froth.

He nodded. 'When the older generation begins to die off, you realise that it's one notch nearer, don't you?'

'Exactly. Very scary.' Their eyes met and they both looked away. She told him about the Swedish folk-picture of life and death.

'The Dalarnatrappe. I know them. They're wonderful, frightening though.' He nodded, and waved to his children. The small girl came towards him and showed him a tiny mark on her foot. He leaned over the rail and examined it carefully, and sent her off reassured, and came back smiling. 'I think she's jealous.'

They laughed companionably, and watched the swimmers. A fat old man eased his way into the water, puffing, concentrating, bald, with mossy white body hair.

'Are you doing that Bath Fair next month that you and Frankie were talking about?' asked Gareth.

'Yes, we both are.'

He nodded. 'Might see you down there. I've got an interview in Bristol around then, and the offer of a cottage; it sounds nice. Think I'll spend a day or two away.'

'It's always a very good fair. I did fantastically well last year. I save up stuff for it; it's quite a high standard.'

'Out of my league, I'm afraid.'

They were silent. Alison, terribly aware of him, his warmth and texture, felt an almost uncontrollable desire to touch him. 'I must go soon,' she muttered, looking at her watch. 'Might be a customer beating at the door.'

'Your husband away too, is he?'

'Yes.'

'I haven't got used to being alone yet,' said Gareth pensively. 'It feels unnatural.'

'I never get used to Philip's being away. It's terribly lonely at first, then just as you've adapted, he's back, and you have to try and get back to where you were, yet it is never exactly the same . . .' She stopped, feeling that she was talking too much, and started to pick up her things.

'I was going to say . . .' said Gareth, and she could have sworn that he too was blushing now, his skin looked so dark. 'To say that it would be nice if you and Frankie would like to come round one night, come and have a drink or a meal.'

She would like that a lot. She nodded. 'Love to, specially with everybody away.' She grinned, waved to the dolphining children, and clattered down the steps into the street, feeling unaccountably happy. As she walked towards the car, she had a thought, what about tonight, if he came too? Turning, she ran back, and startled the old woman who sold tickets by begging to be re-admitted to the spectator section.

Gareth was surprised to see her again but obviously pleased. Breathlessly she invited him for supper with Frankie and herself at eight: it would give her time to read Frankie's letters first.

Gareth eyed his children. 'If I can get my neighbour to baby-sit I'll come. Can I give you a ring if I can't make it?'

She gave him her address, and fled, hoping that he wouldn't notice that her face matched the scarlet of her mohair scarf, or hear the beating of her heart which seemed to make the air reverberate. The ticket lady saw her go, and shook her head at the white-uniformed man beside her kiosk. 'Somebody's got it bad, that's for sure,' she muttered, and handed him a cigarette. She had seen it all before, time after time.

Frankie pounded into the Salveson house at half-past five, pleased with her buys at auction; she dragged Alison out to look who thought most of the stuff had been sensibly bought, though as ever, the pieces of twenties and thirties china did little to enthuse her. There were some good wooden and mother-of-pearl boxes, three decanters, plus some petit-point cushion-covers and an embroidered Biblical text saying 'Bless this House'.

'Super,' Alison approved. 'Cover it all up with a rug and come in, and don't forget your fan mail.'

Frankie came behind her with a large brown envelope, bulging with smaller box-numbered envelopes with many kinds of hand-writing, some typed, some hand-written in green or purple ink. They went through to the sitting-room and sat on the floor, and Frankie spread the letters out as though she were dealing cards. 'Right! Take your pick. I've only had time to glance at them.'

Alison reached for the nearest one and read it out slowly, her voice becoming distinctly Indian in accent as she made sense of it. 'Dear Madam Advertiser, You sound like the person of my dreams; I am a widower, a small bit older than the age-limit specified, but I am slim and active. I have a son of eleven and my own business in the borough of Hounslow. I am very interested in the Dance and Film, and I am intelligent and very Friendly. I hope we will meet very soon. Yours sincerely, Paresh. Telephone 997 . . .' Alison trailed off sadly. 'How poignant. I don't know if I can bear this.'

'Some of them are pretty harrowing,' said Frankie. 'Shall we make a Yes and No heap?' Alison nodded and help up the Indian widower's letter, questioning.

Shaking her head, Frankie picked up another letter, typewritten neatly this time, with a picture of a young man naked to the waist with an oddly self-conscious expression on his half-averted face. She read it, then threw it down suddenly, displeased. Alison rescued and read it quickly. The man was literate and even amusing, but was married (with a dog) and had an open relationship with his wife and was Box number 571 at all interested in exploring sensuality with him?

'I think that's rotten to answer an ad like mine if you're already married.'

'At least he was honest enough to say so.'

Frankie handed her two more letters. 'These are the ones from guys wanting other guys.'

Alison read them and felt sad. 'All that spiel about

his last lover the dentist who left him, and he imagines you must have a specially vital body if you're a dancer. It is sad.'

'It's bloody distressing, and here I am so desperate that I have to advertise.'

'Don't start all that again,' Alison eyed her sympathetically. 'I still think you've done the right thing.'

Frankie raked through the pile, handed a couple more to Alison, and opened two or three more herself.

'Here's a good one,' Alison looked up. 'He's thirty-two, a banker who keeps fit bicycling and walking. Has a house in Sussex, but works in London. Keen on the theatre, gardening, and likes opera.'

'I'm not that keen on opera, it makes me laugh.' Frankie took the letter and read it. 'Five foot eleven, slim, athletic, blond and told he's quite good-looking. What do you think?'

'Put him in the "Yes" heap. He's worth a look. Neat hand-writing, though it's a bit small.'

'Here's a lonely business man who confesses to being older than I want, says he's a little outside my limit, but he's in London on business every two or three weeks, and would love to give me dinner one night.' She gave Alison the letter, and the smaller woman read it swiftly. 'At least you'd get fed, go out, have a happening. Nothing to lose, why not?' She laid it with the Yeses.

'This is quite exciting.' Frankie was cheering up. 'At least I'll meet some people. Aren't they trusting the way they all give their telephone numbers?'

Alison nodded and looked through the letters. 'A lot of them even give addresses, I think that's very brave.'

Frankie pulled another photo out of a letter: 'This one looks super, says he's Canadian, works in computers. Goes to lots of concerts and the theatre. Lives in digs with two other guys, a barrow boy and a solicitor. Sounds an entertaining mix.'

Alison looked at the photo. The man grinned out confidently. The taste of the objects on the shelves in the background was pretty awful, but it could have been taken anywhere. 'How old is he?'

'Thirty-four; plays golf.' Frankie looked dubious. 'Yes or no?' Alison swung the letter above the heaps.

'Let's see his picture again.' Frankie gazed at it. 'He's very muscly, but can you see me with a golfer?'

'Maybe he plays because he's got nothing better to do.'

Frankie nodded. 'He is good-looking. OK, yes.'

At last they had two heaps, and only one letter left. 'That one,' Frankie looked as Alison picked it up, 'for a mad moment I thought that was from our friend Gareth . . .'

'He's coming to eat with us later.' Alison tried to sound natural.

'Eh? Gareth?'

'Yes.'

'Oh.' Frankie watched Alison as she read the letter.

It almost did sound like Gareth – a man left to look after two children whose interests were antiques, pubs and walking in the country. Alison read aloud 'I find London lonely and long for a permanent relationship. Why don't we meet for a drink or meal sometime?' She held it over the heap. 'Yes?'

Frankie nodded, then eyed Alison curiously. 'Did you phone Gareth?'

'I bumped into him by chance.' Alison blushed deeply.

'When is he coming?'

'Eight. I need to make the sauce; I'll do a spaghetti. Will you make a salad?'

'Sure.' Frankie began to pack away her letters back into the envelope. 'I'm dying to phone one of them.'

'Why don't you?'

'Which one shall I phone?'

'How many possibles have you got?'

'Six or seven. The golfer, the one we thought might be Gareth, the blond banker with a house in Sussex, the jazz musician with no money but a good sense of humour, the older businessman who'll give me a meal, and the well-off one with his own business who races cars – he sounded interesting, and there's the civil servant. I liked his letter, but can you imagine me with a civil servant?'

'Try him. He might surprise you.'

'I feel terribly randy after all that,' confessed Frankie. 'Imagining all these men who are just as desperate as me. It's a pity they can't harness sexual frustration and use it as fuel instead of nuclear power. There's plenty of it about.'

'I'm going to cook.' Alison went to the kitchen and chopped and fried, adding garlic and herbs. Frankie sniffed appreciatively.

'Smells good.'

Alison left her mixture to bubble and handed Frankie a large bottle of wine to open and they gulped down a glass each before Gareth arrived.

'Promise you won't tell him about my ad,' hissed Frankie when the bell rang on the dot of eight.

'Don't worry.' Alison smiled reassuringly. 'Your secret rests with me.'

As she went to answer the door she looked at Frankie: 'I forgot to ask you how you got on with your miniature painter?'

Frankie grinned and gulped. 'He's really very sweet and funny. We had a good time. He was telling me about all the awful women he's been meeting from his ad. We nearly go thrown out of the cinema for laughing. Good film too.'

Alison nodded, and disappeared, and Frankie heard

Gareth's deep voice with Alison's chuckle. She was surprised that he was coming, but pleased; he seemed a particularly nice guy: it would be good to get to know him better, but she hoped she would not feel like a gooseberry.

Alison had knocked together a particularly delicious sauce, and with Frankie's inventive and garlicky salad the meal became a feast which, for their various reasons, the three adults washed down with large quantities of wine. Frankie was shattered by a hard day's work, plus the excitement of choosing from her pack of potential lovers: it was all too much, and by nine-thirty she was quite drunk and very sleepy. To keep the conversation rolling she asked Gareth if he had been doing any more protesting lately.

He shook his head: 'Just leafletting. The kids and I popped leaflets through several hundred letterboxes for a couple of hours yesterday; keeps them out of mischief. And I wrote to my MP today: I write every few weeks, we ought to have a beautiful friendship by now. Sometimes as well I run our local stall on a Saturday, and talk to people and sell badges: that's not easy – too many argumentative drunks come out of the pub at lunchtime.'

'You are brave.' Alison, too, felt pretty drunk; the room was whirling a little.

'Not brave.' He looked at her very intensely: 'There's only one way to end this campaign, Alison, like our chairperson said in February. "If there is *Failure* then we will have a nuclear war."'

There was a stricken silence as Frankie shared out the last of the wine. She suddenly felt a pressing desire to leave Gareth and Alison alone to whatever it was that drew them together: it was quite obvious that there was a strong pull between the pair of them, she felt de trop and needed her bed.

Draining her glass, she stood up. 'I've got to go, Alison.'

Gareth also rose abruptly. 'Can I give you a lift somewhere?'

Frankie looked at him. God, he was gorgeous. She wished he really wanted to, but he was obviously just being polite. 'Thanks no, I'll walk. I need the fresh air. I'll leave the car here.'

'Ah,' Gareth nodded. 'Nice to see you again, Frankie. Maybe you two would like to come and eat at my place sometime?'

'Great, I'd love to.' Frankie swathed herself in scarves and gloves, and said goodnight again; they heard the door slam, and Gareth, still standing, looked down at Alison. 'I'd better be going too.'

She gazed up at him, at the dark sombre eyes, the chunkiness of him. 'Must you?'

'I'd better let the baby-sitter go. And what about your reputation – alone in the house with a strange man?' He looked at her quizzically.

Alison stood unsteadily up and faced him. 'Have a coffee, I think we're all a bit pissed.'

He smiled faintly. 'This is true. I've not drunk so much for a long time. I don't usually drink a lot, I don't feel the need.'

'You mean I've had a bad effect on you?'

'No. Not at all. It was nice.' He looked suddenly shy, then flashed a little glance at her, very quick, very straight. 'Very nice it was.'

Alison made coffee and handed him a cup, and they sat and gulped almost in silence. She felt a great yearning for him to stay. She wanted to make love with him and was certain that he felt the same. They sat well apart, and were almost over-polite, trying to ignore the thrum between them. Gareth of all people did not want to cause pain within a viable marriage, as hers obviously must be, seeing the architectural splendour in which she lived. Then, daringly, he said, 'This looks like the Ice Queen's Palace.'

Alison looked a little puzzled.

'But,' he stammered bravely, 'you don't seem to me at all like an Ice Queen.' She was watching him intently.

'How do you mean?'

He looked awkward, wondering if he was saying too much. 'It's just that it seems almost like the wrong setting for you.'

Alison was fascinated, almost tearful at his recognition of what she felt. 'Where do you think I'd fit?'

'I dunno.' He blushed darkly. 'It's cheeky to say . . . I don't really know you, but something warmer, more human.' He paused, he couldn't stop in the middle, even if he had gone too far. 'Fire rather than ice I would have thought, but it's none of my silly business, and, like I said, it is very beautiful.'

He stared at the white carpet for some moments, wishing he could unsay what he had said. Alison was silent too. At last he put down his empty coffee-cup, and stood up beside the clinical plate-glass and steel table. 'Thank you, that was lovely,' he said quietly. The sleeping dog stirred uneasily at their feet as Gareth looked at Alison once more. 'She's a nice girl, that Frankie,' he said. 'Has she not got a boyfriend?'

'No, and hasn't for ages.'

'Surprising.'

'I don't understand it. I think she's fabulous, she'd be a great wife and mother.'

'Is that what she wants?'

'I think so. She certainly wants a fella, and doesn't

have one at the moment.' Then silly from wine, she asked lightly. 'Fancy her, do you?'

Gareth stared at her for a long time, and she wanted to shriek that she wanted him.

'Unfortunately, I don't at all,' he said sadly, 'she's just not my type.' The little wriggle his mouth then made could never be called a smile, but it was trying to say something. She hugged her arms round herself, and he pocketed his hands firmly. Avoidance therapy? she wondered with a tiddly inward giggle of hysteria.

'I'll let you out,' she said. Gareth nodded, and reached for his khaki combat jacket and pulled it on, not looking at her at all now. She led him to the door and the dog almost tripped him up in his haste to run out into the garden. They both laughed, relieved to have a reason to. He nodded almost formally to her. 'Goodbye then; I enjoyed that a lot.'

'Me too,' she said quietly. They did not dare confront each other this time; he fumbled in his pocket for his keys, looked up at the darkness of the night, waved his hand in a sort of salute, and was gone. Alison stayed in the cold doorway calling tiredly for the dog who came running back, redolent of old Kentucky chicken bones which he usually managed to find discarded in the street. She shut and locked the door, leaning against its coolness for a moment. Maybe, she thought, if she was wise, she shouldn't see him again; it was too disturbing; but the thought of not seeing him again was even more disturbing. Shaking her somewhat dizzy head confusedly she climbed the stairs and undressed slowly, reluctant to get into the large empty space of her marital bed which seemed to revolve slowly when she closed her eyes.

Chapter Twelve

Whether it was blessed with the name of hangover or tension headache, it hurt like hell. Alison unwillingly opened her eyes, tried not to think again of Gareth who had occupied her sensual imaginings throughout an almost sleepless night, and remembered that she was alone in the house. Blearily she came to, took a couple of Anadin and shambled downstairs to make coffee. While the kettle boiled, thunderously, she gulped orange juice straight from the pack – something she utterly forbade the children ever to do. Oh Gareth, Gareth, what was he doing today? Was he feeding his children? Was he thinking of her? She remembered the hot chocolate, super-sweet, and smiled. That particular drink would never taste quite the same now: it would always seem extra special, with memories of their extraordinary intimacy as they sat side by side at the pool.

She made real coffee and warmed milk, wondering guiltily how her old father was coping. She must phone, must ask him to stay. And the kids, were they happy? She had so wanted to go away with them and with Philip this Easter, but it hadn't been possible. Soon the children would be too old to want to come away with them, or with her, and the opportunity would have flown. What was it the poet had said? 'Gather you rosebuds while ye may . . .' In other words grab it, girl, whilst it is there to grab, whether it is your own children's youth you want to share, or love, or any opportunity towards happiness – that ephemeral carrot which dangles before mankind.

Still hungover, she went to the bathroom, where to her rage, she discovered dog-pee on a new carpet. She ran downstairs to the back door, waving her hairbrush like a Japanese wrestler gone mad. Pirate, who had just cheerfully administered a lethal dose of urine to the narcissi, heard his mistress's voice and trembled. Alison in that mood was death-dealing to dogs: he fled to the back of the garden where he shook all over. He knew only too well why Alison was coming, but a dog got bored. It was easier just to lift your leg where you were – after all it smelt of pee in there anyway. By the time she had dragged him choking upstairs, Alison felt quite faint. The animal was trembling all over, terrified by her mania. Poor bloody dog, it was not his fault: he had been neglected for ages. It had been a true dog's life. She couldn't even pat him, not yet, he was too scared, too bewildered. She had frightened herself with that overwhelming sudden rage. She was crying, sobbing like a kid.

Still shaking, she cleaned up the mess. She hoped she hadn't shocked the dog's sphincters into perpetual paralysis. She gave him some food, ate a little breakfast, and decided that she must go away.

On the phone, Frankie recognised the urgency in her voice at once. 'What's wrong? You sound dreadful. What's happened?'

'I just nearly killed the dog for peeing in the bathroom.'

Frankie swore that she was not laughing.

'I need to get out,' said Alison, 'I'm feeling crazed. Just for a day . . .'

'I'll be at the shop all day anyway, sanding furniture. Just go, but take somebody with you.'

'I'm not feeling very sociable . . . anyway my next-door neighbour's away, so is my old poet-friend . . .'

'What about . . .'

'You were going to say Gareth, weren't you?'

'Yeah, but . . .'

He'd probably come like a shot. His kids would love the effing dog.'

'Alison?'

'Yes?'

'You mustn't phone him, please, it would be disastrous. I didn't mean to suggest it.'

'No.' Alison's voice was meek and little. 'I'll just take the dog. He's desperate for attention. I could phone Phoebe, I've not seen her for ages.'

Phoebe was an old family friend with whom the Salvesons had a history of shared family holidays which stretched back for years.

'Phoebe's nice, she'll calm you down.'

'I haven't seen her since we went down to their cottage in the autumn.'

'Ring her now. Listen, Allie, I've got to go, my porridge is burning. Have a good time, drive carefully for God's sake.'

Alison immediately telephoned, and was glad to discover that Phoebe was free. Phoebe, married to family therapist John Abrahams, taught art at a polytechnic, and had four children, the youngest of whom, Jake, was a great friend of Mark's. She arrived on Alison's doorstep half-an-hour later, frizzy-haired and energetic, grinning, in purple jeans, granny specs and wellington-boots.

Alison started looking for the dog's chain lead, but couldn't find it anywhere. She summoned the still-shocked dalmatian, who climbed dubiously into the car. Phoebe watched him, amused.

'Don't worry,' she assured him as he cringed on the back seat, eyeing Alison uneasily. 'She loves you really.'

'Do I?' asked Alison.

'Of course you do, you'd miss him dreadfully if he wasn't here.'

Alison parked outside the pet-shop on double yellow lines and ran inside. Decisive all of a sudden, she bought a new lead, a bag of biscuits and a red rubber ball with a bell inside – the latter almost made her cry, it reminded her so vividly of a toy Mark had played with as a toddler. The sound had punctuated the days of her early motherhood. Seeing Alison's purchases, Phoebe smiled. 'You are funny, Alison. So contrary.'

The dog wanted to climb over to Alison's knee, to lick and be forgiven, but she shooed him back. Then, guilty, she took pity on him and removed the red rubber ball from its paper bag. Pirate couldn't believe his change of fortune, and sat with the new toy in his mouth, tail wagging, blissful.

Phoebe sighed. 'Like the rest of us, all he needs is love.'

'Where shall we go?' asked Alison.

'Westwards, we'll get out of town quicker.'

Alison drove fast. The speed gave her a sense of freedom, and when the huge castle appeared on their left, majestic above spring-green fields and pink blossom, she knew that it was the place to go. It was Windsor, and in all her years of living in London she and Philip had never visited it. The castle was romantically impressive, rising from the beautiful English countryside, with the river Thames flowing gently at its feet. They parked a mile or so from it, and let the now-oblivious dog run along the tow-path of the glittering river. He zig-zagged joyously, delighted by ducks, and alarmed yet entranced by the swans at whom he barked, momentarily dropping his new plaything. Alison began to relax: she always enjoyed being with Phoebe, whose wry humour and idiosyncratic sagas of family life were very amusing. After a few minutes the tow-path petered out, and they came to a largish blue pleasure cruiser moored to a quay with a wooden gangway leading up to it. Pleased like children, they paid their money and went on board where they were enchanted to discover that there was even a tiny bar. Alison's headache had disappeared, so she bought two half pints or lager and a packet of cigarettes. They carried their glasses up to the top deck and found maybe ten passengers seated on blue benches set round the newly-painted deck, pristine and shiny. They smiled shyly, and were greeted similarly, and went to stand at the side. The boat was on the move now: Pirate came to stand beside them, just like a fella, thought Alison, and patted him almost fondly, relaxing at last. He wagged his tail softly, and looked towards her, tongue lolling appreciatively.

Phoebe smiled at the dog. 'You see? All is forgiven.'

The captain of the boat had a little black and white Jack Russell bitch who was a flirt and a clown. She summoned Pirate to play with her, and teased and hid beneath the seats; they chased each other, watched like a little circus by the passengers, benign with sun and holiday spirit. The newly-painted floor was slippery as ice, and the dogs slithered comically, excited by the game and its unpredictability. An old man sitting next to Alison chuckled: 'It's the Black and White Mongrel Show.'

Their drinks finished, the women went to explore the boat. They found the sinewy captain at the steering-wheel, his little bitch cradled gently in one arm. Alison watched him idly as Pirate leant against her sensually; she and the man looked at each other amused, almost wry in their glances. It was a strangely intimate male-female exchange, and a longing for Gareth swept over her, her desire for him so strong as to be almost painful.

'What is it?' Phoebe looked at her. 'Is it your Ma?'

Alison shrugged. 'That and other things. We're fighting a lot, Philip and I.'

Phoebe looked at her keenly. 'Marriage is tough, isn't it? It can become so claustrophobic; if one of you changes it can upset the whole balance.'

Alison wanted to cry. 'How are you and John?' she managed to ask at last.

Phoebe gazed emptily at the river and the swans, ignoring the dramatic splendour of the great castle. She sighed deeply. 'Not good, Alison, not good. We could actually do with a bit of John's famous family therapy.'

'You have always seemed so glued together. I used to envy you, you're such a unit.'

Phoebe shook her head. 'Not any more, I'm afraid. It's all changed. We thought we had it sussed, but we didn't. I don't understand sex – it's so combustible, not controlled by intellect.'

'Sex?' queried Alison.

Phoebe looked at her. 'Sometimes I just wonder what it's all about. Do you ever feel like that?'

'Nowadays yes. In the old days I was pretty content. I sort of obliviously accepted everything, and adored

Philip, but it feels so dead sometimes now. We are like strangers. I miss the love.'

'Ah,' Phoebe gazed across the water. 'How can we cope with the loss of love?'

'How about John? Does he feel the same? Is it just that we are all getting older?'

'A natural progression into boredom, you mean?' Phoebe sounded bitter, unlike herself. She turned abruptly. 'John's all right, he's got his bread buttered on both sides. Come on, let's take these glasses back.'

They walked back to the saloon and Alison felt upset, Phoebe obviously wanted to stop talking about it. Alison couldn't imagine the Abrahams really being in schtuck. Their marriage, a famous example of marital bliss, seemed a touchstone pairing. And here was Alison, a woman in her thirties, a long-married mother of two, wife of a well-known architect, utterly obsessed by a dark-bearded man. She must face facts: she had fallen in love, that was for sure, and what was she going to do about it?

They stood at the rail again. Alison looked out at the river.

'It can certainly become an obsession.'

'Sex?' Phoebe looked at her curiously.

'Yes. But what's the cure?'

'For sexual obsession?'

'I suppose so, for being mad about somebody.'

'The only cures I know are to go to bed with the person, or to lose yourself in work, preferably hard physical work.'

Alison grunted sadly.

'Paint a room, jog or something,' Phoebe touched her arm. 'Alison, if you'll take my advice, and you probably won't, you will not pursue the obsession. You honestly don't know how lucky you are.'

Alison nodded blearily. 'Maybe you're right.'

'I know I'm right.' Phoebe's eyes glittered fiercely. 'It doesn't do to mess about, Alison, believe you me, it is not worth it. You will be sorry.'

'I suppose I could paint the spare room and make it into my study. I'd like that.' Alison, gazing into space, saw only Gareth.

Phoebe touched her arm. 'Do it,' she said firmly. 'You'll be glad.'

Frankie was shutting up the shop when to her delight Alison appeared, pulled energetically by the dog. Alison was a little sunburnt, and looked terrific.

'I just thought I'd pop in and see you; I wondered what you were doing tonight, I thought you might give me a hand.'

Frankie wished she had remembered that Alison was alone. 'I'm afraid I'm going out . . .' then she couldn't contain herself, and did a little victory dance, gesticulating like a triumphant boxer. 'I've got a date!'

'Which one?'

Frankie swirled round, displaying the twinkling mirrors of her Indian skirt. 'The thirty-two-year-old banker. He sounds really sweet, Michael . . . from Sussex . . .'

'Ah . . . the keep-fitter?'

When are you meeting him?'

'In an hour. It's very erotic meeting a blind date like this.'

Alison looked at her anxiously. 'Don't get too worked up. Remember Anthony.'

Frankie frowned. 'I know; I need to school myself to expect nothing, then anything decent that happens will be a bonus. What did you want a hand with?'

'Phoebe has talked me into painting the spare-room, so that I have my own space. I've bought five litres of marooney-brown paint, and I'm all set to go.'

'Does Philip know?'

'It will be a paint-accompli. He's got his own workroom anyway, he never goes into the spare room.'

'I'll help. Are you going to put up shelves?'

'Lots. I'll take all my things out of cupboards – the ones he lets me rotate singly on the glass shelf in the sitting-room.'

'When did you decide all this?'

'Today. I ran away up the river with Phoebe and the dog.'

Frankie shook her orange-beaded head. 'Trying to keep yourself out of mischief?'

Their looks locked. 'Maybe.' Alison spoke quietly.

'You didn't see him today, did you?'

'I told you, I went with Phoebe. Frankie, I'm not daft.'

'I'm not so sure sometimes.' Frankie put on her poncho. 'I must go, I'll be late. She hugged her friend. 'I will come and help you with the painting; poor Philip will have to avert his purified aesthetic gaze.'

She swirled out, leaving Alison on the love-seat gazing dreamily into space.

Frankie, with her mind on other things, was a dangerous pedestrian. She ran breathlessly through Trafalgar Square, frightening the pigeons, and hopped across a busy intersection, avoiding honking taxis, and terrifying the drivers. She turned the corner, crossed another zebra-crossing, and peered into the Italian restaurant. A genial Indian wearing a turban instantly grinned welcomingly towards her, but Frankie was looking in dismay at the man beside him. He was a desiccated character, bespectacled, and carrying a furled umbrella. He saw her at once, and moved shyly forward, looking more like a maiden aunt than the keep-fitter he claimed to be, but as he came close, she knew that he was Michael all right. She could not flee them all, but stood glued reluctantly to the spot when he came questioningly to the glass doors, and nodded dolefully as he made to greet her.

Alison was painting the spare room when, later that evening, Frankie rang the bell. She almost fell off the ladder when the Scots girl described Michael in his tight-buttoned raincoat like her father used to wear.

'Honest,' hissed Frankie, 'it was almost a museum piece. We could have sold it in the shop.'

She threw herself down on the dust-sheeted floor and groaned. 'I think this lonely-hearts business is a waste of time. It is too harrowing, and all to fill the gap – in every sense of the phrase. It's five flaming months – six nearly – since mine was filled, but I don't want a poor wee soul like that to fill it, even if he could. He looks like he'd manage it once a year at the most. No wonder his fiancée pushed off.'

Alison rested her brush on the tin. 'He was engaged?'

'Yeah. For eight years. He showed me pictures of them on a tandem. I thought she was his mother, but then he showed me pictures of her too; she seems to be part of the deal with him.' She lay back despondently and watched Alison paint.

'I'll help you in a minute,' she promised and sighed gustily. She gazed at the half-painted wall. 'I was thinking on the way here, what I really ought to do is be specific. What I'd like best of all is a black saxophonist or trombonist. Maybe I should advertise for exactly that.'

'Would a drummer not do?'

'Nuh.'

'But if I were to present you with a thirty-year-old song-writer or film-maker, would you not be interested?'

Frankie nodded, smiling wearily. 'I just find it too harrowing, Allie.'

'Don't give up,' said Alison gently. 'Try another. You've still got half a dozen possibles.'

Heavy-eyed, Frankie nodded and stood up. 'Have you got an old shirt?'

'Through in the kitchen.' The tall Scot disappeared, and Alison heard the phone tinkle; she painted for a few minutes till Frankie came back. She was garbed in an old shirt of Philip's and had a dishcloth wound round her hair. 'I did it.' She said grinning.

'What?'

'Made another date.'

'Good girl! Which one?'

'The muscly one . . .'

'The golfer?'

'Yeah. Sounds quite nice, Canadian. He's called Peter Martensen. We're going to meet at Strand-on-the-Green on Friday.' She looked cheerful, and picked up the spare paint brush as the phone rang.

'It might be one of the kids,' said Alison. 'Or Philip. He usually rings in the evening.'

'I'll go,' said Frankie. 'Stay where you are.'

She disappeared, but came back almost immediately. 'They rang off,' she said. 'I'm sure somebody was there though.'

Alison's heart was pounding. She felt certain who it

was, who she wanted it to be. 'Probably a wrong number,' she said unconvincingly. Frankie looked at her.

'I hope so,' she said, and dipped her brush into the paint with great deliberation.

Gareth Williams' two children sat side by side on the edge of the swimming pool and glumly watched their oblivious father as he swam, grunting, backwards and forwards, relentlessly eating up pool-lengths. Bronwen shook her head as though she were watching somebody who was a little touched. 'That must be hundreds he's done, thousands even; I wish he'd stop. I'm starving.' She stood up, her small body neat in a pink bikini and tried to catch her father's attention as he reached the tiled wall at her feet.

'Dad!' she leaned towards his toiling body immersed in foaming chlorine, aquamarine and almost tepid. His eyes struggled vaguely upwards to her as he touched the end and turned, bubbles encircling his dark shape. 'Forty-eight!' he gasped. 'Only two more!'

Bronwen sat down again beside her brother who grinned proudly, his arms crossed. 'That will be fifty lengths he's done. Good, eh? I bet there's not many people's dads could do that.'

'He was in an awful bad mood at breakfast, I hope he's nicer after this.'

Together they watched the dark head and toiling arms, Gareth's oblivious face surfacing regularly, with a shut-eyed concentration as he gasped in air. They both stood up then crouched together as he came steaming down his final lap, and cheered, clapping their hands on their knees as he at last stopped, gasping, and smiled up at them from the water through his black beard.

'That's better.' Breathless, he climbed up the ladder out of the water and stood dripping beside them. 'Come, let's go home.'

Tenderly, he touched each child on the arm, and led the way to the changing-rooms; Ceri walked immediately behind his father, trying to make his steps as big as Gareth's, and Bronwen, hopping and skipping remembered that it was lunchtime; she hoped she could persuade Dad to make chips.

Frankie's golfer, the Canadian, looked as good in the flesh as his photo had promised. He was big and blond – a real hunk – and her eyes widened when she saw him standing looking out at the racing skiffs on the river near Kew Bridge. He turned towards her as she walked towards him, and grinned with one side of his mouth. As promised, he was holding a copy of *Time Out*, and wore a blue and white zipped jacket, but best of all, and unexpected, was his height. He was not only good-looking, but tall with it, really tall. For once she wouldn't have to walk around on half-bent legs pretending she was normal. 'Hi,' he said, 'I guess you must be Frankie?'

Hours later, after a raucous evening, with much retsina and lamb cooked on a spit, Frankie felt very drunk, but uneasily aware that Peter, though attractive physically – more so with her perceptions so distorted by the wine – was not her type at all. Nevertheless, they were going to sleep together: she had known it before the taramasalata and hummus were even half-eaten. Even if he was as thick as three planks, he was a hunk and that was what she most needed right now, a proper man, but it must be at his place, not hers.

* * *

Alison had played Mozart's flute and harp concerto twice, and had wept at the Amadeus Quartet playing the Schubert *Quintet in C* – surely one of the most poignant pieces of music ever composed. She wiped her eyes and drank yet another cup of coffee, then decided to ring Phoebe for a chat, to tell her that she had painted the room as instructed.

Jake, the youngest Abrahams son, answered: 'Ma's out,' he told her. 'And Pa isn't back yet. He's late at the clinic.'

He sounded as fed up as Alison felt. It was not yet ten; the evening had dragged by, and she still could not clear her mind of her obsession with Gareth. Abruptly, she went to the phone, looked up her address-book and dialled his number, her heart thumping. It rang three times, and she almost fainted when she heard his voice say 'Hello? Hello? Who is there?'

When he met with her breathless silence, she heard him mutter, 'Must be a wrong number', and put down the receiver. She was shaking and almost in tears when she replaced the receiver: it was getting to be crazy, she could not live like this, longing like a love-sick teenager for contact. She almost wished that she was religious, or had someone to talk to who could help to exorcise her from this haunting. Frankie had enough turmoils of her own at the moment, and the children would not be back for three or four days. Her mother would never have been any use, nor would Molly. Her older sister would be judgemental, moralistic, horrified that Alison should even dare to confront such temptation. She wondered suddenly about her father: it was exactly two weeks since her mother had died; she could go and see him on Sunday – you could do the trip down and back with six hours to spend in Torquay all in the one day, leaving early in the morning. Richard had told her about these day trips – always on a Sunday – and very cheap. It would be a long day, but at least it might comfort her father and even herself a little, and perhaps it would help to keep her out of mischief. Hopefully she picked up the phone again and dialled the Torquay number.

Frankie had never felt so explosive with sexual frustration, rage and disgust – both with herself and the situation in which she had landed herself – and at her own desperation, her own needs. Her nipples felt bruised, her female organs abraded. The Canadian was sprawled across the bed, snoring like some great harvesting machine, loud and horrible, while Frankie, another notch on his niblick, lay trying to sleep, still drunk, hating his rank smell, but sleep was impossible.

'Go easy.' she had said, 'I'm not quite there yet . . .' but it was too late, he had gone off on his own rhythm, thrusting, moaning, hurting her, who had suddenly become dry. She felt angrier and more impotent as the green minutes dripped by on the digital clock which lewdly lit the characterless and ugly room. She went through to the bathroom and washed, managing somehow to find her strewn belongings on the bedroom floor; she dressed hurriedly, hauling on her coloured tights and Indian skirt in great haste, terrified of ever having to talk to Peter again. She wanted to cut her losses and get back to her own bed and Hamish the cat.

She was glad that Peter knew nothing about her, her full name, or even where she worked. He was nothing like as intelligent as Anthony: he would never be bright enough to track her down to the actual shop as he had done, thus returning her lost umbrella in person. She crept out of the flat and put on her shoes and clothes on the landing which was lit a ghastly orange from the street lamp outside, then ran down the terraced street, past cars and startled cats, until she succeeded in hailing a taxi at the far end of Fulham Road. Breathlessly, she gave the driver her address, and settled with relief into the dark coolness of the back seat. The man eyed her in his mirror.

'Are you sure you're all right, dear?'

Frankie glared at him. 'I'm fine, thanks. Why?'

He indicated left and turned into North End Road, 'You just look a little upset like, I wondered if you'd had a spot of bovver.'

Tiredly she shook her head and closed her eyes. 'I'm OK.'

Away and tidy yerself up, Frankie, you look like the Wild Woman of Borneo. That was what her mother used to say in Glasgow, her ample huggable body forever wrapped in a floral peeny. Frankie's wildness had always worried her. Frankie realised that she had brought the pink carnation from the Greek restaurant with her, and wistfully sniffed its perfume. The Greek waiter in the restaurant had given her the flower as they were departing; she had been pissed, but terribly pleased, and surprised, as she always was, when her femininity was acknowledged in any way.

Later, when she had paid the taxi man, she looked at the long-stemmed flower, perfect and elegant, and suddenly hurled it away from her with all her strength into the darkened road, where it would lie until it was flattened and destroyed by the wheels of passing traffic. She wanted no visible reminder of tonight's experience, however sweet it smelt.

Chapter Thirteen

Philip lay on a hotel bed in Hong Kong, newly-showered, clad in his white bathrobe, and melancholically wriggled his long slender toes. From time to time he fiddled with the remote control switch for the television, but frowned at the noisy mindlessness of the proffered programmes. He was on his second gin and tonic, and ought really to do some work, but he felt tired, jaded, and not a little lonely. He looked at his watch, it was Saturday back home, he would phone Alison: the kids must be still away. He consulted his diary. Alison: he wished she were here, wished somebody were here, but most of all Alison. He would like to talk to her, it might make her come to a bit. He wanted to reassure her that he felt his wife and family were more than enough, and that he loved her. He asked the receptionist to put a call through to London, and was put out when eventually it rang repeatedly and there was no answer.

He remembered that she might be at the shop; and was glad when she answered. It was a bad line: her voice had a weird echo on it and everything she said was hollowly repeated seconds after she had spoken.

'Hi, darling, how are you doing?'

'Hello. I'm OK, it's kind of quiet back here.'

'Have you heard from the young?'

'Mark sent a wine-stained postcard saying "Vive la France," and I spoke to Jo last night; she's fine, she had the giggles when we talked. Sounded very cheery.'

He told her about the job, complained of boredom, and she was silent.

'Alison?'

'Yes?'

'I thought you had gone. How is business?' He thought he ought to show interest.

'Pretty diabolical. I'm alone in the shop. Frankie had a migraine and stayed home, and business is almost non-existent. We've hardly sold anything.'

'Anything, anything,' boomed the echo.

Maybe she didn't hear him. 'Alison?'

'Yes?' (Yes? Yes? Yes?)

'I love you very much.' (much, much, much . . .)

A silence, then her voice came back, still in tandem with itself. 'Philip, I'm sorry, I've got a customer. Must go. Bye-bye.'

That was it. He held the vacant ticking receiver, then put it down, terribly aware of the silent room and his empty glass. He swilled the last of the melting ice and watched it tiredly. Maybe the time had come to retrench, as Alison was always telling him to do. Let some younger man do the trips, put some more energy into his family. They were growing up so fast they would soon be gone, and he would have lost the opportunity; and she, Alison was becoming more and more distant by the day. Losing her mother seemed to have had a very basic effect on her. He rubbed his face; it felt bloody inane and purposeless being here all alone. He sighed and stretched for his file: he had a lot of bumf to read through before tomorrow's meeting with the lawyer-fellows representing the owners of the site; he must get through it all to be properly primed-up. This was one job he was determined to win. If he succeeded he could afford to ease up a little. He would have proved himself to be the cream de la cream; as an American journalist friend of his used to drawl rather sexily.

Anthony Brownstone had a hard time deciding what to wear to take Frankie to the party. He had settled on his brown velvet suit: it was rather smart – there was even a danger that Jay might mock him for being over-dressed – but Jay usually found reason to mock whatever you did. Frankie, he was sure, would enjoy the party: Jay lived in a large and spectacular flat near Belsize Park, with a vast studio filled with bright abstracts, which sold well, and were much-represented in public collections. Of Anthony's contemporaries, Jay had done best as far as an artistic reputation was concerned. Anthony tried several different cravats and ties on his white shirt, and settled on an Indian silk scarf, orange and brown. He felt good, pleased that Frankie had agreed to come with him, but knew that he must try to play it cool, to make her feel safe and a bit looked-after. He sensed that she needed a bit of cossetting: she was one of these apparently easy-going and forthright people whom most of the world believed to be secure and problem-free. But Anthony knew better: he had felt her vulnerability from the moment he met her, and found it irresistibly attractive, coupled with her impressive body with its crowning glory of flame. He wanted Frankie, and would do his damnedest to win her.

'Down, Fido, down,' he said to his eternally lively

male appendage, and drank a quick glass of water from the tap before putting out the lights in his flat and letting himself out into the street.

Frankie opened the door and saw Anthony beaming with a bunch of anemones held towards her: he looked very nice all dolled up. 'Hi.' She smiled at him. She had obviously been sleeping, her face was pale and softly creased, her expression strangely naked. 'I didn't realise it was so late,' she said, 'I was in bed for most of the day.'

'Are you ill?'

She shook her head – her glorious curly mane – and he tried not to gawp as she took the flowers.

'Oh Anthony, thanks. They are beautiful.' She went to find a vase, ushering him into her multi-coloured grotto, where he stared thrilled, from object to object, each one brighter and more entertaining than its neighbour. 'I just felt rotten, had a bad head,' she called over the sound of tap-water, as she filled a dark blue jar and arranged the flowers with an easy natural talent. She set them on a low table, painted red, and a large black cat leapt up to examine them. The good visuals of the room left the artist Anthony almost breathess.

'Aw Hamish, you're an old wanker,' said Frankie lovingly. 'Sit, Anthony. I just need to do my hair and face.'

He managed to speak in a normal voice, not the emotional squeak he feared might emit from him. 'I like your place; you've got beautiful objects. That's marvellous.' He pointed to a two-foot high Indian carving of a man standing, playing a flute. It was painted red and gold, a ravishing piece.

'I bought that with my first dole-money. My mother nearly slaughtered me, but I kept it. It is beautiful . . .'

So was she; there was colour in her cheeks now, and her hair was glorious. She put on strange glittery earrings like mirrors, and he gulped. 'You look terrific. I don't feel very platonic though . . .'

Frankie glared. 'No, Anthony! I will be your friend. I will come to the party, but we are fancy-free; I am not going to be your bird. You promised.'

He was chastened, like Pirate when Alison shouted at him. 'I didn't promise never to make a pass . . .' he muttered mutinously in a Russian accent.

Frankie leaned against the mantelpiece, a treasure-trove of cards and toys. Her back was towards him, and he yearned to embrace her, to fuck her, fast and dog-like. 'Anthony, I do like you. I can talk to you, but I must be honest . . .'

He wished she didn't feel she must, but listened, knowing what she was going to say. At least, he comforted himself, they were visually, artistically, compatible. Surely that was a start?

Frankie turned to him. 'I will be your friend, but not your lover. OK?'

Anthony forced a jolly grin. 'You don't know what you might be missing. I'm told that I'm a very good lover.' He raised his brows several times and blinked, and Frankie had the grace to laugh. 'Come on, you, let's go to the party and drown our sorrows.' She picked up a bottle from the floor, and took his arm. With difficulty he restrained from clutching her.

'Cheerio, Hamish,' called Frankie. The cat was sitting by the bright flowers, gazing impassively into space, his tail occasionally whisking; he looked very beautiful. Frankie shook her head. 'What a bugger. He's always posing; such vanity, it's too much.'

* * *

Alison enjoyed the daytime journey to Torquay because she could look at the passing landscape and the sea; it was exhilarating after being in the city. There was only twenty minutes to go: she had slept last night in the newly-decorated room, alone in the single bed, enjoying the colour and the objects she had so carefully hung up. It felt like her own space, the way the shop did, and the house never quite had. She wished she could sleep there more often, but obviously when Philip was home she couldn't, but maybe when he was away, as he so often was, she could claim the room for herself. She imagined Mark's puzzled look, and Jo's raised brows, with a finger corkscrewing into her head, denoting her mother's incipient madness. Sadly, she remembered Philip's phone-call and her almost total lack of response. She put away her book of Leonard Cohen poems – poetry was the only reading-matter that had any appeal at the moment. She had not even bought the Sunday papers for the four-hour journey; she simply couldn't concentrate. Poems she could manage, she could somehow tolerate and be comforted by their brevity and intensity. She was in a bad way; she felt empty when she thought about Philip, hollow and miserable, and the Welshman stayed resolutely imbedded in her brain – though where exactly her brain was sited, she was not sure. She remembered Frankie talking about her own mother, who said 'Yer brains are in yer pants,' when Frankie first believed herself to be in love, highly unsuitably, with a married teacher. Maybe that was where Alison's brains were just now, it felt pretty like it.

She was surprised to see both young Richard and her father standing at the barrier this time; her father looked as small and pale as she remembered, but today he was smiling. Amazed, because she had imagined herself sitting comfortingly beside his frail weeping person once again, she walked to greet them. The old man took her hands and said, 'Welcome, my dear, this is indeed a joy.'

Richard led them to his Mini, let Alison into the back, and settled the old man in the front. 'I've got an hour, then I must go back and swot,' he said. 'My first exam is in three weeks, if I don't pass I'll be stuck here for another year, so I've got to pass. I'm sorry, but that's it. However, I'll lend you the car if you like, after lunch, and you can go out somewhere with Grandpa.'

'Lovely.' Alison looked at her father. 'Do you feel up to that?'

He nodded. 'I asked him for the car.' He twinkled, and Alison sensed that he and Richard were now fellow-reprobates.

'What about Molly?' she asked.

The men eyed each other a little uneasily, then Richard took out a packet of cigarettes and handed Alison one. She took one, and he lit it for her.

'May I have one?' her father suddenly astonished her by asking.

'Sure,' Richard handed him one, and lit it carefully. For a moment the old man's face was illuminated brightly by the flare of the match.

'I have never seen you smoke, Daddy.' Alison stared at him. He put his chin out and puffed, his eyes almost closed.

'I used to once. Long before you were born. I seldom do, only on special occasions.' He winked at her.

'My fault, is it?'

He nodded benignly.

'Where is Molly?' asked Alison.

Richard answered. 'She went out for the day, wanted a total break. She may see you just before you go. She's having lunch about twenty miles away.'

It was a relief really, even if it was also an insult. Perhaps it was more honest that Molly had fled her coming, it was certainly better than those awful stilted meetings they usually had.

They came to a pub by the sea, and Alison sat at a round iron-legged table beside her father, from where she could see the ocean above his white frail head.

'How are you, Daddy?'

He looked out and up through the window, and she watched his eyes follow a seagull's wheeling. 'I am a different shape,' he said suddenly.

She did not understand. 'Thinner, you mean?'

He shook his head. 'Freer, looser, relieved perhaps.' Richard brought three lagers, and Alison realised that this was the first time she had ever seen her father drink beer in a pub. He eyed her anxiously. 'It's not that I don't grieve for your mother, but it is a relief that she is at peace. I feel a sense of lightness.'

She was touched by his honesty, and felt tearful. Sipping the lager calmed her.

When his glass was half-empty, the old man stood up. 'I shall get us some food.'

'I'll get it . . .' Richard said, and Alison rose simultaneously. The old man shook his head. 'No; I will go. I want to.'

They sat back, and she watched him march up to the bar, and speak politely and carefully to the barman, who listened intently to her father's faint but precise little voice.

'He's actually cheerful.' She shook her head in disbelief.

Richard nodded, 'He had a fight with Ma yesterday, said she was a beastly bossy virago, and that the sooner he could go home to his own cottage the better.'

Alison's eyes almost popped. 'I don't believe it!'

'He's going too. Ma said OK, go.'

'Can he manage?'

'He's been quite sparky for over a week, after the first shock wore off. He shops, walks for miles, and we've arranged for Meals on Wheels, and the Health Visitor will keep an eye on him. He's got super neighbours.'

'I was half expecting to come down and find him on the blink, he seemed so shattered after the funeral.'

'He's better . . . . He seems to be finding himself. He varies a lot, he's very up and down.' Richard rose to help his grandfather carry the plates. Alison stared, still amazed that her little wimp of a father could at this late date in life have changed to such an extent. Momentarily, he exuded a confidence she had not known he could summon forth.

They ate cheese and pickle, with wedges of French bread, then Richard said he must go. He handed Alison the car keys. 'I'll just run up the hill. See you both at teatime.'

'Would you like more to drink?' Alison shook her head at her father's question, and wondered if he did not want to rest. 'Aren't you tired?'

'No. I sleep at nights, not in the day. How about a walk?'

They walked along the shore, looking at boats, and then along the beach out beyond the town. The old man was surprisingly energetic, he carried a walking-stick, but used it more for verbal emphasis than anything else; after a mile or so they found an empty bench. The day was greyish, but mild. They sat silently together, occasionally pointing out a boat, or admiring a flower. Alison's heart was full; there was a man like Gareth flying a kite on the beach, watched by two small children, and a dog. His eyes were as dark and intense as Gareth's.

When her father laid his gnarled hand on her knee and asked 'Why so sad?' she cried unexpectedly. Wordlessly he handed her a handkerchief. She remembered hating it when her mother used to hold out a hankie wrapped round her finger, frowning, and say 'Spit'. Alison would reluctantly comply, and her mother, intent and unsmiling, would rub hard at her daughter's face, almost sandpapering the fine skin with the hankie and her own warm spittle. She remembered the rubbing sensation vividly. 'I'm sorry,' she sniffed, and blew her nose.

'Is it Philip?' her father asked unexpectedly. 'Is he unfaithful?'

Alison froze. 'No. At least not lately, not that I know of.'

'Has he been? Is that the problem?'

'I don't know.' Alison stared bleakly out to sea. She had dismissed her elderly male parent for so many years as being hopeless, inept, unaware, and suddenly he seemed – like somebody playing 'Hunt the Thimble' – to be getting very warm, without much help from her.

'Marriage is very hard,' said her father. 'It is an enormous commitment, and people are not always strong; they change, and have different needs.'

'Shit!' thought Alison wildly. I can't tell him that what I think I need is a hairy man, name of Esau. He wouldn't like that one.

'How are the children?' asked her father.

She told him and made him chuckle. 'I would like to see them.'

'We will fix it,' Alison promised.

Again they were silent, and watched the man flying the kite. It soared above the beach; they stared upwards, exhilarated by its flight. Once more she felt her father's hand on her knee.

'Is it you?' he asked out of the blue, the question landing on her like a fallen piece of kite. She looked at him uneasily, not understanding.

He looked at her kindly, intently. 'Is it you who has been unfaithful?' He touched her hand. 'I do not want to judge or probe, but I sense great unhappiness in you. Can't you tell me?'

She shook her head. 'Unfaithful? No.' She smiled a little wan smile, and breathed a tiny tired laugh. 'Not yet at any rate.'

She wanted to sleep with Gareth; it was almost the only thing she thought about. Her brains well and truly in her pants, she wanted him out of her head. Out of her head and into her bed. It seemed the only cure.

'Alison,' said her father. 'I cannot give you advice. People never really want advice. But I will say that when the marriage bond is broken, there is hell let loose, and people and children suffer. You will regret it, if that is what you are thinking of.'

'The bond is already broken,' she said sadly. 'Philip broke it.'

'Ah,' said her father. She thought that he was going to say something wise and helpful, that might cure her of her desire, instead he held her hand and smiled sweetly and looked very sad. 'Sex,' he said, shaking his head. 'At eighty I still do not understand it. It causes such torment yet can bring almost transcendental joy to man and woman. It remains utterly bewildering to me. All I can say is try with all your heart to preserve your marriage, but remember that I love you, and I will love you, and will try to understand you whatever thing you do.'

Alison could not speak. She wanted to run naked

along the shore shouting her hatred of Philip's patriarchy, to declare her independence of him, and she wanted to be with Gareth whatever the cost. It was an elemental command that pulled them to one another, irrefutable, irresistible. She looked at the old man.

'I love you, Daddy,' she said simply, and knelt and hugged him, and he patted her like the little girl he remembered all too well.

Frankie had a wonderful time at Jay's party. She talked to everybody, artists, writers, actors, and made them all promise to visit the shop. She adored the huge flat, especially the two striped canvas garden swing-seats which were used instead of sofas, and admired Jay's large striped canvasses. She met a black gay dancer, muscular in a white vest, whom she knew from her dancing days, and sat with him on one of the swing-seats giggling and reminiscing. Anthony felt jealous, and drank a lot of wine. Jay came over to him and handed him a newly opened bottle to replenish his glass. 'That's a very attractive bird you've brought.'

'You're telling me,' Anthony grinned bitterly.

'Big, isn't she?'

'All top quality woman.'

'So I see.' Jay eyed Frankie appraisingly. Jay wore striped dungarees and a torn white tee-shirt, and had spiky punk-blond hair with a long earring that looked like a battleaxe.

'Have you tried for the Academy this year?' asked Anthony. Jay nodded, still looking at Frankie, and lit up a Gauloise. 'Yeah. Twelve bloody quid, and as like as not they'll damage the canvas. Have you?'

'Yes. I did well last year.'

'I didn't get in last year. Very bloody boring; the year before they were all bought by public galleries. Makes you puke.'

Anthony nodded melancholically, 'You have to keep sending. It's the best market place in London.'

'Sure. Good luck.' Jay exhaled smoke and patted him on the back.

'Thanks,' Anthony nodded and gulped. 'You too.'

'What's her name?' Jay was still eyeing Frankie.

'Frankie.' Anthony stared at her too, she was laughing uproariously with the black dancer.

'Are you two . . . you know?'

'I'm working on it,' said Anthony a little bleakly, 'but not so far. Good friendsville and all that.'

Jay laughed. 'Boring, darling, boring. Go and have some trifle.'

'Good idea.' Anthony adjusted his Indian silk scarf, and headed for the splendid kitchen with its laden table of food.

Gareth's two children hung out of the open first-floor bedroom window and watched their father jogging in the dusk: they had jogged round the block with him two or three times and got bored. Ceri leaned his chin on his hands, 'That's seven times he's been round, cor . . .' He watched the toiling figure admiringly.

'He's been running nearly an hour. What's got into him?'

'Dunno. Health kick, I suppose.'

'I'm starving.'

'Me too. What's for supper?'

'Dunno. Bread and cheese probably. I know when he started . . .'

'What?'

'Running. Swimming. All that.'

'Yeah? When?'

'After he went out to dinner last week.'

'No, it's been longer. Easter. The big march thing.'

They watched him disappear round the corner. 'He's been a bit bad-tempered,' said Bronwen.

'It's unemployment. It's very bad for people,' her brother told her. 'Come on, let's get something to eat. You set the table.'

'Yeah.' They raced each other downstairs.

Jay's party went on well into the night, and Frankie – the nastiness of the previous night's coupling almost forgotten in the excitement of this new exciting circle of people – felt happy. She had been talking for what seemed like hours to Jay when Anthony asked if she wanted a lift home.

'Please,' she looked up at him, and his heart melted at the sight of her, legs splayed, colours bright. He yearned to paint her gigantic splendour; he would ask her to sit for him. It was as good a device to be with her as any.

Frankie went to gather up her poncho and green wide-brimmed hat amid roars of farewell and drunken end-of-party song. In Anthony's car, she sighed and sank back in the car seat.

'That was great. One of the best parties I've ever been to. Thanks, Ant.'

'I hate being called Ant,' he said through gritted teeth, as he tried to remember how his car worked. Where the hell did the key go in?

'Oh sorry!' Guiltily, Frankie looked at him. Ants were wee, that must be why.

He started up, did six bunny-hops in reverse, pressed

the horn instead of the indicator, and they were on the way; Frankie was high on all the new people she had met. 'That Jay is tremendously charismatic, don't you think?'

Anthony nodded. 'Good painter too.'

'I thought the big stripey canvasses were really beautiful. Usually I don't like that kind of thing, but they seemed both strong and sensitive.'

'Yes,' Anthony agreed. He felt tired and lonely, and most of all wanted to take Frankie home to bed, but he knew there was no point in suggesting it. He stopped the car outside her flat. 'Here we are, Madame.'

'You are nice to me.' Impulsively, she leaned over and kissed him on the cheek; the yearning she felt emanate from him was almost tangible. 'Thanks, Anthony. I had a wonderful time. I've been invited to Jay's cottage near Monmouth, it sounds beautiful.'

'It is beautiful,' said Anthony wearily.

'Have you been? It sounds lovely.'

'Many times, it is lovely. You will certainly be impressed.'

Frankie climbed out. 'Cheerio,' she said, 'and thanks again. Pop into the shop some time.'

Anthony nodded, his heart heavy. Jay was always stealing people's beloveds. Charismatic, yes, but also ruthless, but Frankie must learn that one for herself. If she allowed him he would try to keep an eye on her; one of these days she might need him. She was worth waiting for.

On the journey home Alison watched a spectacular sunset, filled with awe at the beauty of the passing landscape with its ever-changing orange and purple backdrop. It was unthinkable that it might all be destroyed by man's idiocy.

The train stopped briefly at a station outside London,

and she noticed a middle-aged porter, complete with hat and uniform, with a CND badge on his lapel. Excited like a child recognising somebody in the same club, and touched by his courage, she tapped on the window. He looked quizzically at her, grinned, nodded, and did a victorious thumbs-up through the thick glass window, and pointed to her own discreet little marker.

Molly had not been impressed: she had eyed the badge coldly, and said in a bored tired voice. 'Joined the protesters, have we?'

As the train roared through the gathering dusk Alison thought about her father, the man she had often described as an ineffectual twit in a dog-collar. For years she had despised him for being weak and indecisive, but when she thought about it, he had worn a badge for all his working life. The dog-collar his daughter had scorned was a public statement that he stood for certain principles of peace, love and charity. She had always thought that her father hid behind the symbol of the church, but she was beginning to see there might be more than one way of looking at it.

It was after midnight when she got home; the dog greeted her as though she had returned from the dead. Frankie had been in to let him out, and had left some flowers on the table, along with a note written in sprawling red felt-tip.

'Welcome back.

'Hope your Pa was OK. I met a prince that turned into a frog. Went to a good party with Teeny Ant.

'Jo rang. Says to tell you she's a brilliant cricketer.

'See ya tomorrow.

'FRANKIE.

'PS Room fab.

'PPS I want to elope with Pirate.'

Chapter Fourteen

'Mum, there's no cornflakes left!' Jo was rooting in the cereals cupboard. Mark, by the toaster, turned to his mother, sleepily trying to get herself moving. 'The muesli's finished as well. Will you get some more?'

Alison nodded tiredly. 'There's such a lot to do. We have to pack up all our stuff for Bath today, and I need to stock up here; I feel like crawling back into bed.'

Mark sat down and buttered his toast. 'When does Dad come back?'

'The day after I get home from Bath.'

Jo stretched for a piece of Mark's toast.

'Gerroff!' He made to clout her with the jam jar.

'Oh you! I've put more on the grill. I'll watch it.' She buttered the purloined toast; suspiciously, Mark eyed the toaster. 'OK then,' he grunted. 'And don't be so flaming greedy with my French jam.'

Jo grimaced, and bit into her toast.

'Watch it,' Mark glared at her.

'Shut up, you two. You're both being very boring.' Alison poured herself a second cup of tea.

'What time are you leaving tomorrow, Ma?'

'About five a.m.'

Mark nodded, and there was a smell of burning. He

glared at the oblivious Jo. '*Toast!*' he roared.

'Sorry.' She ran to dowse the flames, and put more bread on the grill. Alison looked at them both: 'I hope you won't fight all the time I'm away.'

'He will,' muttered Jo, and Mark swiped her.

'We won't Ma, promise.'

'I believe you; I believe you.'

'We'll be fine, honestly.' Mark looked credibly earnest. 'And I'll be at the shop all day Saturday.'

'Good.' Alison nodded. 'I do worry, and remember that I don't want Jo alone at night.'

'We know . . .' they chorussed.

'Can I have some money for whites?' asked Jo suddenly, as she stood up to save the next batch of toast from incineration.

'Whites?' Alison was puzzled.

'For cricket.'

Mark held his head and groaned. 'You are so pathetic. Can't you let the poor sods alone to play cricket unencumbered by females?'

'I'm as good as any of them, better than most.'

'Superwoman strikes again. They're fed up with you: for God's sake go and play tennis or something sensible.'

'I prefer cricket,' said Jo huffily.

'You make me puke.'

'Why shouldn't I play cricket if I want to? I scored more goals than almost anybody in the football team, I bet I do just as well in the cricket team.' Jo was flushed, and the perfunctorily-brushed glory of blonde hair was already a bird's nest – she used her coiffure for gesticulation quite as much as her hands.

'Mark's probably right,' said Alison tentatively. 'Tennis is such a good game, for both sexes. I'll kit you out for that if you like; we can get a racquet, and you can do those classes Mark did.'

'They were good. I'd play you tennis,' Mark smiled encouragingly.

'Daddy and I used to play tennis a lot,' Alison tried to help.

'Dad's never here, and you're always too busy. I want to play cricket. I'm going to buy a bat.'

'For God's sake! Use mine!' Mark flung his arms up, aggravated by his kid sister's incomprehensible perserverance with trying to beat the boys. Jo looked at him eagerly. 'Can I?'

'If you must.' He sighed; she was a hopeless case. 'What you don't seem to understand is that boys like to be with boys at your age; you're thirteen now, for goodness' sake, and you should leave them to it. They've got things to talk about, things to get used to . . .'

Jo giggled.

'I give up. Take my bat if it will keep you quiet, but you are so bloody embarrassing I wish I was in another school. It is a pain to be publicly related to you.'

Alison, seeing the hurt in Jo's eyes, intervened. 'Not much you can do about that.' Briskly, she started clearing the table.

Mark rose and went to find his coat. 'Ma.'

'Yes?'

'Can I have some people round on the Saturday night you are away?'

His mother paused. 'How many people?'

Jo started singing to the tune of the Hallelujah Chorus 'Only Susan . . . Susan Richards, Susan Richards. Only Susan . . .'

'Shut up.' Mark's voice was very distinct.

'And she will come for ever and ever . . .'

Mark swore, and chased his wicked little sister round the table; the dog barked, a chair fell, coffee was spilled.

'For heaven's sake stop it! Mark!'

Breathless, murderous, he stood in front of Jo, his hand gripping her arm. 'Ow!' She struggled free and rubbed her elbow.

Alison arms akimbo, glared at her hot-eyed son. 'You may have one or two people here, yes, but no parties. Promise me that?'

Mollified, Mark nodded, and Jo whisked out of the room, pulling the door to. They heard her in the hallway, and just before she called goodbye and the door slammed, there was a further Handelian soprano rendering of 'Susan Richards . . .' which echoed faintly through Mark's bright scarlet ears. He looked at his mother.

'What's the word for murdering your sister?'

'"Sororocide" I suppose.'

'One of these days . . .'

'You would miss her.'

'Don't you believe it,' he growled. 'I must go, I'm late. Bye.' He came and kissed her. She was surprised, he hardly ever did that these days.

She was writing a large shopping-list when the phone rang, she guessed it must be Philip, there were bleeps and un-British telephone clicks.

'Hello?' said Alison, then helloed again. A woman's voice came through, American, assured, not old.

'May I speak to Philip Salveson, please?'

'I'm sorry, he's not here.'

'Oh. When will he be there?'

'Not until Monday next.'

'Oh shit!' The woman sounded very put-out, there was a pause.

'Can I take a message?' asked Alison.

'Oh. No, thank you.' More pause, then: 'Who is this, please?'

Ditto to you, thought Alison, and at eight-thirty in the morning. 'This is Mrs Salveson,' she said precisely. 'Would you like the office number?'

'But I thought he was away . . .'

'Yes.'

'Could you possibly tell me where he is? I'd be most grateful.'

'Hong Kong,' said Alison shortly.

'Oh . . . shit!' said the voice again. She sounded upset, intelligent though, a good voice, classy. 'Hong Kong again, huh?'

Alison said nothing.

'OK.' said the voice, 'Thank you very much. That's kind of you. I can contact him there.'

'Would you like the number?' asked Alison dubiously, but the line went dead before Alison could ask for the caller's name. She looked at the receiver, and slowly put it back on its rest. That was a very odd phone-call: she was sure it wasn't anything to do with business, at least not architectural business. Funny business more like. Was Philip up to his tricks again?

Thoughtfully, she returned to finish writing her list.

Frankie had started packing when Alison came wearily into the shop and slumped on the love-seat, which remained unsold.

'You look done-in? Shall we have some lunch?'

Alison nodded wordlessly, and put down her packages. Frankie looked at the Marks and Spencers labels. 'What have you been buying?'

'Just oddments.' She didn't specially want Frankie to see.

'Show me. Show.' Frankie pounced on the bags as Alison watched uneasily.

'Pants, very nice, I like these.' Frankie held up pale blue knickers with little frills. 'Really nice. And a matching bra?' She rummaged further, and Alison tried to snatch the bag away.

'My goodness, it's a trousseau! More pants, talc, soap, perfume even.' she danced teasingly before Alison. 'Are you planning wicked things?'

'Frankie, shut up. I needed some new things. I was up that way, so I stocked up – I got everybody else stuff as well.'

'Sorry.' Frankie hung her head. 'I was only kidding; I've had a lousy morning. Three thousand mentally deficient customers and only one sale.'

'Any good?'

'The fat guy from Camden Passage. Bought the gold pendant – not bad.' She handed back Alison's purchases.

'Come on, let's eat. What did you get?'

Alison pointed to another bag. 'It's in there.'

Frankie got up to put on a kettle, and they sat and munched sandwiches.

'By the way, guess who came in?' Frankie said through a mouthful of egg and cress.

Sometimes, when Alison was tired, Frankie's ebullience was all too reminiscent of Mark and Jo at their rowdiest. 'Who?'

'Gareth.'

Alison almost dropped her sandwich.

'Hey, you've gone white. Are you OK?'

'I'm fine. I've just been rushing.' She was grateful when Frankie went to busy herself in the back shop. She wouldn't see that she was shaking.

'He just looked in for a minute, said he was passing. He's got this interview in Bristol tomorrow, he's quite steamed up about it. He may come and see us in Bath.'

'Oh yes.' Alison's voice ws meant to sound disinterested. Frankie handed her a mug of coffee. 'Have you seen him since he came over that night?'

Alison shook her head, Frankie was blessedly quiet. The coffee was good, soothing. It had been a very long two weeks of trying not to think about him; for a day or two she almost thought she had succeeded, but it was no good pretending any more. She was longing for word of him, and praying that he would come to Bath.

'Want an apple?' said Frankie, handing her one. Like Eve, Alison took a large bite out of the firm flesh. They crunched in silence, then Alison eyed the boxes: 'Come on,' she stood up. 'Let's get it packed.'

Bronwen sprawled in the big armchair by the fire, and examined her father critically: 'It's lovely. I always wanted you to get a leather jacket. It's really smart.'

'Think they'll give me the job then?' Gareth asked, grinning.

'Yeah. They're mad if they don't. But, Dad?'

'What?' He stood proudly in front of her. Going to the dawn market at Portobello Road had been worthwhile this time, three very good books, a strange, possibly Maori, carving, and his jacket – good leather, apparently unused – for only a few pounds. He hadn't bought himself anything new for a year at least.

'You have got to wear a tie; wear the dark woolly one I gave you at Christmas.'

'Right, Ma'am. Anything else?'

'Shampoo and beard trim.'

'That goes without saying.'

Bronwen sparkled, and jumped out of the chair. 'I'll get the scissors.' Ceri, chewing a pencil at the table, frowned as he struggled with his maths homework.

Beside him a large tortoiseshell cat flicked its tail across his sums. 'Move, cat,' and he shoved the beast gently aside. Insulted, it stood, stretched its elegant body lazily and hopped onto the warm space Bronwen had vacated. Gareth eyed the pulley of drying clothes above his head and reached up to feel a small pair of jeans. 'These are dry; we had better pack your bag. You won't need much, not just for two days. You can just take the one bag between you; it's less to carry.'

Ceri frowned, counting, concentrating. Bronwen came back with the scissors and brandished them at her father.

'I'm not putting my clothes beside Ceri's muddy things.'

'Give over,' muttered her brother automatically.

'You are a silly pair.' Gareth gathered the clean garments into two heaps. 'There now, that's all; pack them yourselves.'

'Come on, Dad, I'm waiting.' Bossily Bronwen handed him a purple towel. Obediently Gareth sat in an upright wooden chair and wrapped the towel round his shoulders; he jutted out his chin and eyed his plants by the window. 'I must remember to water these before we go.'

'Right,' said Bronwen, 'Let's start.'

The beard-trimming was a ritual once every three weeks or so.

'Scissors?' said Gareth.

'Scissors.' she confirmed.

'Towel?'

'Towel.'

'Comb?'

'Comb.'

'Commence.'

Carefully, the small girl combed her father's dark

beard; he restrained from hugging her when she did this for him, but felt overcome with fondness for her little hands which so carefully smoothed his hair and cooled his cheeks. An efficient and helpful creature, she eyed him intently as she snipped and measured.

'Don't take too much off; I need to look beautiful.'

'Why?'

He shrugged, twinkling. It was good to see him cheerful for a change.

Ceri looked over to him. 'Would we have to move to Bristol if you got the job?' Gareth nodded.

'Keep still!' Bronwen shrieked.

'Sorry.' He glanced at Ceri's anxious face. 'We would. The train fare is very expensive, much too much to commute, and it's too far to drive there regularly.'

Both children frowned. Bronwen continued clipping, her tongue sticking out as she tried to level him up. 'I don't want to move.'

'You have to go where the jobs are these days, there's no two ways about it. Bristol's a good place, beautiful old houses, a big river with a magnificient bridge, and lovely hills all round.' Gareth sounded enthusiastic.

'I've seen the bridge on telly,' Ceri had given up doing sums. 'People jump off it, attached to big thick rubber bands. I'd like to do that.'

'I hope you don't ever try it; it's very high indeed.'

'What about your hair?' asked the girl.

He felt behind his neck. 'OK, but only a little, please.'

There was silence, except for the click of the scissors and the hum of the fridge. The cat was asleep.

'Right,' said Bronwen. 'That's done.' Carefully she took the towel from him, cradling the dark shorn locks. He smoothed his neck, shook his shoulders and smiled at her in the mirror over the gas-fire.

'Lovely, *cariad*. Thank you.' He touched her cheek gently. 'You go and have a bath now, I'll pack my gear.'

'Must I?'

'Yes.'

He watched the girl carefully tidy away the scissors, towel and comb, touched by her domesticity. 'I hope you will be all right tomorrow. Your train is at five. Aunt Blod will meet you at Lewes.'

'Dad,' said Ceri impatiently. 'Stop fussing; you're like an old lady.'

Gareth drew himself up, mock-offended.

'I'm only doing my parental duty.'

'We have gone to Aunt Blod's hundreds of times. Why are you making such a fuss?'

Gareth sighed. 'I just worry.'

The children looked at each other and smiled. 'Stop fussing Dad. We will see you on Sunday night, about eight.'

At the shop the packing was done. Alison leaned back from her final box. 'That's that then; it will only take minutes to load up in the morning.'

'God, I'm stiff.' Frankie stretched and touched her toes, then stood up again, bent slowly foward like a giant hairpin, head dangling with her arms in front, relaxed, and slowly unwound upwards and stretched her head sideways, forwards, sideways again. 'Beddibyes for me. When will you pick me up?'

'Five a.m.'

'I was afraid you were going to say that. Were you impressed that I had laundered the Union Jack?'

'Very. I hope we do well.'

'I bet you sell the horsicle.'
'I thought it would go immediately.'
'It's a lot of money.'
Alison nodded. 'What will I do with the big blue and white vase?'
'They wouldn't pass it in Bath – it's a pre-1910 dateline.'
'Maybe Mark will charm somebody into buying it. Even if I get what I spent.'
'If you were daft enough to be conned, somebody else is sure to be.'
Alison put on her coat. 'I'm off. I bought some henna, I fancy trying it.'
'Changing your image?'
'Trying to improve the ravages of time a little.'
Frankie put out the lights, and they went into the streets; Alison carefully double-locked the door.
'I must run. I've got to feed the kids.'
'Cheerio,' called Frankie. 'We shall meet at sparrow-fart. Farewell again, dear friend!' She gestured a Shakespearean farewell, then added: 'By the way, I'm not staying at the bed and breakfast. I'm being picked up by that friend of Anthony's.'
'Which friend?'
Frankie looked hesitant: 'The artist. Jay. I'll be staying just outside the town. I forgot to tell you, I hope you don't mind.'
Alison was first surprised, then hurt. She had looked forward to eating with Frankie after the markets. You needed to unwind after a hard day's selling, like an actor after a performance.
'I wish you had said . . .'
'I'm sorry. I did a blank on it.' Frankie, obviously highly embarrassed, bit her lip. Alison, more and more annoyed the more she thought about it, frowned.

'You so and so, you traitor! Did you phone the bed and breakfast to say you weren't coming?'

'I rang them this morning. I'm really sorry.'

Alison shrugged. 'I'd better take a good book to entertain me.'

'Maybe Gareth . . .'

'Give over, Frankie.' Alison flushed. 'Anyway,' she tried to sound friendly, 'is this Jay nice? You haven't told me much.'

Frankie lit up, then looked bashful. 'Very. But I don't really want to talk about it.' She blushed, nodded, and looked away.

Alison took out her car keys. 'I'll see you tomorrow.'

Frankie nodded an apologetic agreement, waved feebly then walked away. Alison found the car in the mews at the back of the shop and bad-temperedly started it up. Damn Frankie. She might have mentioned it earlier, and why was she being so mysterious? It wasn't like her at all.

Alison and the children had eaten supper when Philip rang from Hong Kong; he sounded fed-up and homesick. The children spoke briefly, then Alison came on the line, and reminded him that she was going away. She remembered the morning's rather odd phone-call, and asked Philip if an American woman had contacted him. She did an excellent imitation of the woman's voice and what she had said.

'She sounded anxious to reach you, and was very annoyed that you were away. Who was she?'

'Silly bitch!' muttered Philip angrily. 'She must have tracked down the number through the directory. Why the hell didn't she ring the office?'

'It was breakfast time. The office wasn't open. Who was she?'

Philip grunted dismissively. 'Just a journalist who

wouldn't leave me alone. Over-emotional. It was nothing. . . . Anyway, darling . . .' he tried to change the subject, which stirred the sludge of old and painful memories in Alison – she had heard him say things like that three years ago. 'I'd better go. I'll see you all on Monday. Good luck with the fair.'

She put down the phone dubiously, and realised with a shock that though she was certainly curious as to what Philip was up to, she didn't really care any more.

'My God, what a time to hit the road,' said Frankie after they had loaded up the car and set off. 'It's even too early for the farming news . . .'

Alison, only half-awake and still angry with Frankie for her impending desertion – which had made her feel sleeplessly unprotected with regard to Gareth's promised appearance – grunted monosyllabically and headed for the M4.

She drove for half an hour, Frankie snoozing beside her, then glanced at her watch. It was news time; she put on the radio and listened gloomily to an announcement of some further Reagan madness with new and more hideous nuclear missiles, then the farming news began, but today she was not comforted by it, and clicked it off. Frankie was awake.

'Are you OK?' she asked in a small voice.

'Yes. Why?' snapped Alison, putting her foot further down. She was doing ninety.

'I dunno,' said Frankie. There was a silence, then Frankie tried again. 'Alison, I'm really sorry about not staying in town with you.'

'I just wish you had told me earlier.'

'I was looking forward to it too,' said Frankie miserably. 'But this Jay thing . . .' Alison's ears pricked up. 'Well . . . to tell you the truth, I felt so hellish after that awful business with the golfer guy, I just feel extra vulnerable at the moment. This has been unbelievably sudden . . .'

'Evidently.' Alison's voice was cold and crisp as lettuce from the fridge.

Frankie struggled to explain, not wanting to cause further chilliness. 'The truth is,' she said at last, 'that I don't want to talk about it, not yet, not even to you.'

Alison shrugged. 'OK. I'll try to understand.'

'Thank you.'

The car covered several miles with the two travellers sitting in strained and formal silence, until Frankie couldn't bear it any longer, and tentatively handed her driver an unwrapped chewing-gum. 'Are you still my friend?'

Alison managed a small laugh and nodded. 'Yes, of course. Let's stop off for breakfast and try not to get hysterical about our prices.'

Frankie had never been in Bath or the Assembly Halls before, and was impressed by the city, which was still quiet when they arrived in the soft morning light. The flagstoned and pillared portico of the halls made her crow.

'What a lovely place. It reminds me of Edinburgh, but without the starkness.'

She gawped at the corridor of dark Chippendale benches past which they carried their boxes, and was deeply impressed with the main ballroom where they were lucky enough to have been given an excellent pitch. Frankie gazed up at the high windows on three sides of the splendidly-proportioned room, and aahed with admiration at the elegant musicians' gallery.

'You can just imagine a wee bit of the old Baroque music emanating from there. What date is this place?'

‘Seventeen-eighty.’

Frankie nodded, eyeing the other tables. ‘We’ve got a good pitch. We’ll be beautifully on show the minute they come in the big door; I suppose they collect the tickets in that octagonal place inside the entrance.’

Alison nodded, and went to fetch another box. ‘You guard this lot till I come back.’

‘Surely they’re too posh to steal here?’

‘You can never be sure.’

‘I’ll lay out the cloths and card-table. I’m really excited.’ She took off her jacket – an over-large man’s black dinner jacket, that had replaced the winter poncho – and stood revealed in a dark blue dress, sparkling with interesting glittery threads. She had tied dozens of pigtails in her hair – each one decoratively baubled with beads of many colours – and looked very unusual. Alison too had dressed with care – fairs were performance-time for stall-holders, especially a big fair like this. They both felt on show.

‘I’m glad to see you’re wearing your gold jewellery,’ said Frankie. ‘It makes you look very successful.’ Carefully, she unfolded the big Union Jack and spread it on top of the deep red velvet cloth they used to cover the front of the stall. Soon they were set up: the glass and silver glittered, the Indian figure on one side of the stall, and the horsicle along with Frankie’s odds and ends of decoration – she had brought a specially-prepared posy of flowers – made Alison feel proud. She carefully set up their shop card ‘TWO BIRDS ANTIQUES’ Moscow Terrace, London W2, which Jo had painstakingly letraset for them, on the very front of the stall. It looked terrific.

As usual, a lot of dealing took place before the show started officially, and the two birds were almost intimidated by the grandeur of some of the most unctuous and self-important dealers, who smiled tolerantly at their colourful display, and at the exotic Frankie and striking-looking Alison. Excitement had made Alison's dark eyes particularly bright today – her newly-hennaed hair was dramatically off-set by her jewellery.

By lunch-time much money had changed hands, and Frankie said she would kill the next old lady that said she had one exactly the same at home. They had sold a lot, it augured well: the large hall was filled with people, dealers and private buyers, and the usual ceaseless stream of gawpers, who came to learn, admire or simply lust. Mid-afternoon they were beginning to droop from the early start; Frankie produced sticky Danish pastries, which they ate, trying not to be seen, crouching behind their laden table.

Alison licked her fingers. 'When are you meeting your friend?'

'Jay's picking me up at five: I arranged just to run out to the car, it's all double yellow lines round here.'

Alison was disappointed: 'I was looking forward to viewing this mysterious artist.'

Frankie looked slightly hunted: 'Yeah,' she muttered. 'Tomorrow or the next day maybe.'

By a quarter to five the place was growing quieter, and both women were drooping, till Frankie spotted Gareth walking towards them, spruce in a brown leather jacket and brown trousers. She nudged Alison, who was peering at a hall-mark on a silver spoon. 'See who's here.'

Alison's heart hiccoughed then somersaulted as she looked up.

'Hello,' he said and their tentative, anxious smiles locked. He eased, then grinned at Frankie. 'How's business?'

They told him, and he eyed the big hall, impressed.

'You look unbelievably smart, tie and all,' said Frankie. 'Was this finery for the interview?' He nodded.

'How did it go?'

He crossed his fingers and touched the gold and red painted wood of the big Indian figure. 'Good. I think I came out very high indeed; I knew a couple of them even, but now of course I have subsided into my usual self-doubt and Celtic pessimism, which' – he smiled winningly – 'is why I came to see you two ladies.'

Alison turned away for a moment, it almost hurt to look at him, she wanted him so much.

'I wondered,' he continued, 'if you were busy, the two of you . . . or if you felt like coming out to eat . . . . I could do with some amusing company.'

What she had both dreaded and longed-for, had happened; he was here, and if she said yes, they would have to confront each other alone.

Frankie was putting on her jacket, 'That would have been lovely, but I'm spoken for; I'm staying the night at a place called Chew Magna, believe it or not.'

'Oh.' For a moment Gareth's mind fused. 'Um . . .' he looked wildly from object to object on the stall, then settled on the equally nervous Alison. 'Er . . . how about you? Do you fancy coming?' Frankie tried to be invisible and groped under the table for her bag, pretending deafness by humming to herself as Alison and Gareth stared at each other. Alison swallowed, nodded, then smiled, 'OK. That would be lovely.'

Frankie's head popped up suddenly from behind the table like a Mr Punch puppet, and she stood up, bag on shoulder, ready to go.

'Right, I'm off! See you tomorrow, Alison. Have a good time.' She fled, swinging down the aisles like a figure-head on a storm-tossed ship.

'What's her hurry?' Gareth grinned after her. 'Whew!'

'A new lover – all very exciting and uncertain,' said Alison fondly.

'Ah,' he nodded shyly.

All over the hall people were preparing to go, putting on hats and coats.

'What happens to the stuff?' he asked as Alison put on her coat.

'There's a Security Guard.' She stood up ready to go and did a final check of the stall.

'What do you fancy doing?' he asked. 'I saw a very nice looking place to eat in a village just outside the town, near where I'm staying. Venison with cranberries, home-made ice-cream – stuff like that – not too expensive.'

'Sounds wonderful. I'm ravenous.'

'Me too. Will you come in my car? I can bring you back.' She felt rather relieved that he was being so circumspect.

'That sounds good; I'll need to check in to my bed and breakfast, and dump my car, and I need a bath.'

He nodded. 'Shall I pick you up around seven?'

She agreed, and told him where she would be; they were both somewhat bashful and business-like. 'Right,' said Gareth. 'I'll see you then.'

Alison smiled shyly, and watched him walk off to find his car with a deafening thumping of her heart.

Chapter Fifteen

At the bed and breakfast, not too far from the centre, in a terraced house of small but sweet proportions, Alison signed-in and relaxed in a bath, listening to Bach's sixth Brandenburg on the cassette-player, with which she always travelled. She had dyed her hair and shaved legs and armpits the night before in preparation, and she knew that it wasn't only to look beautiful behind her stall that she had done all these things. Now she anointed her body with sweet-smelling cream and powder, and dressed carefully, starting by removing the new underclothes from their packet. As she tried to decide which dress to wear – a hard decision, she was fond of them both – she became more and more nervous.

There was an alarming inevitability about this meeting: she knew that it was a point of no return. If she were wise she would plead tiredness, or say she had a headache – indeed, she did feel utterly knackered. It had been a long hard day, and he would be here in twenty minutes, looking so very desirable in his new clothes; she sprayed scent under her ears, on cleavage and wrists, and inhaled the subtle sensual perfume. It was her favourite, used only for special occasions.

What on earth was she going to do? She found herself eyeing her toothbrush, wondering if she ought, just in case, to put it in her handbag, then remembered that she had a disposable one – picked up from the airport Ladies last time she had gone to fetch Philip – she had bought it in an idle moment, slipping ten pence into the slot machine, thinking it would be bound to come in handy sometime.

She shelved the disturbingly practical decision. Maybe after all the dinner would be strained and full of ghastly silences. They hardly knew each other really, it was probably all in her imagination, and silly to presume that there would be any question of her spending the night at his place. She was a mature businesswoman, about to meet a very pleasant fellow-dealer for dinner, that was all there was to it. She looked at herself in the mirror: the deep turquoise dress had won in the decision-making, and she knew she looked good and not at all tired any more. Just ravenous, and longing for his little yellow car with the red and yellow anti-nuclear-sticker to arrive.

'Right.' Gareth climbed into the car beside Alison. 'Would you like to have a drink before we eat? There's a lovely pub in my village.'

'Sounds nice,' Alison nodded shyly. 'I'm starving though.'

'Me too. We can eat soon; I ordered a table for eight o'clock.'

He drove out of the town, and in minutes the car was climbing a hill with trees and dense hedgerows by the roadside, filled with white, pink and yellow flowers. Alison lay back in her seat and gloried in the landscape, whilst Gareth pointed out landmarks. They arrived at a small village, with an old church and small village green nestling in the hillside above the city. Far away, you could see the grey strip of the Gloucester-Bath motorway, where the sun sparkled on passing cars as they whizzed on their way. Gareth halted the car, and they got out. Alison looked round at the village, with tight-knit honey – coloured cottages with stone roofs and baskets of lobelia and lots of flowers everywhere.

'What a beautiful spot.' She smiled at him.

The pub was small and cheerfully busy, and they managed to find seats in the garden; it was cooler now, but just warm enough to sit out. Gareth disappeared, and Alison waited, still nervous, for him to come back with two glasses of wine. He set them carefully down on the table, and took one 'Cheers.' He swallowed a large mouthful and smiled: 'I had need of that.'

Alison gulped her wine fast. 'Me too. It's been a long day.' She relaxed at last. 'This is lovely.'

He nodded, and lay back in his chair, eyes half-closed. 'I love this part of the world. I know it well from student days; I used to escape from exams on my bike, and explore all the country pubs.'

'Sounds like a civilised hobby.'

They were silent, each one worriedly wondering what to say next. Alison was intensely aware of Gareth's proximity, and tried not to look at his furry forearms, so strong and tactile.

At last he dared to speak: 'I didn't ever think you and I would spend the evening by ourselves.'

'Nor me. I nearly died when Frankie said she was pushing off.'

He eyed her curiously. 'Were you nervous?'

She toyed with her glass, and drank again, then looked at him. 'Yes.' She looked away.

'Nervous of me?'

She shrugged, 'I suppose.'

They both examined beer-mats, finding great interest in the brewer's message.

'To tell you the truth,' said Gareth with a small smile, 'I was so petrified I nearly fled past the door of your lodgings.'

'Don't tell me I frighten you?'

He nodded, grinned the beginning of a grin, and looked away.

They sipped in further silence. 'What would your husband say to your eating and drinking with an unknown man?'

'Well, he's several thousand miles away in Hong Kong. Maybe he's dining with a strange woman.'

He nodded. 'How about another?'

'If I drink more before I eat, I shall keel over.'

'OK. Let's go and eat. It's just down the road.'

They walked down the little High Street, which was all there really was to the tiny village. Old ladies stood gossiping in doorways, and dogs lay in front of them, panting. Gareth put his jacket over his shoulder, and they walked side by side; she glanced at him, admiring his intelligent profile. She could hardly bear it when he grinned; it made her feel as though her insides were melting. It wasn't him she had been afraid of, it was herself. At the end of the village was a small restaurant, Gareth touched her arm, 'That's the eating place, but if we walk down the road for a couple of minutes I'll show you my cottage.' They walked in the evening sun until there was a gap in the high hedge, and looked over a wooden gate, across quietly grazing sheep. It was a superb view, with hills far away, and rolling fields in glorious varied greens, starred with buttercups, and an occasional bright-yellow field singing with colour. He saw her looking.

'Isn't it beautiful? That brilliant yellow is rape.'

She breathed in the glory of the landscape. 'I love it. It reminds me of where I was brought up.'

'Were you a country girl?'

She nodded. 'It's only when I come back that I realise how much I miss it, the bonus of beauty in your life, always changing. It is sublime.'

They leaned side by side, peaceful. Gareth pointed to a small cottage a hundred yards or so down a track. 'That's my friend's cottage. I'll show you later if you like.'

'It looks heavenly.'

'It is. So quiet, with flowers and cows all round. I love it here.' He turned to her, and their eyes met, terrifyingly, deeply, as on the march. They both looked away, it was too intimate. 'Come on,' he said, 'let's go and eat.'

The food was as good as he had promised, and they drank much red wine, and suddenly there was no problem, more a problem about stopping the talk in order to eat. He told her about his marriage: he was incredibly open, showing his hurt, his fondness for his children, his loneliness. And she told him of Philip, her parents, and even of the long-lost Gino.

'After my first child was born, Mark, I met a friend of Gino's and we discovered by degrees, from comparing memories and checking on details, that my mother had confiscated all his letters to me. I was shattered because I thought he had reneged on me; I was almost locked up for a while, and sent off to Scotland to au-pair in Aberdeen of all places.'

He was pained for her: 'Did you ever contact him?'

She shook her head. 'No point. I was well-married to Philip by then: I was reasonably content – happy really – I had my baby, it was all water under the bridge.' She savoured her venison and cranberries. 'This is bliss. I feel off the hook. What self-indulgence.'

'I'm glad.' He looked at her again with his piercing look. 'Very glad.'

Almost embarrassed, she said. 'That march we all went on seems a long time ago; I feel as though we have known each other for years.'

He nodded, carefully taking salad. 'I found the last two weeks one of the longest fortnights in my life.'

There, he had said it.

Alison drained her glass, and Gareth ordered more, then ventured a glance at her. She met his gaze fully.

'I found it endless. I painted a room and ran away to see my father.'

He laughed sadly, and watched as the waiter poured wine from a new bottle which had arrived in an instant. Alison glanced at the man whom she guessed to be the boss. 'That was quick,' she said admiringly. He nodded, smiling. 'I can tell where there is a need, Madam.'

'I jogged,' Gareth ironically remembered his toiling body, 'for miles. And swam. My children thought I had gone mad.' He looked at his wine, swilling it gently, deep red in the glass. 'I suppose I had in a way.'

They finished the meal and ordered coffee. Alison went to the Ladies, and looked at herself in the mirror. She looked good.

'Are you going to go back to your bed and breakfast tonight, Mrs Salveson?' she asked her reflection, but it did not answer. She powdered her nose unnecessarily, and combed her hair. She must return to the table: if she did want to go back to the bed and breakfast she would have to go soon, for if he looked at her once more in that way, she would collapse into his arms instantly.

The coffee had arrived, Gareth was obviously relieved to see her. 'I wondered if you had run away through the back door.'

She shook her head and sat down again. 'I thought about it.'

'I'm glad you didn't.' He was shy again. 'I like your dress, you look very nice. Not at all Snow Queenish.'

'Fiery?' she queried, teasing.

'Vibrant, I'd say.' He offered her coffee, and they drank. He glanced up over his cup. 'Alison, I must warn you. I feel a bit pissed; I begin to want to say and do things I should not.'

Challenged, obliquely, she tasted her coffee, found it too strong, and added more cream. 'I've had a lot of wine too. Maybe you should go ahead. I might like it.'

Her hand lay in front of her on the table. Lingeringly he looked at it, and moved his own hand a little forward from where it lay by his coffee cup, until their two middle fingers met in a tentative but highly-charged touch. They each felt a desire to weep, and he put his warm big hand over hers. 'I have found it very difficult not to do that ever since the day you sold me the Ashanti doll.'

She turned her hand round, so their palms met, there was a feeling of having come home. 'I know. I have felt the same.'

'Shall we go? I'll get the bill.'

The waiter laid it at Gareth's elbow before he had time to summon him. On Alison's insistence, they split the bill. 'Business,' she said succinctly, and knew he was relieved.

Outside it was dark. Gareth stood close to her. 'Are you going to come and see my cottage?'

Alison nodded, her face gilded by the light from the restaurant. She was aware of Gareth's breathless gaze.

He took her arm. 'Come on,' he said, then grasping her hand, which she allowed him to take, they stumbled down the dark country lane towards the looming silhouette of the empty cottage.

He let go of her hand, and bent to feel with the key for

the lock, then he stood up beside her, waiting. She could dimly make out his face in his darkness, his beard was black, and she could not really read his eyes. He pocketed the key, and turned to her, she felt his warmth and bulk very near, and was aware of his fingers softly on her cheek. 'Alison,' he said. 'I have a great desire to do something I haven't done for a long time.'

She leaned her cheek to answer his touch, gentle, caressing. 'Yes?' she whispered, and barely restrained from nibbling the strong fingers and cupped palm. In answer, he bent and put his arms round her body, and found her mouth with his, and they stood enfolded, lips, tongues, faces, necks, communing, fondling. It was as though the earth had stopped spinning, and they were held together in its breathless centre. He pulled away at last, and she felt a sense of loss. He breathed, or sighed. 'God, you are lovely. I think you are the most desirable woman I have ever wanted. So beautiful . . . such sad sad eyes . . .' Again his hands cupped her face, and she leaned against his chest, wishing they could stay locked here like this until the end of time.

'Come on,' he said, almost gruffly, 'Let's go in. It's getting chilly.'

He led the way and put on a light, and she saw a squarish room, with timbered floor and ceiling, stone walls, and two vases of fresh wild flowers. There was a stone fireplace in one wall, and a well-designed cooking area opposite. It was simple, tasteful, a rustic paradise, with a wooden table in the centre, and a couple of old comfortable armchairs by the fire.

'What a beautiful place. Who put the flowers there?'

He looked surprised. 'I did.'

'They are lovely.' She bent to look and smell, touched that so male a man would have bothered.

'I'm fond of flowers and plants.' He stood in front of the fireplace; again he looked a little shy, anxious. 'Would you like more to drink? Or coffee?'

She nodded. 'Coffee.'

'Sit,' he told her, and she sat in the biggest armchair, wrapping her jersey more tightly round herelf. 'Are you cold?' he asked anxiously.

'A little, coffee will warm me up.'

He walked past her, touching her head butterfly-lightly as he went by, as though she were a wild animal, and he wanted to reassure her that it was safe to be here. He bent down at the wall by the window to switch on an electric heater, then busied himself at the sink. Alison turned in the chair and watched his firm chunky body as he made two mugs of coffee.

'I don't usually do this sort of thing,' she told him.

He turned, milk-bottle in hand. 'What sort of thing?'

She gesticulated, taking in the room, the place, himself. 'All this. Alone with a strange man in a strange place.'

He handed her a mug, and sat to drink his in the opposite chair.

'I'm not so strange really, quite an average sort of man in fact.'

They sipped and eyed each other. 'I don't either, do this sort of thing. Normally I lead a very quiet life with the two children and a cat.' His look was fond, a little wistful. Alison got up from the chair and walked round the room, peering at a couple of prints of old Bath, and at the mixture of books in the bookshelves – odd paperbacks, a John Fowles or two – and sundry maps. There was a well-thumbed map of the district glued to the one plaster wall beside a neatly constructed new wooden stairway.

'Is that where you sleep?' She looked upwards.

He nodded. 'It's all timbered as well. Very neat, with an amazing view across to the Malverns. It's marvellous to wake up to.'

She smiled. 'Sounds nice.'

He watched her, and drained his mug. He leaned across to where she was standing, leafing through a guide book to Bath, and touched her hand, stroking it softly.

'Alison,' he said quietly. 'Tell me what you want to do. I can take you home if you like, truly.'

She did not respond with touch or voice, but stood uncertain, afraid again.

'Alison. I would like you to stay and see the view in the morning; I would like us to make love. I would like it more than anything in the world. I have thought of little else for weeks, but if you want to go, say so, please.' He stood up, and let go of her hand, and it shrieked its loss to her. She went to him, and laid her head on his chest and heard the thumping of his heart. Softly, he put his hands on her shoulders.

'Are you going to stay?'

Wordlessly, she nodded, and felt tears stab her eyes. He looked very serious, and kissed her long and gently, and she wanted to lose herself in his warm body.

'Come.' He took a candle in a holder from the table and lit it. 'Let's go up.' Silently, she followed him, noticing as she climbed the wooden steps, the mobile shadow of their linked hands on the uneven stone walls.

In the small wooden bedroom, which contained little more than a big double bed, Gareth let go of her hand and laid the candle down by a pot of wild pink orchids laced with bluebells. He turned to her, his face serious, lit by the gold of the flame.

'I thought you were going to leave me back there,' he said, looking at her, his eyes soft.

'So did I for a minute.' Alison looked up at him, then away. He came to her and once more touched her hair.

'It looks red in this light. A fire goddess more like.'

Their faces touched, and they clasped each other with a need and intensity that was overwhelming. In moments they stood naked before each other, clothes forgotten on the floor. He stood almost boyishly, suddenly bashful. 'I'm very hairy, like a bear . . . . I hope you can stand it . . .'

She told him with her lips and hands and eyes that there was nothing she would find more beautiful or desirable than he was; his dark muscular warmth was so different to Philip's pale smooth body, that she felt like a bewitched virgin. At last he pulled away from her, reluctant, clinging.

'Come, *cariad*,' he said. 'Let's go to bed.'

He was sturdy, strong and warm; she nestled in his dark fur, enclosed by his gentle masculinity. His maleness greeted her, tumescent, upright, hard. He kissed her breasts, which crooned their joy, singing through her body a song of love. She had so longed for this, to lie thus, naked, touching, loving. She fondled his hardness, his shaft, his blade, cradling the mysterious soft love-pouches beneath it in her hand.

'I think he likes you,' said Gareth. 'He's obviously impressed.'

His hands, stroking, searching, were so sensitive it seemed as though her complex little knob, her magic switch, were part of him and not of her. She opened to him, and he thrust into her dark harbour, the entry of his implement soft-welcomed by his touch. She pushed and sucked him to her, gentle as a sea-anemone. Her wetness cradled, smoothed, enclosed him. She felt his power within her, and they moved together, slowly, thrumming, touching, kissing, licking, sucking, surging, until they gasped and yelped in an explosion of delight, enfolding, infinite. They lay together breathless, the race both run and won together, and she felt his life-throb pulse within her centre.

There were pigeons fluting, and sun streamed in to glorify the simple bedside posy, when Alison opened her eyes to see Gareth standing quietly by the window, staring at her, his face unguarded, full of love. It had been dawn by the time they had slept, exhausted, like tired travellers from a distant enchanted country.

'Hello,' she turned towards him. 'How long have you been there?'

'Not long. I didn't want you to wake, you looked so beautiful, so pretty.'

She reached for him, and he came to lie beside her, as though they had loved one another for years. He fondled her, and she stroked his dark firm body, marvelling; he entered her and once again they raced together the blissful race, and he lay panting, as she felt his body thrum with hers. The pigeons cooed, and more birds sang, at last he turned to her and whispered:

'Come and see the view.'

They stood naked at the tiny window, her small arm beside his sun-glittering brawny one. Wordlessly, she smiled and compared.

'A bit different,' she said, pointing. He nodded, stroking the miracle of her smoothness, and they looked across the myriad fields and hills to the far off distance, where blue hills loomed.

'What time is it?' she asked at last.

'Eight. When do you have to go?'

'Ten, and I must collect my stuff from the bed and breakfast.'

'Will they think you have been kidnapped?'
'I have a key. They may not even notice.'
They breakfasted in the sunlit garden, multi-coloured with flowers; Gareth made a daisy chain of fat white daisies to hang round her neck. He lay on his back beside her and looked up into the vast blueness of the sky and touched her arm with a long grass.
'Is Frankie with you tonight?'
'I doubt it, unless things go wrong in her rural love-nest.'
'May I see you?'
She smiled down at him, her face young as a child's. 'I think you have no option.'
'I'll cook. Shall I collect you as before?'
'Where will you be all day?' She could hardly bear the thought of being without him.
He laughed. 'Sleeping, I suspect, in the garden.'
'Think of poor me working.'
'The way you look, they'll flock to buy up your entire stall in the first ten minutes.'
'If they do, I'll come and join you.'
'How about Frankie? Will you tell her about us?'
'I don't know. She might simply take one look and know. She's been worried about us for ages.'
He sat up, surprised. 'Was it so obvious?'
'I guess so.'
He shook his head, smiling wryly.
'She will be angry with me,' said Alison.
He nodded. 'Because of your husband?'
'Yes.'
He stroked her face sadly. 'She's probably right.'
'It's too late now.' She looked across the fields into the distance. 'You are the first lover I have had since I was married.'
'Oh God, Alison, I feel terrible.' He hid his face in his hands, and she kissed his fingers one by one.

'Gareth, I don't regret it. It was inevitable. It had to be. Something as wonderful as what we have just shared cannot be bad. I don't believe it; it can only be good.'

He put his hands down, and stared at her, filling his consciousness with her big dark eyes and her beauty that made him want to weep for joy and disbelief. 'I hope so, Alison, I hope so. I couldn't bear to cause you pain. Yet I am fearful of it.'

By the time she reached the Assembly Rooms and met up with Frankie, Alison was very very tired, her eyes were heavy, despite what Frankie at once described as her big pussy-cat smile. 'I can see you had a good time,' she said almost as soon as she saw Alison.

Alison mimed zombie-like exhaustion. 'And you?'

Frankie laughed. 'Ditto. We'll have to take it in turns to stay awake.'

'What is Jay's place like?'

'Amazing. It's a flat in a big old Queen Anne house with a beautiful walled garden, and we drank white wine and got awfy drunk. My head . . .' she groaned.

'I'll go and get coffee,' offered Alison. She didn't feel up to being cross-questioned so early in the day by Frankie as to her intentions re Gareth and was glad of a chance of diversion. She went through the big hall to the coffee stall, and was aware as she waited her turn, of a sort of Doppelgänger image of Gareth which stayed with her and would not go away. Every in and out breath brought an awareness of him, and she remembered the tenderness and emotion and paradisical pleasuring of the night and trembled at the images in her head and body. She did not remember ever feeling so involved and close to a man – and this after one night of love.

The coffee helped; Frankie needed aspirin, which

Alison was able to supply, and gradually they both appeared to be functioning almost normally, though Alison suspected that Frankie's internal imagery was almost as drugged with love as her own: Jay, whoever he was, was obviously having a big effect on her Scots friend. As they stood up to demonstrate or expound upon the beauty and rarity of their wares, Alison noticed that Frankie was wearing a single new earring; it was silver, and looked like a little battleaxe.

'That's unusual, is it a Scottish clan sign or something?'

Frankie flushed, and put her hand up to it. 'It's called a labrys: Jay gave me it.'

Alison become distracted by a well-off woman in a floral dress who wanted to buy a silver-plated fruit dish, and needed a little informed persuasion. The adrenalin was on the flow at last, gushing in fact, and she succeeded very quickly; the woman went away happy, clutching the fruit dish as well as a copper warming-pan which Alison had swiftly persuaded her was an essential to life in her Tudor cottage. Frankie got pretty high as well, and by lunch they were reeling with their mutual brilliance and splendour; 'We'll have nothing left at this rate,' said Frankie, beaming.

'If that happens I can think of much nicer things to do . . .' said Alison, gazing into Gareth's invisible but adoring Doppelgänger eyes.

'You're hopeless,' said Frankie, eyeing her disapprovingly. 'You've got two children and a husband, what more do you want?'

'Gareth . . . Gareth . . . Gareth . . .' she breathed, blinking.

Frankie shook her head, trying to be severe, but Alison's love-sick idiocy was irresistible. 'I just don't want to have to come and pick up the pieces when

Philip blows your head off. He keep a gun in the house, doesn't he?'

'Two,' Alison nodded, still far away, staring with Gareth over the distant blue hills, the daisy-chain round her head.

By lunch they were both ravenous and not a little hysterical. Frankie offered to go for some food 'And some wine?' she queried.

'Better not, we might start swinging from those amazing chandeliers and be booted out.'

'OK. Orange juice. But I feel a need for a bottle of bubbly.'

'No.' Alison shook her head.

'Just a wee bottle?'

'If you bought it and opened it I'd have to drink it to save you from yourself . . .'

'Right,' said Frankie. 'I'll away and get it then.'

She disappeared, clutching her ethnic Indian bag, all mirrored and embroidered; she looked lovely, extra alive somehow, vibrant, as Gareth had said about Alison. Already Alison longed for the night, to see him, to talk more, there seemed so much to say, and to lie in his arms again, her Esau.

'This is nice, is it Persian?' Alison looked up to see a tall, striking-looking woman in green dungarees and a sleeveless white tee-shirt, which revealed hairy underarms. She exuded confidence, had an easy smile, and punky blonde hair, which, as she must be at least thirty-five, made her look unusual and oddly beautiful. Alison looked at the plate, an off-white one, with interesting blue brushwork: 'It is Persian; I think it's seventeenth century. Peasantware. It is lovely, isn't it? I had three, and kept one for myself I liked them so much.'

'What's your trade on it?' The woman looked amused, ready to bargain.

'Are you a dealer?' Alison got a bit fed up with the knowing general public who were always pretending to be trade.

'No. I'm a poor painter, but I need a Persian plate in my life.' The woman grinned winningly, and Alison noticed that she was wearing exactly the same sort of earring as Frankie's labrys.

'That's odd,' said Alison without thinking. 'It's strange because my partner turned up this morning wearing an earring exactly like yours. . .'

The woman laughed, 'It's not strange at all. Frankie, you mean? She's your partner?'

Alison nodded hazily.

'I gave her it. I'm Jay. Hi.' And the woman held out her hand across the stall to say hello.

Bemused, her mind trying to adapt to this huge new piece of information about Frankie's love-life, Alison shook hands, and smiled nervously, thinking my God, Frankie's turned gay. It must be a lesbian earring – a message.

Jay appeared unperturbed, and looked at the plate again. 'How about this? Can we do a deal?'

Alison examined the price label, dazed by her new discovery, her head filled with pictures of the night with Gareth, all confused, swilling wildly. 'You can have it for twenty,' she told Frankie's lover, and Jay took it, pleased, and paid with four fivers.

Frankie returned with a bag full of food, and looked surprised and a little nervous when she saw Jay standing by the stall.

'Hi,' said Jay, very relaxed. 'I just bought your Persian plate.'

'Oh yes . . .' Occasionally Frankie seemed to revert to being a gawky Glasgow schoolgirl. 'Very nice. It will look good with your stuff.' She walked behind the stall to put down the bag, and eyed Alison anxiously, obviously torn by conflicting loyalties. Alison obviously knew that she had gone over to the other side, but the experience was so new and unexpected for Frankie that all she could think of to say was, 'For God's sake let's have a drink!'

'What? Here? In these sacred portals?' Jay was amused.

Frankie took out two plastic mugs and a bottle of sparkling wine and struggled with its cork underneath the table. 'Cough when it pops,' she hissed, 'or we'll be asked to leave.' She grimaced, and a fountain of white fizz spurted suggestively above the Union Jack.

'Yippee!' whispered Jay, and Alison caught the plume of fizz as best she could, whilst trying not to catch the attention of the entire hall, which was no easy task with two such rivetingly unusual people as Frankie and Jay standing there. They drank, and ate sandwiches and pickled eggs.

'Cheers,' Frankie held up her last inch of wine. 'Fizziness for business! Let's drink to that.'

Jay picked up her plate. 'I must go,' she said. She nodded to Alison. 'Nice to meet you; I'll see you again no doubt. I'll pick you up same as yesterday, Frankie.'

Frankie nodded dizzily. 'See you,' she giggled a little hysterically.

They both watched Jay swing through the floral frocks and three-piece suits, then came a rush of post-prandial customers, all jolly and well-disposed to buying from two such splended women. An old ex-military man quite fell in love with Frankie, and almost chased her round the stall, muttering incoherently: 'By God, you're a fine creature!'

He was persuaded to try his charms elsewhere, and the two birds, exhausted from their various rigours, diurnal and nocturnal, drooped somewhat. At last Alison felt able to ask, 'When did it all happen?'

'With Jay?'

'Yes.'

'Very suddenly, after her party. She rang me up and came over . . . . I was still in a helluva state after that golfer guy, and she was terribly sympathetic, and it just happened. Nobody was more surprised than I was, but it all seemed warm and natural. She's a wonderful person . . .'

'I can see she's very strong; she appeares amazingly straightforward.'

'She is. She quite likes to shock people, though.'

Alison was still taken aback; it put Frankie in a whole new light. Would she, she wondered nervously, now start fancying herself as a sexual object?

'I was just very surprised when she said who she was, but suddenly it all fell into place – your secrecy and the suddenness and everything . . .'

'I know,' said Frankie. 'It takes a bit of getting used to. She's trying to make me stop shaving my legs.' She sounded momentarily morose. 'And the earring is a sort of badge.'

'And I thought you were one of the last great heterosexuals . . .'

Frankie grinned bashfully. 'S'funny, isn't it? So did I.'

They meditated for a minute or so on the unexpectedness of life.

'It has obvious bonuses,' Frankie smiled shyly.

'Such as?'

'Well, you don't need to worry about getting pregnant, and women can always do it, there's not all the engineering feats, you know . . .'

Alison hugged her friend. 'You are such a nutter. I don't know what I'd do without you.'

Frankie looked pleased. 'Am I forgiven then?'

'For what?'

'For going gay?'

'Forgive you? Don't be mad. There's nothing to forgive. You're obviously still Frankie, the only difference is that you've widened your experience a bit. It won't affect us will it? You aren't going to become a militant lesbian, I hope?'

'Active yes, militant no. Anyway, I'm bi-sexual, not lesbian.'

Alison tried to look worldly-wise. 'Of course.'

'You get twice as much fun that way,' mused Frankie sleepily. 'If you like both sexes.'

'One's enough for me,' said Alison, tranced.

'Aye,' said Frankie. 'But you can change overnight, like me. There was a time when you were perfectly contented with only one man, and now that's changed.'

Alison felt suddenly afraid. Oh God, she thought. What have I done? I've got two, but I want one. Where will it all end?

They half-dozed, until they were rudely woken by a gigantic lady who wanted to buy a silver thimble, and took almost half an hour to make up her mind which of their several thimbles she most desired.

At five they parted blearily to meet their respective lovers. Frankie waved her index finger at Alison, 'Make sure you get some sleep now, or you'll be hopeless on the stall tomorrow.'

Despite their exhaustion, the stall had done well, and the horsicle had been sold for a great price to a renowned dealer from Chipping Norton. Alison was very pleased with herself by the time Gareth arrived to pick her up. He was relaxed in red sweatshirt and jeans, and looked more handsome than ever, dusky form a day's sun. He greeted her a little shyly, obviously glad to see her, and they headed once more for the cottage on the hill.

They lay on a rug in the small garden watching occasional rabbits hop out of the shrubbery, and listening to birdsong.

'Does the fair finish at five tomorrow?' asked Gareth.

'Yes. Then it's pack up and home. How about you?'

'I said I'd be back not too late tomorrow evening.'

They lay side by side in silence, thinking the same depressing thoughts.

'What is going to happen in London?' Gareth looked at her. 'Can we meet?'

The thought that this was the only night they had together was painful; Alison did not want to go home, to meet Philip, to meet reality. All of a sudden this man had become her reality.

'I don't know,' she said dully.

He hugged her, and their senses swam, and like surf-riders following the surge of a great wave, they abandoned themselves into the roaring crescendo of the tearing, growing, glorious engulfing of the element.

Afterwards, Gareth kissed her face and whispered: 'I am going to miss you.'

'Don't say it,' Alison closed his beloved mouth with her fingers, and wept.

'Come on,' he said at last, comforting her. 'This is madness. Let's not destroy what time we do have together. We still have fourteen hours. It's a longer furlough than some soldiers in the war were given.' He stood up and reached for her hand. 'Come and eat. I've cooked a cassoulet.'

She was impressed, it was good food, with strange

original seasonings; he had put apple with the meat, and chervil. Enjoying his cooking, she told him about Frankie, and her unexpected discovery of Jay.

'Were you shocked?' he asked. 'I must say I'm quite surprised; I thought she gave quite a strong female feedback – maybe I'm losing my touch.'

'I can assure you that you're not. . . . No, I wasn't shocked, just taken aback, bewildered that she had gone so secretive all of a sudden – usually she is unbelievably open about sex, lovers and so forth.'

'Maybe it will pass. People sometimes try it for reasons of loneliness, or just for the hell of it. Or maybe she has found her métier after all these years in the wilderness. You were saying she'd not had a lot of joy.'

'She certainly seems very keen on this artist.'

'Lucky her. I hope she enjoys it for a good long time. I don't care what people do, whether they go to bed with their own sex, cats, dogs, whatever, as long as they are happy and don't cause pain.'

Alison agreed, but the bit about causing pain was worrying. What about Philip? Could she see Gareth in town? It all seemed very complicated.

'Penny for them?' Gareth caught her unease.

She shrugged, 'Thoughts, responsibilities, but they come a little late. Let's go to bed.'

He smiled, drained his glass, and came to embrace her. 'I can hardly believe this is happening. Last night was a new experience for me; I've never felt quite as I did.'

'Nor me.' They looked at each other for a long time, then amalgamated their yearning bodies into a straining creature whose only desire was to give all pleasure possible to its two halves. His half knew without telling what it was she needed and wanted, as did her half, which anticipated his innermost needs and desires before he could have whispered them to himself. It was bliss, and for a while they inhabited another country, a place where only they could speak the language, but the gift of tongues was with them, and they understood each other like a king and queen who had inherited a kingdom together, a golden kingdom, where no other world obtruded, nor shadows dulled the gold.

'God help me, Alison, but I love you,' said Gareth when they rested.

'And I love you,' she said, then wept because it was forbidden and impossible.

Chapter Sixteen

Mark and Jo were watching television when Alison came home, and had not yet eaten. Blindly, annoyed with them for not having seen to themselves – it was almost nine o'clock – she scrabbled in the fridge, maternal guilt automatically urging her to feed her enormous young. She was dazed, tired beyond speech, and highly emotional, having wept nearly all the way home.

She had said goodbye to Gareth at lunchtime: he had come to the fair and they had spent a last half-hour with each other beside the river, happy just to sit together, saying little; it had all been said earlier in that other language in the other country. She had had to leave, to go back to the stall. Aching, they had hugged and he had said: 'I'll see you in the shop, or you can phone me during school hours. Don't let it be too long, please.'

And he had gone away, walking alone by the river, her man, her beloved.

'Are you going to see him in London?' Frankie had asked.

'Don't ask. I just don't know.'

'Oh Alison. You've got it bad, haven't you?'

Alison could hardly see for tears.

'I did try to warn you. I knew it would be like this.'

'I know, I know. It had to happen, it has happened. I'll just have to work it out somehow. It's so painful.'

'Love always is.' Frankie, worried, wanted to make Alison laugh. 'When does The Great White Grope come home?'

'Tomorrow.'

'Oh Lord.'

'My Lord and master. How about you? How's your heart?'

'I'm OK. She's charming, fascinating. I'm not crying. I'm unattached.'

'Don't rub it in.'

Mark looked up when Alison came in; 'How did it go Ma?'

'Fantastic. We brought very little back; it was the best ever.'

'Great. Did you meet nice people?'

She nodded, and yearned to speak of Gareth. 'One very nice guy, I think you met him once – at Richmond – he bought the Ashanti doll . . .'

'Furry fellow?' Mark's mouth was full.

'Yes. He turned up, and we ate together, it made it very pleasant.'

Jo was very quiet, almost unresponsive. 'I'm not hungry,' she eyed the bacon and eggs with distaste.

'I'll eat yours . . .' Mark reached for her plate.

'NO!' she roared, red with fury. 'I'll eat some. Leave it, you sod!'

Mark whisked away a rasher of bacon, and ate it in a gulp like a pelican swallowing a fish. Jo, livid, clouted him. Alison reached for Mark with a wooden spoon and prevented further violence. Jo pushed away her chair, and rushed from the table weeping.

'What on earth has got into her?' Bemused, Alison

looked at the slammed door.

'She has been officially asked to leave off trying to play cricket and football. The boys signed a petition saying they didn't want girls – and she was the only one – in their teams any more.'

'Poor thing.'

Mark munched cheerfully. 'She had it coming to her; she was honestly getting to be unbearable.'

'Still, public failure hurts.'

'She'll get over it. She's very popular.'

Wearily, her family cogs engaged and grinding into motion, Alison rose, intending to try to assuage her daughter's emotional outburst.

Mark pointed to the table with his knife. 'Sit!' he said like the famous female dog-tamer on television. 'Leave her, she'll come back after a good cry.'

Relieved that she might not at this moment be forced to go through the motions of motherhood, Alison gratefully did as instructed.

'You look shattered, Ma. Shall I fetch you a drink?'

Pleased at this adult behaviour, she acquiesced. Mark surveyed the drinks cupboard. 'What do you fancy?'

'Vodka and tonic.' Half asleep, she watched him pour, and hand her a glass.

'Thanks, my son, this is civilised.'

'Can I have one? I've swotted all day since midday.'

'OK. Sherry, a little.'

'Thanks, Ma.' He poured himself an obediently small glass and sat to drink at the table.

'How is the work? The first exam is pretty soon, isn't it?'

'Three weeks.' He sipped. 'OK, I think. I've done a lot. I think at least I'll get them all, except for maths, that's a bit dodgy.' He shrugged. 'I hate all this studying. It's so boring and hard.'

'Poor you. It will soon be over; then France.'

'Yeah,' Mark smiled at the thought. 'It should be super.'

Alison was relaxing, pleased to be here with her son. The dog was delighted that mother had come home, and stood at her knee, gazing up at her, his spotted head sentimentally lying on her knee.

Alison went to top up her glass. Watching her Mark asked if he could have more sherry. She frowned, it made her feel insecure that he wanted more. She shook her head.

'Aw, come on, Ma. You're having more.'

'I'm old and jaded and need it.'

'I'm getting older and jadeder and need it too. I've been very good.'

'No.' Firmly she chucked the empty vodka bottle into the bin. There was an alarming clink; she peered under the lid, and was shocked to see there three empty wine bottles, and a Martini bottle.

'Heavens, are these your empties?'

He nodded, blushing a little.

'How many of you?'

He was embarrassed. 'One or two, last night. You said we could.'

'I didn't know you would be drinking.'

'Ma, for goodness' sake, I'm sixteen, and perfectly responsible.'

'I hope so. That's a lot of booze.' It was bewildering sometimes, the speed with which each hurdle of adult-hood was leapt and left behind.

Lord, she was tired; she had just sat down again, when there was a screech from Jo upstairs, loud and urgent: 'Muuum! Come!'

Alarmed, Alison put down her glass and leapt upstairs. She found Jo in her bedroom, sitting on her bed tearful.

'What is it, love?'

Jo mumbled something she couldn't hear.

'Say it again.'

'My effing periods have started.' The girl was obviously not at all pleased to have become a woman at last.

'That's great,' Alison tried to sound bright and encouraging. 'You're an adult human being, my darling. In France they call it your ménarche, and in the States they have parties to celebrate.' She went to sit by her daughter on the bed and gave her a hug. Jo shrugged her off.

'I hate it. It's horrible and messy,' she started to cry in earnest, 'and I've got an agony tum.'

'Oh honey, I'm sorry. You'll get used to it. Have you found the towels we put in the cupboard?' She had shopped in preparation for this event months ago, when the first of Jo's friends had started to bleed.

'Yes,' said Jo grumpily.

'Tell you what,' said Alison. 'Have a quick bath, that will help the tum, and I'll give you a pill for it, then get into bed. I'll bring up a hot-water bottle.'

'I still think it's horrible. I don't want to be a grown-up.'

Alison felt a little hysterical; she knew exactly what the girl meant. She managed not to laugh, and went to turn on the bath. Back in the kitchen she told Mark what had happened.

'Poor kid,' he said. 'I'm glad I'm not a girl. But it goes to show that they were right to chuck her out. You can't have periods and play cricket.'

'Some women do.'

'Freaks more like,' he said darkly. 'But it explains all her bad temper . . .'

They sat together while Jo bathed – she had locked

the door and obviously did not want company. Alison finished her drink and opened a new bottle.

'You're fairly piling into that,' said Mark, watching her.

'I have had a very gruelling weekend.'

'Please can I have another? To celebrate my little sister's womanhood?' He smiled his most winning smile.

'OK.' She was too tired to resist.

'Thanks, Ma.' He hugged her. 'Are you all right?'

'Yes, why?' she snapped.

He shrugged. 'I dunno. You just seem kind of jumpy. Are you worried about Dad coming back?'

She was silent, moved by his percipience. 'Maybe, a little.' She drank, and felt very sad.

'Susan's parents split up last year.' He wasn't going to give up.

'Was it awful?'

He nodded. 'Ghastly.'

'What happened?'

He shrugged. 'The usual. They just seemed to hate each other and be bored and miserable all the time.'

'Have they got other people?'

'The father has, somebody from his work he'd been screwing for years.'

Alison tried not to wince at her baby's sophistication. 'And the mother?'

'She's pretty lonely and bitter. It's hard for Susan as she's the youngest. The others have all left home.'

Jo summoned Alison, and she hurriedly made a hot-water bottle and cocoa with cinnamon, the traditional family comforter.

'I'd better go up. It's been good to talk. You're a lovely boy.' She brushed his hair fondly with her free hand. Embarrassed, he dodged, but grinned and nodded. 'I'll have a shower. Goodnight.'

Jo was in bed in her nightie.

'How is it?'

'A bit better; the pill helped.'

Alison gave her the hot-water bottle and cocoa, and Jo sipped. 'Thanks, Ma.' She looked up. 'Could you fetch my teddy please?' She tried to look serious, but a smile escaped her when the ageing teddy in his tattered Arsenal strip was laid in her arms.

'You just wait,' said Alison gently. 'One of these days it will be a baby, then you will be glad you are a woman.'

'Yuck.' Jo grimaced. 'Never.' She turned her face away. 'Anyway, the world won't survive that long. We'll all be dead, or sterile. Mark told me; he was reading me bits from that ghastly book about Hiroshima.'

Deeply moved, Alison found it hard to talk sense. The girl's fears were so close to her own. She soothed her brow, sat with her, and listened to her tears and sighs with a heavy heart; it was tragic that the world seemed to hold so little promise for its youngsters – just the inevitability of death, possible holocaust or purposeless unemployment. She felt a great emptiness, and comforted her daughter as best she could, whilst feeling hysterically inadequate. At last Jo seemed ready for sleep.

'Shall I put the light out?'

'Yes.' Her voice was very small girlish. 'Mum?'

'Yes?'

'I love you.'

Alison crossed the darkened room and bent to kiss her newly matured daughter. 'I love you too. Goodnight, sleep tight.'

'Night night Ma.'

Alone in the kitchen she burst into tears. It was all

overwhelming, her mother's death, her father, the loathsome unease with Philip, Gareth, her impossible love for him, and now this breathtakingly speedy growing-up of her children, who still seemed so young and needy, although Mark was almost a man, and Jo was technically physically mature, fit to reproduce, whether she liked it or not. She sobbed alone, watched by the very worried dog, until Mark, newly-showered, in blue underpants and tee-shirt, found her weeping.

'What's wrong, Ma?'

'Everything. It's all too much.'

'Oh Ma.' He came to her, and subliminally she noticed his strong young legs, hairy like an adult's. He hugged her, he could comfort like a man too.

She cried on his chest, and sniffed. 'I'm tired, and a bit emotional. I'm sorry.'

He rocked her. 'Don't be sorry. It happens. Is Jo OK?'

'Yes. She's asleep with her teddy.'

He chuckled. 'She's a wondrous nutter. I can't think who she takes after.'

Chapter Seventeen

Philip's ivory tower, as Alison tended to call it, was at the top of the Salveson house; originally a dark attic bedroom, he had put large roof-lights in, and the gaunt white room now contained little more than a large pine plan chest, a full-sized drawing-board, a bookcase, two guns on the wall and a wooden decoy duck, elegant and decorative. The guns were his hunting guns; one, old and cherished, he had inherited from his father; the other he had bought for himself a few years ago as a reward for gaining an important commission to design a vast shopping complex on the outskirts of North London. He sat at his drawing table now, struggling with a tricky problem on the Hong Kong scheme. The clients had changed the brief when he was over there, and it had become a matter of finding some devious method of fitting too many things into slightly too small a space. The firm, of which Philip was the senior partner, had passed the pre-qualifying section of the competition, which put them into a short list of eight firms competing for the job.

Eight of the office staff had been employed on the project for three months, and it had already cost the firm well over twenty-five thousand pounds to get thus far. He was weary. He looked at his watch, maybe he should knock off and relax; it was quite late. He had intended not to work tonight, and had suggested to Alison that they go out and do something together – eat, or see a show – but he had forgotten that she had a late-night fair at Chelsea Town Hall, and wouldn't be back before ten-thirty. She had not been pleased that he had forgotten; she had snarled that it had been marked on the kitchen diary for weeks, and stormed off. He should have looked, but she had seemed so wound up and worn-out after her big business at the weekend that he hadn't imagined she could possibly want to do another so soon. Ever since he had come home she had been running round like a madwoman, grimly muttering 'I must get new stock,' and going out very early to buy at street markets. He could, he supposed, go over and help her pack up, but she always made him feel that he was in the way. Anyway Frankie was generally there to give her a hand. He stood up, put down his fine line Rapidograph pen and stretched. Maybe there was a film on at the local, or something decent on the box. He wandered downstairs past Mark's room, and saw that the boy was bent over his books.

'How is it going, my son?'

Mark looked up tiredly. 'I've got brain-ache. It's just very bloody boring.'

'Keep at it, not long now.'

'It seems endless.'

'I know it's hard, but you'll be glad you worked so hard when you get the results.'

Mark looked dubious. 'It just seems so utterly pointless; I keep meeting older guys who left school last year and can't get jobs, and even graduates. Why bother to get exams if it leads to unemployment?'

'The economy is looking up; it won't always be like this, I'm positive.'

Mark yawned, stretching. 'I hope you are right.'

Downstairs, Jo, oblivious to the world, surrounded by a vast patchwork of reds and browns, didn't even react when Philip came in. He felt quite hurt.

'Hello, love, that looks impressive. What's it for?'

'Mum.'

'Is it for a bed?'

Jo nodded, carefully clipping six-inch squares of cotton. Philip uneasily imagined the flaming riot of colour in his and Alison's tranquilly pale bedroom. Alison's interior decorating was going too far if this was intended for that particular sanctuary.

'Which bed?' he asked dubiously.

'In the spare room.'

'Ah.' Alison's folly – quite a pleasant folly, womb-like in colour, warm and containing – but he had been shocked. She hadn't said a word, and he had suddenly seen it one day because the door had been left open. He had felt a great confusion of emotions, sort of desecrated artistically, and hurt that he had not been consulted. He paused, trying to examine exactly how he had felt; there had been an alarming feeling of infiltration as well; he had not liked that. He had said very little, there seemed no point. The deed was done, it wasn't like planning permission with buildings, where you could demolish a construction if it was put up without a by-your-leave. Difficult, and certainly not democratic.

He wandered across the sitting-room and looked at the local paper.

'Jo?' The girl – now his little woman, he was moved to recall – squinted up at him. (It was time she did something about that hair, he must talk to Alison about it, get the child seen to.)

'Have you seen *Local Hero*? It's on at the ABC.'

'Yeah.' She resumed her cutting and stitching.

'Do you fancy seeing it again?'

'Nuh. I want to finish this.'

He shrugged; she was her father's child, obsessed with what she was doing, an artist predestined, he supposed. It was probably a good thing. The dog came over to greet him, stretching lethargically.

'Take the dog for a walk,' said Jo, kneeling back. 'He needs it badly.'

The dog had heard the magic word; his ears pricked up, and in a moment he had run out of the room, and returned dragging his chain lead in his mouth, staring appealingly up at Philip. He dropped the lead at his master's reluctant feet and barked.

'Go on, Dad,' Jo had dropped her head back to her patchwork. 'You'll enjoy it if you do.'

It was a sunny night, the laburnum outside was in full bloom. Philip eyed the dog dubiously: he would much prefer to go to a film. The dog barked again, tempting, cajoling; Philip relented, and went to get his jacket amid barks and athletic leaps of joy.

'OK, Pirate, you win,' he told him, and bent to fix the chain round the animal's straining neck.

He walked along Queensway, pulled almost off his feet by the beast, who had obviously not been out for days, and crossed the Bayswater Road into Hyde Park, where, once they had walked some way up the Broad Walk, he let the hound off the leash. In an instant the dog had almost disappeared in the direction of the Round Pond. Philip was pleased that he had come out with the animal; they gave you such feedback, and by God at the moment he was in need of feedback. He smiled sardonically when he remembered his bad temper in the office today: that had been feedback all right – but with a vengeance – the American girl Laura phoning again. He had obviously left an almost indelible impression on her, but today he had roared down the phone at her, almost rabid with fury.

'Do not pursue me to home and office! Leave me alone! I have a wife and family!' And he had slammed down the phone, sweating, trembling with rage. She was a super girl, but one had to be practical in these matters. Enough was enough.

He walked the circuit of the Round Pond, melancholic with the pleasure it gave him to watch the birds squawking, swimming with their scurrying fledgelings. There were dozens of dogs, large and small, as purely bred as you could find – Afghans, red setters, Pomeranians, the lot – and there was a glorious variety of mongrels of many colours and dimensions. He breathed deeply, relaxing, pleased to have re-discovered one of London's basic pleasures. When they had first bought their house they had said they would come often to the park, and when the children were small Alison had certainly done her share of dragging them there so they could walk the dog and sail their boats. Jo, he wryly remembered, had always insisted on having a boat as well as Mark. But nowadays they seemed almost to have forgotten that the park existed, it always felt like such an effort to go, even though it took barely ten minutes to walk there. He sat on a bench, lazily throwing a stick for Pirate to fetch, and watched a woman take a tame duck out of a basket, and lovingly set the bird in the water.

He blushed as he remembered the phone-call, it was damned embarrassing really, because Mary had been in his office throughout the exchange. She had discreetly pretended not to be listening, but obviously she had heard it all; he had been both alarmed and furious.

Later, he had instructed her never on pain of death to allow that particular American through to him again. 'She's a bit disturbed . . .' he had explained vaguely, but by God Mary had looked at him in a very knowing manner. What was it she had said? 'I can understand how she feels.' Then she had gone scarlet, like a pillar-box, no, that wasn't fair, it had been an attractively rosy flush, quite erotic in fact.

A King Charles spaniel, brown and white, well-plumed, sauntered up and sniffed ecstatically at Pirate's hindquarters. Philip smiled wanly, then wondered if it might by some strange coincidence be Mary's dog; she was always talking about it. Tinkerbell or something she called it – she didn't live that far away. There was no sign of the curvaceous Mary however, he would have to do without company this evening. Alison would probably be speechless with exhaustion when she got home, and, if the last few days were anything to go by, she would not be feeling randy either. He sighed; perhaps the two of them should try to get away for a few days, to try and get to know each other again.

The pain of Gareth's nine-day silence after the weekend in Bath had been almost unbearable; they had made no proper arrangement to contact each other, and though Alison knew that she could pick up the telephone any time, woman-like, she wanted him to make the move, illogical though she knew it to be. She longed for his voice, his touch, the reassurance that it had really happened, that they had shared that tenderness and closeness. He remained inexorably in her thoughts, disturbing her beyond belief, but most of all she yearned for some confirmation. When he did at last suddenly appear on Tuesday morning in the shop, she thought her heart had stopped beating, and gazed at him open-mouthed.

He closed the door and stretched up to stop the old-fashioned bell from tinkling. 'Hello there,' he said quietly and smiled his shy innard-churner of a smile. 'I had to come.' They stared at each other, and it was the same. She gasped a little, 'I'm so glad to see you. Come into the back shop.' He followed her, and they collapsed wordlessly into each other's arms. She sobbed slightly, then laughed.

'How are you?' She touched his face, hardly able to believe that he was here at last.

He looked down at her, fondling her hair and neck. 'Bad,' he shook his head. She watched him anxiously. 'Very bloody bad. I thought going to bed with you might cure me, but it didn't. It's worse; I missed you unutterably.'

'And me you. I just longed for some word . . .'

'I got very black; I failed the Bristol job. The usual story – short-listed, hopes raised for days, a second interview – then Friday evening zonk. No deal.'

'I wanted to know . . .'

'I know.' He sat down on one of the two wooden upright chairs they kept for their own use. 'But I knew you would be fraught, with your husband coming home and all that, and I've been busy sending out my book-catalogues and restocking.'

'Don't tell me you were not going to get in touch?' She was chilled at the thought. Gareth didn't answer for a moment, but reached for her, pulled her to him, and buried his dark busy head in her warm middle. 'Oh Alison . . .' he moaned. 'I want you like I've never wanted anybody, but I feel I'm bad news for you. I'm not even a going concern as a man at the moment, living on the dole and my skinny wits.'

She fondled his head, and was appalled to be summoned back to reality by the shop bell. 'Wait,' she whispered, and saw him lean back with closed sorrowful eyes as she went to look. To her surprise and horror, it was Mark. He grinned, then caught sight of Gareth through the curtain, still not quite returned to earth.

'Hi, Ma . . . and hello again there . . .' he added, nodding shyly. Gareth opened his eyes, 'Oh hi . . . . We met didn't we? At the Richmond market?'

Mark nodded. 'And on the march.'

Alison, flustered, said 'Mark, this is Gareth. Gareth, my son Mark.'

The two males nodded uneasily to each other; Gareth stood up and came through to wander round the shop, picking up various items in a serendipitous manner, trying to look interested. Uneasily Alison was aware that he wasn't very convincing.

'I thought you would be in school.' She looked at Mark.

'It's all study periods now until the exams. I need some money; my pen has given out, and I need a couple of new files, I forgot to ask at breakfast.'

Alison wasn't at all surprised that he had forgotten. From all points of view, today's breakfast had been a stunningly bad-tempered affair, which had climaxed when the dog had been monumentally sick in the middle of the dawn altercations – an Albert Memorial of dogsick – She fetched her purse and rummaged. 'Here, will that do?'

He nodded, 'Thanks, Ma. See you tonight.' He waved, nodded to Gareth, and was gone. Gareth watched him.

'He's a lucky fellow, with you to go home to.'

'Do you think he saw?'

'I'm not sure . . . it was a little tense . . . he's a sensitive lad.'

'Oh God.' Alison shut her eyes.

'Alison that's why I didn't . . .'

She caught her breath and looked at him wildly. 'Gareth, it is too late. We are involved. I have broken my bond: we can't go back. The deed is done.'

She looked both beautiful and fearsome. He nodded and stepped towards her. 'I know.'

Alison retreated 'Not here, there are always people in and out.'

'When?'

'Frankie will be here soon . . . I can get out for half an hour . . .'

The doorbell interrupted them once more, and a not very tall, dark-haired man, neatly-built, artistic, in a dark leather jacket came in. He smiled at Alison.

'I was hoping to find Frankie,' he announced smiling, and though his voice was familiar, Alison didn't recognise him. The man spoke again: 'I thought Tuesday was one of her days in the shop.'

'It is. She'll be here any minute.'

He looked pleased. 'D'you mind if I wait? I'll have a browse.'

'Go ahead.' Then it clicked; she looked at him, he was a nice-looking fellow, not at all petite, she had imagined a troglodyte. As usual, Frankie had been exaggerating.

'Are you by any chance Anthony Brownstone?'

He turned from examining the big blue and white vase, surprised. 'Yes. How did you guess?'

'We did speak on the phone once.'

'Ah.' He nodded. Alison decided to make coffee while they all waited for Frankie; she wanted one badly. And, as so often happened at the shop, by the time Frankie had arrived, laden with dirty but interesting junk, there was a small party in progress. Anthony had once lived near Gareth's home town in Wales and soon they were roaring with laughter at the remembered exploits of the locals in a pub they had both frequented. Alison was glad to see Gareth so cheerful. Anthony said he liked the name 'Two Birds', and asked if it was Frankie's invention. Alison nodded.

'Why don't you have a shop sign made, like a pub sign? It would look very good hanging out there.'

'We have actually thought of it, we've just never got round to finding anybody to do it, and we weren't sure how much it would cost.'

'I could do you one.'

'I thought you only painted very small things?'

'Not only. I'm a detail painter, I do complicated sort of primitive-illustrative things. I'd love to do you a sign. I could do two birds with your heads, and the name, all very bright and decorative.'

'I'd have to be a sparrow and Frankie a peacock or parrot.'

Anthony looked excited and thoughtful. 'I'll do you a sketch.'

'What about money? I'd love a sign, but . . .'

'Don't vorry,' said Anthony, sounding like an old Polish dealer. 'I'll do you a beautiful sign, and ve'll do a good deal.'

'Yes . . .' Alison was a little dubious.

Anthony was looking at Frankie: 'How was my friend Jay?' he asked, and an ironic flash in his expression made Alison long to ask him more about the new development in Frankie's life. Frankie's hand went unthinkingly towards her labrys earring, then pulled away. 'Fine,' she mumbled, embarrassed. 'It was quite a weekend.'

'I can imagine,' Anthony turned to Alison: 'Did you meet Jay?'

She glanced at Frankie before answering: 'Yes. She seemed very confident. Strong.'

'She's certainly that. Very successful, obsessed with work. Ruthless in a way. A good painter.'

Frankie, anxious to change the subject, asked Gareth if he had heard the result of the interview.

He held his head and groaned. 'Don't. It hurts.'

'Oh, I'm sorry . . .'

'That makes two of us. Nobody wants my brilliant Welsh talents, dammit. Back to the dole queue, FIS and cheap instant coffee.' He laughed painfully, a sad-eyed clown. 'They say poverty is good for the soul, but it only seems to erode mine.'

'Are you doing many stalls?'

'One a week. I'm not very talented at it, but the books are beginning to sell quite well. I've got a new list going out at the moment.'

'Frankie,' Alison stood up. 'Will you be here for a while?'

'An hour or so.' She nodded.

'I'll be off.' Alison looked at Gareth, who also stood, ready to go. 'Shall we go to the pub?'

'Right.' He nodded to Frankie and Anthony. 'Good to meet you, Anthony. I hope to see your shop sign up soon – I don't think she's a sparrow, something much rarer than that.' He looked at Alison fondly, and Alison caught an expression of concern in Frankie's face.

'I'll get the right image, don't you worry.' Anthony assured her. 'The shop will become a tourist-attraction because of the splendour of the painting outside and the glorious creatures within.'

The large Lebanese restaurant had white linen tablecloths and exceedingly handsome and attentive black-haired waiters in crimson waistcoats.

'Shall we have the aubergine starter?' asked Philip, examining the huge menu. 'And the spiced beef to follow?'

Alison nodded as she took a fat black olive from the generous and colourful dish of undressed salad stuff in the centre of the table. Philip had announced that he had bought tickets for a film called *The Draughtsman's Contract*, and that they were going out to eat. 'I feel that we haven't really spoken to each other for weeks,' he said. 'Let's have a good night out.'

They talked, as they always did when they ate out together, in a self-congratulatory way of their children, of the beauty and intelligence they had unwittingly produced. The food was good, and Philip, confident about the Hong Kong job and therefore relaxed for a change, was touchingly pleased to be with Alison. His face had a youngness to it, a vulnerability which warmed her. As she watched his animation, his eagerness to regain lost ground, she felt once again torn between her two men, the smooth golden one, and the dark opposite, with his burning eyes and gentling hands.

Maybe it was possible to have them both: it seemed to her almost reasonable that she should want both a husband and a lover after all these years. After all, men had for generations succeeded in handling such dichotomies in their lives. Philip had a colleague who had lived for years with his wife, several children, his mistress, their child and the wife's young lover. It had been a huge Tolstoyan household, which had worked in its own unusual way. They had had their cakes and eaten them – until the mistress had got fed up and moved out, having decided that she needed her own domestic territory.

At lunchtime today, Alison had arranged with Gareth to meet tomorrow at her usual street-market, and then to go to his house together. She longed to be in bed with him again; the idyll in Bath seemed long ago. She became aware of Philip wiping his face and grimacing: 'Whew! Those chillies are hot!'

The handsomest waiter, with big moustaches, leaned over them. 'More wine, sair?'

Philip nodded: 'Same again please.' The waiter left them, and Philip smiled at Alison: 'What great thoughts are you thinking?' He reached for her hand. She let him take it listlessly, it felt strange with the memory of Gareth's touch so recently imprinted on her. She shivered.

'Nothing really . . . just lifestyles and marriage, things like that. I was actually thinking about the Hobbses and their strange household.'

Philip gulped wine. 'Mad, that was. He was a very stressed fellow – responsible for that army of people. I don't know how he kept sane. He's a lot better in the office now, smoother and more efficient.'

'Where is he living?'

'Mostly with the second family, but he sees the others quite often. Why, are you thinking of getting a young lover?'

Alison stared at him, 'I might be. How would you feel about that?'

'I'd shoot him,' said Philip simply; he smiled blandly, and got up to go for a pee.

When he was away the handsome waiter came to Alison. 'You have everything, Madame? Everything you want?'

'Yes, thank you,' she smiled, and he let her admire him, flirting outrageously. She pushed away her plate. 'More than everything. Too much really.' He grinned lazily, dark-eyed – his eyes were as dark as Gareth's.

Philip was back. 'Want a pudding, darling?'

'Just coffee.'

They were both in a mellow mood when they arrived

at the cinema. Philip was annoyed with himself; he had wanted to explain about that inopportune telephone call from the States, but somehow the moment had never seemed right. Maybe he could do it later. He was sure that the alienation which had so much intensified since Easter and the business of her mother's death, would evaporate if he explained that it was nothing and tried to reassure her. She had been very odd since he came home, and obviously deeply uneasy about something.

The film was a period piece with exceptionally beautiful camerawork. The story was of an architect, with dark curls rolling over his shoulders, who was commissioned to do drawings of the estate; there was much sex, and a strange running gag – which totally mystified Alison – of a statue which was in fact a real man. She hated the film, but Philip declared it to be brilliant. By the time they reached home they were shouting at each other. It seemed to Alison that Philip would simply not permit her to entertain an opinion that in any way differed to his.

'It was tedious meaningless rubbish!' she yelled. 'I loathed it. I didn't understand any of it, and I have no desire to unravel its inner meaning. I just wanted to get up and go I was so bored!'

'You cannot say these things,' said Philip. 'It was a brilliant, beautifully acted, beautifully constructed piece of work, with some of the finest camerawork you will ever find. A masterpiece of cinema! How can you not see? You have to bring some intelligence to work on a piece of visual machinery of that standard. I think we should go again. You obviously didn't watch it properly. It's worth seeing over and over, it was very densely textured – aesthetically and emotionally. Brilliant.'

'Dense, yes. Brilliant, no.' Alison's face and teeth were set. 'It was a wank from start to finish, camp wank of the first order.'

'Nonsense, darling. Listen, woman, the whole symbolism of the man who was summoned to perform both professionally and sexually was an image of . . .'

'Philip!' roared his little wife, eyes like flames. 'Stop it!' She put her hands over her ears. 'I don't want to be told what to think: I have a very strong opinion about the bloody film, and I refuse to waste another moment of energy on it. I beg to differ. Finito!'

She shouted the last word as they entered the house. Mark, pyjamaed and making himself a hot drink, looked up in alarm as they came into the kitchen.

'Hi, how was the film?'

'Terrific,' said the father.

'Shit!' hissed his mother.

Mark eyed them uneasily. Alison tried to calm herself, and went to make herself a cup of tea. 'How's the work?'

'Awful. I'm too tired to work properly, I'm going to bed. Goodnight.'

He left them, and Philip eyed Alison as she sipped tea, her back against the sink. 'It's that phone-call that's made you so angry, isn't it?'

She looked at him coldly. 'I don't think so. We are just seeing things differently, it can't be helped.'

'Please, can I tell you about it? I'd like to explain . . .'

Alison felt very angry, sickened. She shook her head, eyes closed. She didn't want to know. 'No. I don't care, I don't want to be told about your affairs or your might-have-been affairs, I simply do not care. Do what you must, but please don't expect me to be interested because I'm not.'

She rinsed out her empty cup. 'I'm going up to bed.' Philip watched silently as she bent to pick up the empty milk-bottles.

She went upstairs, passing the newly painted room. It looked cosily peaceful with Jo's new patchwork laid enticingly across the bed. Minutes later, Philip met her coming back down the stairs, carrying her nightie and toothbrush.

He looked at her bewilderedly: 'Aren't you coming to bed?'

'I'll sleep in the spare room. I'm too tired to wrangle any further, I need to be alone.'

She walked past him. 'Goodnight,' she said dully, and shut the door. He stared after her in dismay, shook his head frowning, then heavily continued his way up the stairs to the master bedroom.

Alone in the spare-room Alison remembered the previous night in bed with Philip. He had tried quite desperately to get a response from her, and had hugged and touched her, sobbing almost.

'Please darling, please . . . speak to me. Give me some sort of feedback. I hate this sort of cold war we are living.'

Her eyes had slid sideways, murky, half-closed. 'I can't think of anything to say. I just feel numb . . . empty . . .'

He had covered his face with his hands, and detachedly she had watched him. Then, moved by the suffering in his expression, she had patted him abstractedly as one might soothe a dog or child. He had wept and tried to smother his sorrows in the comfort of her body. She had responded, dutifully, caressing his pain away almost automatically, like a good nurse. He had made her come – as he usually could. Betrayed by years of habit she too had found relief in the meeting of their warm familiar bodies, but when she came she wept, yearning for Gareth. Her pity had turned from alarm to disgust. She felt territorially occupied by this desperate man who still hoped to gain what was already lost, and he, bewildered, believing that she had come back to him, misread her tears for ones of joy.

Frankie sat on her bed with Jay smoking a joint and listening to David Bowie singing 'Let's Dance'. Hamish the cat, large and black, purred beside them.

'Loud, loud purrs . . .' said Frankie dreamily. The purring and the singer's voice, aching, thrumming, filled the room, which appeared to be bathed in a golden glow; the small posy of marigolds by the bed burned bright, almost as though they were on fire.

'Orange flames . . .' she murmured, pointing at the magic happening. She knew they were pulsating, sending out the colour.

'So bright . . .' said Jay, she warmed her hands at the glowing blooms. 'Hot . . . loud cat . . .' she giggled, and rolled towards Frankie, touching her smooth underarm.

'Why?' she nuzzled her. 'Why do you want them smooth?'

Frankie found it terribly funny, and touched in turn Jay's unashamed, dark, curly underarm. 'A forest, little lost fingers . . .'

'I'm very hungry.' Jay sat up. Frankie got up and danced a little, the music filling her head, the flowers aflame. 'Dancers,' she said, laughing more – it did seem very funny – 'they shave. You need to have purity, a clean line – no pubes or underarms, dancers don't . . .'

'S' not right,' said Jay. 'Not natural. It's a male image of woman, not real.'

'I'm real . . .' Frankie danced and stretched, grinning, 'And ma underarm's got a bald heid . . .'

'I'm starving.'

'Honey. You want some honey?'

'I want honey, honey, yeah. And bread.'

Frankie disappeared and came back with two pieces of bread and honey.

'You can taste the flowers.'

'Everything tastes more intense with a joint.'

'Mmmm . . .'

'Frankie?'

'Uhuh?'

'Have you discarded my love-token already?'

Frankie felt her empty ear-lobe. 'I just took it off for a while . . .'

'I'll forgive you.'

'It's just . . . I actually don't like wearing a badge like that all the time; after all I'm not gay. Not always . . .'

'No?'

'No, I'm not even a lesbian; I'm me, I'm Frankie, I'm a person. It's just at the moment we . . . . We're friends.'

Jay massaged her feet. 'Lovers, darling.' She kissed Frankie's red-painted toes, one by one, smiling lazily. 'I thought I had totally converted you.'

'I'm exploring like . . .' Frankie tried to explain.

Jay's lips and fingers moved further up from toying with Frankie's decorative extremities. 'I'm exploring too.'

Frankie laughed. 'God, you're a terrible woman.'

'Speak for yourself.'

What Jay was going with her lips and fingers, as she gazed ironically up at Frankie's relaxed and splendid body, was something Frankie's mother would neither have approved of nor understood, yet it was so comforting, so friendly. The softness, the lack of appendage, and breasts which were not her own which she encountered when embracing another female body still came as a shock to her. It reminded her of being cuddled, years ago, by her Glaswegian Mammy, then all of a sudden it wasn't a bit like that. She swayed to Jay's rhythm, her fondling gentle rhythm, and absent-mindedly stroked the cat's smooth black fur, purring, rocking, soft, fondling.

'Nice pussy . . .' she said, and giggled again.

Chapter Eighteen

Alison woke at six next morning and was momentarily surprised, then relieved, to find herself alone in the spare room. She crept out of the house without saying goodbye to Philip and climbed sleepily into the car, wondering if Gareth was awake yet. It was grey and drizzly, and only took her a few minutes to drive over to the street market where she found her usual parking-place in a side-street with scrawled hoardings and rotting terraced houses, half of which were boarded up and had ghastly overflowing rubbish bags and cartons in front of them. She got out and locked the car, taking her big leather bag, and checked the purse she wore round her neck – stuffed with cash for speedy dealing. You had to be very alert, find your bargain, grab it, fix a price, pay, put it in the bag and move on to the next one. There were always a few black youths hanging around this area, and older white men – meths drinkers – and she felt a little nervous as she walked a couple of blocks to the actual Portobello Road. After all, she came here often – was a known figure, small, easy prey – and some of them must know that she carried a lot of cash, often, like today, a fat wad of notes. The black boy on the other side of the road was a Rasta, with dozens of tight black pigtails and a huge bulbous knitted beret, striped red, yellow, black and green. 'Black for my skin, green for the green grass, yellow for the sun, red for the Lord's red blood . . .' one of Mark's West Indian school-friends had told her.

Even though it was drizzling, there were all the usual stalls set up: she smiled at the couple who sold clothes heaped into a mountain on the ground, and at old Jimmy. Everything on his stall used to cost ten pence, but he had recently put the price up to twenty, he mostly sold clothes and rags, but occasionally she found worthwhile linen, silk, or embroidered things. She started grovelling, but didn't find anything she wanted on the first couple of tables; it took time to get warmed up, to get her eye in. She wandered further down the road and bought a tablecloth and a couple of bowls, and said hello to the tall Chelsea dealer, blond, gay and infinitely amusing, who always had a silver-topped cane and a fur collar.

'Morning, dear, any luck so far?'

'Not really.'

He smiled blandly, and showed her a couple of cloisonné vases. They were undamaged and very fine. She hissed as he winked and waved his cane at her. She hunted and bargained, filling her bag slowly, leaving the larger purchases to be collected later. Time was the important thing: you had to be decisive. Her faculties were at last pumping along full belt, and the drizzle had stopped; it was going to be a good day. She didn't see Gareth on her wanders, though she looked out for him. At eight o'clock, as they had planned, he was standing under the motorway bridge, in an area crammed with slightly superior stalls, where she nearly always did well. He looked at her across the crowded market place, and smiled. He walked over to her, and they leaned against each other, her forehead resting on his chin.

'Hello there.' He hugged her gently. It was very public here; and they were both known dealers. She drew away, catching sight of a red-haired lad behind a stall: he was watching her curiously. Confused, then alarmed, she turned away.

'What's wrong?'

'That boy on the coin stall, he's a friend of Mark's. He left school last year; he was watching us. He's been to the house . . . . Damn!'

'I'm sorry, we'll need to be better behaved, and not fall into each other's arms like that.' Gareth frowned.

'In public. In private is OK.'

'OK for today?'

She blushed, and nodded, glancing up at him.

'Have you done enough buying? Or do you want to do more?'

'I'd like to walk the full length just once more, for half an hour or so.'

'Me too. Let's meet in the caff,' he pointed just beyond the bridge, past a birdcage and a wardrobe rail of Afghan coats and army surplus.

They breakfasted in the workman's caff. When Alison and Frankie did this together, Frankie always used to amaze her by the size of the meal she could eat at this time of day, though the two or three hour battle to find junk did leave you feeling very hungry. Frankie would stuff herself with bacon and egg, chips, beans, tomatoes, mushrooms, the lot – and so did Gareth. 'I've got to fuel my boiler,' he said and smiled. She looked at him over her pale milky coffee, and found his eyes staring back.

'Do you want to do what I want to do?' he asked. She

nodded, and their feet said hello under the table. Swimming with love, she finished her coffee, and stood up to find her bulging bag. There was a queue of people at the counter, and she saw the red-head again. He nodded, almost imperceptibly, and she did likewise. Uneasily, she wondered if he and Mark ever spoke these days.

They drove to Gareth's house, Alison followed his bright yellow car with the anti-nuclear sticker, flashing to go left or right when he did, trying not to lose him at lights; it felt exciting and romantic. His home was small, but pleasant, with a sitting-room made from what were orginally two rooms, connecting through to a good kitchen. There was a pulley with clothes drying on it and well-tended plants everywhere. There were lively photos and prints – electric, visually strong – on the walls, the furniture was all stripped wood, mostly old and well-designed. There was a huge table at one end of the room, obviously used for everything, where a tortoiseshell cat sat impassively by a bowl of oranges; on the mantelpiece she was pleased to recognise the Ashanti doll.

Gareth shut the front door behind them, and looked at her. 'A poor place, but mine own. It's nothing like as splendid as your Ice Palace.'

'I like it. It's warm and friendly. That's nice.' She eyed the big dresser along the wall opposite the fireplace, full of china, obviously much-used.

'We stripped about ten layers of paint off it. Can I take your coat?'

There was a sudden awkwardness between them. They were here to make love by mutual consent, and, perhaps because it was on his territory, and not in the limbo of the cottage near Bath, it felt very serious, and once more almost frightening, a commitment. Alison slipped off her coat, and he went to hang it up.

'More coffee?'

She shook her head. 'We've played this scene before.'

He nodded, smiling with a quarter of one side of his mouth, and looked at her. 'I'm glad you came, I was afraid you'd funk it.'

'No. I wanted to, it has been too long.' She touched his furry wrist, he stroked her cheek with a crooked forefinger. 'Shall we go to bed?'

'Yes, please.'

'When do you have to be at the shop?'

'Not for three hours.'

Once more, but this time without a candle to light their way, Alison followed Gareth upstairs to a strange bed, and once more they gave each other indescribable joy, and were both moved beyond belief by the emotions that they felt. It was too happy, too good to possibly be evil: she felt innocent, guilt-free, filled only with enchantment that such a transfiguration of the everyday should have so unexpectedly occurred in her mundane life. She felt as though she had lived in the shade for years, and had suddenly discovered that it was possible to sit in the sun, and be warmed by its glow, that life did not have to be passed in the chill shadow. Gareth, with his warmth and fun, seemed like the sun, and Philip, cold, remote but beautiful, as detached as the pale full moon.

After lovemaking they lay together, he half-asleep, his arm sprawled across Alison's body. Tenderly, she watched his peaceful face, and stroked him.

'Gareth,' she whispered, kissing him, her lip like a falling petal. He woke and smiled and they gazed into the dizzying depths of each other's eyes; he caressed her face with the back of his hand, and she stopped his finger with her mouth. 'I need to go soon. Can I make some coffee?'

He sat up rubbing his eyes, and face, 'I haven't got anything drinkable, only ghastly brown dust I foolishly buy for the sake of economy.'

She climbed out of bed. 'I'll get some.'

He watched her dress, sick with love, and held his hand out to her. 'I don't want you to leave me . . .'

She bent for a long kiss, 'I'll be back. There's a threat.' He smiled lazily.

'You'd better.'

She left the door on the latch, and went through the broken garden gate, hanging on a single rusty hinge. He really needed a new gate but no doubt could not afford it.

She was making coffee when Gareth appeared, silently in socks and jeans. The sight of him dressed thus, chest exposed, made her reel, and she melted against his warmth, blindly exploring the texture of him with her cheek and mouth.

'Thanks for the coffee. What do I owe you?'

She shook her head. 'Another mug, another day.' She stared at him, as he took the coffee in both hands and sipped appreciatively.

'There's a letter for you.' She pointed to the dresser.

He took the envelope, opened it with a knife, and read it swiftly, frowning.

'Damn.' He crunched it up and flung it into a wastepaper basket, and looked wryly at Alison:

'Edinburgh. Not even an interview.' He shook his head. 'It's getting beyond a joke.' He sat at the table, and motioned her to do likewise.

'When do you have to go?'

'In about fifteen minutes.'

'Are you hungry? It's lunchtime.'

'I am quite.'

He rummaged in the fridge, and pulled out an end of

cheese, a couple of tomatoes, and brown bread. 'Help yourself.'

'What about your children?'

'It's not that bad, Alison. I've got to shop today anyway. Eat. I'm starving; you work me too hard, you snake charmer, you . . .'

She sighed. 'It was lovely.'

'More than lovely. You are a miracle.'

They ate, then he eyed her. 'When can I see you?'

She frowned. 'I don't know.' It was so complicated. 'I should really have been cleaning up all the stuff I bought this morning.'

'Me too. I usually come straight home and do that, wash, polish and repair. I've got a market tomorrow. I only hope I do better than I did last week. I only managed to pull in nineteen quid, and the stall cost ten. It was diabolical.'

'It happens to us all sometimes.'

'It happens to me all the time. I'm simply not very good at it; I'm OK on books, but the rest no.'

Alison had seen his books in the bedroom, which doubled as an office. There were hundreds of them on pine shelves he had cunningly constructed round the walls. Logically and intelligently collected, there were travel books, Edwardian, Victorian, modern, and books of anthropological interest, along with primitive art from all over the world. His catalogue was well-designed and organised. She was pleased and touched to see that he had used the Ashanti doll as a symbol on the cover – a simple but effective black and white graphic he had drawn himself.

'I hoped you would bring me luck,' he said.

Alison, struck by this evidence of his individuality and perseverance, had hugged him impulsively. 'I'm impressed.'

He had a brilliance when he talked about his books; he had shown her several of his favourites, handling them with fondness and excitement, pleased by their rarity or good writing.

'I love them, I love books. The passing on of ideas and information, it is a sort of magic,' he said now.

She looked at him. 'I'll never look at old books in the same way again. I'm impressed.'

'I just love them,' he grinned.

'I'm jealous.' She hugged him and he pulled away, 'Hey, I've got something to show you.' He got up and went to open one of the drawers in the wooden dresser, and pulled out the bundle of African necklaces she had seen in a local shop weeks before. He extracted the most beautiful one, with three flat squares of beads, black, dusky pink, and blue. She remembered it well. He handed it to her. 'Do you like that one?'

'I tried to buy it.'

'From drunk Willy?'

'Yes. He said a bearded fella had bought the stuff; I was quite put out.'

'Would you wear it?'

'Why yes . . .' She didn't quite know what he meant.

'Take it. I saw it, and thought of you at once. Please.' He thrust it at her. Suddenly shy, she said 'But you should sell it . . . it's a good one, they're quite pricey these days.'

'Alison.' He looked quite fierce. 'Please. I want you to have it, to have something from me. Here.' He bent gently over her and put the necklace round her neck. She was aware of him fiddling with the brass button clasp at the back, and felt his simple kiss beside it. He looked at her and smiled, proud, admiring. She felt strangely domestic and happy here in this plant-filled room, alone with the man she loved.

'You look beautiful. Go and look.'

She stood to view herself in the mirror above the mantelpiece, and saw him watching her fondly; she did indeed look beautiful. Their eyes met in the mirror, and she turned to hug him. 'Thank you. It is lovely. I'll wear it lots.'

'It won't raise suspicions?' He looked worried.

'No. I occasionally keep an odd piece of jewellery that I fancy.'

He glowed. She eyed the big clock on the wall. She wanted to stay, never to break the spell. 'What are you going to do this afternoon?'

'Write letters mostly, applying for jobs in Toronto, Philadelphia and Newcastle.'

She was chilled at the thought that he might have to go away. 'Would you really go so far?'

'Don't panic,' he stroked her. 'I've failed everything I've applied for so far; the odds are very long. I want to stay right here, preferably in bed with you, *cariad*.'

She felt safe in his arms; loved being called *cariad*. Had he called her 'darling' as Philip did, she could not have borne it, but *cariad* was part of their secret language. She never called him darling: somehow the word was part of her marriage, but its meaning had decayed, and she could not use it for Gareth, partly for fear of the same decay and pain setting in, and partly because it was Philip's word.

'Don't cry,' he looked down at her. 'Let's be positive.' He kissed away her tears, cupping her face in his hands. 'Same time next week?'

She nodded, and wrenched herself away.

When she got back to the shop Alison found Frankie in bouncy mood.

'Hi,' she greeted her. 'You look terrific, what have you done to yourself? And what a fabulous necklace . . .' She danced across the shop to examine it. 'It's great! Did you get it this morning? I couldn't be bothered to get up early. We had a crazed night. She's a nutter, that Jay. Can't stop talking sometimes. Where did you get the necklace, which stall? And I've just met a *Time Out* guy for a lunchtime drink, and I'm going to the opera – God help me – with wee Ant tonight. He begged me to go, said I needed the culture, but opera just makes me laugh . . . . Whew! And look! More suitors!' She flourished a large brown envelope breathlessly at Alison, who reeled back, laughing.

'One at a time, woman! You say Jay can't stop talking, what about you?'

'Oh sorry . . .' Frankie's hand went guiltily to her mouth. 'I'm a wee bittie hyped. We had some dope, and I've been a bit hyped all day . . .'

'So I see.'

'Where did you get the necklace? I'm envious.'

Alison momentarily wondered if she could fib to Frankie, but thought better of it: 'I was given it.'

'Oh oh. That's why you look so good. Gareth?'

'How do you always know?'

'When you've been getting it?'

'Yes.'

'It's obvious, you change from being a forty-watt bulb to a two hundred-watt one.' She sat down suddenly. 'I'm knackered. I can't keep up this hectic life.'

Frankie was wearing an Indian dress – the weather was getting to be quite warm now. She also had, Alison noticed, bare legs and sandals. She examined Frankie approvingly, but paused at the legs – they were disturbingly hairy. She frowned: 'Frankie?'

Blushing, Frankie hastily crossed her legs underneath her skirt.

'Are they awfully noticeable? Gorilla-like?'

'They are a bit.'

'I know. I feel really self-conscious; I usually shave my legs in summer.'

'What's the problem then?'

Frankie frowned. 'Jay. She's terribly bossy. It's a sort of philosophical point with her, an obsession. Be natural: females have hairy legs, ergo don't shave them, but I want to put my wellies on to cover up.'

'But she's utterly illogical; she dyes her hair like crazy. Anthony told me she really has almost black hair . . . That's not natural.'

'That's right.' Frankie considered. 'It's a sort of power mania: she seems to want to take me over and build me into a superdyke.' She grinned a little awkwardly.

'Do you want to be a superdyke? It's rather a quick change you're undergoing . . .'

'I dunno, really.' Frankie bit her lip. 'This guy at lunch was really nice, I rang him on the spur of the moment when I got a whole new batch of answers to my ad, and he said he was up this way, so we met for a drink.'

'So you haven't entirely gone over to the other side?'

Momentarily, Frankie looked like a guilty six-year-old, as she shook her head, and pretended to suck her thumb. Alison guffawed. 'Thank God for that! You are a creature of such extremes. I was quite upset that you had deserted me.'

'I hadn't really . . .'

'What? Earrings? Hairy legs? Not, I know, that all gay women go in for such things . . .'

'Well, Jay is unusual to say the least. She seems to

have about six lovers on the go, of all sexes and ages.'

'That would worry me sick, what about herpes and AIDS and things?'

'Only haemophiliac Haitian homosexuals get AIDS, but I was a bit worried. Imagine if all six of her lovers have another six lovers . . . you'd be in touch with an awful lot of . . .'

'Exactly.'

'Oh Gawd.' Frankie looked very worried. 'Do you think I'll be OK?'

'Probably. Jay seems pretty responsible.'

'I'm not so sure. She's been quite aggressive, wanting to manipulate me; but she's a great laugh. Apparently she and Anthony used to have a thing . . .'

'Lovers, you mean?'

Frankie nodded. 'She said he was fantastic in bed.'

'I quite believe it. I think he's a really nice man. You were awful about him. Gareth says he's almost his height, and *he's* not small.'

'Really?' said Frankie.

'Really,' said Alison, and blushed.

Frankie suddenly stood up. 'Listen can you lend me fifty p?'

'Sure.' Alison handed her the desired octagonal coin.

'I'll be back in a minute.' Alison watched, dazed, as Frankie tornadoed out of the shop, hair streaming, dress flapping. She was away for a few minutes, during which time Alison sold a pale man in a suit a couple of thick old-fashioned beer-mugs. Frankie soon returned, breathless, flourishing a small white paper bag.

'I've decided. I can't stand it!'

Puzzled, Alison watched her go into the back shop. Moments later she emerged grinning, her dress held high, pirouetting on smooth legs.

'Am I a lovely girl?'

Alison nodded approvingly. 'Much better. Are you going to keep on seeing Jay?'

Frankie frowned. 'She's very good fun, and I've learned a lot about myself, so probably yes I will, but not exclusively. As I said, this guy at lunch was nice, and it made me realise that I'd mebbe only momentarily been put off men.'

'Are you going to see him again?'

Frankie grinned. 'Nuh. He was married, obviously seeking an excuse to get out of it, I certainly don't want any of that. It's not worth it. But he was very attractive . . .'

Alison was quiet. She sighed a little, 'You're wiser than me.'

'I know that. I tried to tell you often enough. What are you going to do, you with your two handsome beasts?'

Alison moaned. 'I don't know . . .' She shut her eyes and frowned, then gazed at Frankie's newly smooth legs. 'I love him,' she said simply. 'I don't know what to do.' She met Frankie's anxious eyes tearfully.

'Has Philip any idea?'

'No.'

'What do you think would happen if he knew?'

'He says he'd shoot any lover of mine.'

Frankie's eyes grew very big. 'Would he?'

'He might. I hadn't really thought about it, but it was something he said when we ate out the other day. He said it as though it was a joke, only I didn't find it very funny.'

Frankie looked very serious. 'I don't see how you can possibly have two men and make it work.'

'But you just said Jay had lots of lovers.'

'Aye, but she's a free spirit. It's different. There are no children involved.'

'Don't,' said Alison unhappily. 'I think Mark may have picked up something the other day, when he saw me with Gareth.'

'Oh Allie . . .' Frankie's face was full of compassion. 'What are you doing to yourself?'

'Why can't I have them both? Some people can make it work. It seems perfectly reasonable to want a husband and a lover.'

'Not very many make it work.'

'No?' Hopefully.

'No.' Emphatically Glaswegian. 'Definitely not.'

'What am I going to do?'

'Knowing you, probably carry on as you are until the faeces hit the fan.'

'You put things so elegantly, Frankie.'

Frankie smiled smugly. 'I know.'

'Let me see your new letters.'

Frankie stretched across to hand her the big brown envelope. 'They actually came about a week ago, but I couldn't cope, not with Jay as well; I almost threw them away, but I heard my mother's voice saying "Dinna waste anything; you never know when it might come in useful." I don't think there are any real soul-mates there. Anyway, I don't feel desperate at the moment, because apart from the mind-blowingness of thinking I'd gone gay, I've had a good time. Anthony is a hoot – as a friend I mean – and he knows a great lot of people.'

Alison leafed through the nine letters which constituted the second batch. A man wrote in green ink that he was lonely and highly-sexed, but had a lot of love to give. The matter-of-fact simplicity with which he wrote about his frustrations, needs and hopes was very moving. She read it carefully: 'I bet you he's nice.'

Frankie nodded. 'Sad, isn't it? This one sounds nice as well, but terribly young, heartbreaking . . . all that stuff about being alone in London. It's more or less how I was feeling, he's a student, probably only twenty or so.'

'Young men make good lovers, so they say.'

'No, he needs stability that one, wants a Mammy.'

'Don't we all?'

'Aye,' sadly. 'Love and stability, that's what everyone wants.'

'But Frankie . . .'

Frankie looked up innocently from her reading. 'Yeah?'

'If you start meeting strangers again, you must be careful. Promise me?'

'I will, honest.'

'No getting steaming pissed and leaping into bed first meeting; it's dangerous, you could easily meet a real nutter, a hatchet man . . .'

Frankie frowned. 'Oh God . . . imagine if that Peter bloke had been really violent. Nobody would have known anything about it . . .' She looked worried, then glanced out of the window and jumped. 'Help! Hide the letters! Here comes Anthony. He said he'd pick me up here.'

Alison shoved the letters into the bulging envelope and stuffed it behind an embroidered cushion on the love-seat, as Frankie rose, beaming, to greet Anthony, who once again struck Alison as being unusually intelligent and amusing. They were both very interested when he produced a sketch for their proposed shop sign from a small dark green portfolio, the decorative, bright and witty sketch had clever suggestions of Alison's and Frankie's heads. They were both flattered and loved the fairy-tale quality of the birds. The shop name 'Two Birds' stood out bright and clear, in red.

'I'd like us to have it,' Alison was decisive. 'The only problem is how much?'

'Anthony pointed to the love-seat. 'How much are you selling that for? I have lusted after it ever since I first saw it; I need it to complete my life.'

'We're asking four-fifty for it . . .'

'How about a straight swap? No money to be exchanged? I'll make the sign painted on both sides – it ought to cost you at least five hundred pounds – after all I have three pictures in the Academy this year . . .'

'Honest?' said Frankie, impressed.

'Yes,' Anthony smiled. 'I usually do in fact.' He went to the love-seat and knelt to examine it closely, and Frankie froze as he touched the embroidered cushion – a beaded parrot.

'This is nice,' Anthony picked up the cushion, and to her horror, Frankie's hurriedly hidden envelope fell over, spilling out several of the would-be suitors' envelopes with box numbers on the corners. Blushing, she rushed to rescue the packet, praying that Anthony hadn't seen, but he looked at her wryly.

'That particular brown envelope looks heartbreakingly familiar . . .' He put the cushion back decisively, after examining the price-label.

'Right ladies.' He became bent and Polish, gesticulating, accented: 'I said I'd do you a good deal. I paint you ze sign. veather-proofed, superbly beautiful and unusual, like ze original two birds . . . and in return you giff me ze loff-seat? Hend-delivered of course, to mine house . . .'

His accent had slipped from Polish to German, but he was very entertaining. The two women looked at each other, considering: the love-seat had cost them three hundred pounds, but had been around for some time.

'I'd like us to have a sign,' said Alison.

Frankie nodded, 'Me too.' She had hidden the envelope away in the back shop by now, and was trying to recover her equilibrium. 'But how would we put it up?'

Anthony waved his hands, and wobbled his head from side to side in a very foreign gesture. He rubbed his forefinger along the side of his nose. 'For you my dears, anozzer suggestion.' He bent down and picked up the parrot cushion – it was a particularly fine piece of embroidery, priced cheaply at forty pounds. 'You giff me zees, I construct, mit ze help of a friend, a metal bracket, strong and safe. It's a standard job, they use it for pub signs all the time.' He smiled appealingly over the cushion, and the women looked at each other and nodded.

'How soon,' asked Alison, trying to be businesslike, 'could you paint it?'

'Two weeks, Madame.' Anthony touched his forelock.

'I had no idea you were so good, Anthony,' said Frankie enthusiastically.

He pulled himself up to his full height. 'I have many talents you have yet to discover my dear. One of these days you must come and view my atelier. We'll have an installation ceremony for the love-seat.'

'What if someone come in and wants to buy the love-seat tomorrow?' asked Alison. 'It's bound to happen . . .'

Anthony was adamant. 'You mustn't let them have it. Put a sold label on it, please.'

Alison and Anthony busied themselves briefly with pen and paper. Having signed his name, he stood with the cushion held across his chest. 'May I take it with me? It will brighten my bachelor grotto – or should I say grot? – no end.'

Frankie and Alison looked at each other and nodded. Anthony hugged the cushion, pleased.

'What are you going to see tonight?' asked Alison.

'Prokofiev's *The Gambler*, at the Coliseum.'

'Bet you it will make me laugh,' muttered Frankie. 'Opera always does.'

Anthony grinned. 'Come on, let's go. See you, Alison. Give your friend my regards, the Welshman, Gareth, was it? Nice man . . .'

'He is nice.' She blushed. 'He enjoyed meeting you.'

He went out of the door, clutching the cushion, and Frankie, wrapping a big black mohair cardigan, sprinkled with giant-size silver sequins round her shoulders, made to follow. As she left, she whispered to Alison 'Are my baldy legs all right? Not too pale and interesting?'

'They're fine. You look great. Have a good time.'

'Good *Time Out*, eh?' she grinned. 'Cheeribye, hen.' She waved, her wave turning into a grope, and left. Alison tidied the shop, dealt with a last pair of customers, put a 'Sold' sticker on the love-seat, and looked at the time. With a sinking heart she realised it was time to go home.

At the office, Philip signed a large batch of letters, beautifully and intelligently typed, and stretched, yawning.

'Well done, Mary, that lot is ready for the post. Is there anything else we have to do tonight?'

Mary stood up, delightful in a short pink frock. 'No, I think we're done. I'll just put them in their envelopes. I've addressed them.'

'For goodness' sake don't send Svensson's mail to Hong Kong, or vice versa.'

'You should know me better than that by now.'

'I do, Mary, I do.' Placatingly, he touched her

shoulder. 'I need a drink before returning to the fold. How about joining me?'

She flushed, 'I'd love to.'

'Have you tried the new wine bar? The Italian job with the bay trees outside?'

'No, it looks lovely.'

'Right. It's about time I took you out for a drink; I promised to after you were so helpful at Easter.'

Efficiently she sealed the last few envelopes, and looked up. 'How is your father-in-law? You said he was in a bad way.'

'I believe he's now very chirpy. Learning to drink and smoke aged eighty. She was a tough old bird, my ma-in-law. Very bossy.'

'He sounds sweet.'

'He is quite, a self-effacing old thing.'

She stood up and went to fetch her bag and jacket, a white cotton garment, rather classy. 'I'll just freshen up.'

'You look lovely as you are.' It amused Philip to make her blush; she did it so delightfully.

She disappeared, and came back into the office to pick up the letters. Philip watched her. 'What would I do without you, Mary?'

'You'd manage . . .' She eyed him.

Philip sniffed, 'Nice perfume, lily of the valley?'

'Diorissimo. My favourite.'

'Very nice too. Suits you.' He inhaled deeply and held open the door.

On the fourth Friday Alison and Gareth went to bed together after meeting up as usual at the early morning market. After they had made love, Gareth become very emotional and clasped her, his face agonised: 'I don't know if I can go on like this. I can't bear the times apart. I want us to be together, Alison, for always.'

Alison was silent. Part of her constantly longed for this as well, but what about her children, and Philip? How could she destroy their unit? She could not imagine living with her children and Gareth's children – all in this small place, with its broken gate and rotting window-panes – any more than she could imagine her children tolerating Gareth as a surrogate father. After all they already had Philip, and Gareth was poor and unemployed. It was impossible.'

'Alison?'

'Yes?'

'I mean it.'

'I know.' She sighed.

'Could you see yourself living with me?'

'Here alone, yes, or in the cottage, just the two of us, but what about all the others?'

He lay back, his eyes shut. 'It must be solvable. I must get a job soon.'

'I don't know.'

'You always say that. It's your refrain . . .'

'I'm sorry. I say it because it's true.'

Gareth was silent, watching her sadly. She looked at her watch: 'I'll have to go.'

He glowered. 'You always go; you always leave me.'

She touched him, soothing, 'I always come back, my love. I need you. I love you.'

It was a long and painful weekend: Alison could think of little other than Gareth, and his loneliness. Their next meeting seemed aeons away. Her period arrived early within minutes of saying goodbye to him, and she worried as to whether or not it would be over when they next went to bed. She longed simply to be with him, to comfort him, but knew that because of his children she dare not call him at the weekend – he was understandably adamant about that. Philip, still obsessively intent on reinstating himself as a family man, had insisted on arranging a series of dinner parties for Saturday nights, even volunteering to do most of the cooking. This time the Abrahams and Curtises were coming. Alison had not seen Phoebe or her husband, John, since the trip to Windsor. The Curtises were both architects, and all three couples had teenage children, and therefore much in common, but Alison felt alienated even from them, and let the guests and Philip do most of the talking. She was imprinted indelibly, it seemed, with Gareth, and did not want to be here at her own elegant dinner table, presided over by Philip, who was in excellent form, making everybody laugh, as he described how good that ghastly boring film had been. Alison was glad when both the Curtis man and Phoebe voiced their reservations about it, and she was activated once again to say how much she had hated it. Then, as usual, the subject of politics was raised, and Alison's heart sank as Philip filled the guests' glasses and laughingly said that his wife had become a CND zealot, and believe it or not, even wore a badge.

'You haven't, Alison, not really?' Peter Curtis looked at her in amused amazement. 'They are so naïve. We need a decent defence policy, it's pie in the sky to think if we withdraw our weapons that Russia and the Jews and Japanese will all be nice guys and say "Yes, yes, you're right and moral, and we'll all lay down our arms too." He gazed at her, grinning in disbelief.

'I have not become a zealot,' she said through gritted

teeth. 'I just feel a basic gut-reaction; to me nuclear arms are immoral. I have children, they are afraid of the future, they honestly don't believe they will have a future; and I would like my children's children to be born and to survive and not produce cancer-wrecked monsters.'

Phoebe shuddered. 'I don't think Alison is at all naïve, it's you men who are naïve. Think of Three Mile Island. They were fifteen minutes from meltdown, and that was a simple mechanical failure that could have destroyed half of central America, and rendered it uninhabitable for generations.'

Philip, John and the Curtis man shook their heads. 'Nonsense,' said John Abrahams. 'Nonsense, you're being a panic merchant. The men in control know what they are doing; they don't want conflagration any more than we do, but they know that we need proper armaments as a protection. That's why we haven't had a war in Europe for nearly forty years.'

Alison got up from the table, glad to leave the jeering and pontificating, and set about making coffee. Phoebe came to join her.

'Are you all right? You seemed very upset.'

'I'm all right, I just get sick of these arguments. Neither side will ever persuade the other, I think they are blind romantic fools, and that's what they think of us.'

Phoebe sighed. 'I am very glad that there's such a growing peace movement. I've joined up since I saw you last. I feel that same sort of gut thing, religious almost. Nuclear warfare destroys nature, and not just one generation, it destroys things genetically.' She cocked her head backwards to the dining-table, where Philip was holding forth: 'The American Civil War, that's where it all started. They used machine-guns, trenches and barbed-wire for the first time, and people said it was inhuman and appalling, and war must end, then they invented mustard gas, and said the same, but we must be realistic. The only possible way to have peace is to hold the balance of power . . .'

Viciously, Alison hurled coffee into the pot, and had a vision of battering it down on his bland blond head.

'Take it easy, girl,' Phoebe touched her lightly. 'Are you still suffering from the extra-maritals?'

Alison stared at her: 'Is it so obvious?'

Phoebe signed. 'It takes one to know one. I think John and I are about to bust.'

Alison was shocked; the Abrahams marriage was even older than hers and Philip's, and she had hoped that Phoebe's unease of a month earlier was a passing thing. 'You aren't really? I can't believe it.' She stared at Phoebe.

Phoebe shook her head. 'Not now . . . too public . . . suffice to say we thought we were emancipated sexually, and could cope. John has a bird, and says he needs us both, and I'm not willing to put up with it.' She looked on the brink of tears.

'And you? Have you been naughty?'

Phoebe sniffed, and took a lump of brown sugar. 'I did toy, but I'm really a monogamous soul. I can barely cope with one man, and I'm used to that idiot there.' She rolled her eyes backwards to indicate John who was doing a painfully bad imitation of Margaret Thatcher as Queen Victoria. 'He's gone SDP. That's where he met this girl, addressing envelopes, can you believe?'

'Are you really going to split? I can't imagine it.'

Phoebe nodded. 'I suspect so. We're waiting till Josh finishes A-Levels and goes off to university. We are trying to be what they call civilised.'

Alison stared at the coffee, 'I know the feeling,' she whispered bitterly, and tried not to cry. Phoebe patted her. 'Let's have lunch together soon.'

Alison nodded. 'I'll ring you next week.'

Later, when the guests had shouted farewell, Philip, brimming with good brandy, was in mellow mood, and wanted to make love.

'I don't want to. I've got a period anyway.'

'I don't mind, darling. Come on . . .'

'No!' she snapped.

'Oh, like that is it?' Taken aback, he went for more brandy, and sat swilling a hefty portion in his favourite eighteenth-century goblet – the first present Alison had ever given him, when she still worked in the auctioneers in Worcester.

'That was a good evening,' he said at last, easing his shoes off and lying back on the bed. 'Did you enjoy it?'

'Not very much.'

He turned to her 'You mustn't get so uptight about this peace movement business, you know. You need to know all the arguments, then you'll seem a little more viable. You can't simply be emotional about politics, it's serious stuff. The military and the politicians know their stuff. You must expect to be teased.'

Alison did not answer.

'Alison?'

She looked at him, it was not a friendly glance.

'What the hell has got into you lately? You're not still angry with me are you? And this not sleeping together is a pain.'

She shrugged, and stared deadly at the bedcover.

'I told you it was nothing. Nothing happened.' Philip reiterated yet again.

She eyed him, this stranger she had lived with for seventeen years. 'Did you know that John and Phoebe are about to split?'

She felt a small sense of satisfaction when he almost choked on his brandy. He stared at her: 'Never! Not because of this SDP bird?'

'You know about it?'

'Yes' – a long drawn-out 'yes' – it was old, tired, boring news. 'John always has a bird, he needs it as an ego-booster.'

'When did he tell you?'

'We play squash often enough, I always know where he's getting his end away.'

'You never told me.'

'There was no point. Phoebe will never let him go anyway.'

'I wouldn't be so sure; I think she's had enough.'

Philip finished the brandy. 'Well, well, well, who'd have thought it? Poor old John hoist by his own petard.' He laughed briefly. 'It's quite funny really. He's a family counsellor these day's isn't he?'

'Yes.'

'Heh!' Philip laughed again, and Alison, seeing his thin arms, shut her eyes to rid herself of the image of Gareth's muscular body.

'I'm going to sleep.'

'Goodnight, darling. I think I'll wander down and do some clearing-up, use up some of my surplus energy. I didn't think you were due till next week.'

'I wasn't.'

He leant over her, still brandied and randy, 'Can't I persuade you to a little something?' His erection muzzled her ear.

She shook her head, her eyes shut.

'Philip, I'm tired.' She tried not to snap.

'Oops! Sorry ma'am,' he sighed, got up from the bed a little unsteadily, and tiptoed noisily out of the room, chuckling as he went. 'Poor old John, heh heh.' She listened, and was relieved to hear him pad downstairs. At least they had avoided another bloody fight; she didn't have the energy for more of that. Fortunately the brandy had rendered him benign. She put out the light, and went to sleep imagining Gareth making love to her, like it had been only thirty-six hours ago. He made love like an angel, only angels weren't meant to be sexy, were they?

It was a relief to Alison that Philip was staying in Birmingham for two or three days. She had felt much freer this morning at Gareth's house, knowing she would not be cross-exmained by her husband at night. It had been idyllic in the secret kingdom upstairs in Hammersmith, but now an evening at home with nothing to do stretched drearily ahead. Hopelessly, she succumbed to her yearning and phoned Gareth.

'I just wanted to hear your voice. I miss you.'

'I miss you all the time. What are you doing?'

Thinking of you, feeding my son. I'm tired.'

'That makes two of us,' he said fondly, 'And no wonder. I was just thinking, it's probably mad, but say you came round – tonight I mean – late, after my two are in bed, I could feed you . . .'

'What time?'

'After half-past nine. I'll leave the door open so you don't have to make a noise.'

'I'll be there.'

'We're crazy.'

'I know.' Trembling, she put down the phone. It was a disease, an obsession, this love-business: she could think of nothing else, but at least he wanted her as much as she did him.

She blindly watched half a film on television until at last it was time to go.

'What time will you be back?' asked Mark when he saw Alison put on her jacket. Jo was at Charlotte's for the night.

'Late, I expect, I'm going round to Frankie's.' She noticed that he looked at her a little curiously.

It was dark when once more she entered Gareth's house. He came to meet her and quietly shut the door behind them, glancing uneasily upstairs as he did so.

'I ordered early beds and baths, and was very bad-tempered, poor little sods. Come and eat.'

She handed over a bottle of wine, and in moments they were seated at the table. 'This is insane,' she said.

'Quite mad, but I felt we needed it, the pair of us. We won't see each other for a couple of weeks with the two half-terms. We've got ourselves in a bad way. I don't think you can go on like this, it's too stressful.'

'I can't not see you.'

'I don't want it to be like that, I want more of this, eating together, talking, sharing things . . . . It is a constant pain to be apart. I want to be with you, Alison.'

She leaned on the table, and covered here face with her hands. He soothed her, and handed her a glass of wine. 'Drink up, my love. We mustn't panic; we are adults, we went into this thing open-eyed.'

'Did we?' Her eyes were wet.

'I did.'

'I didn't know it would hurt so much. My chest really hurts.'

He smiled at her tenderly.

'It doesn't only hurt, does it? There's pleasure too?'

After eating they sat by the fire, intensely aware of

the sleeping children upstairs, wanting each other more than ever. Alison wanted to tell him things that she could only tell with her body.

'Let's go out to the garden,' he whispered.

They stood outside, lit by a small moon, watched curiously by passing cats, and embraced like teenagers.

'This is no good, girl,' he said at last. 'We can't do it on the concrete. Shall we chance it indoors, a silent service like?' She giggled, and entwined, they returned to the sitting-room. Gareth dowsed the lights and came to lie on the brown woolly hearthrug beside her, also giggling. They had started up again when Gareth reared up, listening. A small high voice wailed 'Daaad!'

'Damn!' Gareth fumbled with zip and buttons. 'What is it?' he called.

'I've got a sore ear . . .'

'I'm coming, don't worry. Stay there. I'll bring you something.'

He looked at Alison helplessly.

'I'll go,' she said. 'Earache's awful. I'll leave you to it.'

'Thank you.' His kiss was the whole world for an instant. He got up hurriedly, pre-occupied, a parent now. The lover had fled. 'She wasn't feeling good at supper, had a sore throat. I'm sorry . . .'

'I'm gone,' said Alison.

'When will I see you?'

'Friday morning? Same as usual? Under the bridge?'

He nodded towards the stairs. 'If she's OK. If not, I'll ring you at the shop.'

It was only eleven when she got home, and Alison was surprised and annoyed to find her best bottle of Macon empty on the kitchen table, along with the remains of two suppers. She noticed that her carefully ripening giant avocado had also been consumed. The dog came to greet her, and sniffed at her with great curiosity, no doubt smelling Gareth.

Puzzled, Alison went upstairs. Jo's room stood dark and empty, with the door open. Mark must still be working, but on a bottle of best Macon? It was just not good enough. Angrily she thrust open his door and marched into the room, prepared to give him a good telling-off, and was shocked to be greeted with a loud girlish scream, and the sight of Susan Richards and Mark, both naked, and definitely on the job.

'I'm terribly sorry!' she gasped, and shut the door quickly. Filled with mixed emotions, she wanted simultaneously to cry, giggle, and shout with rage. Instead, she went downstairs, switched on the telly, and watched it, still in her coat, unseeing. It was a difficult one to handle; Mark ought to be swotting, not drinking and making love to a minor. Was Susan a minor? Probably not, but she was very young, and what abour her parents? And were they taking precautions?

After a few minutes she heard voices on the stairs; she saw Susan Richards' face, red from weeping, her blonde hair everywhere, as, overcome with embarrassment, not looking anywhere but out, she flashed past Alison towards the front door. There were whispers, scufflings, an audible sniff, then the door banged shut.

'Mark?' She had to confront him. He stood in the doorway, hastily dressed, truculent in bare feet.

'I thought you said you'd be out till midnight.' He glared at her. He had his shoes and socks in his hands.

'I changed my mind, I was tired and wanted to come home. That . . .' she pointed to the dead bottle, 'was my best Macon, being saved for a special occasion.'

'I'll replace it. I didn't know it was special.'

'It's not easy to find; it costs a fiver a bottle.'

Mark winced. 'I'm sorry.'

'Don't do it again.'

'Do what again?' he asked sulkily.

'Help yourself to my booze.'

'Sorry. Anything else?'

'Well, I was surprised to say the least. What about your exams?'

'I needed to unwind. I've prepared enough.'

Alison didn't quite know what to say to this one. 'How old is Susan?'

'Oh Mum . . .'

'Don't you "Oh Mum" me, my lad.'

He glared uncomfortably at the carpet; she still had a fierce desire to laugh, but tried to control it. They both turned simultaneously as they heard the key in the front door; the dog barked like mad, and there suddenly was Philip, pale and worn-out, standing in the doorway.

'Hello,' he said wearily. 'I just wanted to get home, I couldn't face yet another strange bed.' He looked at Mark, still defensive, and Alison, not yet out of her street gear. 'What's going on?'

They both spoke at once. 'Nothing,' said Mark. Alison tried to give a slightly edited version of the events of the last few minutes, and Philip picked up the truth pretty quickly. He didn't seem worried about Susan Richards as much as he was annoyed that the boy had not been swotting.

'She is terribly young . . .' said Alison again.

'Mark glared at her: 'You can talk; don't moralise to me! You told me you were at Frankie's but she rang, asking to speak to you. And what about you and your hairy Welshman, touching each other up in the bloody street in front of my friends!'

With which bombshell he turned, red-faced and teetering on tears, and stormed out of the house, still bare-footed, shouting 'I'll see you tomorrow!'

Philip and Alison looked at each other, paralysed, shocked to a numb silence.

'I thought there was something funny going on,' said Philip, slowly taking off his pale raincoat. 'That's why I wanted to come home.'

Chapter Nineteen

By the time she arrived at the shop next morning and saw the brightly-painted new sign swinging in the breeze, proudly declaring the name 'Two Birds', with an idealised humorous portrait of Frankie, and a strikingly mysterious one of herself – 'A black firebird, he's made, the clever so and so . . .' Gareth had said admiringly when he saw it – Alison felt half dead, drained entirely of physical or emotional energy. She and Philip had had little sleep; he had alternately shouted, wept and ranted for at least half the night. Then, desperately, he had made love to her – but it had been violent, she had felt used, that he was staking his claim of ownership on her body. She had been too frightened to refuse him his marital rights – indeed his desperation and almost operatic frenzy had filled her with a half-crazed sort of pity. Virile with rage and despair, he had staked his claim on the territory of her body, and she had wept as she came, betrayed by years of habit.

She must phone Gareth, must see him, she needed his comfort; somehow a viable way must be found to extricate them all from this mess. And Mark running off like that into the night; they had been so involved, and Philip so wildly angry at what Mark had said about that hairy Welshman, that they had simply allowed him to go.

'He'll be all right!' Philip had roared. 'It's you I want to speak to. I knew! I knew! You've been so bloody dewy-eyed, like a lovesick kid for weeks . . . . I'll kill the bastard!'

Mark had come back for breakfast, pretty hangdog, not saying much. He had nodded wearily to them both, and grunted 'Susan's', when Philip asked where he had slept.

'Fair enough,' Philip looked sternly at him, 'I can accept that you are a maturing young stud, and have to do what you have to do. Only my son, be discreet, be careful, and don't ever stay out for the night again without telling us your whereabouts.'

Mark had mumbled that he was sorry, glanced at his mother and looked away, and sat down wordlessly to consume a giant breakfast. Later he had gone to shower and change, and go to school for his French exam. He slammed the door, and left without saying goodbye, and Alison thought her heart would break. Philip was sitting at the table reading *The Times*, apparently immersed. Looking at him it was hard to realise that this aloof and elegant businessman was the same person as the nearly demented naked creature of the night before.

'Are you still seeing this man?' He looked up suddenly from the paper. Alison, trying to eat yoghurt and fruit which tasted of sawdust, gazed at the table, her eyes listless, and said nothing.

'Alison! I want to know.'

'Then yes. I suppose I am.'

'What does he work at?'

'I don't want to talk about it.' She could just imagine

how he would jeer, an unemployed lecturer, with a beard, a CND badge, and a rusty ten-year-old car.

'I would like to know about this man who has been making love to my wife.'

'You're not going to. I'm certainly not going to tell you. *You* can talk.' She stared at him, and was almost afraid of the hatred she felt welling up. Sometimes these days, like yesterday, when he was travelling by train, she did actually wish he would die, neatly disposed of in a crash. It would be so simple, the perfect solution.

'Alison,' Philip was very pale, and his eyes were shut as he concentrated, with a pained expression, 'we have been married for a very long time. We have two wonderful children; please don't let's throw it away. You cannot do this. You cannot have a full-blooded love-affair and expect the marriage to survive.'

Her eyes were black slits of loathing. 'You broke the bond in the first place; you destroyed my trust.'

'But I knew not to get involved. At least I was adult about it. I knew when to turn my back, not like you, who rushes in like a kid and falls head over heels, grandly thinking . . .' here his voice went falsetto '. . . it's all right; I'll have a lover, my husband won't mind, he's so civilised . . .' His voice changed back and became deep and menacing. 'But Alison, I warn you, it is not all right, I do mind. You are my wife and this is my home, and I intend to keep it intact.' He stood up and stared at her with as little love as she stared at him. 'I advise you to grow up, Alison, to turn your back, same as I did . . .' Alison imagined gypsy violins playing for Philip's lost love. She despised his sordid little affairs, his two-facedness. He was staring down at her, and the expression in his face was frightening.

'You are my woman, Alison, and *I'm* your chap, not anybody else. I'll fight for you, and don't you forget it.'

Her mind clanged with replies, silly ones, sad ones she wanted to weep and scream for what was irrevocably lost between them. Wearily she pushed away her uneaten food.

'I'm going to the shop. I have a lot to do today.'

Philip was silent, then he asked in a quiet dead voice. 'Will you be here tonight?'

'I do live here.' She got up, busying herself with the breakfast debris, and he went out of the room.

Later, before she left the house, she wondered where he was, and grew afraid again: he had had a look of desperation. She looked in the bedroom, but it and the bathrooms were empty. He must be in his ivory tower. Uneasily she climbed upstairs, and tremblingly opened the door of the stark white workroom. She was horrified to find her husband sitting with his back to her, bent over one of the guns which normally hung on the wall. Terrified, she stared at him, silhouetted darkly against the bright sunlight which streamed in through the rooflights.

'What are you doing?'

Startled like herself – he had been absorbed in whatever it was that occupied him – he turned, the gun held across his chest.

'I was just cleaning this.'

Her heart was still thumping. She saw that he had a tin of 3-in-1 oil and cotton wadding beside him. He stood up and hung the gun back on the wall, and came to her. He was very pale, and looked vulnerable and agonised. 'There is some hope for us, isn't there?'

Alison shook her head tiredly. 'I don't know,' she said slowly. 'I don't know.'

Tentatively, he put his hand out and touched her face as though he were bestowing a blessing. She turned to go and could barely see her way for tears. She could not help that she no longer loved him.

*   *   *

She let herself into the shop and eyed the phone. Gareth. His children would have gone to school by now. She must seem him, tell him, before she and Jo went off to Devon for half-term. She was reaching for the receiver when the shop bell clanged and Frankie was there, frenziedly filling the shop with a dramatic sense of emergency, wild-eyed and breathless.

'It's wee Ant! He's been mugged! It's awful, I tried to phone you from the hospital last night but Mark said you were with me.' She looked at her, her eyes huge and alarmed. 'You mustn't do that, I've told you I'll not tell lies.'

'I'm sorry . . . . It was an impulse, it was silly . . . tell me about Anthony.'

'Oh . . . . It was so hellish. He was just set upon by these two guys for no reason. He'd been in the pub with a friend, and I think the friend had had a joint. Anthony isn't very interested in smoking dope . . . and they just grabbed him on the way home and beat him up, kicking him almost to bits . . .' She covered her face with her hands. 'Poor guy . . .'

Horrified, Alison listened. 'What bastards!' She imagined Anthony battered, his laughing face bloody. 'How badly injured is he?'

Frankie took a swig of Alison's coffee. 'He's actually very lucky. No broken teeth, and his eyes – though he can hardly open them – are all right, though for a while last night he couldn't see properly. It was unbelievable; I've never seen anybody in such a mess. And his poor back and bum were kicked – he can barely walk or even sit down . . .' She was breathless. 'I'd like to kill them, I really would.'

'How did you find out about it?'

'A nurse from the hospital phoned me. He'd tried another friend but he was out; he needed somebody to help get him home. He was in casualty for about three hours. Poor guy, it was heartbreaking.'

Alison shut her eyes. 'How awful. Where is he now?'

'He's in his house; I was going to take him back to me, but he wanted his own place. I've just come out to buy some groceries and painkillers – the hospital gave us a prescription – but I wanted to tell you.'

'Poor man. Shall I come over and see him?'

'Aye, maybe, but remember he can barely talk. Poor soul; his flat is absolutely lovely, and his paintings are just great.'

'I'm not surprised.'

Frankie stood up, 'I'll have to be getting on.'

'Did you spend the night there?'

'I had to; he wasn't fit to be left. He's got two cracked ribs . . .'

Alison wanted to cry; the world seemed particularly black today. She must see Gareth somehow.

'Frankie . . .'

'Yeah?' Frankie had gathered up her things, and was poised to go.

'Philip knows.'

'Oh God . . .' Frankie sank into a brown Victorian balloon chair. 'Tell me.'

Alison poured out the story of Philip's rage as Frankie gasped and listened.

'And Mark, last night . . . . I found him in bed with his girlfriend . . .' Alison groaned at the memory.

Frankie snorted. 'What a wee chancer! Was that when I phoned? I thought he sounded pretty funny.'

'No doubt,' said Alison drily. 'He'd had a whole bottle of my best Macon.'

Frankie guffawed, and Alison began to see the funny side. She chuckled ruefully, then wiped her eyes. 'It's not funny really.'

'Allie, if you can't have a laugh, life's not worth bloody living.'

'Your text of the week?'

'My text for life. Listen, I've got to go.'

At which point the phone rang: Alison picked it up and froze as she heard Philip's voice. 'It's Philip . . .' she hissed to Frankie, who nodded wisely.

'I just wanted to speak to you.' Philip's voice was almost reserved. 'What's happening tonight?'

'What do you mean?'

'Food and things, will we all be there?'

'Yes. There's a chicken defrosting.'

'Do you want me to buy anything?'

'No. We're quite well stocked.'

'Right. See you tonight then.'

'Right. Goodbye.' Brief and formal, her stranger, her husband of seventeen years. She was shaking when she put down the phone.

Frankie was watching. 'He loves you Allie; he doesn't want to lose you.'

Alison sighed. 'The trouble is he thinks I am his chattel; I don't think he actually knows me any more. It's an image he loves, a sort of Madonna, a mother-cum-wife-cum-homemaker all rolled into one and put on a pedestal. And in a way it's the same for me: I think of him as a father, a professional man, an escort, I can see this sort of golden solvent person, but it's an image. We've lost each other as real people along with our innocence. I don't really like Philip as he is any more, any more than he can really tolerate what I have become.'

'What have you become?'

'I don't know . . .'

'Alison!' Frankie was getting angry. 'Don't cop out. Think: what exactly do you mean?'

'It depends on how you look at it. You could say I have become a love-sick irresponsible idiot,' Frankie nodded grimly at this, 'or you could say I have grown up, and I have discovered my own needs. But half of the time I feel like a lunatic; I dread the boredom and misery of home, dread the unexciting sex where we both try so hard for old time's sake. Yet, I also wonder, does being grown-up mean that one has developed an ability to tolerate boredom?' She looked at Frankie, tears once again near, and shook her head helplessly. 'Frankie, I just do not know.'

'Well,' Frankie spoke briskly, 'I'm glad you're going away for a week; it will give you time to think. You will have to choose: you can't go on like this. You and Gareth are involved, over-involved, to the point of marriage-wrecking and misery.'

'He wants us to be together.'

'And you?'

'I love him, I want to be with him . . . but it's not just him, is it? I love my children, I can't leave them . . . take them away from Philip.'

'Could you leave Philip?'

'Sometimes when I'm with Gareth, I feel that I never want to see Philip again, but the children love him . . . he's a good father really . . .' She paused, and added bleakly, 'When he's there . . .'

'Oh, Allie,' Frankie hugged her. 'What are we going to do with you?'

'I don't know.'

'I don't know either, but I must go and see to wee Ant.'

'Are you going to stay with him again? Why you?'

'I'm quite happy to; he's a real friend now. He'll probably feel a lot better tomorrow. As it is he's been so badly bruised he can hardly shit . . .'

Alison winced. 'Give him my love. I'll try and pop in with a bottle of wine before I set out tomorrow . . .'

'You have enough to think about. Cheerio, I'll see you tomorrow.' And she was gone with a hug and a grin.

She tried Gareth's number, longing for the comfort of his voice, but the number was engaged. She put down the receiver, wondering if he might be phoning her, but there was no ring. After a few moments she tried again.

'Hello?' It still made her melt, the deep Welsh sound.

'It's me.'

'Oh, hi. What can I do for you?' He sounded oddly formal. She wished she didn't cry so much these days. 'Gareth, can I see you today sometime? I need to see you . . .' She hoped it didn't sound as much of a wail as she suspected it did.

His voice was guarded. 'It's a bit difficult right now. I've got Bronwen here, sitting in the chair; she's quite bad – got terrible earache – I was just going over to the doctor with her, but my car's dead, so the doctor is coming over here in an hour or so; so I can't possibly get out. I'm sorry.' He paused. 'Are you all right?'

'I . . . I just need to see you . . .' she sobbed. 'Before I go to my father's . . .' There was a pause, then he grunted. 'Oh God. Look, I'll phone you back later. Are you at the shop?'

'Yes. It's Philip. He knows, and Anthony Brownstone has been beaten up . . .' She hadn't meant to tell him that.

'Oh . . .' He was at a loss for words. 'Oh God, what a mess. I'm sorry . . . I'll ring you later. I have to go . . .'

Obviously the child needed him, but so did she. She felt like a bloody child. She put down the phone shaking; suddenly terribly tired. It was all too much, and to her horror here was the dreaded Hilary coming smiling in the door. She took a deep breath and smiled back. On with the show.

It was the longest, loneliest stint Alison could ever remember doing in the shop: she dealt with her few customers in a haze, and tried to be nice to a couple of regulars, one of them the old widower, who rarely bought anything, but often came in for a chat, and on his luckier days, a cup of coffee. It was now four hours since she had phoned Gareth, and she didn't want to ring him back – she knew that he wanted to keep his children innocent of the affair, 'until we sort ourselves out,' he used to say when they made plans to meet or phone. If he didn't ring by five that would be it for today, because she had to be home for Jo and cook supper. Poor Mark, she didn't know what to say to him, or when they would get a chance to talk. She certainly wouldn't get much opportunity tonight because the whole family would be there: she remembered Mark's sullenness at breakfast, and his hatred last night. There was a lot of lost ground to be made up: it was heartbreaking.

At a quarter-to-five Gareth phoned from a coin-box. 'Alison? I'm sorry, I've been waiting till my neighbour came back; she's keeping an eye on the youngsters for an hour. I managed to take the car limping into the garage: I'm at Hammersmith. Any chance of meeting you now?

She thought quickly: Philip would be paranoid if he were home first, he'd be convinced she was with her lover – and he would be right. She consulted her tube-map. 'Can you get to Notting Hill? We can meet for half an hour. I'm off to Devon in the morning.'

The pips went, she heard him swear and put more money in. 'OK. See you very soon. North side. By the book shop . . .'

Chapter Twenty

In her father's house one night Alison had a strange dream. As she slept, she saw the three men she had loved, Gino the Italian, Philip and Gareth; all three were dressed exactly alike in dinner-suits, looking like members of an orchestra. In the dream they were coming towards her and she watched them uneasily, realising that, like Paris with his apple, she had to make a choice between them, only she didn't know which one to choose, for in the dream each one seemed to her equally desirable. The three black-clad men were walking towards her, smiling enigmatically, when she woke feeling very disturbed indeed.

It took three days to clear up her father's cottage; she threw out many bags of rubbish – old tattered linen, towels, and weevily half-used packets of sugar and flour. In the months before her illness, her mother had evidently not been as much in charge of her housekeeping as she used to be. Molly, Alison gathered, used often to come over to give him groceries or an evening meal, but she had been overtired for some weeks, and not coping.

One night when she and Jo had been at the cottage for almost a week, and the old man had retired early to bed, Jo, gazing out of the cottage window at the night sky, suddenly asked:

'Mum? Why was Dad so funny and bad-tempered about our going to visit that poor artist-man before we left?'

Alison, reading by the fire, paused, then looked up. 'I don't know; maybe he was tired or something.'

'Pre-menstrual tension,' Jo giggled, 'or maybe he was jealous and thought he was your lover . . .'

Alison froze. Surely Mark hadn't said anything to Jo. She couldn't bear it if he had; she had managed a few moments alone with Mark before they left. She had said, feebly perhaps, that adults sometimes found themselves behaving like characters in a Feydeau farce, and that she hoped he would forgive her. She had also said that she loved him, and was not always perfect, but she knew that he needed stability, and had promised that this was not threatened. He had stared sulkily at the belt of his brown towelling dressing-gown.

'Are you still seeing him?' he asked like an inquisitor. Alison paused and looked at him coolly.

'That is actually none of your business, Mark. I don't probe you closely about your private life.'

'I'm not married.'

'Indeed you are not, nor are you an adult.' She felt unaccountably angry, it was not a clever riposte, but the only one she could think of.

He had shrugged, not wanting to look at his scarlet woman of a mother. She had felt pretty helpless: what could she say after all? In the end when she had hugged him, he had grudgingly submitted to her embrace.

'Anyway, I'm off for a week, you'll be left in peace. I hope the work goes well with your two wild women away.'

Mark had almost smiled, but not quite, and she had

ruffled his hair, which was a mistake, for he shrank from her hand before saying goodbye with a deadpan expression, which made her very sad. She missed him when he was there now; it was horribly similar to the sort of cut-off Philip so often did which used to make her miserable.

'Is that Anthony, Frankie's boyfriend?' asked Jo, still at the cottage window.

'No. They are just friends.'

'I think he quite likes her, do you?'

Alison nodded. 'I'm sure of it.'

'His paintings were really good, weren't they? I loved the one of a princess, the one that looked just like Frankie.'

'Yes. He's very talented.'

'Yuk. His bruises looked awful.'

Alison remembered the almost-closed bruised eyes, and the painful way Anthony moved about his beautiful flat. 'Terrible, I've never seen anyone after being beaten up like that. He said he wouldn't be able to do any work for at least a week, his hands hurt so much.'

'I'd like to kill them,' said Jo.

'That's just what Frankie said, but killing doesn't answer the problem.'

Jo was silent, gazing thoughtfully out over the moors. Alison remembered Philip's expression when she had announced at supper that she was going to look in on Anthony with a bottle of wine. His eyes had gone a menacing gunmetal grey and he had stared at her icily. She had explained that Anthony was Frankie's friend, and the artist responsible for the shop-sign – which even Philip had admired – but it had not helped his mood. She had realised then that it wasn't only a lover Philip felt threatened by. It was the whole thing –

the business, Frankie, the shop and the social life it generated – all these things plus Alison's growing independence of him, financial and emotional. He wanted her to stay home and be his little Allie again, the good wife and mother, always on call – but it was too late. She had taken Jo with her almost in desperation, hoping to shut Philip up and to allay his suspicions. They had only spent half an hour with the battered little Ant, till Frankie had arrived with a Chinese take-away. Before they left, Anthony had presented Jo with a beautiful copy of Aesop's *Fables* illustrated by himself. She had been thrilled. 'I'd like to do that one day, painting and illustrating books.'

'I think you will,' said her mother. 'You've been an artist almost since you could walk.'

On a sofa in Susan Richards' mother's flat, in a large Edwardian block of brick-built apartments, not far from the Greek church and opposite a pâtisserie in Moscow Road, Bayswater, Mark watched helplessly as Susan cried. She had been crying for ages, and didn't want him to hug, kiss, or even touch her at all. He felt bewildered, angry and helpless. Ever since Alison had surprised them in bed – it had been the first time – Susan had been cold and awkward, and he didn't know what to do.

'Do you want a coffee?' he asked. Susan shook her head. She looked awful, red and swollen-eyed; her hair, usually sleek and blonde, was tangled and messy. Tentatively, he tried to put his arm round her, but she pulled away.

'Susan, what is it? Can't you tell me what's wrong?'

The girl sniffed and shook her head. Mark stood up and leaned against the mantelpiece, his back to her, and rocked uneasily, his forehead resting on his hands, then he turned round.

'Look, I promised I'd be back by half-past eleven. Pa was furious the other night. I'd better go. You seem to want me to go anyway.'

She looked up at him, still tearstained. 'Were your parents furious about me? They must think I'm awful.'

The boy shrugged. 'They didn't say much about that; I got a lecture from Pa about being discreet, but they were furious because I rushed off after you without telling them where I would be. Will you be OK?'

'Yes,' listlessly.

'When will your Mum be back?'

'Dunno.' She shrugged, her eyes dead.

Mark turned round, and went over to her, tentatively putting out his hand. She pulled away.

'You'd better go.'

At the door she did allow him to kiss her, but it wasn't the same any more, it felt sort of middle-aged and worried. When Mark got home, Philip was watching the late-night movie, half-asleep.

'Hello lad, how was your evening?'

'OK.'

'Were you with the lovely Susan?'

Mark nodded.

'Nice girl, I admire your taste.'

'She's all right,' muttered Mark, and wished that it were true. Maybe she was pre-menstrual. Unthinkingly he put his hand out to touch the door; touch wood for luck – he hoped that that was what was wrong.

'When is tomorrow's exam?'

'Two o'clock. I'll do some work in the morning.'

'How do you think they have gone so far?'

The boy shrugged. 'Dunno, I think I messed up my physics.'

'Mark . . .' Philip suddenly switched off the remote sound-control switch and the television was silent. 'I'd like you to tell me about this hairy Welshman as you called him.'

He looked squarely at his son. Mark's face was impassive. He had had enough for one night.

'What do you know about him?'

'Nothing really . . .'

'You must know something, or you wouldn't have said what you did. I want to know.'

His father looked pretty grim, but he didn't want to make more trouble with his parents, it was nasty enough these days.

'It was just a guy I know who said he'd seen Ma with a man at a market . . .'

'Doing what?'

'I dunno . . . being a bit friendly . . .'

'Have you ever seen this man?'

'I may have . . . there are always people in the shop, it goes like a fair sometimes.'

'Mark, I want to know.'

'Well, if it's who I think it is, he's Welsh, he's bearded, and he seems quite a pleasant guy. There's probably nothing to it.' He wanted to protect his mother now, not to cause any more dramas.

'Do you know this man's name?'

'Garry or something. Look . . .' He turned in appeal to his father. 'I don't know anything about it. I was upset the other night, it was terribly upsetting for Susan – I'd drunk all that wine and didn't mean what I said – I just wanted to get at somebody. I'm going to bed . . . . Goodnight.'

He went out, shutting the door behind him. Philip switched up the sound again. Garry, was it? He must find out more. Sort the bugger out. Philip was not prepared to be sophisticated as far as his wife was concerned, no way. He glared unseeing at the screen.

On the way back to London from Devon Alison made a detour so she and Jo could spent twenty-four hours in the Abrahams' idyllically situated country cottage in Somerset. Phoebe was there with Jake, her youngest, now seventeen, and the two women walked the familiar lanes where they had once wheeled pushchairs side by side. The cottage was fairly primitive, with candlelight and an old stove for heating and cooking on. From every window you could see rolling fields, rich tangled hedgerows, and sheep.

The worst discovery of the week for Alison had been that her father was incontinent. This fact was made self-evident by a bundle of old sheets she found hidden away, obviously recently, in the garden shed. With difficulty she had persuaded him to tell her about it; he had been very embarrassed, like a guilty child who has wet the bed, and had called her by her mother's name.

'It just happens sometimes,' he had said reluctantly. 'I wake up dreaming that I need to go to the lavatory, but by then it is too late. It simply happens, it's old age, Meg.'

She sighed as she remembered. She was leaning on a gate looking miles across the rich green fields; she had worked hard to arrange for reliable local help for him, and hoped he would be all right for a bit.

She felt Gareth's letter in her pocket, and fondly read it once again. It was the first letter she had ever received from him, and had come to her father's cottage bringing joy.

'My love,

'I just want to say I miss you terribly, and I meant everything I said to you about how I feel.

'No luck with jobs yet. I have sent out another batch of applications to Toronto, Sydney, Aberdeen and Croydon. From the sublime to the ridiculous, but I have had a very good reaction to my book-list. We've got a packing-factory here.

'I love you more than I thought I could ever love anybody, and long to lie beside you once more. I embrace you.

'XXXX Gareth.'

'You look very absorbed, what great thoughts are you thinking?' Phoebe appeared beside her and also leaned over the gate to enjoy the view. Alison reluctantly put the letter away and told Phoebe about her father's incontinence and what arrangements she had made for him.

'What are you going to do?'

'I don't know. I think another winter there alone would be too much. We may have to share him out, only he has told me so often and so adamantly that he hates the city and doesn't want to be in London, that I don't know how we could persuade him to come to us.'

'It is a terrible problem.' Phoebe sighed. She gazed across to the distant blue hills, her eyes wrinkled. 'My old ma is becoming so messy, so forgetful, and that beastly radio blaring away day and night. It makes me terribly aggravated, poor old love.'

'I turned Daddy's off every night – it was always tuned to the World Service – and he never said a word.'

Phoebe shook her head. 'I never dared; my Ma looks so horrifying in bed, I can hardly bear to look at her, she's like a poor old toothless monkey.'

'He actually told me that he would prefer to go into a home when it all became too much. There's a place for retired church people not far from Exeter, he gets letters from a couple of old friends there.'

Phoebe shuddered. 'I dread the thought of facing old age alone.'

'You might be lucky and be the first to go.'

Phoebe stared bleakly at the twittering birds on a nearby hawthorn. 'I suspect I will be by myself.'

Alison hugged her. 'I'm sure things will look up between you two.'

Phoebe glanced at her. 'I've been on Valium, you know. I still am.'

'You said.'

'It makes me so idiotic and weepy.'

'Phoebe, it's nothing to be ashamed of. You're just having a rough patch.'

Glumly, Phoebe bent to pick some pale yellow primroses, and Alison saw that her eyes were full of tears.

It was dawn when Mark heard the sound of his father's car return. He had slept badly, rattled by exams and worried by Susan's continuing remoteness. At supper that night he looked as worn as his father.

'That was an awfully late dinner-party yesterday, Pa.'

'It was a bit. I'm not sure what time I got home, two or three I guess.'

'It was six.'

'It can't have been; you must have heard a neighbour.'

'I don't think so.' Mark looked at him; it was quite an amusing role-reversal, with Philip looking guilty and Mark putting the questions.

'Nonsense,' said Philip. 'It really wasn't that late. It was a damned good dinner-party all the same. Very entertaining people, mostly fellow-architects.'

Mark nodded. He didn't believe him, it was all so reminiscent of what Susan had told him of her home life before her parents had broken up. It made him feel very uneasy.

Philip looked at his son: 'It's a bit quiet without the girls, isn't it?' Mark nodded morosely.

'Why so gloomy, my son?'

Mark shrugged. It was impossible to explain about Susan, that she just didn't seem interested in him any more. 'Just exams, I'm knackered, it's hard, I hate it. Sometimes I wish I could just get the hell out and forget everything – and I really do think I messed up my physics.'

'Oh . . . that's rotten bad luck. But we all feel like that sometimes. I'd like to run away from the office and the responsibilities, it all gets me down at times.'

'Competitions and things?'

Philip nodded. 'Right now I'm waiting to hear about three enormous projects, especially the Hong Kong one, which I'm reasonably sure about, but you can never be really sure. A war or some political upheaval might change the whole thing. It's when you aren't in control that it's hard to take.'

Mark nodded. He knew exactly what he meant.

Philip looked at his watch, 'I'm hungry, what about you?'

'I'm starving, what's for supper?'

'To tell you the truth I hadn't even thought about it. It's awfully quiet here, isn't it?'

'A bit depressing, yes.'

'How about a meal out? Can you spare the time off work?'

Mark lit up. 'Yeah!'

'Well there's all of Queensway to choose from. What d'you fancy?'

'Indian?'

'Fine. Let's go.'

'I'll just get my jacket. Thanks, Dad.' The boy was grinning.

Frankie pounded into the shop to welcome Alison back. She was extra cheery, even for Frankie, and dressed as entertainingly as ever, this time in red baggy trousers, a bit clown-like, with a black cotton top with huge white spots. She waved her arms like a triumphant athlete.

'I've done it!'

'Done what? Won the pools? Bought a Canaletto for five pence?'

'Naw . . . . I've just told Jay to go and stuff herself!'

'Oh, I thought you were resolving your differences.'

'No, darling, the differences were too basic. She wanted my soul as well as my mighty body; anyway, I've decided that I am after all one of the last heterosexuals!'

'I'm glad. What happened?'

'You knew it was going a bit funny, with all that stuff about leg-shaving?'

Alison, heading for the kettle, nodded.

'Well she got all heavy about that, saying I ought to come out, and I said I didn't feel that way, that it was just a beautiful friendship that I needed at the time, and she got all morbid, wanting to own me. She even got jealous of my Florence Nightingale bit with Ant – and he's one of her oldest friends. So I just said "Piss off, hen," in no uncertain terms, and I feel really relieved.'

'Do you think you'll see her again?'

'Yeah. Probably. She's a good mate. She's just a giant-sized nutter, with the ego of a megalomaniac.'

'The artistic temperament . . .'

'Aye. Come on there, Frankie needs coffee toot sweet.'

'How is Anthony?'

'Still bruised, but he's moving around OK. Says he'll get working this week. I'm really fond of him after looking after him.'

'Is his hand OK?'

'Yes; but his ribs still hurt. It was an awful problem, because it hurt him to laugh, and you know me, I kept making him laugh . . .. Ouch!'

They drank coffee, and Frankie briefly recounted what had been sold, or was hopeful: business had been sluggish, except for the bonus of at last getting rid of the mock Japanese jar for a tenner less than Alison had paid for it.

'I think the American who bought it thought he was going to make his fortune at Sotheby's, same as you did.'

'If he did, then I'd really be upset. I'm awfully glad its' gone. It made me feel guilty, sitting there accusingly reminding me of my mistake.'

'How about you? How's your Pa?'

'My old Dad's very sweet, sometimes incontinent, but coping.'

'And the home front?'

'Philip's very beady. He started asking me about this last night, just as we were going to bed . . .' Alison fondled Gareth's necklace. 'Said I was wearing it an awful lot, and asked very piercingly exactly where I'd got it from!'

'Oh God. You do actually wear it nearly all the time, and that's not typical. Give it a rest.'

'But I like it . . .'

'You're a love-sick eejit, I'm getting fed up with all this. You know I had Philip along here on Friday, very aggressive, wanting to know all about your friend Garry, which I presume means Gareth?'

Alison felt herself go suddenly cold. 'What did you say to him?'

'I told him everything, of course. You know me, honest Frankie . . .' She saw Alison's sudden pallor, put down her coffee mug and rushed over to hug her.

'Of course I didn't say anything. I wouldn't, but it was very heavy, and I do not like telling lies, as I've said many times before.'

'Oh Frankie, what did you say? How much does he know?'

'He knows he's Welsh from Mark's yelling at you, and he thinks he's called Garry. I swore I didn't know anyone called Garry, crossed my heart, and fibbed and said I didn't know anything about anything.'

'Oh . . .' Weak-kneed all of a sudden, Alison sat down.

'He ranted on and on, saying you'd broken the bond, which he'd never done, even though he's had affairs and still had plenty of women after him. It was hefty stuff, believe you me. I actually had to ask him to go.'

'Oh Gawd, what will I do?'

'I've told you before, you can't keep two men, not with Philip and the kids. You can't have your cake and eat it . . .'

She watched helplessly as Alison's eyes filled with tears. They were both quite relieved when a customer came in looking for silver spoons.

'Saved by the bell . . .' muttered Frankie as Alison went to bathe her face. 'I must go Allie. It's my buying day. Think I'll try over the river. By the way, wee Ant is going to take me out for a slap-up meal, to Langan's Brassière, or something . . .'

'Langan's Brasserie – it's lovely, all Hockneys and good modern paintings, off Piccadilly – you'll love it. Why so grand?'

'Because I've been so wonderful . . .' Frankie pirouetted. 'And he's sold all his pictures in the Royal

Academy. Jay was furious, she had two rejected this year, and the one they did take hasn't sold. Artists . . . they're all mad!'

'Like antique-dealers.'

'True, true. Well, I'll love you and leave you. Byee!'

She was gone leaving a terrible silence behind her; the very air seemed numbed by her exit.

Chapter Twenty-one

The mid-term break, with little word from Gareth, except for the letter and one strangely unsatisfying phone-call to the shop, seemed endless. Alison longed for him with a dull and constant ache and at home things were very strained. Philip was so paranoid about wanting to know her whereabouts, and when exactly she would be home, that sometimes she was tempted to shout at him that Gareth was away, and he had no need to worry, not this week.

They slept in the same bed, only rarely making love, and when they did, it was wordless, and usually reduced her to tears, it felt so meaningless now, after all the years they had made love and said 'I love you.' Philip looked fraught, they talked little, and slept back to back like the two dead men who drew their swords and shot each other. He was home most evenings, but generally retired to his workroom to work after supper. Mark seemed very silent too, and all too aware of the tension between his parents; he still had several exams to sit, but appeared preoccupied, and ensconced himself on the telephone in his parents' bedroom for hours on end every night, until finally Philip, complaining about Mark's lack of work and the huge telephone bills, cut his calls down to two-minute ones.

'It's ridiculous,' he told his glowering son, 'you see the girl all day, part from her for ten minutes, and you're immediately on the phone to her. What with you and Jo, your mother and I hardly get a chance to use the damned thing.'

It was a relief when, on the Friday night, Philip said he had an architectural meeting. This was unusual, Friday not being a normal time for such things, but Alison did not care; she wished he would take himself out every night, instead of playing at being her keeper. Both children were still out when she got home, and she relaxed, watching the news and evening chat shows. She felt more cheerful: she would hear from Gareth on Monday, and would, hopefully, be in his arms on Wednesday, and there was nothing Philip could do about it, unless he was insane enough to hire a private detective – which he might do if he became any more obsessed.

Home did not exist with Philip any more for Alison. It seemed an empty place, a black hole where the children grew and were fed, but were not at the moment well-nourished spiritually. It made her very sad because she felt it to be beyond repair. Glazed, she thought of Gareth. She had told him once that she liked his shirts – he tended to wear bold stripes or checks – and she wished he was here now so that she could tell him, her dear gorilla, that she liked his hair-shirt best. She was woken from her reverie by Mark's coming home. He came in, as glum as ever.

'When's supper?' was his cold almost inaudible greeting.

'Seven o'clock.'

He nodded, eyes dead, and went up to his room. It was heart-breaking: she must try somehow to break through to him again. It was too lonely to live like this. She had fallen for Gareth, unconsciously hoping it would replace the emptiness she felt with Philip, but she had never expected to lose her son in the process. Jo was still out, it was late for her – another half hour and Alison would have to ring Charlotte's house and try to track her down. She was chopping onions when she heard the phone ring: she sweated it out with Mark to see who could be bothered to answer it; she was glad to hear him take it, she wasn't in the mood to talk to anybody. She decided to make a special effort with the supper. Maybe if she cooked something extra nice her lad would at least raise a smile.

Mark gave her such a fright by appearing suddenly behind her in the kitchen that she only just avoided cutting herself. She clutched her chest, her heart jumping. 'Oh! I simply didn't hear you come in.'

The boy was beaming: 'I'm sorry, I didn't mean to startle you. What are you cooking?'

'An extra divine beef stew, and we can have avocadoes.'

'Great! I'm starving.' This was a real change, he had hardly eaten supper properly for days. He sat at the table and grinned.

'Why so cheerful all of a sudden?'

He rocked backwards on the chair, and she was about to stop him with the usual warning about wrecking the wooden joints, but held back, she didn't want him to go bloody-minded again, not so soon.

'No reason.' He grinned again.

'Really? You seemed so fed up when you came in. Who was on the phone?'

He smiled. 'Susan.'

'She must have said something nice.' Alison continued chopping.

He smiled his sweetest smile. 'Ma, I've got something to tell you.'

She paused in her chopping, intrigued.

'You're half-way through your beastly exams?'

'I am, but thats not it.' He got up, and she was relieved to see the chair still standing.

'So tell me, what's this all about?'

He leaned against the wooden worktop, and smiled, breathing out in a sigh of what looked like relief.

'Promise not to tell Dad or Jo what I'm about to tell you.'

'I'll try to, but it's difficult to promise before I know what it is.'

He nodded, then glanced at her, 'I want to inform you that you are not after all going to be a grandmother.'

'A what?'

'A grandmother.'

'My God!' Alison stared at him, 'Did Susan think she was pregnant?'

He nodded, a little bashfully.

'You poor things. You must have gone through hell.'

'It was awful. I was nearly bonkers.'

'And poor Susan; what happened?'

'She was two weeks overdue, we were all set to get her a test tomorrow, but she just phoned screaming, "It's come! It's come!" The period, I mean . . .'

'Oh, Mark!' Impulsively she hugged him, and he clutched her back, still bashful, blushing a little. 'You poor, poor things. Does Susan's mother know?'

'No, and *please* don't tell her, she's very neurotic just now anyway, with the divorce and everything. I was sure she couldn't be when I really thought about it, but she was in such a state. Crazy almost.'

'I won't tell anybody. I promise. I'm so glad you told me. I thought you were still angry with your wicked mother.'

'I'm sorry, but I felt crazed too. I hope I haven't effed up my exams.'

'Do you think you have?'

He grimmaced. 'It's hard to tell. I've been so preoccupied, I've thought of nothing else.'

'Shouldn't she be on the pill?'

'I guess so, unless it's put her off for life.'

'It might put her off for a bit.'

'It already has.' He looked worried. 'Do you think it will put her off me?'

'I hope not. When are you going to see her?'

'Tomorrow.'

Alison nodded. 'Well, my son, let that be a lesson to you.'

'Don't you worry, Ma, it's almost put *me* off.'

'But not quite?'

He grinned. 'Not quite.'

'I'm glad. And I'm glad you're speaking to me again. I missed you.'

He nodded. 'It's been horrible.'

The dog barked, and they both turned to greet Jo, who came in and flopped down by the table, dropping myriad bags, jacket and books. 'Hi,' she said vaguely, 'sorry I'm late.'

'Where were you?'

'We went to the caff.' She was wearing a blue and white striped tee-shirt, and a red skirt, and looked Alison noticed, quite blotchy. She peered at her daughter, 'What have you done to your neck?'

Jo blushed scarlet, and her hand flew to cover her neck.

'Hay-fever?' she asked hopefully. Alison was puzzled. Mark got up to examine her more closely, and pulled her hand away from the pink and purple marks.

'Leave me!' yelled Jo, furious. Mark looked, and bellowed with laughter.

'Love-bites. You are so pathetic. Third years always seem to need to give each other love-bites. Silly turds.'

'Mark . . .' warned Alison dangerously, 'People in glass houses . . .' He immediately let go of his sister, and looked down at her, friendlier.

'Honestly, it is a bit duff, Jo. It looks so pathetically obvious. And they hurt, don't they?'

Jo didn't answer.

'Bet it was Concorde . . .' Mark laughed again.

'Shut up!' Jo glared, and stormed out of the room.

'Who's Concorde?' Alison, puzzled, watched the door slam.

'Remember when she got kicked playing football?'

'Yes.'

'Well, Jo is now going out with him, he's got a very big nose, that's why they call him Concorde.'

'Isn't she a bit young?'

'It's like that these days, Ma. Times have changed since your youth in the vicarage.'

Alison threw a dish-towel at him. 'Evidently. I hope she won't sulk all night.'

'I'll go and calm her down, have a brotherly chat. Concorde's OK. He goes to another school, but I know him.'

'How old is he?'

'Fifteen. It's a status-symbol to have love-bites at that age.'

'It's all very confusing,' said Alison.

'You'll get used to it.'

'I don't seem to have much option.'

As Mark went upstairs to placate his naughty little sister, Alison made supper, and mused, a little bewilderedly, on the passing of time. Yesterday she had met Jo from school to do some shopping for clothes, and she had noticed that when they passed a group of bare-torsoed workmen digging in the road, it had been Jo they had eyed appreciatively, and had whistled at, even though Alison looked quite good in a new red dress. It had made her feel quite old and depressed. They were all travelling up the staircase, like the Swedish folk-picture. Fortunately she still had a few years to go before she reached the summit and started to go downhill, and she intended to make the most of it. She finished cooking, and they ate. Mark had worked some magic on Jo, and they had a joyous family evening, just like old times. Alison was glad that Philip was not there, this was how she liked it. Had he been there there would have been the usual awful tensions. It was good like this: she liked being in charge by herself, and soon, soon she would see Gareth, and her cup would be full.

She was at the shop with Frankie, planning the week, when the long awaited phone-call came. Her lover was back at last.

'Alison?'

'Yes?' Breathless, swooning.

'Is it safe to talk?'

Alison eyed Frankie, who busied herself with brass polish and pretended unconcern. 'Yes, Frankie's here . . . I missed you . . .'

'Too long it was. Can we meet up today?'

'I have to be here all day. You'd better not actually come here, in case . . .'

'Mark or your husband walk in . . .'

'Yes.' Her voice was small.

'When then?'

'Wednesday? Same as usual?'

'Two whole days!'

'I could meet you for a quick lunch today.'

Gareth groaned. 'Then I can't touch you . . . but I

want to see you . . . . OK, just for a short time. I'll meet you at one, the Frog and Firkin.'

'Right.'

'I still love you.'

Frankie saw Alison blush, and mutter, 'The same this end . . .' and put the phone down.

'Allie, you're a naughty girl. You'll have to shut the shop, you know I'm out from eleven onwards.'

'I'll only be an hour, just for the lunch-break. I promise. Oh Frankie . . .'

'Tut,' Frankie shook her head sternly. 'I'm just worried for you; Philip was in a helluva state when he came over here the other day, and the kids, what about them?'

'Mark's friendly again, thank goodness, and Jo and I had a good trip down to Devon. I feel confident about my children. They'd opt for me rather than Philip if we blew.'

'If? How would you describe your present situation if that's not blowing?'

'I'm still married . . . . I live with my husband; it is tolerable most of the time, just . . . . We entertain most weekends, and we went out to dinner last night with friends – it was OK.'

'Gareth obviously wants all of you, so does Philip; I'm just worried about you coming in here one day with one arm, one leg and half a head . . .'

Alison wasn't really listening; she was sitting with a beatific smile on her face, lost to the world. Gareth, she was thinking, Gareth, Gareth. Frankie waved a mug in front of her eyes, and spoke in a deep Welsh voice, 'Drink up your coffee, *cariad* . . .'

'What?' Startled, Alison stared up at Frankie's grin. 'Oh sorry . . .'

'You are hopeless, and you worry me.'

'I worry me too, but it will solve itself, it's got to; things never stay the same. How was your big night out with Ant by the way?'

'Amazing.' Eagerly, Frankie recounted the evening, the paintings in the restaurant, the food, and the entertainingness of Anthony. 'I really like him you know.'

'I'm glad. We must have him to supper some time, would you like that?'

'Me and him you mean? At your place?'

Alison frowned . . . she had meant that, but her image had been of Gareth as host, not Philip. 'Yes, I'll fix it – do you think he'd like Philip?'

'Of course he would.'

'Pity I can't ask Gareth too . . .'

'Away you go, you idiot. Anyway, Ant's gone up to Scotland, he's got a job painting a goat.'

'I wonder what colour he's going to paint it . . .'

'Tartan, probably.'

A bell tinkled, announcing the first customer – a sad little man in a grey raincoat. Frankie wondered if he had ever put an ad in the lonely hearts column; he looked as though he could do with it.

Alison, busy in the back shop, was thinking about Philip. He had walked the dog yesterday afternoon, and obviously had not wanted company – he had put Jo off when she had offered to come with him. He had been out for ages, said he was thinking through some design problem.

When he came back, he had pecked Alison dutifully on the cheek before disappearing upstairs for a shower. She had noticed then that his aftershave had an unusual smell – not the normal discreetly musky scent, but a lighter, sweeter one. She had been busy in the kitchen at the time, but now that she remembered, it was an odd smell for a man, too floral. Strange. She must look at his various toiletries in the bathroom cabinet some time. It wasn't like Philip, normally he was very choosy about his aftershaves, and used only the one kind, with which he stocked-up on his trips abroad. He was off to Dublin soon for several days. Alison was relieved about that; they needed a breather.

Gareth, waiting in the big corner-sited pub, a five-minute drive from the shop, looked terrific. It was hard not to give up all plans for work and rush off to bed with him.

'Wait till Wednesday,' he said. 'It's less than forty-eight hours.'

They lunched, and tried not to clutch each other too publicly.

'Alison,' he said intensely, 'when I was in the country I so often imagined us together there. We could sell antiques from a country place. I could strip and polish . . .'

Their hands touched and they gazed at each other, wordless. At last Gareth drained his pint. 'It's almost two, you'd better go back.'

Alison stood up reluctantly. 'Any news of jobs yet?'

'Nothing. Croydon is a possibility still. They wanted a couple of references, which I've sent, but Croydon has little charisma, and it's a lousy journey from Shepherd's Bush, but I'd take anything that was offered. It's almost a year now, and I've written over a hundred applications.'

'They must be mad not to want you.'

'You must be mad because you do. Anyway,' Gareth stretched, and she watched his furry arms muscular in his purple and white striped shirt, 'I have various plans:

I'll tell you about them. I may learn to do woodworking, do a government course. They pay you to learn a trade. A philosophy lecturer friend of mine did that, and now he's got his own business making and mending furniture; he's a happy guy. All that could tie in with a country life . . .'

He walked with her to her car, where they embraced publicly, foolishly, unable to keep apart. Alison drove off shaking, and burst into tears. Why did it have to hurt so much? Why could she not simply treat him as a bonus and enjoy him as such? On the way back she passed an antique shop where she sometimes bought, and stopped off for a look. She came away very excited, having paid out a heart-stopping eighty-five pounds for an old Bristol cream jug; the girl in the shop was obviously pleased with the sale, but Alison knew for sure that it was worth much more, perhaps eight or nine hundred pounds, it was well marked – 'Bristoll', it said – and perfect, the best buy she had made for ages. She would sent it straight to Sotheby's. She was almost cheerful when she unlocked the shop door and heard the familiar tinkle of the bell.

Chapter Twenty-two

Phoebe Abrahams arrived unexpectedly on Alison one day in the shop; she looked utterly distraught, and her frizzy hair seemed suddenly to have become much greyer.

Alison sensed from her quavery voice and unkept looks that she was in a bad way – Phoebe was usually very much in command of herself. Within moments of seeing Alison she was weeping almost uncontrollably. 'I'm sorry to come unannounced,' she said, 'but it's John . . . he's actually left, gone off to live with his damned SDP girl of twenty-something – about half his age. He says he can't stand it any more. He called me a frigid bitch!'

Alison, alarmed to see her normally controlled friend in such a state, left Frankie to keep shop and took Phoebe out to eat round the corner, where she sobbed her way through an Italian lunch and a large quantity of wine.

'I told you we were trying to be civilised until Josh finished doing his A-Levels? Well, we did try, but John was coming home later and later, and pushing off for so-called seminars every weekend – any excuse not to be with me – and when he was home we fought and he said I nagged, and I felt nothing I could do was right . . .' Here she almost howled. 'And how can I at forty-five compete with some dolly bird twenty years younger, with no stretch-marks, or varicose veins?' From Phoebe, who was still a most elegant and attractive woman, highly successful in her work, this was almost laughable, but she was in no mood to be cheered up by being told so.

'I hate him! I hate him!' Hysterically she clutched Alison's arm almost painfuly and stared at her with wild eyes, then later, after more wine and divulgences of rows, tears and insults . . . 'I love him, I've never loved anybody else, but I cannot live like this . . .' She wept again, bitterly, apologised, drank more wine, and wiped her face with the white linen napkin, as Alison listened and tried to be of comfort.

'It's always sex, isn't it?' said Phoebe, calmer now. 'Sex or money. It's classic; John, for all his family counselling, messes up his own life in the same messy way as the clients who have made him famous and pay him God knows how much an hour for his psychiatric services. And now here we go – I scream at him that he's impotent, and he screams at me that I'm frigid, and actually we just don't fancy each other any more, but I am tied to him . . . . You can't destroy twenty-odd years of loving and friendship just for a slip of a girl he wants to sleep with!'

'Oh God . . .' said Alison. 'It is so sad. The loss of love . . .'

Phoebe sniffed. She was a little calmer now, and actually started to eat her seafood salad, pausing only a couple of times to wipe her eyes. 'Poor Josh . . . he saw us screeching, he knows the whole thing. He is so torn – he adores John. Thank goodness the other children have left home.'

'They do seem to pick up every frisson, don't they?' Alison remembered Jo's anxious face last night when she had discovered Philip and herself wrangling about the summer holiday. Philip had just accused Alison of not wanting to be with him because of her damned Welshman, when Jo had walked in and looked very uneasy.

'Why are you always arguing?' she had asked. 'It's horrible; I wish I went to boarding school.'

Philip had immediately tried a jolly-father act, as though nothing had happened, but Jo wasn't fooled.

Phoebe looked drained, suddenly much older than her years. 'How will I ever find anybody at my age?' she said, shaking her head hopelessly. 'I don't want to be alone for the rest of my life.'

'Maybe he will come back.'

'Never. I don't think I could bear it now. I wouldn't want him after the pain he has caused and the lies he has told . . .' The tears flowed again. 'I cannot imagine a life without him, and I don't want anybody else, yet I am afraid of being alone.'

'Oh, Phoebe. I always thought you were a perfect pair, glued together. I am so sorry.'

Phoebe tried to smile. 'The glue must have got metal-fatigue or something. Anyway, how are you? You seemed pretty fraught when we last met.'

Alison shrugged. 'I don't know. We are in the middle of a most uncomfortable time; Philip has hurt me terribly in the past, and I in my turn have gone off the rails, only . . .' She looked at Phoebe, and now she too was tearful, 'I have done the forbidden thing and fallen madly in love.'

'Oh God, it is all so bloody painful.' Phoebe shook her head frowning. 'I thought you were looking extra beautiful. That explains it. Maybe we should all be speyed like cats so that we don't want sex any more, it would certainly solve a lot of problems. Is your man married?'

Alison shook her head. 'Divorced, looks after his two children by himself – pretty heroically.'

'What's his job?' Phoebe smiled sadly as she reached for more wine. 'I'm sorry, darling, I know I sound like a maiden aunt, but it's interesting to know.'

'He's an unemployed lecturer in sociology. Very poor, very handsome, kind, intelligent, amusing, brave . . . . And he sells antique books.'

'Oh dear, you have got it bad. Poor you. Poor Philip. How is he?'

'He's just booked a three-week holiday in the south of France for the whole family. He's madly trying to be domestic and play the good husband.'

'He's not pissing about?'

'I don't think so, not at the moment . . . why do you ask?'

Phoebe looked a little embarrassed. 'Just something John said, trying to justify himself that his behaviour was normal.'

Alison was puzzled. 'I don't think so, he's being so jumpy about me, intermixed with being grovellingly helpful domestically, but mind you, we both work so hard that we often talk very little except about domestic arrangements, and lately we zonk into bed and simply sleep. I've been quite relieved about that to be honest, because for a while I cried every time . . . but he's almost left me alone for the last two or three weeks.' She gazed thoughtfully at her green salad topped with decoratively sliced radishes, 'Though come to think of it, that is pretty unlike Philip . . .'

'Maybe he *is* otherwise occupied . . .'

Alison was adamant. 'He couldn't be such a hypocrite; he's so paranoid about what he thinks I'm doing.'

'I wouldn't be so sure, my dear. Men are strange creatures, they like to own us body and soul, yet to be free in what they do themselves.'

Alison shrugged. She had a sudden memory of the last time she had made love with Gareth, two days ago. She had arrived at his house fraught and juddering from an argument with Philip – though what the argument had been about she could now hardly even remember. They often seemed to have these almost ritual confrontations these days, all about nothing; Gareth had taken one look at her and told her to take off her shoes. She had done so, and he had made her sit down and had massaged her naked feet with such loving tenderness that she had wanted to weep; he had relaxed her; and loved her until she felt in balance with herself again. He had an unerring instinct for what she needed. She could not do without him, yet could see no easy solution to the situation. It was a deadlock.

'A marriage is an awful lot to dispose of.' Phoebe was getting heavy again. 'Think hard, Alison; count your blessings. You have an intelligent and responsible husband, and remember all those years when it was all right.'

'I know, I know, but you know how suddenly you see your whole past in a different light? How you read it as a different pattern, and start feeling resentful about things that happened, or that you weakly acquiesced to, even years ago?'

'All too well,' Phoebe sighed. 'But here I am at the end of the road, and the bleakness of the future is almost unbearable for me.'

They ordered coffee, and Alison succumbed to buying cigarettes – her first packet since she had smoked secretly when staying with her father, desperately trying to hide the fact of her smoking from Jo by hiding in the garden or the fields behind the house.

'I didn't know you smoked,' observed Phoebe, taking one.

'I don't, not often.'

'Nor do I.' They smiled painfully, and lit up.

Phoebe was certainly calmer than she had been on arrival when Alison at last paid the bill. As they hugged farewell, promising to keep in touch, Phoebe clutched Alison tightly, 'Don't do anything hasty, you have a lot to lose, probably much more than you realise. Believe me, it is only when you lose it that you realise what you had, and I think you and Philip have a lot going for you.'

'You're probably right, but I suspect logic has very little to do with it.'

'Alison, you are playing with fire, hotter than you know.'

'I think I do know,' Alison looked back at Phoebe levelly. 'It's already pretty hot. We're in a fiery furnace.'

'Anyway, goodbye, thanks for listening.'

Alison watched her friend lurch unsteadily towards the tube-station; she felt drained and shaken by the meeting. How difficult people's lives seemed to be: how she hated people's need to possess each other. She despised Philip for his jealousy now, yet she had been consumed with agonies of rejection and jealousy when first he had been unfaithful. It seemed insoluble. She was glad to have the shop to go to, glad to be able to potter about tidying and mending oddments, even glad for once to do the VAT. It took her mind off the agony of it all.

Mark Salveson and Susan Richards, both young, blond and melancholy, sat in the evening sun on a wall overlooking the river Thames in West London and looked at the boats and ducks on the river. Below them, a couple of dogs ran along the mud-flats chasing seagulls, and a lone treasure hunter wandered by the water, clad in wellington boots, his metal detector nosing hopefully from side to side in search of coins or even something grander. He had been there for ages, as had Mark and Susan – who was gazing morosely into her half-full glass of shandy which glinted in the evening sun.

'Why can't we, though?' said Mark.

Susan was vehement, and somewhat weepy. 'I just don't want to. I never want to be frightened like that again.'

Mark looked at her anxiously; she had gone all remote and difficult to talk to again, and he didn't know how to get through to her. He sighed, and watched the dogs – one of which had given up chasing seagulls and was busily gnawing a disgusting-looking bird-corpse. 'I think you've gone off me.'

Susan didn't answer, but her eyes brimmed; Mark eyed her uneasily, drank a large schlurp of beer, put down his glass, and gently felt for Susan's hand and played with her flaccid fingers. 'Have you?'

Susan took ages to answer, Mark wanted to scream at her to talk to him, wanted her to respond as she used to, all warm and willing, wanting him to touch her, but she stared across the river, and helplessly he watched the tears trickle down her cheek.

'Susan, for heaven's sake tell me what's wrong?'

'I don't know, I just feel different about things . . .'

'About me, you mean,' he said glumly.

'It doesn't seem simple any more.'

'I feel like that too, but we won't ever get into trouble, I promise.'

'I just feel the only safe way is not to start anything.'

'Oh God,' Mark shook his head bewilderedly. 'That's crazy.'

'I'm sorry you think I'm crazy,' said Susan stiffly, and sniffed. 'Have you got a hankie?'

'Here,' he handed her a tissue. 'It's not very clean, sorry . . . I used it on the bike.'

To his relief Susan laughed a little, and wiped her nose. 'Very romantic.'

'Do you want to stop going around together?' He watched the dog intently: it was bound to be sick if it ate all that gunge; come to think of it he felt pretty sick himself.

'I don't know,' said Susan at last, and gazed with obsessive interest at a passing boat crammed with people waving.

Mark dropped her hand. 'You must know.'

'What do you think?'

'You know what I think; I think we usually have a really good time, but we both had a hellish fright – you most of all obviously – but it won't happen again, I promise.'

A long silence, then: 'Maybe we shouldn't, not for a bit.'

'Not do it, or not go out?'

She shrugged. 'Both maybe.'

'You're giving me the heave. Why can't you come out straight and say so?'

'I'm not saying that.' She was crying again.

'Yes, you are, or if you aren't, what are you saying?'

'Maybe we should stop going out for a bit . . .'

Mark was silent; he wanted to shout, to cry, to hug her into sense, and to thump her all at once. Instead he stood up and took the empty glasses in his hands, which he noticed with shame were trembling. 'I'll take these in.'

Susan looked painfully up at him. 'I'm sorry.'

The boy shrugged. 'It's your choice.' He tried to smile, but his mouth and eyes weren't doing the right things. He turned to go into the pub, and having put down the glasses, escaped to the Gents. He peed, zipped himself up and went to the basin; he still felt quite sick, kicked in the guts. He simply did not know how to cope with this one, and he hadn't cried for about four years. Shit. He didn't want her to see him red-eyed. He washed his face, and took as long as possible to buy crisps. They crunched them in silence as they walked towards the tube; neither of them could think of anything to say. They travelled back on the train with barely a word exchanged, and when they arrived – they got off at the same station – Susan looked at him: 'I'll just go home by myself.'

'Goodbye, then.'

She turned to go. 'See you tomorrow.'

'Tomorrow's Sunday.' They usually spent Sunday together.

'Oh,' she nodded, blushing. 'See you on Monday then.'

'OK. Bye.'

'Bye.'

Mark turned quickly and lost himself in the evening jostle of Queensway with its swarms of people of all nationalities. There were enticing food-smells from at least twenty restaurants and take-away places. He bought himself a couple of samosas and went to eat them near his old primary school, where there was a low wall he could sit on in front of some flats. When he was small he used to watch an old woman feed the birds here every day. He had always thought she must be very rich, because she had a new packet of birdseed every single day, and Ma used to tell him how small old-age pensions were. He ate his samosas slowly as several fat pigeons fluttered hopefully near him. He threw a couple of tiny pieces to them and looked at the time. It was only nine o'clock, the night was young, but without Susan to play with it loomed endlessly and depressingly ahead. He decided to go home: he hoped that somebody would be in, and that if they were his parents would not be bickering. He would watch the late-night film, there wasn't anything else to do.

Frankie had not spent a Saturday night in – washing her hair – for ages: there had always been something happening – the fair in Bath, the affair with Jay, Frankie's various dancer and singer friends, plus the odd encounter with a lonely-heart stranger – and of course there had been Anthony, who had taken up quite a lot of her time of late. It was odd with him out of town, it made things seem strangely piano.

She was tired. She had risen early to do the Bell Street market which was always a bloody battle to get at the best things – people became quite violent sometimes – and it was one of the few occasions when she was glad she was big, because she could elbow her way through the smaller dealers to flick out the garments and objects she spotted in the mêlée. She had done well this morning, and passed a pleasantly busy day at the shop refurbishing, washing and polishing her various buys. She had decided to stay in tonight after turning down an invitation to another of Jay's parties. She still felt sensitive about the whole business, and thought she would give it a rest for a while: Jay was sure in mid-party to make some very public joke about Frankie's brief entry into her world, and her even briefer exit. She blushed at the memory, then smiled, because she had sold the labrys earring to a shy bespectacled American girl today; she wished her luck. Maybe she actually had found her niche. Frankie wasn't Scots for nothing.

She finished drying her hair, and shook her head to make the fiery curls stand out more. She felt very lonely: maybe Alison was in. Impulsively she tired the number: Mark answered in a rather subdued voice.

'Hi, Mark, it's Frankie, I just wondered if by some miracle your Ma is in?'

'Sorry. They're both out at some big architectural dinner. I'm by myself.'

'By yourself!' Frankie was surprised, 'On a Saturday night? What have you done with your beautiful blonde?'

'We had a bit of a thing . . . . I'm not seeing her . . .'

'Oh Mark . . . I'm sorry. When did this happen?'

Reluctantly, Mark admitted that it had been tonight.

Frankie immediately felt maternal: 'What are you doing?'

'Watching telly.' He sounded very low.

'Is Jo in?'

'She's at Charlotte's.'

'Mark, have you had supper?'

There was a pause, 'I had a couple of samosas . . .'

'Are you hungry?'

'I am quite . . .'

'Would you like some fish and chips or something?'

'Yeah, I would, but . . .'

'Would you like me to bring some round? And could I please watch your telly with you? I won't yatter, I promise, 'I'm feeling pretty frail myself, and a wee bit lonesome.'

'OK.' Mark sounded more cheerful. 'That would be great, but I've no money . . .'

'Fear not, my son, Auntie Frankie will provide. I'll cycle over; see you in about fifteen minutes.'

Several hours later, when Alison and Philip, dressed formally – Philip resplendent in dinner jacket and black tie – arrived home, they found Frankie dozing on the sofa, wth Mark sprawled on the floor, watching the final captions of the late-night movie. Alison was pleased and surprised, and at first somewhat puzzled by the combination, but fetched Frankie a sleeping-bag and insisted that she stay the night; it would improve breakfast no end to have Frankie there. She didn't question Mark's presence – she guessed from his face that something had happened – but was tactful enough to leave the boy alone. She and Philip had had quite an enjoyable evening for such a formal affair: the food had been good, and Philip had been happy talking business, extra-cheerful because the Hong Kong job was, as he put it, at last in the bag. He always used to say at such events: 'Must go and mingle darling, Michael Angelo had to hustle to get the Sistine Chapel commission.'

They both looked good. Alison had talked to several people she liked. Briefly it had felt almost like old times, when they used to be a normal married couple. The entire evening passed without any bickering, perhaps because they were both on public display, being images rather than realities.

Chapter Twenty-three

Alison and Gareth managed to meet regularly, barring the odd dental appointment or sore throat in Gareth's ménage. Their love blossomed: the terraced house remained an oasis for Alison, and she could not imagine life without her lover, though the pain of being parted from him was increasingly agonising, and, as the holidays loomed not far ahead there was a desperation and poignancy to their love-making which made it all the more intense.

Philip, high on his Hong Kong success, and now also involved in the building of a big new factory for an American company in Dublin, was away a lot, and when at home was cool, preoccupied, but still manically domestic, which, though she had long resented him for not being, Alison found bizarre, and occasionally demeaning. He would arrive back from Heathrow, pale and tired, put on the 'Happy Days' apron and wash up or cook chicken in some new exotic fashion. Jo teased him, calling him Philippa, but she, along with the rest of the family, was pleased enough to eat and admire his excellent meals. For the moment he had laid off questioning his wife as to her doings, though he remained aggressively curious as to her daily whereabouts, but his own pressure of work was so heavy that there was little he could do in the way of keeping close tabs on her.

One evening he arrived home from work early, and summoned the whole family out to view a split-new silver Audi which he had bought that afternoon, without a word to anyone. Mark, soon due to sit his driving test, was particularly cheered by the sight of the car, and Jo, filled with admiration for her brilliant father, clung close to him, smiling proudly and they all laughed when the dalmatian leapt into the driver's seat, tongue lolling.

Alison felt numb: that very morning she had bought and planted two new rose bushes at the front of the house. They were both acting as though the marriage was going to continue, both making acts of faith in the future, but she could simply not imagine a future without Gareth. Philip, seeing the newly-planted roses, became very emotional, and hugged her, his pale eyes swimming with tears.

'We are going to be all right, aren't we? France will be good.'

'I hope so,' she said doubtfully.

Philip – once more without consulting her, as with the car – had booked a house in France for three weeks in August. It was forty kilometres from Bordeaux, right on the sea, and there was a maid as part of the deal; the big new car would make the long drive down very comfortable, but she dreaded the thought of no Gareth for all that time – he would be cut out of town for six whole weeks. Nevertheless she liked the car, and was aware that she perversely took pleasure in the good living Philip provided. That night he took the whole family out for a celebratory Greek meal, and she watched her children, both glowing, as they enjoyed their father's munificence, and once more felt torn between the two men, the dark and the golden.

Gareth's electricity was about to be cut off because he could not afford to pay the bill. Alison could not imagine herself sharing that sort of ménage. Gareth became upset when she offered to lend him money: 'I would never borrow from you; I want to look after you, not be beholden to you.'

It was very different to the Salveson finances. Alison herself was doing well: Sotheby's had valued her Bristol jug at over a thousand pounds, so she was feeling pretty smug businesswise, and it depressed her to see the man she loved in the same old pair of shoes and the same few shirts, however much she admired his taste. On Gareth's birthday – his thirty-eighth – she gave him a new shirt in brown and white stripes, and a golden yellow pullover. She saw that though he was pleased and touched, he was also embarrassed by the different in their finances. Obviously it made him feel less of a man.

Philip, confident that he was winning back his errant wife, was so obviously attractive when she thought about him objectively, even though she was no longer sexually stirred by him. Alison felt as bewildered as ever; there was no doubt that she enjoyed the good life, and found Gareth's poverty hard to view. There seemed no end to it – none of his job applications had gelled despite a couple of abortive interviews – but in bed, in his arms, conjoined with him, all such problems melted away. She did not think of the future, only of the now.

In his double bed with bright green pillows and duvet, Anthony Brownstone bemusedly watched Frankie's glory of curls spread over the green and thought he was in heaven; he lay entranced watching her sleep, her mouth slightly open, the expression on her face sweetly vulnerable, her beautiful arms spread behind her head like a baby's. The morning sun, filtering through the white window-blind made her hair glint with gold, and he wondered if he should draw her, and was about to reach for his sketch-book – which always lay beside the bed – when she opened her great green eyes and smiled up at him.

'Hi, Ant. What's the time?'

'About eight.'

She lay quietly, and reached across to stroke his chest; he felt her touch go through him like some glorious lightning, and pulled away gently, stroking her magical hand.

'Do you want some coffee?'

'Mmmm, lovely. How long were you lying there watching me?'

'Just a few minutes; you're very beautiful. I want to paint you.'

She smiled again, snuggling sleepily into the duvet. 'I actually think you're beautiful too. That was amazing. What a night . . .' She leaned towards him, and they kissed slowly, deliciously.

He looked at her, abandoned and relaxed: 'I knew the minute I set eyes on you that we would be good together.'

Frankie giggled, 'And I ran, fleeing into the murk . . .'

'Ah, but you left your umbrella.'

'This is true.'

He stood up, and she admired his compact but strongly-made body. How could she ever have thought him small or unattractive?

'Croissants for Madame?'

'Wonderful, have you got some?'

'There's a delicatessen round the corner. I'll only be a minute.' He pulled on jeans and tee-shirt and busied himself with socks and shoes. She watched him amused.

'Do you always wear odd socks?'

'Usually. I keep them paired in odd colours, it saves hassle when the washing-machine eats them.'

'Funny, I'd never noticed.'

'I have hidden depths, there's a lot you can learn about me.' He stood, shoes tied, belt buckled, ready to go.

'So I'm beginning to find out,' Frankie turned over on her side. 'Don't be too long, Ant. I'll miss you.'

He went out, switching the electric kettle on in the kitchen before he left. His plants had never looked so bright and alive as they did this morning; everything seemed sharper, more beautiful to him and his body was charged with a humming sense of being extra-full of energy. The blood was surely flowing faster.

He hummed as he bought croissants: 'Somebody's veree 'appy today . . .' said the fat lady behind the counter.

Anthony grinned. The woman handed him a bag and took his money, cheered to see him in such a good mood; she had been very upset when she saw his injured face a few weeks ago, and muttered angrily about the 'orrible people in London to her melancholy French husband.

When he was out Frankie lay in a disbelieving state of happiness. She had missed Anthony dreadfully when he was away, and was just beginning to realise why. When he had come rather shyly into the shop on his return from Scotland she had felt an immense surge of delight at the sight of him, and immediately they had talked and talked, laughing, breaking into each other's sentences, breathless with the rediscovery of their friendship, which had now turned – for Frankie, unexpectedly – into a different and much deeper sort of friendship. They had gone for a Chinese meal when the shop closed, and had drunk only China tea, and almost before the almond cakes were consumed, they had clutched each other breathlessly, and confessed how much they had missed each other.

Moments later, it seemed, they had been in Anthony's green bed. She felt a sense of wonder and delight: it had been rapturous, highly emotional, they had talked and made love with amazing fondness for most of the night; her bleak months of loneliness slipped away, and already seemed a thing of the past. She was certain that this was something that would not be over after a night or two. It was more special, more precious than anything she had ever felt. She wondered what Alison would say – probably that she had expected it for ages. Trust Frankie to be the last to realise, but it was wonderful, there was no other word for it. She looked round the white-walled bedroom, with its healthy plants and many pictures, all detailed and unusual and to her, beautiful. He was a very special man.

Alison was writing lists when Frankie flamed into the shop, burning bright and beautiful: 'You're looking very cheery. Have you found something that will make your fortune?'

Frankie sank into the Victorian button chair, legs splayed, and closed her eyes. 'Nothing like that. No.' She shook her head, a beatific smile on her face.

'What's happened?' Alison was intrigued. The woman was positively radiant.

Frankie opened her eyes. 'You'll be relieved to hear that I've decided that for certain I am definitely heterosexual after all, not bi, not gay, but infinitely hetero.'

Alison rose from her papers. 'Coffee time I think; shall we have real coffee?'

'If ye haven't got champagne, that will do fine.'

Puzzled, Alison filled and switched on the kettle and peered at her: 'Frankie, have you fallen in love or something?'

Frankie looked momentarily worried. 'Yes, mebbe, but I don't know, I've never been in love. Does it make your toes tingle?'

Alison laughed. 'It can do, and quite a few other bits too.'

'Ahhhh . . .' Frankie sighed.

'Don't tell me you've met another lonely heart?'

'Well, he was once . . .'

Alison stared, coffee-pot in mid-air. 'Anthony?'

Frankie nodded almost shyly. Alison put down the pot and walked over to her friend.

'Frankie, that is the best thing that has happened for ages. I had almost given up hope. It's wonderful news; he is a lovely guy, perfect for you.'

'He's awfy wee . . .'

'Nonsense! He's not very tall, but so what, Napoleon was tiny, Mussolini was tiny, Dudley Moore, Roman Polanski . . . . There are lots of fabulous small men, and I know loads of people who are taller than their men – what about Princess Di and Charles?'

'I suppose it doesn't really matter if you like each other . . .'

'Of course it doesn't. Ant has been mad about you for months.'

'I know. Poor guy, I've given him a bad time.'

'You haven't; you've needed that time to explore yourself.'

'And a few other people . . .' Frankie smiled lopsidedly. 'Oh Allie, he's just so nice . . .'

'I'll get out my violin.'

'Please do, a wee bittie Mozart to start the day.'

They drank coffee, and dealt with a customer or two, though Frankie remained in a haze for most of the morning. When at last they ate a picnic lunch in the back shop, Alison managed to get the Scots girl down to earth to make plans for the next couple of weeks.

'We are setting off for France in a fortnight, right?'

'Right, and I'll be here.'

'Now,' Alison took her lists and looked earnestly at Frankie. 'I'm going to that country auction in Somerset next weekend, it's on a Tuesday, I'll drive down and view on Monday, and either be back late Tuesday or Wednesday.'

'Are you going alone to Somerset?'

Alison paused, 'Maybe not, if he can farm his kids out, and I can borrow the Abrahams' cottage.' She spoke quietly.

'Surely they won't be using it mid-week?'

'I'm not sure; Phoebe Abrahams is pretty hysterical, she phoned again yesterday, she sounded really bad. It's awful to see.'

'Yes well . . . that's what happens . . .' Worried, Frankie eyed Alison. 'How's Mark's broken heart?'

'He's got about ten tubes of cream to fight his spots, that's taking most of his energy.'

'He's plooky is he?'

'What's plooky?'

'Pussy spots, boils and things. Zits, the Americans call them. I prefer plooks myself, it's more onomatopoeic.'

'How do you mean?'

'Plook!' said Frankie simply. 'It's the noise they make when you burst them.'

'Frankie, you are disgusting.'

'I know,' Frankie beamed and munched.

Alison, looking out of the window, suddenly winced. 'Oh God! It's Hilary!'

Frankie moaned and peered. 'Where?'

'Over there, heading this way . . .' She stared round in panic, 'I cannot face a Hilary session, what will we do?'

'We could hide . . .' Frankie was panicking too, but suddenly stood still, staring. 'It's OK, it's not Hilary, it's somebody else, older, look, honest – but it does look like her . . .'

'Thank goodness for that! What a fright you gave me! You!'

Alison threatened her partner with a newly-acquired pair of elk-horns. They were large, flat with several points, attached to a skull, a hefty weapon.

'Sorry! Here, we ought to fix those to the wall, they'd look quite good, they're a bit bulky just sitting there.'

Frankie rooted under the sink and produced nails and a hammer; later, when Anthony came in to greet his beloved and take her home for supper, he found her up a ladder cursing, her mouth bristling with nails, fixing the huge horns to the stripped pine wall.

Philip was uneasy about Alison's imminent departure to Somerset and obviously distrustful. 'Why isn't Frankie going with you? She usually goes on buying trips with you.'

'Frankie's staying at our place. Anyway, she's involved with Anthony and wants to be with him.'

'Who is Anthony?' asked Philip aloofly.

'You know, the artist who did our sign – the man who got beaten up.'

'Oh,' said Philip. He had not met this person, therefore he was not of interest. He stared coldly at Alison. 'I hope you don't have any plans to have company down there?'

Alison flushed, and hoped he couldn't hear the thundering of her heart. 'What are you talking about?'

'You know very well what I'm talking about. Your Garry or whatever; I might just take a trip down and join you if I get bored in Dublin.'

'Please do,' Alison got up from the breakfast table and clumsily began to put the supper dishes into the dishwasher. She was pretty certain that he wouldn't do that; she had seen his agenda last week, and he really needed to be in Dublin – he was leaving tomorrow, like Gareth and herself – but she felt very frightened when she imagined Philip bursting in on herself and Gareth with a gun.

'I saw John on Friday by the way,' said Philip; he seemed oblivious to her confusion. 'You know he's moved out?'

'Yes, I saw Phoebe.'

'You didn't tell me.'

'We haven't exactly been talking.'

'Anyway, he's with his bird; he says Phoebe is being very difficult and emotional, keeps phoning up in tears and making the girl cry. Silly bitch.'

'How can you say that? She's very unhappy.'

'I've always thought she was a silly bitch; John's a fool too, but Phoebe is old enough to accept reality.'

Just like you eh, thought Alison bitterly, and had yet another fantasy of crashing some heavy culinary item down on her husband's unwitting head. She was alarmed by her own imagination, she could almost see his brains pulped on the floor and the blood.

'We are so lucky,' she had said to Gareth; 'I never thought we would manage time like this together again, it just seemed too difficult.'

'Don't ever say we're lucky again.' He laid his hand on her lips. 'Don't tempt fate; but I am happy that we're going, we need time together. I hate it more and more when you always have to run off because of work or my kids coming back.'

'At least this time I won't nearly have a crash every time I see a yellow car. On the drive down to my father's I kept seeing yellow cars and veering off the road.'

He put his hands on her face. 'I love you, you daft woman.'

'I love you too.'

'Are you happy?'

She nodded. 'Very happy.'

'This cottage we're going to, you've been there before?'

'Often, but not to stay for a year or so.'

'Have you gone there with the family?' He meant Philip.

'Yes, in the past, and I was there with Jo recently. The owners are very close friends – or were – they have just split, and the wife is terribly upset.'

'Are there neighbours?'

'There's a farm a couple of hundred yards down the road; we collect the key from them.'

'What about me? Won't they be curious? They'll notice that I'm not tall and blond.'

Alison frowned; she had been so obsessed with

getting away with Gareth that she hadn't thought about that. 'We'll have to keep a low profile; I hardly know them; you stay away, I'll do the talking.'

'OK.'

At last they were actually in Somerset and were able to walk along the beach, dizzy with joy at being alone. She smiled at him. 'Two whole days; I can't believe it.'

They went to the nearby auction house and viewed, and saw a lot of hopeful things. After chatting to a local they discovered that there was another auction that night in a country pub about twenty miles away. Alison grew very excited.

'Let's go. I'm desperate for new stock. We'll fill the back of the car right up.' Gareth was happy to do anything she suggested, though he didn't expect to buy much, except for the odd book or two.

They came to the Abrahams' cottage at tea-time, with home-made buns and cakes from a country baker. Gareth quickly got the old stove going; Alison loved to watch him do things in his quiet muscular manner, he was very practical and efficient. After tea they lay on mattresses in front of the roaring stove and made love; Alison was enchanted to look beyond her lover's dark-bearded head out of the window, which was filled with field and sheep – no sky was visible. It was like a Samuel Palmer painting, bosky and overflowing with life. She could imagine a painting by Anthony of lovers in front of a stove with a green sheep-filled window like that; she wished she could commission him to do one for her and Gareth.

In the late afternoon sun they wandered behind the house and lay together in a buttercupped field with ladybirds crawling over them like a mobile jewels. It was an idyll, and Gareth once again said that he would like to be with her always.

'I could sell my house and we could buy somewhere in the country together and run a business: I know I have not your visual flair or knowledge of antiques, but my book-list is doing quite well, and if we sold furniture I could be very useful, stripping and polishing and restoring. I'm good with my hands, and I may still do the course I told you about. I'm giving myself another two or three months of applying for academic jobs, then if I have no luck I shall stop trying. It's too demoralising. I'm not good at being penniless.'

'Who is?'

He shrugged. 'Nobody, but you have only seen me like this. I was quite respectable once, you know.'

'Of course you were,' she tickled him with a long grass, and they kissed and watched a rabbit hop across the buttercups.

'I'd like to stay here forever,' said Alison.

'I'm asking you to do something like that,' Gareth leaned over her and stared earnestly into her worried face. 'We can't go on like this, something will give, or erupt, and it might even be me.' He sat up and stared across the hills which hid the sea, his face grim.

'Give me time, Gareth.' Alison leaned against him. 'It's hard, and there are all our children.'

'Children can adapt; mine have. They're well-enough adjusted.'

'Who wouldn't be, living with you?'

'Well then?' He looked at her, his eyes full of yearning. 'I need you, woman.'

That was what Philip kept reiterating. She felt weary of being needed. She stroked his face. 'I don't know, not yet.'

Gareth grunted almost angrily, and stood up to walk

to the wooden gate. He leaned on it staring blackly at the green glory, the butterflies and cows, and the sheep which bleated plaintively amid the bird-calls. She watched him, and felt as black as he did; maybe after France, she would at last be able to reach some sort of decision. She was certainly not happy with Philip, but was she unhappy enough to do what John Abrahams had done, and to do it to Jo, to Mark and even Philip? She was not sure; but she did want Gareth, of that there was never any doubt. He returned to her, and held out his hand to pull her to him. The problem faded. All time and all the world was in his arms. Nothing else mattered.

'Come on,' he said. 'Let's go back.'

They walked hand in hand, but when the farmhouse was in sight they wordlessly let go of one another.

Gareth looked at her: 'I could pack my bags and go, Alison, if that's what you want.'

She was shocked. 'You know that's not what I want. I couldn't bear that.'

'No?'

'No!' vehemently. 'But I can't just dump my family and life . . . not just like that.'

'And husband?'

She did not answer; they walked in silence till they came to the cottage. Her eyes were full of tears. 'When I'm with you it seems so simple, but when I'm at home, it seems very difficult.'

'I understand, but I don't think you can go on like this, and I'm not at all sure that I can. I'm clear about what I want, but do I actually have any hope?'

She tried to silence him with the oblivion of an embrace, but he pulled away and she felt rejected by his gesture. Almost fiercely he put his hands on her shoulders and stared into her eyes, his own murky and darker than ever.

'Listen, my love, I want you, I want you more than anything or anyone I have ever wanted, but if there is no future for us I would rather cut and go before I get any more hurt.' He stared fiercely at her tears, then kissed them dry. 'Men can cry too, you know.' Alison remained almost numb, speechless; she did not know what to say or how to answer him. She wanted him as much as he wanted her, but she wanted the rest as well, her family, her home, and her children with their father. She wanted them all.

'Anyway,' Gareth's voice was gentle now, and a little husky, 'soon we will be parted for the whole summer. Maybe that will give you the time you need to decide what you are going to do.'

There was a rabbit of panic lolloping round and round her stomach; she nodded faintly: 'Time, Gareth, I need time.'

'OK,' he said. 'Today and tomorrow we have stolen time, it's your limbo you're always talking about; let's try to enjoy it and not destroy the now.'

Later, they set off to view the evening's auction. Gareth concentrated on the driving, the road was windy and narrow and the scenery spectacularly distracting and they spoke little. Maddeningly, through Alison's head the words of a nursery game repeated themselves meaninglessly over and over:

'The farmer's in his den, the farmer's in his den,
Heigh ho my daddy oh, the farmer's in his den.
The farmer wants a wife, the farmer wants a wife,
Heigh ho my daddy oh, the farmer wants a wife . . .'

. . . and so it went on and on until she was nearly stupid.

The pub was in a small village with lush gardens and huddled cottages, many of them ancient and thatched.

Alison buzzed as she marked her catalogue with much excited anticipation.

'I can stock up for months on this lot if the prices are right.' Her face was glowing, eyes bright. There was a lot of sporting paraphernalia, fishing-rods and reels, and several five guns. Philip would have been fascinated. . . . She bit back the thought, but seventeen years of living with Philip had made it automatic to think of him when she viewed such items. She pointed to one particular gun, a beautifully-made Holland and Holland twelve bore with intricate chased patterning on the metal.

'That's worth at least a couple of thousand, it's a real goodie.'

Gareth looked a little helpless, 'I feel so damned ignorant with you, I'd have guessed a couple of hundred at the most.'

'You know about things I know nothing about, that's how the whole business operates.'

The excitement of two auctions in one day got to Alison, and he watched admiringly as she confidently placed bids. He bought a few books, and seemed pleased, but spent about two hundred pounds compared to Alison's nearly two thousand. She was sure of herself, and a little manic, but the quality was there. There were a lot of high-class dealers competing, and Gareth was amazed like a boy at some of the prices. He glanced at Alison when the gun she had pointed out sold for two thousand, four hundred pounds. She had never bought so much or so well, and was high when late at night in the darkness of the pub car park they packed the new acquisitions into the car.

'You're so bold.' Gareth grinned as he lifted a cardboard box of glasses and china into the car boot. 'I was amazed at you, going on and on, up and up . . . it would terrify me.'

'You get used to it. It's all superb stuff. I'm so glad

we came . . .' She looked at him, '. . . even for the business I mean . . .' She smiled, and they stared at each other, lovestruck, senses whirling.

Back at the cottage, both painfully aware that this would be their last night together for weeks if not months, Alison wordlessly fumbled round for candles, and Gareth livened up the stove before they undressed and climbed into the bed they had made up on the floor. They shared a glass of wine, lit by the glow of stove and candle; it was magically beautiful, and they tried not to think about their imminent parting.

They were making love when the phone rang. It was utterly unexpected, an intrusion. Alison had already rung home from the pub and spoken to a giggling Jo, who told her Frankie was feeding them haggis: she had also reported that Philip had just rung from Dublin sounding quite cheerful.

'I'll have to go . . .' she clambered, naked in the firelight, trying to remember where the phone was. Gareth followed, also naked, and obviously interrupted, lighting her way with a candle.

'It's here by the door,' he said, and laid down the candle on the table. Alison glanced at her watch, it was well after midnight: she picked up the phone.

'Hello?' she said, eyeing Gareth and fondling his erection.

It was a man's voice, familiar. 'Is that you, Alison?'

'John . . . yes it is, hello . . . we . . . I'm just enjoying your lovely place, it is bliss . . .'

'Alison,' John Abrahams' voice was low and serious. 'I'm sorry to disturb you so late.'

Alison was suddenly very alert. 'What is it, John?'

'I just wanted to tell you . . . it's Phoebe . . . . She's dead.'

'Dead!' Alison almost shrieked. She had known

Phoebe for as long as she had known Philip. 'What on earth? I saw her only last week.'

John's voice was old, tired and world-weary. 'She killed herself. Josh found her early this morning.'

'How? What?'

'An overdose. She was on lots of tranquillisers, that plus most of a bottle of gin.'

'Oh my God . . .' Alison's knees almost gave way. Gareth handed her a chair and stood caressing her shoulder, listening anxiously.

John wasn't very coherent at the other end. 'She was terribly fond of you, Allie, said you were her best friend. God, it's a mess.'

'John. I'm so sorry . . . how's Josh? And the others?'

'Shocked, very grown up really. Antagonistic to me, understandably, specially Josh.'

'When is the funeral?'

'Wednesday, one o'clock, Golders Green Crematorium. Is Philip with you?'

'He's in Dublin.'

'Of course . . . with whatsit from the office . . .'

Alison was puzzled. 'What?'

'His PA. Sorry, Allie, it doesn't matter, will you tell him?' He was sobbing a little now.

'Of course. I'll be there, John, on Wednesday. Anything I can do before then?'

'No, we're coping, thanks, Allie. Goodbye, I'll see you then.'

Alison, numbed, put down the phone. Gareth made her come over to the fire and handed her a glass of wine, but she shook her head. 'Oh my God, poor Phoebe; I knew she was unhappy, but I didn't think she was suicidal . . .'

'She killed herself? The owner of this place?' Gareth was aghast.

Alison nodded dumbly, memories of her lunch with Phoebe and earlier memories of inter-family holidays and picnics welled up. 'She was so lively, so intelligent . . .'

'And so unhappy?'

Alison nodded dully. 'Her husband had just left her after years of so-called happy marriage; they were a sort of touchstone pair, he's a family therapist.'

Gareth grimaced 'How bloody sad and wasteful.'

'Yes.' Her voice was very small; she pulled the duvet round her and detachedly watched the muscular beauty of his naked back and strong flanks lit orange. 'I feel quite sick.'

'Here.' He knelt by her, his furry body comforting, his sex shrunk small and tender. He gave her a warm mug of coffee and patted and stroked her like an animal in need of comfort. 'I'm sorry, my love.'

She wept in his arms for Phoebe and for her own lost marriage.

'Oh, my love,' he said, 'cry, cry if you need to. It's good to cry sometimes.'

'I should have realised . . . I should have phoned her after having lunch. I was so bloody preoccupied with me and you. What a waste, and her boy is only a year older than Mark, they are great mates.'

'You can't blame yourself. People do these things because they want off the wheel, because they can't cope or it hurts too much.'

'She was always such a good coper; I used to go to her for advice.'

'It happens, it happens.' He soothed her, and once more with his body he comforted her and told her he loved her, till at last she lay peaceful in his arms, the crying stopped, her breathing soft again.

'Gareth, I do love you so.'

'I love you, I shall love you for ever.'

They gazed together into the fire.

'But I still don't know what to do . . .'

'I know, I know.' He stroked her hair and looked earnestly into her sad small face. 'Just remember that I love you, and that I will wait for you.'

Phoebe's funeral was awful. There was the distracted silent Josh, shocked and large-eyed, and the new widower, John Abrahams, who had aged, it seemed, fifteen years, plus the two older sons, grown-up now, white and almost speechless. Philip had arrived back from Dublin half an hour after Alison got back from Somerset tearfully parted from Gareth, and was in a weird remote mood. As they prepared to go to the crematorium he suddenly accused her of having been with her lover.

'You have that satisfied-pussy look about you again, that and the sunburn; I know you have. I knew you were going to be with him . . .'

They wrangled and she denied it, terrified of his temper. She was sure that he was capable of real violence towards her, and it probably did show – after all, Frankie always knew.

'Please shut up,' she said as they dressed. 'Mark is bound to hear us, and he's upset enough without our making it worse.'

The three of them, dressed sombrely for the funeral, were quiet in the car; Jo had opted to go to school. Alison, trembling from Philip's aggression, felt rattled by everything – the future which loomed ominously, and no Gareth for six whole weeks – he was going to the country to help a friend do up an old house. She shut her eyes against the pain.

'Ma?'

She leaned back to look at her son in the back seat of the new Audi.

'Yes?'

'I was wondering about Josh after all this. I wonder what he's doing for the summer now; he was going to be at the cottage for a while with Phoebe . . .'

How bitter, poor Josh.

He looked at her anxiously, 'What if we asked him to come with us? To France, I mean? I know that the other two are going off abroad, and Josh is with John just now – and it's bound to be even worse since Phoebe . . .'

Alison glanced at Philip to see if he was listening: this was definitely a family decision. Philip looked grim, the boy was bound to be very mixed-up and hard to cope with. He wasn't at all sure that it was a good idea, particularly with the Salvesons in the state they were in.

'I need to think about that, Mark,' he caught his son's eyes in the driving-mirror, 'it could be awkward.'

'Please, Dad . . .'

'I'll think about it.' Philip frowned, and indicated to go right.

'I'd like him to come,' said Alison. She was fond of Josh, and it might ease the family claustrophobia to have him with them.

'We'll talk about it later,' said Philip firmly. 'I'm not keen.'

There was an uneasy silence as they parked at the crematorium. Later, Alison remembered little about the ceremony except that it was stark and simple. Phoebe had not been religious, any more than John, and though they had both been brought up Jewish, neither of them had practised any religion since they were young.

Phoebe's old mother was there, a tragic bent figure in a fur coat and brown hat. She stared at Alison and received her kiss on the cheek wordlessly and simply shook her head, her face haggard, eyes brimming.

Mark and Alison spoke to Josh, white-faced, his wiry hair brushed flat for once – normally it foamed round his head like a black halo. He almost broke down when she asked him what he was going to do for the summer, and said that he didn't know anything, except that he didn't want to be with his Dad, with which he glanced at his silent father who was uneasily watching them.

Alison was determined that he should come: it would leaven the family bread. Nervous enough about the whole French trip anyway, she was convinced that with an outsider in their midst she and Philip would fight less, and Josh looked so lost and unhappy – normally he had a wide, winning smile that stretched right across his face. She hoped that it would not rub salt in his wound to be with a family that was at least publicly complete.

It was a dreadful day, and an even worse night: Philip, at what had been John and Phoebe's home in Highgate, became very gloomy and drunk. He was ensconced for ages in a corner talking to John Abrahams who no longer lived there, and whom the family obviously blamed for the tragedy, until it was time to go.

Back home, the Salvesons had a morose family supper, after which Philip, hungover and exhausted, went upstairs to sleep it off. Alison, alone with the two children, was worried when she heard them talking almost clinically about divorce as though it were inevitable: Jo, spooning raspberry yoghurt into herself at top speed, remarked that if Mum and Dad got divorced like everybody else seemed to be doing she wouldn't like it very much, but she would rather live with Alison '. . . Because Dad's always away, or working anyway. . .' and Mark, still spotty, and depressed from seeing the havoc wrought in the Abrahams family, remarked in a frighteningly detached manner, that that was obviously what would happen if their parents split. Alison, pretending not to listen, automatically wiped the kitchen surfaces, and tried to dispel her images of Phoebe's tears and her last sort of gypsy's warning that one didn't know what one would miss until it was lost, and wished that she could tell her youngsters not to worry.

The yoghurt finished, Jo set about demolishing a loaf of bread and a pot of Somerset honey: 'We would keep Pirate, wouldn't we?'

Like hell they would. The dog was Philip's responsibility: he would have to take him. Momentarily she thought of Gareth and his dream of a country life, but she knew that it would be her as a country wife and mother of four, and she knew she did not want that; she did not want more children and to share Gareth's debts. She wanted her own space, but maybe it would be possible to keep their separate spaces, so that he still saw to his own family, and she to hers. It was Philip she wanted to go, but after viewing the Abrahams family agony today it all seemed more impossible than ever.

Alison hoped that Philip would stay asleep if she were late enough. She was exhausted from the dramas of the last three days and did not want a set-to with her husband. She would have liked to sleep in the spare room again, but felt afraid of Philip's strange mood. He had been very pissed and odd, and full of aggression. She was as quiet as possible in turning off the light, she jumped when Philip spoke. He didn't sound sleepy at all.

'You can't go on having this affair, you know.'

She got gingerly into bed lay back quietly and decided to say nothing.

'I know you've been with him; it's written all over you, that moonstruck look. You would think you would learn from Phoebe.'

'You thought that John's running off was all very jolly and entertaining only a few weeks ago, if you remember.'

'Humph,' grunted her husband. They had barely made love for weeks, but tonight, once again, Philip became violently physical. She found it an agonising intrusion so soon after the glory and tenderness of Gareth, and wept bitterly. Her husband knelt above her, his desire spent in a frenzy of territorial statement, and put his hand across her mouth almost viciously; his eyes blazing with hate. She was afraid he was going to beat her with his other hand, but he thought better of it, and roughly grasped her shoulder instead, leaving bruises which were to last for days. She gasped at the pain.

'Just quit that damned wailing. It's time you grew up, Alison, and faced your responsibilities. I want you to promise that you'll stop seeing this bastard, this Garry, this Taffy, whoever he is . . .'

'I can't see him anyway . . . we're going on this happy family holiday aren't we?' She stared up at him. She had never felt so frightened of Philip, he looked like some mad cardinal conducting the Inquisition.

'I want your word on it, otherwise I don't know what I'll do. I understand Phoebe only too well, but if it was me it would not be suicide.' His fingers were still on her shoulder, his other hand rested near her neck. Momentarily she wondered if she should summon Mark, but that would be terrible, the end . . .

Philip's fingers tightened again; such hatred radiated from him that she was paralysed with terror, like a hypnotised animal.

'I want your word on it. It's got to stop. You are making me into a madman.'

Exhausted almost to the point of hysteria, afraid, and desperate for peace, she capitulated. 'I'll not see him . . . I'll stop . . .' It was an exhausted chant. And she wouldn't see him, not for six weeks anyway.

Philip's grip relaxed. 'You promise?'

Anything, anything for peace, for oblivion. 'I promise.'

They lay in a terrible separate silence for what seemed like hours. Later, when Alison got out of bed, Philip reared up.

'Where are you going?'

Wearily she turned to his dark shape: 'I am going to sleep downstairs; I can't sleep here.'

Philip suddenly switched the light on. Blinded, they both blinked.

'You're not going to him?'

Wearily, wearily she looked at this man who was almost mad, whom once she had loved. She shook her head.

'I couldn't anyway. He's got children; they don't know about us.'

' "Us"!' he hissed, 'Christ, woman! How can you say "us" to me?' He held his head and rocked, sobbing, grunting, cursing, she couldn't tell which.

'I need to sleep, Philip; I am going downstairs to the spare room. I must sleep or we will all be mad.'

He put his hands down and stared at her, a cold uncomprehending stare. 'I've got your car keys, and I've locked the house and have the keys.'

'What?' She was dumbfounded. 'You're keeping me a prisoner?'

'I thought you were going to him.'

Alison, too tired to fight, was still afraid of murder.

'I am going down to the spare room,' she spoke very quietly, zombie-like. 'I am going to bed; we both need to sleep.'

'You promise?'

'I promise.' It was a litany, gibberish, the world was in chaos.

She stumbled downstairs and climbed between the cool sheets. To her surprise she slept, and woke with a start in the morning to find Philip dressed, standing by the bed, looking down at her.

'What time is it?' she asked blinking.

'Eight. The kids are having breakfast; I told them to leave you because you were exhausted.'

He looked tired, but normal; the madman had disappeared for the time being. He had brought coffee. She sat up and sipped it warily.

He looked at her. 'Can I sit down?'

She shrugged.

He sat, and neither of them spoke for some time; she drank the coffee. Bewilderedly she remembered about the keys. And the violence.

'I have to go to the shop and unload the things I bought.'

Philip nodded, still not looking at her.

'Can I have the keys?'

Wearily he felt in his pocket and put her keys on the patchwork cover; they lay on a patch made from an old grey-striped shirt of Philip's which she had loved to see him wear, long long ago, when he had seemed beautiful to her.

'I'm sorry.' He was still looking away.

Alison did not answer. She remembered her terror, he had almost tried to throttle her.

'Alison, it's easy enough to find someone to sleep with. I can do that.'

We all know you can do that, she thought, looking at his bent head, his quiet demeanour.

'But . . .' he looked at her, vulnerable, sorrowful, 'I want it to be us, you, me, Mark and Jo. Us, here in our home that we have made. It's too much and too many years to throw away.'

Alison's mind mumbled nonsense:

> 'This is the house that Jack built . . .
> This is the rat that ate the malt
> that lay in the house that Jack built . . .'

Why could she only think of nursery rhymes at times like this?

Philip was talking again: 'I know that you have been unhappy, that you have felt left to do everything on your own, but I have been trying, and I'm willing to try again, to try harder.' He looked at her, begging for forgiveness, for comfort, but she lay still, watching him. She could think of nothing to say, no gesture to make.

'What happened last night . . . we can't live like that.'

'No.' She met his gaze fully.

'I was frightened . . .' Philip reached towards her and passively she let him hold her hand. 'I was as frightened of me as you were . . .'

Only who would have been the survivor? She remained silent, and with her free hand fingered her bruises. He saw them, hid his head and groaned, then looked up.

'You made me a promise last night, that you would stop seeing this man. We are about to go to France, perhaps even plus poor Josh, please can we try at least to be kind to each other, to be civilised, to make it good?'

Alison too yearned for peace, for an end to hostilities. She barely had the strength to nod her slow, tired nod.

'Please don't cry . . .' He wiped her face, his voice breaking.

They turned as there was a knock on the door and Mark called: 'Dad? Can I come in?'

'Yes,' they answered unwillingly together, and their son stood there, uncomfortable, embarrassed to see his parents thus.

'What is it?' asked Philip. He stood up, hiding Alison with his tall body.

'I can't open the front door, and there's no milk.'

'Ah . . . I must have locked it by mistake last night. I was pretty pie-eyed.' Philip felt in his pocket and handed Mark the key.

The boy peered past him at his mother: 'You ill, Ma?'

'No, just exhausted and upset about Phoebe, I couldn't sleep, so I came down here.' Her voice was weak; Mark did not look very convinced, but nodded.

'Are you feeling better?'

She smiled feebly and nodded.

'D'you want a coffee?'

'No thanks, Pa got me some.'

'OK. And Jo needs money for shoes or something, she said you'd told her you'd give her it this morning.'

Real life was obtruding. Philip felt in his back-pocket and took out his wallet.

'How much does she need?'

'A tenner,' said Alison. Philip handed his son a note, and he went, shutting the door carefully. He turned to Alison.

'We have two very nice children.'

'I know.'

He sat beside her again. 'Anyway,' he said, 'Can we agree to try at least to be kind to each other?'

Gareth, Gareth, Gareth; it hurt to think. She nodded feebly, her eyes shut.

'And you will stop seeing this man?'

She had no option. All the emotions she had felt so often lately were there. Pity. Duty. Fear. Love? They puppetted her weary head into submission. Her husband hugged her. Doll-like, she allowed him to.

He let go of her. 'I'm sorry, I'm sorry I frightened you.'

Alison didn't answer, then shifted the bedcover. 'I must get up.' She said it quietly.

'Yes, it's time for me to go. I'll see you tonight. I'll be back early, and we can synchronise arrangements for the holiday.'

He left her, with the empty coffee-cup in her hands, staring vacantly at the dent made by her car keys on the grey-striped patchwork square.

Chapter Twenty-four

It was only half-past nine on the Friday morning when Alison, fraught and desperate arrived on Gareth's doorstep. It was much earlier than she had said she would appear, but she had already sat in the car for some time rehearsing her farewell speech with a breaking heart, and could bear to wait no longer.

He was overjoyed to see her: 'What a bonus to see you so soon. Come and have breakfast with me.'

There was a fresh pot of coffee on the table and as she entered the room two pieces of toast popped up from the toaster. She sat, and watched Gareth busy himself with cups and plates.

She had come to tell him that all this happiness, and the loving and touching had to stop. For the sake of her family.

'Good coffee,' she said faintly and promptly burst into tears.

Gareth stared in concern: 'Hey, what's the matter with you? Do yo need a foot-massage again?'

She told him, as simply as she could, that they must stop seeing each other, then she wept and became almost incoherent.

'I have to try for my family's sake . . . I don't want to

. . . I can't imagine being without you . . .' she cried, and he rose from her side and walked up and down the room.

'Was it your friend's suicide that made you decide?'

She sobbed: 'Partly that, it certainly brought it all to a head at home, and Philip knows I've been to Somerset with you . . .'

'Did you tell him?'

'No . . . he just knew. I guess it was obvious . . . it's hard to hide things when you've been together so long, you can't tell lies in bed, I can't anyway . . .'

'Has he been threatening?'

She cried more. 'Yes . . . and sad and crazed. It's awful, and we're all going off on this holiday. The kids need it and I think we're taking Phoebe's son, Mark's friend . . .' She looked up at him, his handsome, concerned face, the man she loved: 'I feel I must put my heart into it and try for the children at least.'

'But what about us? What about after the summer?'

'I don't know!' shrieked Alison despairingly.

Gareth nodded. He looked more serious than she had ever seen him. 'So at least there's some hope for me?'

She collapsed sobbing on the table. At last he came to her and she was comforted by his touch. He rocked her in his arms like a babe.

'Alison, these things are hard, believe me, I know all too well how much they hurt.'

'I'm sorry; it's not what I want to do, but what I feel I must do. I can't cause all this unhappiness. I must at least try.'

'We can't see each other anyway for six or seven weeks; I'm off to Kent with the kids in a week for the whole summer, and you've already said next week may be impossible. Maybe you will at last sort yourself out and decide what you really do want.'

‘I don’t know . . .’

‘And how about now?’ asked Gareth softly.

She turned to him numbly, ‘How do you mean?’

‘He shrugged, ‘I mean here, now, this very morning. Are you going to be strong and go away from me right now, or are we allowed to say goodbye properly?

He looked at her, but made no move towards her, and it was as it had been so long ago on the Good Friday march, when they had looked into each other’s souls and touched fingers for the first time.

Gareth smiled at last. ‘I thought for a minute I’d lost you. Please will you come to my bed just once more?’

He held out his hand to her.

She wished that it could all end, here and now, in this small room with him. All the pain, the indecision.

‘No.’ She shook her head. ‘I can’t. We’ve got to stop. I must try.’

Gareth gazed at her with great intensity, still not moving towards her.

‘When you are in France, my love, and you are away from me, I want you to remember this: I want you to remember that I love you, that we love each other and need each other; I believe that, and I believe that you will one day come to me. Only remember that I will be here waiting for you.’

She stared at him, too numb for tears, longing only to lie once more on his warm woolly chest, with no other thing to obtrude, no tasks to be done, no life to be lived but this.

Gareth moved away from her, and stood by the window, still gazing at her intensely.

‘I will love you for two thousand years, Alison, and remember too, that I would never force you to come. I want you, but I want you to come to me freely, of your own volition.’

At last it was time and more than time to go. He stood in the doorway, very serious. 'Can I not write to you?'

She shook her head.

'Nor you to me?'

'No.'

'That's it, then? Goodbye?'

She nodded, and drenched his shirt with her tears when at last he universed her in his arms.

'I've got to go, Gareth.' Her voice was muffled in his chest.

'OK.' His voice ached. 'Go, but remember. Remember all I said. I'll be waiting for you.'

She wrenched herself from his warmth; it was like tearing her own body in two. Down the path, past the broken gate, the world a haze of anguish. She drove to the shop, almost unaware of the other traffic on the road and the angry hootings which punctuated her crazed course.

Frankie it was, dear Frankie, who with tea, words and tender friendship, wiped the tears, soothed and listened till the storm was spent.

'Allie, you had to. You've done right. After the summer you'll know if it is too unhappy to continue at home, but at least you will have tried properly.'

She made Alison up a bed in the back shop where they had a couch large enough to lie on, pulled the velvet curtain across, and left her to sleep; she even unhooked the bell so that Alison would not be woken by the clang of the door. When closing-time came she woke her friend gently with tea, and said she was coming home and would cook supper. Like an invalid, Alison acquiesced; she could hardly talk, but catatonically allowed Frankie to organise everything.

At the house Frankie put Alison to bed in the spare room, telling everybody that she had a screeching headache. She cooked a vast and delicious stew and entertained them all, so that when Philip eventually looked in on the way up to bed, he asked no questions; Frankie had told him that Alison was exhausted but had done what he asked. Embarrassed, he had poured himself and Frankie large drinks, held up his glass to her and muttered 'Thank God for that. Thanks for telling me, Frankie. Here's to us all.'

On the Sunday morning that the Salvesons set off for France Frankie lay in Anthony's bed and looked down at the floor beside them.

'He's a nice dog, isn't he?' Pirate looked lazily up at the sound of her voice and thumped his tail in a leisurely Sunday-morning manner.

'He's lovely.' Anthony turned to admire the dalmatian who, excited by their attention, came over to the bed and rubbed himself along it, then tried to jump up on top of them. Anthony pushed him, 'Down boy, good lad.'

'I hope he won't be a nuisance; Allie was almost off her head when her neighbour who'd said she would have him slipped her disc. I thought she was genuinely going to flip her lid. Thank goodness you offered.'

'I like dogs, and he's very paintable.'

'I hope they'll be OK,' muttered Frankie.

'Alison and co?'

Frankie nodded, frowning.

'Has she really given the Welshman the heave?'

'She's certainly trying to. They aren't communicating or anything.'

'He seemed such a nice guy; I thought he was her

husband when I met him. You could tell that they adored each other. What's her husband like?'

'Philip. He's good-looking, very successful and ambitious, but a bit cold for my taste, though I used to quite fancy him.'

'You did, did you?' Anthony nuzzled her fondly. 'And do you still?'

'No,' Frankie grinned. 'I've been converted to miniature painters.'

'Did you ever have him?'

'Naw, but he's quite a womaniser in his own quiet way.'

'So what's all the noise about, especially if this is her first affair?'

'He says it's different for men and women. He's insanely possessive.'

'He sounds like a shit.'

'But they're a lovely family, the kids adore him as well.'

'How long has Alison been unhappy?'

Frankie wrinkled her nose. 'I've known her for a couple of years, and she'd been fairly miserable for at least a year before that – he'd been affairing and she had found out about it. She's been pretty miserable for ages, and was getting more so till Gareth arrived.'

'Well, I believe in love,' said Anthony, admiring her profile.

'So do I, but what about the family?'

Anthony shook his head. 'My parents stayed yoked together in misery for years because of us, and it was not good; it was very sad to grow up with. They'd have been better apart. His love-affair was with the police force.'

'Maybe you're right . . . she's so happy with Gareth, she looks different when she's been with him.'

'She should go where the love is.'

'And if you could have seen her on Friday; I thought she was going to kill Philip – and this was after her telling Gareth it was over.'

'What happened?'

'She had this big fair booked months ago in a big hotel in Brighton – a really important one, and she'd spent a fortune on stuff for it,' Frankie paused.

'Yes?'

'Well, Philip knew all about it, but he went and autocratically booked the ferry for today, the day after it. That was bad enough, then the so and so upped and announced that he absolutely had to go back to Dublin for Friday and Saturday, otherwise he wouldn't get some massive design job, and he was originally supposed to do all the packing and buying of stuff and last-minute arrangements for France when she was doing her fair, but the bugger had the cheek to say that his trip to Dublin was more important and worth much more money than her fair.'

'My God. What did she do?'

'She had to cancel it, lost her deposit. She was in a helluva state, though actually, with the dog and the extra boy they're taking whose mother committed suicide last week because her husband ran off with a twenty-year-old . . .'

'Hold on there, you're losing me . . .'

'It doesn't matter.' Frankie kissed him lingeringly. 'She had too much to do anyway, and she was quite relieved not to do the fair in the end.'

'Dramatic friends you have . . .'

'They are quite. I hope they're going to be OK . . .

'You said that before . . .' Anthony rolled over onto Frankie's large and magnificent body.

'You did that before too . . .' Frankie's laugh enchanted him, like everything else about her.

'I did, shall we do it again?'

'Yeah . . .'

They did and the dog barked, and they laughed, and the white room with bright green bedcovers was filled with happiness.

On the boat sailing for France Alison at last began to relax. Maybe they could make it work. The young people were all excited. Even young Josh had managed to summon up a half-smile when they drove onto the ferry, after sitting pale and silent all the way to Dover. Philip, after their enormous battles about taking Josh, and then his last-minute trip to Dublin which had forced her to cancel the Brighton fair, was being easy and cheerful, and had offered to do most of the driving. He found driving relaxing, whereas it made Alison tense. She had been very angry indeed about missing the fair, but doubted now if she could have managed it and still have remained on her feet. The days since saying goodbye to Gareth had been insanely hectic, with trips to organise passports which were suddenly discovered to be out-of-date, pricing and organising the things she had acquired in Somerset, seeing to the house and the dog, and packing what the four of them needed, insurance, new shoes and swim-gear. It had seemed endless, but at last they were on their way, and she wanted to make it good if she was able to. She tried to stamp out thoughts of Gareth, tried not to imagine how the trip would be if she were with him, and hoped that he would be happy in Kent with his friends and children.

Philip had gone for a walk to explore the boat, and Alison found herself a bench on the sunny side of the upper deck where she sat herself down with a magazine, determined to enjoy the trip.

'Hi, Mum.' She looked up and saw her big daughter standing smiling at her in white shorts and tee shirt; Alison, in denim skirt, red-checked shirt and sunglasses also felt holidayish.

'Hello, love, what are you up to?'

Jo plonked herself down beside her mother and snuggled in close.

'I've come to ask a favour.'

'I thought you had come to wheedle me. What do you want? I might even say yes.'

'You know the duty free shop?'

'Y-e-e-s,' dubiously.

'Oh please, Mum, please . . .'

'Tell me.'

'I'm dying for some perfume; I've never had any of my very own – proper French stuff – and I've seen the kind I've been longing for . . .'

Alison tried not to laugh. Last year the only things Jo had wanted had been flippers and goggles, or a football.

'How much is it?'

It was a lot, but she gave her the money. Jo danced off saying, 'Thanks, Ma, you're lovely!'

A few minutes later she was back, beaming ecstatically, clutching a carton of perfume. She gave Alison the change and hugged her. 'I've been dying for this, it's the only perfume I really like, I've tried all yours and Frankie's, but they're all too strong. This one's like the flowers in Granny's garden.'

'What is it?'

'Diorissimo.' Jo opened the carton, and wonderingly broke the seal. It's a spray, look . . .' She thrust out her chin and sprayed under her chin, then applied it to her wrists as she had so often watched Alison do. A scent of lily-of-the-valley wafted from her as she thrust her slightly grubby wrist under Alison's nose.

'It's lovely, yes . . .' Why was it familiar? she wondered. 'How did you know how to pick that one? Did they let you test it?'

Jo put the bottle back into the carton. 'I didn't need to. That Mary girl from Dad's office, she always wears it. She let me use some when she taught me patchwork.'

Suddenly, horribly, the jigsaw fitted together for Alison: Philip had smelt like that the other day, and once or twice since . . . she had never remembered to ask him, and Phoebe . . . and something John had said about Philip's PA in Dublin . . . . Mary. He had been sleeping with Mary. The bastard, the two-faced hypocritical shit.

'Where's Dad got to?' she asked lightly. Jo was inhaling happily from her wrist.

'He's in the bar, said he needed a cognac to celebrate being on holiday.'

'Here,' said Alison handing over she didn't know how much money. 'Go and find the boys and have some chocolate from the shop. Feel free.'

'Ooh, thanks, Ma; will you keep my perfume in your bag?'

'Yes,' said Alison thoughtfully, 'I'd like to.'

Jo handed it to her and skipped off happily, and Alison saw her find the boys and go off with them all grinning, even Josh. She found Philip standing at the bar.

'Hello, darling,' he said easily. 'Come and have a cognac, it's just the job.'

'Thank you,' she said politely, 'I will.'

Obliviously, he ordered her drink and another for himself. 'Is it nice on deck?'

'Very. Jo just bought herself some perfume.'

'Really? By God, that makes a change.' He laughed at the vagaries of life and teenage daughters.

Alison took the carton out of her handbag, slowly extracted the bottle and sprayed some on her wrist, then, just as Jo had done to her, thrust it under his nose. 'Nice?' she asked.

He sniffed. 'Very nice . . .'

'Familiar?'

He eyed her, 'I don't think so . . .'

She thrust her wrist towards him again. 'Try once more and think hard.'

He made to sniff, then retreated uneasily. 'What is all this about, Alison?'

'I think perhaps you know.'

He looked at her blankly.

'The office? Mary? Sweet young thing who's so very helpful?'

'Oh God.' He turned to the bar and reached for the brandy.

'You must think I'm an idiot.' She was steaming, her eyes flaming sparks. The other people in the bar were beginning to become interested. Philip handed her the glass he had bought for her. 'Let's go over there, it's more private.'

They went to sit in a corner, and he plonked himself down helplessly.

'You bastard.' She drank a large mouthful of brandy and looked at her turd of a husband.

'You can hardly talk,' said Philip. 'I needed somebody. You've not been exactly welcoming in bed of late.'

'All that stuff about regenerating the marriage, how you'd turned your back, how I must end my affair, all that sob stuff. How could you do it?' Her voice was getting louder with every word.

'She was warm and comforting when I was in need of warmth and comfort. It was just a physical thing. I never changed my allegiance, I never turned from you, it didn't mean anything. You really broke the bond which was a totally different thing.'

Alison shook her head. 'If I were strong enough I would throttle you here and now.'

'Alison, for heaven's sake . . .' He tried to sound reasonable, placatory.

'I hate you, Philip,' she hissed. 'I hate you for being weak and a liar and hypocrite. After all the threats you have made to me, all the accusations, how could you?'

'Alison . . .'

'Shut up! I don't want to hear; we are going on holiday with three vulnerable kids, and I for one intend to try to make the holiday work. I will as we agreed be polite and civilised to you, but don't ever again try to tell me what is right and what is wrong.'

'I never changed loyalties, Alison. You did. I knew to turn my back if there was a hint of love.'

'More fool you.' She looked at him tiredly, and handled the brandy glass meditatively; her imaginings were alarmingly full of violence. She stood up.

'I'm going up on deck, lest I do you an injury.' She was trembling all over. 'I'll see you at the car.'

'Alison . . .'

'Fuck off!' She said it very loudly, and two red-faced men clapped as she exited from the bar.

She went back on deck and stood in the stern watching the gulls shrieking and wheeling in the wake of the ship. She imagined Philip being churned up by the propellors, all blood and blond hair, and imagined hurling herself into the foam, but she recognised them for the dramatic thoughts they were, and thought melancholically of Phoebe, and her own mother, whose cottage-garden flowers had smelt as sweet as Philip's young mistress. The betrayal of it was what was so appalling. All the time he had been screwing that girl whilst she was with Gareth; the only difference it seemed to Alison, was that she and Gareth loved each other, and that was good, not bad. It was Philip's loss, but how dare he behave as though he owned her?

Jo found her, and they went to the car together, as the ferry was approaching Calais. They disembarked, and drove for the rest of the day with the car reeking of Diorissimo.

Alison did not speak to Philip for three days, except to communicate about practicalities, meals, the itinerary, and finally the house where they were to spend two and a half weeks together. The house had a tiled patio overlooking the sea and balconies in front of the bedrooms. There was plenty of space, a woman came in to tidy up every day, and they ate out in a good inexpensive restaurant most night – delicious seafood, bouillabaisse, artichokes, beautiful salads, olives, and always plenty of wine. For lunch they bought food in the cornucopia of the local market. The swimming was good, the weather generally perfect, and the youngsters water-skied, wind-surfed and swam all day long, and after a couple of days had found a group of young people of their own ages and seemed very content. Josh would occasionally become very silent and white, but Mark and Jo were incredibly kind and sensitive with him.

Every day Alison took herself for long walks along the beach and rockier areas within half a mile of the house. She thought of Gareth often, but tried to eradicate her feelings for him, they hurt so much;

though she did have a strip of four photos of him which she looked at sometimes and wept. She tried to be cheerful and pleasant, though to Philip she was remote and polite, and their eye or body contact was almost non-existent. They had not made love together since the night when he had so frightened her, and they slept in separate beds. Philip had accepted her desire for celibacy more easily than she had expected; he seemed to respect her need for space, and was sad and cautious with her, and read a lot or walked alone.

There was a strange hard core developing in Alison as though she were dead in the middle; at times she felt almost content – after all if you were dead inside, it didn't hurt, and to be without pain was a relief. She wept surprisingly little, and at least they weren't fighting, and the youngsters appeared pretty oblivious of the uneasy parental truce.

One night towards the end of the holiday Philip asked her to come for a walk along the beach with him. They had eaten well at their usual restaurant and had drunk a fair amount of wine. It was a starry night with a full moon, and they watched its reflections which sparkled arbitrarily and magically on the waters, hypnotically beautiful.

'Can we talk?' said Philip.

'By all means,' said Alison in the polite tea-party manner that had become her norm.

'I mean talk properly, not just make conversation.'

'Yes.' Her reply was almost a grunt. She shrugged, and wished she didn't want to cry.

He looked at her, his face silvered and intense in the moonlight. 'I don't know about you, but I feel very lonely the way we're going on.'

Alison concentrated on the reflections on the waters.

He tried again. 'How do you think we are doing?'

'What do you mean?'

'Alison.' He stopped in front of her and caught her shoulders. 'I mean us, you and me, our marriage, our future, our children's future. Can you bear to go on in this way, this sort of pretend way, where we more or less ignore each other, where we have no sex, no friendship, no love?'

'I don't know,' she said, and had a wild desire to weep.

Philip dropped his hands and raked his hair distractedly.

'Please talk to me; don't just cry or say you don't know; I don't know either, but I do know that I still want us to try. I know that we have hurt each other, perhaps beyond repair, maybe by simply being ourselves. I'm not assigning blame, I am simply trying.'

She looked at him straight. 'I'm trying too. I've been trying as hard as I can.'

'But this coldness, this lack of communication, it is very bloody lonely, isn't it? It feels so destitute.'

She nodded, and this time she did cry.

'Please,' he said. 'Would you at least try to be my friend again? I'm not purely bad, I'm fallible and weak, and I can understand your anger; I probably wanted to get at you by having Mary – though believe me she was a pretty irresistible young thing, and she was nuts about me – but it is you I love. You are the mother of my children, and you are the woman I choose to live with. I will never sleep with Mary again, if that is what you want.'

'I think your promise may be too late.'

'Too late for what?'

'Too late for me to care about. I cared about your hypocrisy, not what you were doing.'

Philip sighed. 'Men are different.'

'The way I see it, that is an excuse to do what you want.'

'Maybe it is. I don't know. But what are we going to do? Do you want to keep trying? I know that I do.'

Alison heard Gareth's voice saying 'I will love you for two thousand years,' and 'We need each other, we love each other, I will wait for you . . .'

'It's this man, isn't it? You can't forget him?' Philip's voice had a desperation to it.

'It isn't easy.' She tried to reinforce the deadness of her core, to damp any flame in the ashes, to keep the pain at bay, to exorcise his image.

'Oh God,' said Philip. 'What is a trap is sex and love. Here we go round the mulberry bush . . .' His voice broke.

'I'm trying, Philip. I'm not in touch with him, I have told him it is over. I, too, long for peace and not to feel lonely.' She looked at him.

'I'm sorry for having hurt you,' he said. Painfully aware of the shrieking space between them, they walked slowly side by side along the water's edge. '. . .But sometimes I feel that I should apologise for being me, but I can't actually help that. I am what I am.'

She sobbed or laughed, she was hardly sure which. 'That's exactly what I feel . . .'

'But shall we keep trying?'

She sighed. 'I'm willing, but I don't want us to sleep together. I can't confront that yet.'

Philip grunted, a small baffled grunt, and she wondered if he would suddenly lose his temper again.

'I'm sorry,' she said, 'but that is how it has to be.'

They walked in silence. He glanced at her, sadly, fondly. 'You look very beautiful; I find that part difficult; I'll try to contain myself. But Alison . . .'

'Yes?'

'Kindness. Can we try some of that?'

She nodded.

'Will you try to be my friend?'

'Yes,' a small quiet voice.

He laughed sadly. 'We sound like ten-year-olds.'

'We behave like them sometimes.'

'Come on, friend; let's go home.'

She nodded, hardly able to see him for tears, and they walked towards the house together, both very moved, with his hand tentatively on her shoulder. Mark, sitting with a pretty French girl in the lee of a rock, was overjoyed to see his parents thus enclasped; he had in fact been all too aware of Alison's icy politeness, and the lack of any real warmth between them. He returned to his conversation with the girl with renewed vigour.

'Please,' he said. '*Je t'implore* . . . . I'll be very careful . . .'

'*Hein*?' said the girl.

'*Je serai tres* careful . . . um . . . *tu seras saufe* . . . no baby . . . *je te promis* . . .'

'OK , Marc,' said the girl, and he grinned from ear to ear.

From the balcony in front of his bedroom at the house, young Josh Abrahams was also watching his married hosts walking in the moonlight; it reminded him bitterly of earlier, happier times, when his mother was still alive and they had spent family holidays together, and he went to bed and wept desperately. Lonely, lonely, lonely.

Chapter Twenty-five

Gareth was working at the top of a ladder leaning against an old oast-house in Kent, which he was helping friends to convert to a home and pottery. He enjoyed being outside, especially when it was sunny like today, and he could wear little more than an old pair of shorts; he was brown, well-fed and healthy, but lonely. With every pinkish terracotta tile he fixed with a galvanised nail to the new roof – replacing the old rotted wooden pegs – he thought of Alison. He hadn't seen or heard of her for over a month now, though he knew that she must be back in London. He presumed that because he hadn't heard, she was still trying to reinforce her marriage. Many times he had been tempted to ring the shop, if only to speak to Frankie and get some news, but so far he had refrained, even though he had entered the phonebox on the corner of the village green, money in hand, more than once. When she came to him – and he still believed that she would, their bond was too strong for her not to – he wanted her to come of her own free will, with no pressure from himself. He crawled up a second ladder fixed to the roof and carefully hammered more tiles in place. It was satisfying work, he was good at it, a meticulous craftsman, and he enjoyed watching his children running wild, screaming with joy, among the orchards where the trees hung heavy with apples, and relaxing at night with a pint of beer in the timbered kitchen, which was gradually being made habitable for the winter. He hoped that one day he and Alison might live in this sort of house, together at last, peaceful after the pain and storm of their separate lives.

'Dad!' He looked down from his eyrie and saw Bronwen, brown and grinning, squinting up at him.

'What is it?'

'Tea time, Jim says you've to take a rest.'

'Two more to go, then I'll come; don't eat all the buns. I'm hungry.'

'I might, you'd better hurry up!' She ran off, frightening a couple of hens which squawked in panic and fled.

London at the end of August seemed very desolate. The Salvesons had been home for a week, burnt brown from the French holiday. Frankie, when Alison arrived at the shop bearing a bottle of wine and a string of garlic, had gasped at her colour: 'You look like some Indian maiden – especially with the beads.' She had taken to wearing Gareth's beads again, they somehow comforted the ache in her centre.

'I missed you,' said Frankie. 'It's been so quiet without you, but we've sold a lot, the Somerset stuff has gone down very well.'

Alison looked fondly round at the shop; she felt terribly pleased to be back. 'I missed you.'

'How was it? Your cards were all about food, wine and sun, but I want to know the real stuff. How were you and Philip? And that poor boy?'

'At the moment it's almost tolerable. We're making massive efforts, being nice to each other, but it's a strain, neither of us is exactly blissful.'

She described to the enthralled Frankie her discovery of Philip's affair with Mary.

'That upper-class bird from the office? The one with the dog called Twinkletoes or something?'

Alison nodded.

'My God, what a cheek! And this all the time he was on at you about Gareth?'

'Yes.' Alison sat down with a cup of coffee, she felt more at home here than in the house.

'You must have felt murderous.'

'I did.'

'And now?'

'I've been disciplining myself not to think at all; it's easier that way, and Philip is walking on eggs to be pleasant to me, almost driving me mad with his solicitousness sometimes.' She sighed. 'It's pretty bizarre really; I am so glad to see you. There was nobody I could talk to there at all. I communed with nature, and enjoyed the food and wine.'

'How's the kids?'

'Josh and Mark are still in France, Jo went straight down to the Isle of Wight again, and Philip has to do the Hong Kong trip once more; when are you going off?'

'I'd like to go in a couple of days if that's OK. We always said I'd go when you came back.'

'Have you decided where?'

Frankie beamed, 'Scotland of course.' She danced a quick Highland Fling.

'To see your folks?'

'Yes, but actually I'm going camping . . .'

'Alone?'

'No, me and Wee . . . I mean Ant.'
'Great. It's still good, I take it?'
'Marvellous. He said he'd bring the dog into the shop today at lunchtime.'
'How was he? The dog I mean.'
'Adorable. Anthony drew him a few times.'
'It's going to be very strange with everybody away . . .'
'Have you been in contact with Gareth?'
'No. Nothing.'
Frankie was touched by the sadness in her friend's face.
'That's good, Allie, I'm sure it's right, don't you feel the better for it?'
'You must be joking.'
'Oh Allie, is it no better?'
'I have been trying so damned hard, but you can't just switch off your emotions like a light, at least I can't. I miss him dreadfully, but I try to ban all thoughts of him, but oh Frankie . . . it hurts, it hurts.'
'Oh dear. Here is me hoping you'd come back cured, all starry-eyed about Philip and family life again.'
'I'm afraid not.'
'What are you going to do?'
'Nothing as yet. I'll give it more time. Seeing that boy and hearing what his family went through was awful. I'll keep trying.'
'Good girl. I might even knit you a gold star if you're good.'
'Thanks a lot.'
'I've not seen him at all, I half thought he might look in.'
'He's still away, he's away till school starts.'
'What will you do all alone, with us all away?'
'Sell antiques, talk to the dog, listen to music and cry no doubt.'
'Oh Allie, I'll send you a postcard from Loch Lomond.'
Alison felt quite a pang when she waved them off, they

looked so young and carefree. Philip was preoccupied with business, and worked in his upstairs studio most nights. They were civilised to each other, but there was no spark, and she often found herself inventing things to say, purely to make conversation, to give some semblance of life to the relationship.

She didn't ask about the situation with Mary, though she knew he must see her every day at the office, and he never enquired about Alison's lover, but was remote, polite and as helpful as he could remember to be when he managed to switch his mind off work. They behaved together like brother and sister – and a rather old and bored brother and sister at that. But at least they weren't at war for the moment; it was easier to live that way, but the years ahead, especially when the children had gone – and Mark would be gone in two years, off to university and the outside world – yawned ahead like a cold desert. Often, when Alison was alone in the shop – and a day without Frankie to swoop in and entertain her was very empty indeed – a silly little verse went round and round her head:

'The buttercups are dead,
The ladybirds have fled,
The grass is hay
Where once we lay
What is there now instead?'

Then, melancholy with thoughts of Gareth, she would put on some music or set about polishing or tidying the shop, to try to break her relentless memories of their happiest times together.

Philip had dreaded confronting Mary. When he was away, he was confused by how much he missed her availability, intelligence and enthusiasm. Her unreserved adoration of him was undeniably a great bonus. He had spoken to her several times from France – office phone-calls – and had muttered things like 'It's a bit difficult . . .' and 'Yes, I miss you . . .' Then he had told her that Alison knew.

'Oh my God . . . how?'

Philip told about the perfume.

'But what will we do?'

'We'll have to stop seeing each other – privately, I mean – at least until all this blows over . . . . Bear with me, Mary. It's too complicated . . . my marriage . . . my children . . .'

Mary had cried and put down the phone.

When they did meet at the office, Mary was white and miserable, and Philip wanted to go and enfold her in his arms and lie obliviously as he had so often done in her Laura Ashley papered room with the King Charles spaniel watching. But he looked at her sadly and did not move towards her.

'I'm sorry,' he said simply.

'You're staying with Alison?'

'I must.'

For a moment she thought she might faint, but she stood, and remained upright, a true soldier's daughter.

'I think I should resign.'

That he couldn't bear. He shook his head palely. 'No. I beg of you, don't leave me. I need you, I rely on you here. Please . . . . Let's be professional. Just give it time to settle.'

Dammit, he felt near to tears himself. He tried not to remember the sweet wickednesses they used to perpetrate together, and gripped his pigskin briefcase tightly to him. Pained, he implored her: 'Please, Mary . . . don't go. Try it for a bit. Bear with me . . .'

* * *

When Philip was away, Alison spent the evenings, which seemed endless, tidying out all the cupboards in the house. She told herself that she was doing the spring-cleaning she should have done at least two years ago, before her so-called domestic breakdown. The most pleasurable thing she did in his absence was to have an enormous bonfire in the garden of garden rubbish and household junk. She found great exhilaration as she watched the flames soar. Fires were always cathartic.

In a mad moment she took her much-fondled strip of photographs of Gareth out of her wallet where, miraculously, nobody in the family had ever discovered them, and added them to the fire in a desperate hope that seeing them burn would finally dispel all thoughts of him from her mind and body. She wept bitterly as she watched them catch fire and curl up in the heat, his four beloved images distorting then disappearing in a sharp orange flame. She regretted the act immediately, and howled like a beast alone in her garden which was filled with flowers and the rampant bushes of high summer. Now that she had not even his pictures to remember him by she felt more bereft than ever.

She felt dead in the middle, and sometimes actually wished she was dead, it would be an end to the pain; she understood Phoebe all too well, and often almost envied her courage, as she also envied the courage of her friends who had actually divorced. But Alison was afraid, a coward perhaps; she was healthy, opulent, with an ideal home, husband and children; maybe she expected too much from life, and ought to be simply grateful to be alive and healthy, and not care about the emptiness. Happiness was after all a luxury of sorts.

She decided to go and visit her father one weekend. He seemed well, and the daily woman Alison had organised and paid for had proved to be excellent. They sat together one night after she had cooked him supper and listened to Beethoven's *Fifth Symphony* which was being relayed on both the television and Radio 3. It was particularly beautiful, and when it was over they both had tears in their eyes.

Her father turned to her: 'Your mother loved that symphony. When we were first married she had it on 78s, conducted by Dr Adrian Boult, as he then was, it was splendid.'

Throughout her two-day visit she wondered if he might refer to their conversation on the beach, when she had felt so unhappy, before she and Gareth had become lovers, but he never talked about it, nor did she. It had become too complicated, too painful.

Alison had been in touch with Molly several times, who had obviously not approved of their French holiday. She considered it selfish that they had gone abroad and not spent the time nearer their father; Alison refrained from explaining that she had been trying to save her marriage at the time. Molly would only have disapproved of that too, and of the fact that Alison could be so decadent as to have a marriage that needed saving.

Frankie and Anthony ended their three-week trip to Scotland in Edinburgh. They had camped by Loch Ness and spent happy hours searching for a glimpse of the famous monster, and been washed out on the Isle of Skye, where Anthony had become almost delirious with the grandeur of the scenery. In Glasgow, Frankie took him to meet her folks and he charmed her plump old mother and drank whisky with her father. In the local pub, near where her parents lived, Anthony talked for hours to Frankie's seventy-year-old, purple-rinsed Auntie Jean, who, full of whisky and goodwill, was dressed splendiferously in peach-coloured silk with hundreds of pleats down the back. 'It's second-hand, ye ken,' she whispered huskily to Anthony, 'but it's got the Jenner's label – I like fine tae dress up on Saturday night . . .' Then the whole pub sang, 'I belong tae Glasgae . . . . Dear old Glasgae toon. If I have a couple of drinks on a Saturday, Glasgae belongs tae me . . .' till tears streamed down the worn working faces.

Anthony was enchanted by it all, though saddened by the alcoholism and cultural poverty evident in the pubs. When he hugged Auntie Jeanie goodbye, the old lady glanced across the room to where Frankie was roaring with laughter with her mother, and clutched Anthony's arm.

'She's a fine lass that, gaither her up,' she told Anthony in a whiskied whisper.

'I'm trying, Jeanie, I'm trying, there's a lot of her to gather,' he said, smiling.

In Edinburgh they wandered through the city, which they were fortunate to visit when the sun was shining. They peered down closes and wynds, and admired the elegant New Town with its grey rows of spacious streets and pale sandstone buildings, interspersed always with gardens and views of the sea.

'Every street seems to have a view of hills, gardens or the sea,' said Anthony, entranced, as they walked hand in hand, pointing out each new building or delight. He was impressed by the castle rearing magnificently up on its black volcanic rock right in the centre of the city, and bought himself a jersey of multi-coloured stripes from a delightful shop which reminded him of Frankie's bedroom with its brilliance and variety of garments.

Eventually they climbed to the top of Salisbury Crags, a long sheer cliff of red rock which rises starkly behind the city, and is part of a large hill shaped like a lying-down lion, called Arthur's Seat – nobody seems to know why. They picnicked on the Crags, overlooking the city which stretched with its castle and many spires, splendiferously to the sea and the hills of Fife beyond.

'God, it's beautiful,' said Anthony. 'I could live in a place like this, just for the sheer aesthetics of it.'

'It's very cold in the winter, grim and grey; that's one of the things I like London for, the better climate,' said Frankie. 'But I love coming back to Scotland.'

They gazed at the grand panorama, and leaned against each other.

'I have been very happy these last weeks,' said Anthony putting his arm round her shoulders.

Frankie was dressed in a sort of baggy jesters' jacket of many colours, with pink trousers and bright yellow clogs. 'Me too.' She looked at him, the midget she had fled, 'It's been fantastic.'

They gazed in silence for a long time, pausing occasionally to sip coffee from a thermos, or to gnaw a piece of chicken.

'Frankie.'

'Hmmm?' She was dreaming, watching a small boat – at least it looked small because it was so far away in the Firth of Forth.

'Seriously, Frankie . . .'

'Hmmm?' She was still far away, trying to imagine exactly where that little fishing village in Fife they had visited was in relation to the hills on the other side of the blue water.

Anthony tried again. 'What would you say if I asked you to marry me?'

Frankie smiled a little, and continued to gaze at the view.

'I'd say I thought you would never ask.'

'You mean it?' He couldn't believe her. 'We're on then?'

'You haven't asked me yet . . .'

Anthony leapt up and plucked an instant bouquet – a daisy, a buttercup and a purply thistle-like flower – and knelt before her.

'Miss MacGregor, would you do me the honour of marrying me?'

'Aye, I'd like that fine,' said Frankie, and they fell, both kneeling into each other's multi-coloured arms, breathless, tearful and overjoyed.

'Oh, I love you, Ant.'

'Thank goodness for that,' he wiped his eyes. 'I thought you'd never say it.'

'I was scared.'

'Me too; I've wanted to say it for weeks, months . . .'

'Good old *Time Out*, eh?'

Anthony laughed. 'I'd almost forgotten that was how we met. I was just so damned lonely I had to do something.'

'Me too. Alison forced me to answer your ad. Just for the hell of it.'

'And here we are.'

'Yes.' They stood up and looked at each other, blissful. Frankie smiled, 'And to think I used to flatten my hair!' She bent down to pick up her bouquet, and Anthony picked up the picnic bag.

'Come on,' he said. 'I want to buy you a ring in the Royal Mile.'

'Are you sure you can afford it?'

He did his Polish accent. 'Don't you vorry my dear. My voman's an antique dealer, she'll get it trade. It vill be a good price . . . I'm a practical man.'

The summer was over; the children back to school, the nights drawing in, and the leaves beginning to fall. Alison felt melancholy enough without the dying of the year to help her on. She knew that Gareth must be home, but still she refrained from contact. She had even stopped going to the Friday morning market for fear of meeting him. The pain she knew it would cause was too great to precipitate. The only good thing in her life, it seemed, was Frankie's happiness with Anthony. Frankie came back from Scotland blooming, gloriously in love, wearing a beautiful Victorian engagement ring with three large Scotch pearls. They intended to marry at Christmas, and to find somewhere larger to live in than Anthony's flat, but meanwhile seemed blissfully content to sleep together at whichever place suited them best at the time.

The Salveson marital truce was much more difficult to maintain with everybody at home and working hard. There were meaningless wrangles with Philip, and Alison felt constantly tired and ill and looked awful. Finally she went in desperation to her doctor who tested her for glandular fever, but the result was negative.

'Are you worrying about anything, Mrs Salveson?' he asked.

Alison shrugged, what could she say?'

'A lot of ladies of your age feel like this, children growing up and all that. Try a holiday.'

'I've just had one,' said Alison palely.

She found Jo crying more than once, usually after she and Philip had had some stupid argument. One night, after Alison knew she had been particularly bloody-minded at supper and shouted unnecessarily that they were a damned lazy lot, she found Jo sobbing her heart out, the mouldering teddy resurrected and clutched to her still-burgeoning bosom.

'I hate it here; you and Dad are so horrible to each other. I wish I could go and live at Charlotte's. Why do you hate each other so much? I like you both.'

'We don't hate each other, darling. I'm sorry, I'm just awfully tired just now . . .' Alison tried not to start crying too.

'You're always tired or depressed, and Dad's always stuck at his drawing-board or he's not here, and when he is here it's horrible.'

Alison felt helpless; it was all true. Mark, miserable and monosyllabic, locked himself away the minute supper was over, and used the house like a hotel, asking wearily if his clothes were washed or when they would be, ironing his jeans and shirts with an expression of such high martyrdom that Alison felt, for no good reason, guilty – the boy was quite old enough to iron his own shirts. Philip's answer to the unease and lack of communication was the usual one of overwork, and sometimes it seemed that days went by without their speaking to each other, except to agree as to who was cooking or to ask for salt or pepper at the dinner table.

One Friday, at the end of September, she did, in desperation, go to Portobello Road, and wandered through the market like a wraith, seeing nothing, but looking for her long-lost lover. She bought almost nothing, except a bowl which turned out to be cracked, and had coffee in the café where she had often been so happy, but the only familiar face she saw was that of the red-haired boy who had originally told Mark about Gareth. She came home feeling half mad, and hours later was in bed with a fever which developed into bad flu.

She was in bed for three days, very unusual for Alison, and had terrifying bloody dreams of Gareth, Philip and her dying mother mixed into macabre and frightening images, with everybody inter-changing. She longed for some warmth and comfort, but Philip was away for most of the three days, and the sight of their mother ill appeared to affect Mark and Jo with alarm and despond more than compassion. She was feeling very sorry for herself when at last she was fit to stagger shakily into the shop, but at least Frankie was welcoming and pleased to see her.

'I don't think I can go on like this, Frankie; it is too unhappy, and the children are suffering.'

Frankie, kind as ever, tried to cheer her up. 'You need a break; and you've got post-flu depression. It won't seem so bad next week.'

But it did. The winter loomed like a black misery in front of her, and when she went to bed – which she did, alone, often and early – she longed for sleep but dreaded the coming of the day. There seemed to be nothing whatsoever to look forward to, and she missed sex but did not want Philip.

Philip was equally unhappy; things were bad at home, but at the office they were very strained indeed. Mary had wept and again threatened to leave, but he had begged her not to. He missed her warm young body and welcoming arms much more than he had expected to, but, doggedly, he still hoped that by some miracle the relationship with Alison would resurrect, even though his friend John assured him he was flogging a dead horse – a changed tune for the once-persuasive re-uniter of unhappy families.

'But what about Phoebe?'

'Even if I had stayed she might have done it. She was pretty depressed off and on; she was as miserable as I was with the marriage. I don't think my staying on would actually have made her any happier.'

He was rationalising, of course. Then Philip was invited to Sweden by one of the major timber firms the architectural practice dealt with; a week in Sweden, based in Stockholm, with an elk-hunt thrown in – and bring the wife. It was irresistible, though secretly Philip wished he could simply push off and pretend he was married to Mary – who was, he was sure, sobbing in the lavatory while he was on the phone to Stockholm – but of course he couldn't. Life was never so simple. Maybe a foreign trip together would do the trick, tip the marital balance and stop all this celibacy nonsense. Alison had been depressed and unwell for ages now. It was worth a try. He felt quite excited when he accepted his Swedish counterpart's invitation. He hadn't hunted for ages, but the Swede assured him on the telephone that he would arrange some practice for him before he was actually confronted with an elk. He decided to take his big Winchester and a 12 bore.

Alison watched Lars, their tall blond Swedish host, put away their suitcases and Philip's guns into the boot of his big Mercedes. She hadn't really wanted to come to Stockholm. There had been a panic-stricken madwoman in her head who said what if Gareth phones? It was the same madwoman who still jumped with hopeful hysteria every time the phone rang – indeed, some days when she was alone in the shop, she used to sit for minutes on end willing it to ring, and for it to be Gareth . . . . But it never was, and she never rang him, though more than once she dialled the first few digits of his number until she put the receiver back, feeling almost sick. But here she was in Sweden, and in fact quite alert and interested for the first time in months. Flying over the many thousands of islands which made up the Stockholm archipelago had been invigorating – it was such an amazing sight, the complexity of green against the all-encroaching sea.

Lars closed the boot and his wife, Birgitta, equally tall and blonde – and a judge, they were surprised to discover – motioned Alison into the car. She smiled.

'We will give you a small tour if you are not too tired from your yourney.' They found that many Swedes could not manage to say 'j' and tended to substitute it with a 'y'. It was faintly endearing in the middle of all that shamefully articulate and correct English.

They drove past lots of lakes, sea-lakes mostly, and dark fir forests which stretched for miles. There was a great sense of space, and the houses were never close together. Out in the country the houses were all wooden, simple and elegant, and mostly painted a dark reddish-brown. Alison loved the colour against the mysterious dark green of the trees – it was exactly the colour she had used for the spare room.

The Swedish flag was much in evidence. It hung proudly outside many of the houses – often a tiny dark red shack would have its own flagpole for the bright cerulean blue flag with its egg-yolk-yellow cross. Stockholm itself was beautiful, built on several islands. There was water everywhere, and lots of green.

Before they parted Lars invited them to supper, and Birgitta drew a map of the best shops and museums for Alison to see.

'I can show you Stockholm tomorrow morning if you would like that,' she said, 'but in the afternoon I have to be a yudge.'

The hotel was in the old part of the city, on an island which also contained the Royal Palace, where earnest blond young men stood on guard in grey uniforms. Alison was amused to discover that the hotel was right next to a shop which sold only tartan – she sent a card to Frankie to inform her of this bizarre fact.

'The Svenssons are very friendly, aren't they?' she said as she undressed for the shower.

'So they ought to be. I'm worth an awful lot of money to them.' Philip grunted smugly and lay back on the bed, arms behind his head.

In the old days at this point of a holiday they would probably have made love, or at least celebrated being alone together in a beautiful environment. But now neither of them wanted the other; they were neutral, cool. Her heart sank when she saw his eyes close, not because she wanted him to desire her, but because his switching-off acknowledged the death of their relationship. Sex was still non-existent between them, and after the shower she came and lay on her own bed and thought how like two neutered animals they were, disinterestedly sharing a basket.

Philip was snoring, something he only did when he was very tired. He had put out a lot of business energy today, impressing, amusing Lars and Birgitta with jokes, questions and comments which to Alison were like some tired old tape played over and over until it was misshapen and sagging, like her droopy tits and his wrinkled cock. She felt worn, unattractive and used-up, and for the first time in weeks she allowed herself to think of Gareth, of his warmth, his love-making, of how they always wanted each other. It was up to her: he had stated his case clearly enough, but she felt pretty certain he would still feel the same. Briefly she panicked, wondering if some female in Kent had caught his interest and comforted his loneliness. She felt bitterly lonely, and fantasised about quietly dressing, taking her bag and leaving her sleeping husband – simply walking out of their mutual life – or half-life as it was now, but to where? And what about the children? Always, always she came back in a circle to the same insolubles. As Philip had said 'Here we go round the mulberry bush . . . round and round.'

The Svenssons's flat was large, spacious, with white walls and much wood. There was an eclectic mix of modern pine, simple, clean and satisfying, and several old pieces of furniture which Alison enormously admired, including a white clock – a rustic piece, a grandfather from 1810 – with flowers painted on it, and several chairs with gentle curves, also white-painted, with woven seat-covers. On the walls were several more weavings, made by Birgitta's grandmother, woollen, in gentle natural dyes, strange greens and soft grey-blues. They were welcomed with drinks and met the children of the house, also tall, golden-haired and stunning-looking. Mark would reel at the sight of Kerstin, the seventeen-year-old girl, and Magnus, who at eighteen, had just sat his Studentsexamen – the Swedish A-level, but treated with more ceremony than its British equivalent in that the successful candidates were garlanded with flowers and given caps – was already a large handsome young man.

After dinner the men took themselves off to Lars's study with cigars and brandy, and Alison wandered admiringly round the large sitting-room. She stopped at a large framed photo of Lars, grinning happily with a garland of flowers on his head.

'That's lovely, what was that for?'

'That was at midsummer, we yenerally have a big party outside with also much singing. We had yust got married.' Birgitta smiled fondly at the image.

'You had just got married . . . but it looks recent.'

'Oh yes, it was only two summers ago.'

'But . . .' Alison had felt almost envious of this happily-married pair with their lovely children. It had made her feel quite inferior.

'We are both divorced; the children are mine, Lars has four more, but his wife, his old wife and her new man, they have his children.'

'I am amazed.' Alison looked at the tall cheerful woman. 'I presumed you had been married for years . . .'

Birgitta chuckled, 'We have, but with other people. Now I am very happy but it was not so happy for a long time.' She laughed humourlessly as she remembered, then shook her head. 'Not good, not easy, but now very common.'

'Indeed,' Alison sighed.

'And you? How old are your children?'

Alison told her.

'They are Philip's?'

'Oh yes.' She looked at the candle-flames wistfully, and remembered being in bed with Gareth in the cottage near Bath.

'Your husband; I think he is very clever, a successful man; my Lars is impressed with him. And handsome . . .'

'Yes, he is, all of that . . .' And cold, remote, and she no longer loved him . . .

They were silent, Birgitta got up and poured them some more coffee – comforting coffee – in English cups. Spode, it was a pattern Alison knew well.

Birgitta was obviously longing to probe further, but

her Swedish reserve held her back from being too full-frontal.

'I was so unhappy only three years ago; but now it is like a new life, I am a new person.'

'And the children?'

'Children are adaptable animals; they like fact, stability. They hate doubt and not to be secure.'

Alison nodded. Gareth would love this place, love the wood everywhere, and the space.

'You look very sad,' said Birgitta. 'Are you tired from the yourney?'

Alison, perhaps from the wine and the schnapps, laughed. 'The journey through life, you mean?'

Birgitta laughed too. 'That can be very tiring if you are not happy.'

'Right.' Alison nodded, and they looked at each other. Birgitta was very sympathetic. It made Alison dare to become personal: 'Were you unhappy for long?'

Birgitta frowned, and Alison wondered if she had done wrong to ask, but it was the memory, not the question that affected her hostess.

'Quite long, yes. When you fight it's bad, and so awful for the children, and then when you don't even want to fight, you don't love each other enough to fight, then I think it is saddest. I felt like a dead person until I met Lars, but he made me alive again. I think it was the same for him.'

Alison could not speak, the lump in her throat was so large. She felt Birgitta's hand on her arm. 'Alison, it can be better; nobody is unhappy for ever, even if you feel it will always be black.' She pointed to the picture of Lars with flowers in his hair. 'You would not have recognised him a year before that; he looked like a white old man, and he was drinking too much. It was good what happened, I believe that.'

The men came back, still busy talking; now it was hunting, politics, guns, elk, killing. Man-talk.

In the old town of Stockholm next day Birgitta took Alison for coffee in an old-fashioned coffee-shop where they ate spicy biscuits called pepparkakor. Next to the coffee-shop was a sort of peace-shop, filled with books, leaflets and badges celebrating bicycles, Greenpeace, and nuclear disarmament. Alison enjoyed browsing there amongst the long-haired blond young men and girls. She was suddenly reminded vividly of Gareth and his peaceful ideals. She almost wept at the memory of the Easter march and their first magical contact, and decided to buy herself a red and yellow sticker the same as Gareth had on his car. It was like a secret love-token – Gareth's was exactly the same design, and said 'Nuclear Power No Thanks' where the Swedish one said 'Atomkraft Nej Tak'.

Birgitta had smiled when she saw her buy it: 'I am not very political, but you know Sweden is neutral. We do not fight wars, but Kerstin and Magnus, they are very anti-nuclear, and for Greenpeace and conservation. We have a lot of problems in Sweden with pollution, many many of our lakes are dead now from factory pollution; it is very sad.'

Philip had seen the sticker when she got back to the hotel, and had predictably jeered and commenced another of his violent diatribes: 'You are so damned romantic, woman. What about Russia, don't you know about Russia? What about those poor Afghani tribesmen with only a few old rifles to protect them, and Czechoslovakia? And Hungary? And Poland? Do you want us to be like that? Over-run, dead, in prison-camps. You are a fool. A child.'

They had looked at each other with murder in their eyes.

'If you really think that, why are we here? Why are we staying together?'

Philip glared at her. 'Sometimes I wonder, I really do,' he said quietly.

They stood staring at each other in a mutually shocked silence, then he muttered 'I'm going to have a shower,' and disappeared to the sound of gushing water as she stared dumbly out of the window at the river and wondered how Gareth was. She thought about murder: she imagined Philip dead and bleeding in the shower, like some Hitchcock film, and she imagined herself, hurled out of the window, smashing bloodily onto the cobbles below. Death, or major surgery of some kind seemed to be the only answer; somehow, she had to sever herself from this man who had been flesh of her flesh, and she of his, for all these years, but the flesh now seemed rotten, gangrenous and unhealable; they had tried for long enough. But how? And where? And what? As usual she had no answer.

Chapter Twenty-six

The country place where Lars drove the Salvesons was a large old stone mansion set by a famous salmon river; it belonged to an aristocratic family who ran the shooting syndicate, and Lars and his Swedish associates had arranged for about ten guns on the shoot, which, from the sound of it, was nearer to a cull than anything. The Swedish elk were so large and prolific and so damaging to cars and drivers, that they had to keep the numbers carefully controlled by killing a certain amount each year.

Several of the men had brought wives, and the group were superbly catered for in the big house at night, but the Salvesons and Svenssons were to sleep in a small red-ochre painted wooden house in the forest a few kilometres away, much nearer the site of the elk hunt. In the evening, before it was properly dark, after Earl Grey tea and pepparkakor biscuits Alison went with the others to find their house in the woods. On the way Lars stopped the car by a large dark lake and summoned them to look.

It was one of the most impressive and dramatic settings Alison had ever seen: there were dark fir-woods all round, dense and gloomy, and you could imagine trolls lurking not far away. There was an old boathouse nearby, with dark reeds swaying in the water. The boathouse was the usual dark red, timbered and beautiful, and the sides of the lake were strangely smooth and curved – she was reminded of the curves of the concrete skate-park in London. Lars explained that the country here had all been glacial, and that the movement of the ice over thousands of years had made the grey stone so smooth.

'In the summer we swim here, and we can slide straight down deep into the water,' he told them. It did look lethally slippery, and the lake loomed black, deep, mysterious and secretive. Near the place where they were standing in the darkening light tall straight pines stretched up to the eerie purple of the dying sky. Beside the pines, in a small green clearing was a tall dark man-made structure of two enormous pines, like vast rugby posts, built from straight tall trees, still with the bark on, but stripped bare of twigs and branches; there was a crosspiece fixed firmly between the two, made from a similar felled tree. It was strangely powerful, like some primitive sculpture or weird religious structure. It was a frightening place, haunting, with an extraordinary atmosphere, as though there much had happened, and not all that had happened had been good. Alison's mood was black anyway, and the place matched her sense of doom.

They dumped their bags in the forest house – again a well-designed spacious Swedish dwelling – with striped rag-rugs, and wooden furniture. She and Philip unpacked, and he lovingly checked over his Winchester, oblivious of his watching wife who viewed him as dispassionately as an anthropologist observing some alien tribesman. Alison lay under the duvet and tried to sleep, but felt rattled and miserable. Restlessly, she sat up to light one of her rare cigarettes.

'Must you?' Philip turned from caressing his gun, a pained expression on his face.

'I'm sorry, I need one.' She continued to puff, not caring if he hated it, knowing it was stupid, anti-social and lethal. She watched him and felt lonelier than ever. 'I wonder how the kids are . . .'

Philip didn't look up. 'Why don't you ring them? There's a phone downstairs.'

'Do you want to talk to them?'

'Not specially.' He didn't really want to talk to anybody.

Alison wandered down the wooden stairs, past several massive elk horns, bigger than the set she and Frankie had in the shop, and admired an old oak chest with a curved top and iron clasps. She was glad to find Birgitta sitting reading. They chatted a little, then Alison phoned Jo who sounded happy and was full of the wonders of Anthony who was teaching her to draw.

'You sound a bit miserable, Ma. Is Pa there?'

'He's busy getting ready to hunt, sends you lots of love . . .'

'Are you miserable? You sound it.'

Alison felt quite choked. 'No, I'm fine, we're having a super time.'

Birgitta took one look at her when she came back. 'I think it is time for a drink. Sherry or yin?'

'Gin, please.' It might help keep the yanglings at bay.

In the morning the men set off early; Philip in khaki outfit and wellingtons looked militaristic except for the orange neon band which the hunters had by law to wear on their hats. He wore an old tweed deerstalker which once she had adored him in, but now found faintly ridiculous. He looked like a kid dressed up, with his set serious face. Birgitta was driving them to the hunt, and had some shopping to do; she invited Alison to come, but she said she wanted to go for a walk. Birgitta showed her where it was safe to go.

'Every year,' she explained, 'there are some people killed in the elk-hunting season, usually hunters, that's why they have to wear the cap band; we don't want to lose you. Have a good walk, goodbye,' and she left, with her odd, sweet formality.

Alison wandered along the river bank, overcome with a sense of gloom. It was snappily cold. She was glad of her sheepskin coat and warm boots. She still felt rattled; her solar-plexus was juddery and her heart heavy, but the dark beauty of the place was breath-taking. She sat by a pool in a river and watched a small waterfall cascading down onto granite boulders, and admired the fir trees and the orange and yellow of the autumn-tinted oaks which had been speckled with frost when they first saw them at breakfast.

The sky was a crisp clear blue and the sun bright. Alison walked for an hour wondering what she must do with her life, and always, always she saw images of Gareth, peering like ghosts from behind the lines of fir trees which stretched darkly into the secret depths of the forest.

She stopped at a big tree, and stood beside it, hugging it with her arms, her face sad against the warm rough bark; it was strangely comforting, and she knew she must look very odd, alone in this Swedish forest, tears streaming down her cheeks, embracing a pink-barked tree. Frankie would laugh herself sick. She laughed herself, and within moments she recognised the reason for her change of mood. Her period had arrived, she felt it flow, the damned menstrual cycle which somehow contrived to make life even more of a crazed roundabout of emotions for women than it had to be.

She went back to the lodge to change, and met Birgitta who was ready to take her out for the day.

'We will enyoy nature, and leave the men to kill it,' she said.

What Alison had expected to be a leisurely wander through the pine forest turned out to be the most entertaining day imaginable: Birgitta took her first to the sea where they bought smoked eels and pots of home-made mustardy sauce. They bought honey from an old lady of eighty-three, dressed in a long skirt with a pale blue kerchief on her head, who jabbered to Birgitta in Swedish, and toothlessly grinned at Alison and pinched her cheek to demonstrate friendship. This was followed by a visit to a potter where Alison acquired a simple but beautiful bowl with a deep blue-green glaze. Its bottomless depths of colour reminded her of the lake last night. Thence to a farmer's wife, fat and fifty, who wove the rag-rugs, and offered them real coffee and home-made cardamom cakes.

They had a late lunch back at the house in the woods, Swedish cheese, yoghurt – quite different to the yoghurt at home, thinner and tastier – rye bread and honey. There was even a strange brown goat's cheese that tasted almost like fudge.

After they had eaten and were relaxing in front of the old tiled corner stove, Alison thanked Birgitta.

The Swede smiled: 'I enyoyed myself very much. I felt you needed to be taken – what do you say? – inside-out of yourself,' she paused. 'I think that is not quite what you say?'

'I think you mean "out of myself", and yes, I did need that.'

'I am sad because I can see you are not happy.'

'Is it so obvious?'

'Oh no,' Birgitta was at pains to reassure her. 'but we like you both. Lars has known Philip in business for a long time now.'

'Oh God,' said Alison, the despair returning. 'It is so sad, so difficult. Why can't we be simple?'

'People are not simple. When I fell in love with Lars we were not simple. Our two marriages and six children . . . eight, because his wife now has a man with two more children. It was awful . . . . You and Philip are very different people, perhaps you have got more different . . .'

'We have. So different that we are now like strangers.'

'Perhaps you need to be apart?'

'We came to Sweden to be together, to try to make it better.'

Birgitta looked at her. 'I am so very sorry.'

It was getting late, and would soon be dark. Birgitta stood up.

'Shall we go to see our little boys, how well they have killed?'

Alison nodded; she rose, and went to the big Swede – she was even bigger than Frankie – and hugged her.

'Birgitta. You've been lovely.'

'No . . .' said Birgitta, hugging her back. 'Yust human, yust a woman. But all I can advise you is do not be afraid of change, sometimes change is good and necessary.'

They took the car in the dying light of day to the strange almost mystical place by the lake with the huge crucifix-like wooden edifice, and were greeted by a scene of carnage. Elk carcasses, huge and tragic, hung from the posts, heads downwards, their great flat horns heavy, shaped like giant troll hands. There was blood everywhere from the eviscerated corpses and Alison was horrified to see the normally cool Philip flushed with blood-lust – euphoric, it seemed to her – from having shot two of these majestic animals, kneeling with a huge knife and an even huger smile, carving up the belly of a monster elk-corpse whose insides spilled onto the ground. The men, all happy and excited, were drinking schnapps from hip flasks, and there were several dogs tearing at the livers of the dead animals – their reward for the day's work. The women were greeted with shouts and cheers. Birgitta, obviously used to the sight of blood and massacred animals, pragmatic and Swedish, smiled and strode over to hug her victorious Lars, who had also killed two elk. It had been a splendid day for them, and there was much noise and joy. Alison watched Philip, in shirtsleeves, hatless, his hair pale beneath the dark trees, with the gloomy and fearful lake in the background. His arms and hands were steeped in blood, his look manic.

'Come and see, darling; it's a magnificent beast.'

Alison paused, then turned, she felt sick, hysterical.

'I'm just going to the car,' she said, and left them to their jollity and all the blood and death. She ran stumbling to struggle with the door of the Mercedes, got into the front seat and sat alone in the shadow of the tall dark trees. She was not a squeamish person – she had often watched Philip hunt – and was objective about the process of killing animals to eat. Years ago she had decided that she was a confirmed carnivore. But she now realised coldly and realistically that it was over: her marriage, Philip, the two of them together. It had to end. It had ended ages ago; it simply had taken her until now to acknowledge it with her conscious mind. She felt extraordinarily relieved; it was obvious now that she could accept that it was all over.

At night, again at the big house, after more good food, wine, and extravagant tales of other heroic hunts, the Salvesons went to bed. Philip, who had washed off the elk blood and dressed in a white jersey with pale trousers, undressed dreamily, pulling off shoes and socks, still full of the day's euphoria. Alison undressed too, and prepared for bed by putting on a long striped red and white cotton tee-shirt she had bought in Stockholm. She felt strangely peaceful, almost friendly to this man she was about to leave.

Philip, naked, leaned towards her: 'You look wonderful, how was your Swedish day?'

'Magnificent,' she said, and smiled. It had all been good. Cathartic.

For the first time in months she wanted him. She wanted sex, as Philip, still flushed and triumphant, obviously did.

She looked at him. He lay back eyeing her appraisingly.

She smiled ironically: 'I'm a bit bloody.'

Philip looked at her hopefully and moved towards her. 'Aren't we all?' He clutched for her, and she allowed him to pull off the long striped garment with precision and an arousing gentleness.

They made love for the first time in months with a fierceness and passion that matched the gory and jubilant scene by the lake. Alison felt liberated, abandoned, like a prisoner who has been set free. Their language was one they both knew well, and they retired between bouts breathless and astonished that this could still happen between them. It was an oblivion of passion. Life, death, and pleasure were bloodily intermixed. They were on some strange plane, momentarily liberated from all bonds of hatred or love. It was lust, pure and simple, but earth-shaking.

Philip slept at last, spent, ecstatic, and Alison watched him, his head a shadow on the pillow. She sang a jubilant song of freedom within herself. Then she too slept, a deep dreamless sleep, refreshing, like she had not had for years it seemed.

In the morning she told him, quietly and straight. She wanted out of the marriage, a separation if he insisted, but she would prefer a divorce. He was thunderstruck and stared at her in disbelief. For a moment she wondered if the violence would return.

'But we fucked, we fucked like we never have . . .'

A final fuck it was, a fuck to end it all. She nodded. 'We both needed it, needed each other. I mean it, Philip. I want out. I think if you are honest, you feel the same.'

He stared at her with his uncomprehending cold stare. 'Are you going to your Welshman?'

'I don't know, I haven't contacted him or he me for over three months. Anything might have happened. He may have somebody else. I want us to part regardless of alternatives.' She found that she had picked up her red and yellow 'Atomkraft Nej Tak' sticker, and was holding it in her hand like a talisman to give her courage.

Philip eyed her warily. The bloodstained victor of the night before looked a little raddled.

'Don't tell me you're going to rush off and join the dykes at Greenham Common?'

'I might. Anything can happen, and they're not dykes, I heard two speak, and they were magnificent.

'Magnificent, huh,' he said. Then he looked at her, his little dark-haired, fierce-eyed wife, whom once he had so adored. 'You mean it, don't you?'

She nodded. 'I really mean it. I've tried my hardest, there's no going back.'

Again, with the guns lying beside them in the room, she wondered, almost abstractedly this time, if he might kill her. He rose from the bed abluted, then dressed in silence putting on the pale clothes of the night before. He said nothing, but when he was ready he pulled on his green wellingtons and khaki jacket, and picked up one of his guns. If he did choose to kill her it would all be part of the master-plan, she thought mindlessly, but he turned to stare at her once more, sitting apparently tranquil on the bed in the long striped nightie, then he cursed her:

'Damn you, Alison, *damn* you!' She quailed, then, clutching the gun, he banged out of the room. She wondered, still in a strange state of numbness – as though she were the eye of a tornado – if he would hurl himself down the slippery granite slope of the lake and drown himself in a demented despair similar to Phoebe's, or if he would shoot himself instead of her, and add his splayed and brilliant grey matter to the bloody gore already festering by the lake. But she was beyond pain, beyond caring. She dressed in a skirt and jersey, and tremblingly put on gold earrings and a chain, and went downstairs. Birgitta had gone over to the big house, on some errand, and Lars was peacefully putting holey Swedish cheese on rye bread.

'Good morning Alison. You are well? Coffee? I think Philip has gone out; I saw him with his gun. He is a keen man, yeah?'

She smiled faintly and sat down at the table. Lars was an undemanding and easy breakfast companion. They talked amicably in intermittent three-word sentences. After a while Birgitta appeared clutching a letter.

'For you? A surprise?'

It was from Frankie, Alison had begged her to write some silly note to cheer her up in Sweden. It was a miracle that it had reached her here; she opened the envelope, which contained a short scrawl from the Scots girl in red felt-tip, written at the shop, plus an envelope, quite fat, which, again in Frankie's writing, said 'Accounts'. A little puzzled, she laid that one aside and read Frankie's note. Short and sharp, it said everybody was happy and hoped she and P. where OK and please to open the enclosed envelope in private, underlined.

Lars disappeared and Alison helped to clear up the breakfast mess, and Birgitta asked where Philip was.

'We had a bit of an argument,' Alison told her.

Birgitta looked concerned: 'A bad one?'

'I told him I want a divorce.'

'Oh my God!' Birgitta clutched her. 'It's not my fault?'

'Of course not; it had to come. Last night I just knew, and I feel sure.'

'And Philip?'

'He was very angry, he went off with the gun . . .'

'What?' yelled Birgitta. 'Is he safe?'

'I don't know . . .' said Alison.

'We had better go and look for him.' The big Swede was obviously very worried.

'I think he's OK. Honestly . . .' Alison felt numb, detached. Birgitta, watching her, said, 'You stay. I go. Maybe it's better.' She pulled on her smart fur-lined English Burberry, and boots, and went off into the woods.

Alison decided to go out too; it was a crisp bright morning, and she wanted to sit by the lake. Booted and furred, she strode past the fir-trees and orange oaks and birches, and came to a part of the lake beyond last night's scene of carnage. It was fairly dry under the pine-trees, where there was a thick carpeting of brown shiny needles. Filled with curiosity, she sat down on a rock and curiously ripped open Frankie's mysterious second envelope. Inside – and her heart almost stopped for a moment – was a second envelope from Gareth, addressed to Alison in black ink in his strong simple hand. She looked at it for almost a minute before she summoned up courage to unseal it. At last she tore it open. It was written on white plain paper, with no address, dated four days ago.

'My dearest Alison,

'Our mutual silence has now been so long and so painful to me that I can now no longer bear it. Hence this letter.

'Forgive me for intruding on your life, and please ignore and destroy this if it arrives at a time when you have succeeded in finding happiness in your marriage once again. With all my heart I long for you to be happy, and if this is to be your way I will try to understand.

'If this is not the case, and I hear from Frankie that you have not had a very easy time, I want you to know that I still feel as I did about you, and if there is the slightest chance that we might make a life together I am still here waiting for you as I promised all that time ago when we said goodbye.

'Please, whatever your situation, may we at least meet once and talk, if only as friends, for old time's sake? I will contact you on your return from Sweden.

'Still no luck on the job front, and I continue to be untalented as an antique dealer, though I improve slowly in the book business.

'I must tell you that I am seriously considering emigrating, possibly to Australia; it sounds like a fine place. It would certainly be a good country for the children, who thrive.

'I ache for you, and will love you for ever,
'I embrace you,
'Gareth.'

She wept, gasped and laughed; this letter of love, this almost mystical happening, had arrived at the moment she needed it. She had often talked to Gareth about the almost extra-sensory communication that happened between people who were deeply in love. It was unbelievable, but here it was in her hand, the proof of it. They loved each other still, and maybe they could actually make a new life together, like Birgitta said. She looked with swimming eyes at the beauty of the deep dark lake and beyond to the depths of the forest surround. One day she would like to come here with Gareth.

Then she heard the shot. The loud report went through her head with immense shock; there was a commotion of shrieking crows cawing in their crazed crude way; and a disturbance in the sky above some lakeside trees a few hundred yards away. A moment later Birgitta came running towards her, terrified.

'Is it Philip? We must go and look . . .' She was panting. Alison stuffed the letter into her pocket and they ran in the direction of the shot, past tree-trunks, branches tearing at their heads. Then they saw Philip, and stopped dead.

He was walking towards them holding the gun in one hand, and the corpse of a pigeon in the other. He held the bird with splayed wings up to them and smiled crookedly.

'Look what I got.'

Speechless, breathless, the women stayed still and watched as he walked up to them. Alison's heart was churning away like a mill-pump, Birgitta was white as Swedish snow.

'Am I too late for breakfast?' asked Philip. 'I'm starving.'

The three of them walked back to the house where Birgitta poured coffee, then, saying she had things to do, she left them alone. They drank in silence until Alison could bear it no longer.

'You gave me such a fright with that gun-shot.'

He looked at her uncomprehendingly: 'What?' Then . . . 'Oh Alison, you're always so dramatic; surely you didn't think I would go and do what Phoebe did?'

She didn't answer. She thought of the guilt, and wondered how on earth she would have told the children.

'I'd never do that.'

She looked at him and nodded. He drank more coffee, then eyed her seriously.

'I've been thinking about what you said.'

She felt very tense; he looked quite threatening again. 'And?'

'I must have full and easy access to the kids,' he was fierce, intense, 'otherwise I won't go.'

'Of course . . . they need you . . .' She was crying now, tears pouring out; he was actually agreeing to their parting. She felt his hand on her shoulder. 'Please stop it, Allie, or we'll both howl.'

So it was agreed. Exhausted, Philip slumped in his chair and gazed at the pale pine table-top, and Alison, her forehead cupped in her hands, gazed at a spot a few inches to the left. Neither of them spoke, and it was thus that Birgitta found them when, five minutes later, she had the courage to knock on the door.

'I am sorry to disturb, but I think we must think of starting our yourney; it's far to go, and we want to show you some good places on the way.'

Philip smiled bleakly up at her:

'OK, Birgitta; we'll get ourselves together.'

Chapter Twenty-seven

Alison and Philip arrived home to their empty house late on a winter afternoon after a painfully silent journey during which they had both wondered if this might be the last time they would publicly be seen together as man and wife. They were greeted by the hysterically welcoming dog, which made Alison, almost before the door was shut, tell Philip that he must take the dog with him when he moved out. In seconds, all her old bitternesses flared up into a sudden hideous wrangle, like petrol ignited by a match, and Jo and Mark were shocked when they arrived home to find them both shouting and glaring.

At supper they announced their decision to part. Jo stared at them in disbelief, then burst into tears, which alarmed the dog, and she collapsed on the floor with him, hugging the animal, blindly sobbing.

Mark took the whole business more quietly: he watched them intently when they said that Philip would move out, then shrugged hopelessly.

'I'm not exactly surprised, how could I be?' Then he looked at Philip. 'When will you go?'

'For the moment you will all stay put; we'll have to sort out finances and things, and that takes time. I shall find a flat; maybe John Abrahams will put me up until I do, he's living in quite a big place, and he's offered more than once lately.'

This was news to Alison, but a relief, Philip had obviously been as uncomfortable as her with the situation of the last few weeks.

'I'm also taking the dog,' said Philip.

Jo wailed very loudly, and the dalmatian licked her, his tail thumping an anxious overtime.

'Please Mum, please . . .' Tear-stained, she appealed, but Alison was steely: 'I'm sorry; he's Dad's responsibility. You'll see him lots.'

'Of course you will,' Philip looked anguished.

'But you're always away . . .' Jo gazed at him, tears spouting.

'We can take him when Dad's away abroad, how about that?'

Mollified, the girl nodded.

'You haven't taken him for a walk for months,' Alison reminded her gently.

'I did! I did! I took him for a walk yesterday with Anthony and Frankie.'

'Only once . . . in how many months?'

Jo glowered, 'I don't know.'

Mark stood up from the table: 'I've got a lot of homework . . . . Do you mind if I go up?'

'OK. We'll clear up,' his mother looked at him anxiously; she was sure that he was going to his room to cry. Mark mumbled something incoherent and fled.

Frankie was already busy when Alison arrived at the shop next morning. She was squinting as she re-threaded a long string of amber beads. She leapt up grinning when Alison came in the door:

'Hi? How was the frozen north?'

'Not at all frozen, lovely really . . .' Then she broke. 'Philip is moving out. We've decided to split.'

Frankie stared at her aghast, 'Oh Allie, no. I thought you would come back all sorted out and together again. You've both been trying so hard . . .'

Alison shook her head emptily.

Frankie moaned: 'I knew I shouldn't have sent that letter on, but Gareth was so desperate just to contact you . . . . I felt I had to.'

'It's OK.' Alison sat down tiredly. 'I had made up my mind long before that arrived, honest. It came after I had made my decision; Gareth or no Gareth, I want out.'

Frankie was crying now. She lurched up from the table, tipping it a little, and dozens of orange beads of different sizes skidded randomly across the shop floor. Frankie swore, but was too concerned with the news of the family demise to do anything about them.

'I so wanted it to be OK. I love your family, I'm fond of Philip too – when I first met you I thought you were the most ideal, beautiful wonderful family I'd ever seen, or would ever see . . .'

'I used to think that too.'

They both bawled, and Frankie became angry.

'Why? Why? Why? You're intelligent lovely people . . . why the hell do you have to go and split?' She howled amid the strewn amber beads, bewailing the passing of her ideal image of family life. Alison, who was fast becoming used to the whole hellish business, rose and went to comfort her friend, who sat sobbing in the Victorian button-back chair.

'It makes me worried about getting married . . . I can't bear to think of ending up hating Ant . . . of hurting him . . .'

'Oh Frankie, I know, I know.'

Frankie groaned and started crawling over the floor, swearing quietly in Glaswegian as she grovelled to find the lost beads. She was under a table, her long body stretched out as far as it would reach, her arm under a small chest of drawers with claw feet, when Gareth walked in wearing the saffron yellow jersey Alison had given him. Alison, standing in the curtained doorway of the back shop holding two mugs of coffee immediately dropped one and it smashed, spraying coffee everywhere.

'Oh Lord!' he said seeing the chaos and Alison's shock. 'Shall I go away again?'

Frankie turned to look at him and clutched her head, half-sobbing, half-laughing. 'This is all too much, I cannae cope!' and lay on her back shaking her head, a handful of beads in her hand. Alison put down the other mug carefully and walked over to Gareth.

'Please don't go,' she said. 'Please don't ever go.'

They were in each other's arms, speechless. There was no need for words, yet such a lot to say. They hugged, and like some weary traveller who has been away for years, Alison felt that she was home at last.

Frankie finished harvesting the beads and laid them neatly in a saucer, whilst Gareth picked up the broken china; Alison, after wiping sprayed coffee off porcelain, elk-horn and velvet, made more drinks, and the three of them looked at each other.

'I gather that I arrived in mid-drama.'

Frankie shrieked, 'No, no darling, it's just a typical morning down at the shop!' She looked at Alison, sitting close to Gareth, glowing.

'Listen, I'm gonna push off; it's OK for Gareth to be here now, isn't it?'

'I suppose it is.' Alison blinked at the thought.

Frankie picked up her bag and poncho. 'I'll go. I've got to feed the cat and view an auction. I'll see you about teatime. OK?'

A customer arrived, an old lady who wanted to sell some oddments of jewellery: Alison dealt with her, then looked at her dark furry Esau; he was even better than she had remembered. 'Come into the back shop,' she said. He followed her and she pulled the curtain across, and for an hour they outpoured and wonderingly touched the flesh that was no longer forbidden fruit. His kisses champagned a rampage through her limbs.

'So what happens now?' asked Gareth when the sagas of France and Sweden were unfolded.

'It is hell. Who takes what. Whose is which. The kids are in a bad way. It will not be easy, but Philip has agreed definitely to move out.'

He looked at her and caressed her face gently. 'I can hardly believe this. When can we meet properly? It has been terrible not to see you, not to touch you . . . . I've been half-mad.'

'You must be mad to still want me.'

'I still want you. You know that.'

'I guess you must . . .' The gaze, the contact, the magic, it was all still there.

'Let's try to meet on Friday as usual . . .'

'Wednesday's sooner.'

'I hardly know what day it is – we only got back last night. OK, Wednesday it is.'

For the rest of the day Alison felt freer and happier than she had felt for years, but at home it was different. Philip, never one to waste time, had arranged to move out immediately, to put his gear at John Abrahams' and to sleep there until he found a flat, which extraordinarily, he did not anticipate would take more than a few days. He packed quickly and efficiently; Mark retired chalk-white to his room, speaking to nobody; and Jo sobbed ceaselessly, or lay on the sofa catatonically watching telly, sniffing and sucking an old woolly scarf. Alison helped Philip to pack, found bags and boxes, and they were icily polite.

'We will have to see lawyers, both of us. I'll use Tim Marcus as he's an old friend. You'll have to find someone. We'll talk about the house later, when we've got lawyers. We'll probably have to sell so that we can both have somewhere big enough for the kids to stay; they must be free to come and go.'

Tim Marcus was also Alison's friend. She would have liked to use him too; she didn't know anybody else.

'Why can't you go tomorrow, Dad?' asked Jo, red-eyed. 'It's almost nine o'clock, nearly bed-time.' She looked at him bewilderedly, clutching the dog, who hopefully thumped his tail.

'I'll see you lots. You can come for weekends.'

'But I don't know where you'll be . . .'

'Nor do I,' Philip's face was set. 'But I'll be away, that's for sure.'

He left complete with dog, and Jo locked herself in her room, sobbing. Mark made himself a cup of tea in stunned silence, said goodnight to his mother tonelessly and went upstairs. She sat on the sofa for ages, till she grew cold in the small hours of the morning. She was full of doubts and distressing memories of earlier, happier times swirled through her head. She was awake till three a.m. The next thing she knew Mark was shaking her awake on the sofa:

'Ma, wake up, Jo's being terribly sick.'

Jo was very ill and feverish next day.

Crazed, Alison phoned Gareth to tell him that Wednesday was out. He was more than sympathetic, and very loving.

'Maybe Friday . . .' she said dubiously, 'but I'm not sure. The doctor said she must rest till the fever's done, and he's given her antibiotics.'

'I can't do Friday anyway, I've got a big interview.'

'Where for?'

'Sydney, Australia.'

'But that's the other side of the world . . .'

'It's a good country; I've done a lot of research. One of my mates is a professor there; I'm quite hopeful.' He sounded very optimistic. 'Don't worry, we've waited long enough, a day or two more won't make us love each other any the less. Australia could be wonderful!'

Jo was ill for a week; Philip came one night like an uncle or family friend to visit her, and Alison managed to see Gareth in a café for half an hour. It was anguished, they only wanted to be in bed together.

'How was the interview?'

'Marvellous, I think I'm in with a chance.'

'But what about us?'

'You'll have to come,' he said firmly.

'Those dreams we had, of a life in the country . . .'

'They were good dreams. Maybe we still will, but in Australia. Listen, girl, I've missed every job I've applied for so far; let's not get worked up about this one yet.'

It was true, the odds were against it. But the children needed a London base, needed their friends and Philip.

He hugged her and her senses reeled. 'The sooner you and I get into bed together the better.' He kissed her, and there was nothing but his lips, his touch. It was the centre of the world.

'Next week, surely next week we will . . .'

'Of course we will, otherwise I'll break in.'

'You can't be at my place, not yet, not with the kids around.'

'I know.'

Mary had been delighted when Philip had embarrassedly announced that he was looking for a flat, and asked if she could help as he was so busy.

She smiled hopefully. 'I've got my spare room if you're stuck . . .'

'Thanks, Mary, but I can't. I need somewhere big enough for the children and the flaming dog.'

'The dog?'

He nodded sheepishly. Poor man, Alison must be a mad virago; Mary had always had her doubts about Philip's little wisp of a wife.

'Of course I'll help. Where do you want to be?'

'Near enough for the children to come and go freely, not too far from the office, and near a tube, and a park I suppose.' He frowned as he thought of Pirate, who had peed on John's sofa last night and broken some new plants in the garden.

'Would you like to come and eat one night?' Mary asked at last. Philip, staring blackly out at the dull grey river, turned to her, frowning.

'I'd like to . . . but I don't know if I should . . .'

'Just to eat . . .? It must be a bit odd staying with your friends after what has happened.'

'It is. It is very bloody weird.'

'Please come?' Mary tried not to show the enormous emotion she felt. 'It might even do you good, take your mind off it all.'

He looked up, his eyes were empty, like thumb-marks gashed on wet clay. 'I'd like that, if you can put up with me; I'm pretty lousy company at the moment.'

'Tomorrow?' She longed to touch and solace him.

He pulled out his diary. It all seemed such an effort; he felt chronically exhausted, ill almost. He eyed the pages of blank evenings. 'I do happen to be free.' He nodded wearily. 'Could I bring the dog?'

'Why don't we walk them in the park first, that might make it easier.'

Philip managed a faint chuckle. 'You're a practical woman, Mary, that's what I always liked about you.'

She smiled, and turned away to hide her tears. It was all she could do not to hurl herself into his arms.

The feeling of bereavement brought by the end of her marriage was something quite unexpected for Alison, but at last she regained the love and comfort of Gareth, with whom she was sexually reunited. It was as good as ever, and for the few short times they managed to lie together, her problems temporarily faded and seemed surmountable, but often, when she was alone, she would be overcome by grief for her loss of love and for the death of the marriage. One day one of her favourite customers came in, Solly was an old Jew, who dealt in jewellery and was meant to be retired, but had found he couldn't stop buying and selling. Alison had known him for five years, and was particularly fond of him. He was straight, honest and informative, and had taught her a lot about the trade. As usual she gave him a cup of coffee and listened to his rambling stories of his wife, children and grandchildren. But this particular day he was even more full of pride and delight than usual, because he had just celebrated his golden wedding-anniversary.

'I'm still mad about Bea, you know,' he said. 'Ever since I set eyes on her I've loved her. Fifty-one years ago she sold me an apple, and I knew that I was going to marry her. She's a wonderful woman, my wife.'

When he left, Alison wept bitterly. She remembered how she used to imagine Philip as an old man, with Jo's or Mark's children. She had looked forward to a marriage like Solly's, permanent, loving, with the fruits of old age to compensate for no longer being young and beautiful. But maybe they might be friends, though at the moment – what with talking to lawyers, and Philip who kept appearing unannounced to pick up this or that record or domestic item that he reckoned they could do without – it was hard to imagine.

Still, she had Gareth. She loved him like that now. Soon they would have to get to know each other's children, but they were taking that slowly. They had agreed that they must give it time for Mark and Jo to accept the situation. Typically, Philip had been speedy and efficient about finding somewhere to live; he had announced, only two weeks after leaving that he had found somewhere off Kensington High Street. It was within easy reach of the tube, and the children were enthusiastic about it, and excited at the prospect of staying with Dad, only that worried her too. What if they liked it so much that they decided to go and be with him permanently? The idea was almost unbearable.

Last week she had met Gareth's children: he had persuaded her to come and eat with them. Gareth had cooked a chicken and been relaxed and cheerful. The children, whom she had only seen once before, seemed very sweet and had eyed her curiously. Obviously their father did not often invite strange women to supper. She had liked them, though the little girl seemed rather clingy, and still, at nine, sucked her thumb.

At home, Jo, first with her illness and her now almost constant stroppiness, was not at all easy, and Mark had become as remote as his father used to be. He was still tense and uncommunicative, though Alison had been pleased when he dropped into the shop one day with Susan and bought a brooch for her birthday – at least that had seemed to be going for him again. He had obviously been quite proud to show Susan his mother's place, and to display his fairly extensive knowledge of antiques. It was a side to him she had never really been properly aware of – he must have learned by osmosis.

She met Gareth at Portobello Road just as they used to do in the old days, and this time they hugged freely, not caring who saw or reported them. Alison felt incredibly happy as she watched the first snowflakes of the winter fall onto his head, and kissed them off his beard.

They ate enormously at their usual caff, and went back to his house to make love where she realised, with a growing sense of liberation that they could now even go to her house. Later, when they lay in bed, holding each other, she talked about the weekend.

'Mark and Jo are going to Philip's for Saturday and Sunday. Is there any chance that you could come over to me?'

'There's an offer a man can't refuse. I'll fix a baby-sitter. The kids will be fine. That will be paradise, my love. And we must talk and plan.' He looked almost severe.

'I agree, we must.' It was time that they made some sort of plans, and knew exactly what they were going to do. It was a new life now.

Gareth got out of bed and stretched: 'Oh . . . I feel so good. I always feel good when we are together.'

'Me too.' Smiling, Alison lay back watching his dark muscular body, her man, her beloved.

'Are you happy?' He looked down at her.

She shut her eyes, blissful, and nodded, then opened them to admire him again. 'I'm always happy with you.'

'And you will always be with me now. Always.' He came to her and they embraced again, one creature, naked in harmony.

Frankie, who was always concerned about Alison's welfare, knew all too well about the spasms of grief and doubt that overwhelmed her friend and was worried about her first weekend with no children.

'What are you going to do?'

'I'm seeing Gareth on Saturday night; Sunday night I'll just potter.'

'Like hell, you will.' Frankie was decisive. 'We'll spend it together; I will feed you, Mrs Salveson, I insist. Ant's away anyway, painting some dog in Sussex, so I'll be a wee grass-widow. Will you come?'

Alison nodded. Sometimes Frankie was almost too good to be true.

On the Saturday the youngsters went off expectantly to stay with Philip. He was doing it in style; typical Philip, she thought bitterly, anything other than having to actually be with them and talk. They were going to *Cats* and no doubt he would take them out for a meal. They would probably never want to come back to their dreary Mum after Philip's set-piece.

It was snowing a little when Gareth arrived clutching a bottle of wine. He seemed shy at first: 'I feel strange being here again, and knowing it's OK and all that. Philip won't suddenly arrive and shoot me, will he?'

'Of course not. I think he's quite enjoying being a bachelor.'

'Like me, eh? Here we are two unattached people of

a certain age . . . . What will happen next, I wonder?'

Alison cooked whilst Gareth pottered, listening to *Don Giovanni* on tape, and exploring the many art books in the sitting-room.

He was amazed and delighted to be fed steak, and said wonderingly: 'I don't know when I last ate as well as this, Bath I suppose, in that lovely place . . .' He smiled. 'You're too good for me you know, above my station in life.'

Sated with food, they lay in the white sitting-room entwined, and he caressed her breasts as they drank wine and listened to music – mostly Mozart opera, with a little bit of Purcell and Handel. Late in the evening, Gareth had a great desire to sing the *Hallelujah Chorus*, and she told him about the strange man who had reminded her of him at her mother's funeral, who had sang so entrancingly, like a woman. As lovers do, they remembered all their early meetings, the Ashanti doll, the swimming-baths, the march, and Bath, where their love had been consummated by candlelight.

'Have you got any candles?' he asked.

'Mhum. Lots, and I've got a new Swedish candlestick.'

Birgitta, as a farewell present, had given her a simple white porcelain candlestick which held five candles. She put out the lights, and came back into the room naked, bearing the five candles aflame.

Gareth humming along to the poignant aria of the wronged husband in Don Giovanni, turned to her: 'Is my fire goddess giving me a subtle hint or something?'

'How did you guess?'

'I'm a very percipient person.'

Alison could not bear to make love with Gareth in her marital bed – there were too many memories, both good and bad – so they slept together in the sitting-room on cushions covered with bedclothes from the spare-room. The five candles lit their love-making, and for them both it was unsurpassed by anything they had shared before.

'After that time together in the cottage, the first time . . .' said Alison.

'I thought nothing could be better.' Gareth, golden, vibrant in the candle-glow, looked at this heaven-sent woman. Maybe she was a goddess: it seemed more than any mere human could desire, this joy they shared.

'Nor did I.' She looked up at him, so strong and dark, and could not speak. She could only touch and tell.

They made love off and on for most of the night, till the five candles guttered and extinguished themselves, one by one. Each orgasm was a parable of life and death – the tumescence, the flowering, the glory, and the stillness, the peace that followed. Late in the night, in the darkness, Gareth whispered 'Alison, we must talk, you know.'

She stirred, and in turn she made him hard again, wanting only to possess her, to explode within her magic centre. 'We're talking . . .' she said. 'How much better can we talk than this?'

'Really talk, I mean . . .'

She kissed him to a glorious silence. 'Tomorrow my love, tomorrow . . .'

There was snow on the ground when they woke, and the morning was half gone. They looked from the window at the new-born world, white, with no footprints on the ground, and the trees glorified with a white layer, each branch delineated and softly coated in white.

'It is so beautiful,' said Gareth wonderingly. Alison put on a Bach Brandenburg for them to listen to as they gazed out at the shrouded garden.

They went back to bed and dozed, then woke then

slept again, sated, never so happy, each of them bewildered that such joy should have come their way.

Gareth had to be home for his children at three, so they made breakfast, read the papers, and pretended that neither of them were watching the clock with its inexorable curfew. At last, the food eaten, the dishes washed, he said he must tell her something. She sat opposite him, he on the sofa, she on a black leather chair.

'Something very important has happened.'

Anxious, she looked at him. He sounded very serious. 'What is it?'

'I want you to come away with me.'

'Where?'

'Australia.'

She stared at him. 'Australia! You mean you got the job?' She had put it out of her mind, like all the other jobs, the hundred-and-God-knows-how-many jobs . . .

'I've been offered a lectureship in Sydney University, with good money, security of tenure, and help with travel expenses – the lot.'

'But I can't come to Australia!'

'Alison, I can't refuse this offer. It's a good place; I have friends there, it's a country with potential, and maybe there's a tiny bit more chance there of survival.'

'But I can't leave my children . . .'

'Bring them. Come with me. We will make a new life. They'll be able to see their father for holidays sometimes. I have to go, it's the only way for me.'

'They need to see their father, Mark has his A-levels . . .'

'Alison, Alison, it is all soluble. We need each other, that is established. We need to be together. You *must* come with me.'

She shook her head. 'I can't. It is not possible . . .'

'You must. You will; I know you will. I have had sixteen months of being unemployed, of being half a man, I can't go on like that. I like teaching and doing research. I know my subject, I'm good at it; I miss work, I miss money, I hate bringing up my children in poverty.'

'But . . . our country dream?'

'We can have it there . . . we could have acres maybe, all of that. And you could do fantastically well with your knowledge and contacts. The Australian antique market is full of opportunity for somebody with your knowledge:'

'Why didn't you tell me last night?'

'I only heard for sure yesterday. I have accepted the job. I feel I have to go, for my own and my family's survival.'

She looked at him then shut her eyes. 'Yes; I can see that you probably do have to go.'

'I feel that I have no option.'

'But us . . . me . . . my kids . . .'

'Come. Come with me. People have to be brutal sometimes in order to survive. We need to survive together. I could keep you, look after you. I'll be well-off and doing work I love in a fine place. I want to go. I need to go.'

She felt icy cold, and stared at him like one condemned.

'I cannot come, Gareth. My children are rooted here; I couldn't do it to them or to Philip. In fact they wouldn't come.'

'Come yourself, then. They are almost grown-up; they have their father. They'll survive.'

'No,' said Alison, and she thought her heart would tear asunder. 'I couldn't. I have my life here, my business, my partnership, and my family. No, no, no.' She shook her head despairingly.

'I have to go, I have no option.'

'Then that's the end for us.' She could hardly force out the words, and stared at him in disbelief.

'It can't be. I will not accept it; I must go, then you can come and see how it is.'

'Maybe.' Alison felt unable to speak, to talk or think. She stared into mid-air, and shook her head, it must be a nightmare. She would have nobody, no husband, no lover. Nothing. No Gareth, Gareth, Gareth.

He knelt by her, hugging, loving, begging. 'We need each other. I thought you would be glad.'

'I am glad for you. It's right, but for me it's not. I cannot come.'

'Oh God . . .' he buried his head in her knees, and abstractedly she stroked his dark beloved hair.

'When are you going?'

'In about a month. Christmas on the beach.'

'Send me a postcard,' she said faintly, and bitterly they wept together.

Then he was gone, back to his children, to his planning and packing and his new life, wrenched weeping from her, his *cariad* who sat alone in her deserted Ice Palace with the snow soft outside and wondered if she were mad. She sat as though frozen for a long time, hours perhaps, then stumbled to the phone. Frankie was there, cheerful, bright. Her lover would return.

Alison's voice was an incoherent mumble. 'Are you busy?'

'I'm just going over to the shop, I've got a couple of oddments to do. Come over there. You sound terrible.'

She drove blindly, slithering on the Sunday snow, and Frankie hugged her like her old fat Glasgow Mammy taught her. 'What on earth has happened?'

Bit by bit, stumbling, sobbing as though she would turn inside-out, the story was sicked-up.

'Oh God . . . but he must go; I can see that. But Alison, it's not the end. You love each other so much, I can see that now; give it time. Maybe he'll hate it, or maybe you'll go . . . in a year or two . . .'

However long, without Gareth it would be an infinity of pain and emptiness. At last, like a child who is too tired to cry, she could breathe and talk again.

'I like it here,' she said at last. 'I like my work, my friends, and the children need to be here near Philip.'

'Yes they do, and you do have a good life. My God, what a problem.'

Alison wandered round the shop mindlessly; on a shelf near the sink she discovered her forgotten Swedish peace-sticker.

Idly, she picked it up and looked at it. 'He's going because he says it's a better life there.'

'Well, maybe he's right. Mebbe we should all emigrate . . .'

'And Philip and the children . . .'

'And the dog . . .'

Alison actually laughed. 'That bloody dog! Just before I came over to you just now, when I was about to stagger weeping into the car, and the end of the world had come, guess what?'

'Pirate?'

'Yes, the effing dog arrived, barking like a maniac, tongue lolling, tail wagging, all pleased to have run home to Mother.'

Frankie shrugged. 'Well he loves you, it's a compliment, I thought the kids were with Philip . . .'

'They are; he must have run away.'

'Back to Mummy.'

Alison looked at her sticker, 'I'm going to put this on the car.'

'Now? It's snowing, it won't stick.'

'It will stick,' said Alison grimly, and went out armed with a cotton cloth. She came back looking better, flushed from the cold.

'I brought some medicine for you,' said Frankie, rootling in a cardboard box which was stuffed with twinkly bright fabric. 'I've had it in the fridge for a year. A rich lover gave it to me.' She produced a bottle of champagne. 'It's still cold.'

Frankie found two goblets and carefully popped the cork. The liquid foamed gloriously as she filled the two goblets. 'Drink it up like a good girl.'

Alison felt the bubbles tickle her mouth, and took a good half glass.

'Lovely medicine.'

'It should be. It's fifteen quid a bottle.' Frankie leaned over the cardboard box. 'I bought super things today, at the Horticultural Halls; I was just back when you phoned, it was a good fair.'

There were Indian silks, and a black long pair of stoles with pieces of silver all the way through the fabric, golden baggy trousers, a turquoise silk jacket, bright, with buttons, and scarlet saris and purple.

'You put that on.' She handed Alison a yellow turban with a massive orange feather in front. It must have been used for some quality theatrical production. Frankie put on a red fez, and they continued to drink and drape themselves in silk, gold and silver.

'My sticker's come loose.' Dizzily, Alison looked out of the window; the car was on a double yellow line, but it was Sunday, and you couldn't see the yellow lines for snow. 'I said I'll make it stick and I will.' She marched out, the feather on the turban trembling indignantly – she also tinkled loudly – she had added the black and silver stole to her outfit – it trailed behind her splendidly. She rested her glass giddily on the snow-covered roof of the car – it would cool the champagne very well – and rubbed determinedly at the car-window. This time the sticker stuck. She was pleased, and took another swig of alcohol.

'Philip wouldn't like it,' she said loudly, and giggled a little hysterically. Through the shop window she saw Frankie dancing, trailing coloured silks, dancing to the elk-head which she draped with a shimmering gold and red brocade sari, then she kissed the nose of the stuffed bear which she had, to Alison's disgust, produced last week. Alison smiled, then, dimly, she heard somebody calling 'Cooee!'

She turned, and to her horror, a hundred yards up the street, saw the unmistakable figure of Hilary, in black and purple, with a monstrous black fur hat stuck on her head like a dead sheep, waving her scarlet umbrella and heading firmly in their direction. Alison ran, skidded into the shop, making the bell clang like a fire-alarm. 'Help! It's Hilary! She's coming right now! Hide!' She dived behind the stuffed bear.

'Don't you worry,' said Frankie. Champagne bottle in hand, she marched firmly to the door and shot the bolt, then leaning into the window to undo the string of the blind which they rarely used, she struggled with the knot – a little hampered by the champagne bottle – just as Hilary leered in, butterfly specs and awful black hat feathered with snow. Frankie waved at her, grimaced and yelled, 'Sorry, we're closed!' and pulled down the blind with a resounding rattle, then did the same with the door blind.

They clutched their stomachs and giggled. Frankie looked at the bottle.

'Here, there's another glass each.' Carefully she filled the goblets to the brim, making sure that they got exactly the same amount each. 'I'm not Scots for nothing, ye ken,' she said.

'Oh Frankie, what am I going to do?'

'I don't know,' said Frankie gulping, 'but I'm sure you are going to have a lot of adventures.'

'But I only want Gareth . . .'

'Patience, hen, maybe even with him.'

'Oh God . . .' Alison wept and shut her eyes.

'God won't help you – you don't even believe in him.'

Frankie was dancing again. She embraced the stuffed bear: 'You want to dance, my darling?' she asked him, then looked at Alison. 'Even if we do enjoy it, it won't last. We'll not be here one day!' She grinned. 'So let's enjoy it while it's here.'

They quaffed their glasses and Alison burst into tears.

'It's not funny you know . . .' she sobbed, then, as Frankie took down the elk-horns and held them on her head, she laughed as suddenly as she had cried.

'I'm not laughing,' said Frankie, dancing. 'Cheers, hen.'

'Cheers,' Alison's eyes were still wet: 'And I'm not crying.'